After a few seconds of walking, I heard it again. Footfalls of something heavy and sharp almost perfectly in cadence with my own. *Step, step. Clip, clop.*

The corner of the boulevard yawned ahead. I picked up the pace in tiny increments, trying not to make it look like I was running.

The boulevard was fifty yards…forty… I made it to a light trot. *Clip clop clip clop clip clop.*

Hex *that*. I ran. Now there were more of them, and I swore I heard whispers and cries and fluttering wings…

At the mouth of the street I pulled my Glock, thumbed the safety, spun, and aimed. "Hex off!"

Nothing was behind me except old lampposts, wrecked cars, and piles of trash that rustled in the wind. A breath I hadn't meant to hold rushed out of me.

So there was nothing behind me, and never had been.

I believed that until the sidewalk in front of me started to burn.

It started with the crackle of a working, and grew into a whooshing roar that liquefied and then became solid again in a glowing orange sigil that seemed to change and bend as I watched. My eyes ached, and feedback screamed in my ears, until I realized that it was me screaming.

NIGHT LIFE

CAITLIN KITTREDGE

St. Martin's Paperbacks

This is a work of fiction. All of the characters, organizations, and events portrayed in this novel are either products of the author's imagination or are used fictitiously.

NIGHT LIFE

Copyright © 2008 by Caitlin Kittredge.
Excerpt from *Pure Blood* copyright © 2008 by Caitlin Kittredge.

ISBN: 0-312-94829-8
EAN: 978-0-312-94829-0

Printed in the United States of America

St. Martin's Paperbacks edition / March 2008

St. Martin's Paperbacks are published by St. Martin's Press, 175 Fifth Avenue, New York, NY 10010.

10 9 8 7 6 5 4 3 2 1

For my mom
I always said I'd dedicate the first one to you.

ACKNOWLEDGMENTS

This book could not have been published without the tireless assistance of my fantastic agent, Rachel Vater. Rachel, you are awesome in every sense of the word.

Thanks are also in order for my boundlessly enthusiastic editor, Rose Hilliard. We've come a long way since that first draft.

Night Life couldn't have been written or sold without the support of my friends and fellow Urban Fantasy Grrls: Jackie Kessler, my all-around Jedi Master; Richelle Mead, my wacky evil twin; Kat Richardson, my ferret-loving voice of common sense; and Cherie Priest, with her knack for proving that real life is *much* stranger than writing fantasy.

Sara, thank you for knowing me since I was fifteen and never publishing any embarrassing photos, and also for believing me every time I said I was going to write a novel. Ravenna, thanks for making undergrad creative writing classes go by a little faster. Holly, Vern, Ann, Corin, and all the Writer's Weekend alums of 2006, thank you for reassuring me that I wasn't crazy to write a book about a werewolf detective.

I'm exceedingly grateful to Agent Heidi Wallace, ATF, for the information on firearms and to Professor Rebecca Sunderman for teaching such a comprehensive class in forensic investigation. Any errors are mine, not theirs.

Finally, thanks to my mother, Pamela Kittredge, for instilling me with a love of books, a desire to write, and for never, ever telling me that I needed to get a day job.

NIGHT LIFE

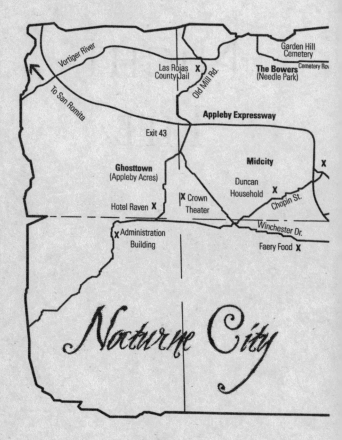

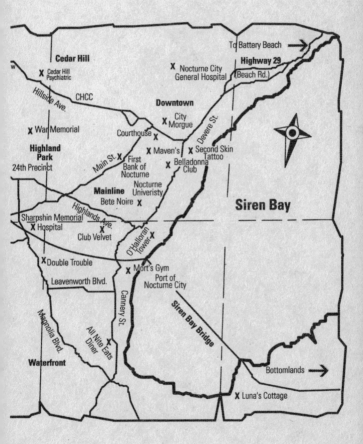

ONE

I smelled the girl's blood and saw her body in a pool of neon light. Signs from a bar facing the alley painted the scene dreamlike, the pavement slick and bottomless and the body's skin pink and hard.

I could smell her blood because I'm a werewolf.

I had gotten the call because she was dead.

A uniform stopped me with an upraised hand. "Ma'am?"

I drew my jacket aside and showed him the Nocturne City Police Department detective badge clipped to my waist. He squinted at it in the ineffectual light and then nodded. "Sorry, Detective . . . Wilder. Go ahead."

He even lifted the tape for me. I rewarded him with a smile. "Call me Luna, Officer . . . ?"

"Thorpe, ma'am." He smiled back, tired blue eyes lighting up. I tend to have that effect on men, even when it's 3 AM and I'm wearing raggedy blue jeans and a T-shirt stained with fingerprinting ink. Not my off-duty attire to be sure, but you try cleaning blood out of a silk halter.

Thorpe called after me, "Hope you didn't eat dinner. She's juicy!"

Fantastic.

I walked into the red light from the beer signs, moving between CSU techs and a photographer snapping a digital Nikon. I stopped, the pointy toe of one boot just shy of the body, and looked down at the girl. Her throat was opened in a wide gash, obscured by dried blood. What hadn't been left inside her—and that wasn't much—was coating the blacktop, giving oily life to the ground below her. Her left index finger was severed neatly at the knuckle, a raw red-white disk with the blood coagulated.

Someone spoke from below my line of vision. "Another night, another dead girl. Nice to have a routine, isn't it?"

Bart Kronen, one of the city's three medical examiners, crouched next to the body, his bald head as red as everything else. I mimicked his posture and bent over the girl's corpse.

"*Nice* wouldn't be my word for this." Closer, the blood wasn't the only smell rolling off the girl. A sharp, musky odor lay under it, and that only meant one thing. I slid a glance to Bart to see if he'd figured it out yet, but he was busy with a thermometer and a stopwatch.

"Killer took time to get a souvenir, so make sure you print her skin before the autopsy. Any idea what made that gash in her throat?" Other than the obvious, of course— the musky scent was the panic of a trapped were, panicked because she had wandered down the wrong street and been jumped by a rival pack.

Kronen chuckled, plump cheeks crinkling. "If this happened before the Hex Riots I'd say you've got an outlaw were that needs to be put down, but as it is . . ." He shrugged and began packing away small evidence bags filled with cotton swabs taken from the body. He didn't pick up my instinctive flinch at the phrase *put down*.

Weres don't kill people, and never did, except the few who can't take the phase and go insane. Were attacks were the fuse that lit the bomb of the Hex Riots over Nocturne City in the 1960s. If you got the bite, you pretty much resigned yourself to living with the constant, twitchy fear that someone would discover your secret and take matters into their own hands. Witches and weres don't enjoy many civil rights in this day and age. On paper, sure, but when a self-righteous plain human with an aluminum bat is after you, it's another story.

"Detective."

I put my attention back on Dr. Kronen. "Hmm?" Great, could I manage to seem like more of an airhead? Maybe if I showed up for work tomorrow in a pink sweater set.

Kronen gestured to the dead girl's hands. "You may want to take a look. She's got some nasty defensive wounds."

I slipped on the proffered glove and took her right hand in mine. Her fingers dangled limply, flesh stripped off the tips, nails torn and broken. Good girl. You fought like hell. You scratched him and kicked him, and made it hard for him to hide what happened.

"I'm also guessing we'll find evidence of sexual assault."

"Why do you say that, Doc?"

He rolled his eyes at me and stood up, brushing non-existent dirt from his khakis. "Cause of death appears to be peri- and postmortem mutilation, and coupled with the ritual of severing the left digit, I'm guessing this is a sex crime."

"Isn't mutilation usually a secondary trait in sex crimes?"

Kronen nodded. "Usually, but I can't find another obvious cause. I'll know more when I can screen her blood for drugs and cut her open to have a peek at her internals. Your skin may lie but your guts never do."

"Kronen, your reverence for victims never fails to amaze me."

"In this line of work, Detective, if we didn't laugh we'd all be prey to the wolves of insanity before the night was out."

Wolves again. What was it with this guy? Well, as long as he was harping on it I might as well put my talents to good use and see if I could find anything he'd missed.

I took a second look at the girl, inhaling deeply as I let my eyes focus in on her skin, her hair, the creases and crevices where trace evidence could hide. The telltale sting told me that my eyes were starting to turn from their normal gray to deep were gold, and I blinked fast to clear them.

Grease, urine, blood, garbage, and the smell of wet brick from the recent rain all mingled. It wasn't what I'd ever describe as pleasant, but there was nothing out of the ordinary, either.

The girl herself looked about twenty, with porcelain skin and black hair, a lighter color showing at the roots. Leather skirt, black platform sandals, and a shocking lime-green halter top made out of stretchy material that showcased her chest. No bag, wallet, hidden money roll, or anything else that would help me ID her. And it wasn't exactly like I could go knocking on her pack's door for information. An Insoli like me would get a boot in the ass at best, a torn throat to match the dead girl's at worst.

I walked with Kronen back to the ME's van. "So, any theories?" he asked me, tossing his gear into the back.

"Based on the neighborhood and the outfit . . . pro. John gone bad. Always tragic, but it happens a lot around here." Kronen was a good medical examiner and a decent guy, but he shared the human attitude that Were = Bad & Scary & Okay to Hurt. Best to feed him the party line for anonymous dead hookers.

Kronen got into the driver's seat and shut the door. "Prostitute murder in a downtown alley? How rare. Shocking, in fact."

"Absolutely shocking," I agreed, glad that he let it go at sarcasm.

"I'll page you when the autopsy is scheduled."

"Thanks. Night."

"Morning," he corrected me. And it was, nearly four thirty.

I walked back through the tape and sat in my 1969 Ford Fairlane. Black, shiny, fast, and a hell of a lot better than an unmarked vehicle from the motor pool.

I was a liar. Even as I voiced my theory to Kronen, I knew it was a bad excuse. The torn throat, the fierce defensive wounds, and the missing finger joint all spoke to something far more violent than a business transaction gone sour or a were pack warning a pro off their turf. Lots of packs did street-level dealing and sent their mates out to work the streets, but run across one of those puritanical pack leaders and you were in deep crap. Usually the offending were got away with some nasty bruises and a humiliation bite. Killing just made it bad for all of us.

It could have been a human who killed her, a savage one, but I dismissed that as quickly as it popped into my head. Even without phasing, a were could fight off a human three times their size. We're strong. Not Spider-Man strong, but we manage.

Attempts to rationalize failed, which meant I was right. She had been killed for a reason. A heightened five senses comes standard with being a were, but I firmly believe it gives you heightened instincts, too. Now I would use them to find out why the girl in the alley was dead.

I looked at the dashboard clock as I pulled away from the scene and turned onto Magnolia Boulevard, once the heart of downtown Nocturne City. If it was a heart now, it was one in dire need of a quadruple bypass and a pacemaker. Boarded-up storefronts glared at me like empty eye sockets, illuminated by broken streetlamps and holding enough shadows to hide a multitude of sins.

The clock read 4:42 AM. With no means to ID the girl with until she was fingerprinted and x-rayed at the morgue, I had nothing to do for the rest of my shift except go back to the Twenty-fourth Precinct, file my report, and see if any progress had been made on my seven other open cases. That, I doubted. Working the midnight-to-eight shift in homicide does not lead to a high clearance rate, or a lack of bags under my eyes. Some nights I swore I should invest in the company that made my concealer and retire.

Magnolia intersected Highland and I made the right turn, crossing over into the old Victorian district. Highland Park was one of the few neighborhoods where the residents had been able to stop the city from widening the street and chopping down the hundred-year-old oak trees. It also housed the Twenty-fourth, tucked neatly into a skinny brick two-story that had once been a fire-house, back when fire trucks were horse-drawn and the Hex Riots weren't even a puff of smoke on the horizon.

The grazing lot for horses had been transformed into a parking lot for cops, and I pulled my Fairlane into the only free space—if the tiny margin between two patrol cars deserved the title. As a detective, I had an assigned spot, but someone was already in it. The Fairlane scraped against concrete, and I winced. That didn't sound like it could be repaired with a fine brush and a dab of Black Magick nail polish.

I got out and looked at the license plate of the car that had taken my hard-earned spot. The small rising-moon crest told me *city vehicle,* a black Lexus with tinted win-dows and no other identifying marks. What it was doing at the Twenty-fourth, *in my parking space,* was a mys-tery I wasn't up to solving at the moment.

I satisfied my frustration with a kick to the Lexus's bumper, and went into the precinct.

At some point in history, the department had de-cided that fluorescent lights were not only cheap but also flattering to the complexion, and in-stalled them on practically every inch of ceiling. Other than that small addition, the fire brigade had their way. There was still a brass fireman's pole in the corner of the squad room. Sometimes, at Christmas, we wrapped tin-sel around it.

My single desk, tucked into a corner, held just enough space for my computer, a hanging file, and a picture of me, my cousin Sunny, and our grandmother from when Sunny and I were kids. Sunny and Grandma Rhoda were smiling. I was not.

I went for coffee before I settled in to type up the report on the dead girl. She'd be Jane Doe number three this year among my cases.

The squad room was deserted, but the desk clerk waved at me as I walked by.

"Long night, Wilder?"

"The longest, Rick."

He clucked in sympathy.

"Heard you caught a mutilation homicide down on Magnolia."

I've given up trying to figure out how the police gossip network disperses information. It could give you a headache.

"That's right" is all I said.

"So, how's Sunny doing?" he asked me, smiling shyly. Rick has been in love with my cousin ever since she moved here. Whether he's figured out that she's a witch or not, I don't know.

"She's fine. Teaching meditation over at Cedar Hill Community College. How's your little one?" Rick's wife had left him three years ago, leaving him saddled with a five-year-old son and a job that kept him working nights. As far as I could tell, though, he did okay. He was attractive, in that quiet dark-haired way, and stable as a cement pylon. He would be good for Sunny. But he was also a plain human, and I wasn't going to encourage them.

"Great. He's growing like a—"

A bang from the frosted-glass door down the hall opening interrupted us. Wilbur Roenberg, captain in charge of the Twenty-fourth, stepped out. Seeing him working at this very early hour made my gut clench. Roenberg and I didn't get along even when I'd had a full night of sleep and wasn't on the tail end of a bad shift.

"We'll talk, Wilbur," said a shortish man in a dark suit, with hair and eyes to match. He shut the captain's door and took clipped steps down the hallway toward Rick and me. He carried a black briefcase, and his shoes were highly polished. I realized the dark suit was a tuxedo. He wore a red silk tie, the only hint of color on his monochrome frame.

Roenberg wiped his face with the back of his hand before disappearing down the hall toward the men's room.

"You have a nice night, sir!" Rick called as the visitor passed. The guy turned and gave Rick an evil eye. I heard Rick gulp. Tuxedo kept staring, his hand on the door to the outside. His posture had the reptile quality of someone who knew how to fight, and probably fought dirty.

"Shouldn't you be doing your job instead of flirting?" he finally asked, pure dark eyes flicking to me.

It was my turn to provide a hostile stare. Tuxedo didn't flinch, but his full lips curled up slightly.

"Is there anything else I can help you with, *sir*?" I asked, adjusting my loose tee so that my badge and my service weapon showed clearly.

After a long two ticks of the clock, he looked away. Point, Luna.

"The name is Lockhart. And I doubt very much that you can, Officer," he said, before turning on his heel and striding out like he had a badger nipping at his ass.

"What a butthead," muttered Rick, punching a few keys on his computer.

I walked over to the door and watched Tuxedo leave. I wasn't surprised when I saw the black Lexus screech out of my space and speed away down Highland. A city bigwig named Lockhart. I'd remember the name. See if he got a warm welcome next time he needed someone to fix a parking ticket.

Walking back to my desk, I almost ran head-on into Captain Roenberg. He jumped aside, face flushed and stale coffee on his breath. "So sorry, Detective Wilder."

"That's fine, sir," I told him. He wasn't sorry. Roenberg was a throwback, and it was apparent every time he deigned to make eye contact that he was really seeing me in pumps and a frilly little apron. Fair's fair. Every time I was unfortunate enough to see him, I wanted to plant a solid left in his smug little mouth.

"Yes . . . ," he said absently, hurrying past me toward his office.

"Don't get any cooties on you," I muttered, glad I was going the other way. At least not all cops in the Twenty-fourth felt the same way as Roenberg. Most of them could deal with my being female. It was the were part I kept under my hat. Not that I wore a lot of hats. They make my head look like a dinosaur egg.

I decided to type up Jane Doe's report and clock out early. Those other seven cases weren't getting any colder.

Name? the computer prompted me. I typed *Jane Doe*. Age? *Unknown*. I filled in all the boxes for physical description and forwarded the file to Missing Persons for a cross-check. In three weeks, if I was lucky, they'd tell me they found nothing.

Cause of Death?

My fingers stopped. I saw the girl lying on the wet pavement, dried blood on her tattered throat. Wet blood under her, matting the long black hair. The tight clothes that left no room for any ID. Torn, bloody hands reaching out to fend off . . . what?

I blinked. The night had been too long and too full of death. Under the COD field I typed *exsanguination* and checked the box to indicate that the autopsy was still pending. The printer spit out a hard copy of the report, and I attached the appropriate forms and tucked it into my open-case file, which was really just a tattered accordion folder sitting on top of my desk.

Jane Doe: filed and processed and tucked away where she needed to be.

I got up, stretched, and slid into my scuffed motorcycle jacket. The telltale point in my lower back twinged. Definitely time to go home. I had made it to the squad room door when I heard a voice bellow, "And where does that sweet ass think it's going?"

Turning brought me face-to-leering-face with David Bryson, a fellow detective—if *fellow* could be classified as the occasional lewd comment and a burning desire on my part to kick him. The only thing keeping me from phasing out on him was the hope that he'd be fired for sexual harassment and I'd get to watch.

"Hey, Wilder," he panted. A younger Hispanic man was attached to Bryson's arm via handcuffs. The kid had gang tats and a bloody gash on the side of his head. "Be a good girl and help me get this piece of crap to interrogation," Bryson said, detaching himself from the kid and recuffing him.

"What the hell happened to his head?" The gang-banger smelled like sweat, cheap weed, and fear. Bryson gave off adrenaline and coppery, impotent rage.

He grinned at me. "*Vato* resisted. I showed him he couldn't resist the hood of my car."

I sucked in a breath. "That's great, Bryson. Really great. What's on the menu for the rest of the night? Toilet bowls and telephone books?"

"Aw, who's he gonna tell? Dumbshit doesn't even speak English." He shoved the banger into a chair by his desk. "Am I right, Pedro?"

"Su madre aspira martillos en infierno," Pedro muttered. I turned away quickly so Bryson wouldn't catch my snort and grin. Red-faced, he didn't even notice me.

Instead, he grabbed Pedro by the neck and slammed him face-first into the brick wall of the squad room.

Pedro moaned once before he slid down and curled into a ball on the linoleum at our feet. "You think that's some funny shit, don't you?" Bryson shouted, drawing back his foot for a kick.

I stepped over Pedro and put out my hand, palm up. "Enough, Bryson."

He glared at me, foot still poised, big shoulders hunched. I'd spent enough time in my kickboxing dojo to handle an opponent bigger than myself, but Bryson was not only big, but also armed and a cop with training of his own. This standoff definitely called for sugar rather than round kicks.

"He had it coming," Bryson snarled at me when he realized I wasn't going to move.

"Leave it alone, or I'll help this poor kid file a complaint against you right now," I told Bryson. "And you can bet I'll be calling Lieutenant McAllister at home to make sure he sees it."

After another long second, Bryson stepped back and fixed his tie. Pedro got up and ran like hell.

Bryson heaved a dramatic sigh. "Shit, Wilder. You can be a class-A bitch sometimes." His eyes traveled down to my chest, lower, and back up. "If you weren't so cute I might pop you one." He reached around and patted me on the bottom. "Thank that sweet ass."

Bryson squealed as I grabbed his index finger and

bent it backward, applying pressure on the knuckle and creating a vise that could snap bone with a few milligrams more pressure.

"David, I know that the time for this conversation is long overdue, and that's my fault, because up until now I couldn't believe that you could really be such a gigantic dickhead. But apparently you can, so listen up."

"That's my trigger finger you got!" he yelped.

"Then you shouldn't have put it on my ass." I pinched harder. "I couldn't care less what you think of me. But for the record, I think *you* are a violent, incompetent psychopath who has no business being a police officer." Somewhere between the dead girl and the Lockhart jerk from the city, my annoyance had boiled over into rage, and I was feeling it deep down in my gut. Bryson just happened to be the closest target. Not that he didn't deserve it.

"Now that we understand each other, David . . ." I squeezed and relished the cry of real pain I elicited. "Take your opinion of me and stick it up your ass. If there's room next to your head, of course." I twisted his hand to the snapping point, realizing how easy it would be to hurt him. How easy it would be to lean in and feel his hot breath as I tore his throat. My hand clamped down and the joint let out a popping sound.

I let go, jumping a step back.

Bryson stared at me with wide eyes, holding his hand. Then he turned without a word and practically ran out of the squad room. The big baby.

As soon as he was gone, I bolted for my car.

Shit. It had never hit me so early before a full moon, and so hard. A full seven days still. I stroked the chain under my shirt and felt the cool kiss of the silver star pendant against my skin. The rage I'd felt in the squad room still demanded satisfaction, a hunt brought to a bloody close.

Weres are all instinct and nerves, loosely held together by the thin veil of humanity that covers us when the moon is new. When we get angry, control is a memory. You can hurt people, and probably will at least once. Wearing silver when you're human is a good deterrent, or a little wolfsbane next to the skin if you don't mind smelling like an old lady's medicine cabinet. But when were rage really grips you, nothing on this earth can stop it.

I breathed in, out, and turned on the car, forcing my hands to stop shaking. Bryson was an idiot and a terrible cop, but what I had done was unforgivable. I had lost it. Something had awakened the were and I didn't know what. That scared the hell out of me.

I kept my pentacle outside my shirt, touching it every few seconds with my free hand. It did little to calm me as I drove home while the sun came up.

TWO

By the time I got home, sunrise had become a fluffy pink line across the horizon, deepening to lava orange at the heart. The dilapidated one-and-a-half-story cottage Sunny and I shared sat on a hill that sloped to the ocean, on the opposite side of Siren Bay from the city proper. It may not have been the trendy address, but there sure was less pollution, and there were fewer gunshots at night.

Salt smell wafted toward me when I got out of the Fairlane and I heard the gentle whoosh of the waves like they were right next to me. The humid air curled the wild roses that climbed the front of the cottage, but aside from that it looked like the front of a Hallmark card.

A light glowed from the kitchen window, and I shouted, "I'm home!" to Sunny as I came in the front door and kicked off my boots.

Sunny padded into the front room on bare feet, wearing sweatpants and a tunic. If I could look as good as my tiny cousin in what amounted to basically a sack of cotton, life would be sweet.

"Morning," she said, swirling a tea bag in her purple ceramic mug.

"I will never, ever understand why you get up this early when there's no earthly need to," I told her. "I'm so damn exhausted I could sleep through the Hex Riots."

Sunny shrugged. "Witches greet the dawn. Doesn't hurt to remember where you get your gifts from."

"Guess there are some benefits to missing out on the legendary Swann witch blood," I said. Swann was my mother's maiden name, Sunny her niece by my aunt Delia. Delia, Sunny, and my grandmother had all gotten the blood. I hadn't. My grandmother blamed Vincent Wilder, my father and a plain human. Privately, I thought she was probably right, but to everyone who mattered I couldn't give a flying broom whether I had the blood or not.

Sunny extended her mug. "Green tea? Chai, maybe?"

I shook my head. "The only thing I want right now is a hot, hot shower and some sleep."

"Your loss," she informed me with a wink, taking her knobby wooden caster and a plug of sage incense for the dawn-greeting.

"I'm sure," I said, shrugging my jacket off. Its thick leather had kept my skin off the road or a suspect's knife out of my ribs more than once. The jacket went on the coat tree next to Sunny's moss-green shawl, and my shoulder holster with it. My Glock went into the middle drawer of the old desk that served as our toss-all table for letters, keys, and miscellaneous junk. I locked the drawer and hung the key around my neck. That image of the hardened cop sleeping with a gun under their pillow is crap. Cops get their heads blown off with their own guns at home just as often as civilians.

Sunny watched with mild disapproval, as she always did when I took out my weapon around her. Caster witches usually came with all the pacifistic trappings you'd expect from white magick users. I always felt slightly deceptive when I made a show of putting the Glock away. We both knew that it wasn't the gun Sunny should be afraid of. I was way more hazardous to her health.

She asked, "Did anything bad happen during your shift?" No, not psychic, but with a witch's sense of when energy was disturbed.

"Homicide," I said, rubbing my eyes. They felt like some of the beach sand we constantly tracked into the foyer had gotten caught under the lids. "A girl. A young woman, probably twenty or so. She was . . . it wasn't quick."

Before I could react, Sunny's arms were around me and she was holding me close. "I'm sorry, Luna," she murmured.

Normally I would have flinched, or at least backed away from Sunny's overwhelming sympathy, but right now it just felt good to have contact with a human who wasn't in handcuffs or trying to touch my butt. I patted her shoulder in return and then extricated myself. "Thanks, Sun. I'm going to go catch that shower."

She nodded. "I need to get outside before the whole dawn is over." She went out the front door, still barefoot.

I stood in the center of the living room for a few seconds, then turned and jogged after her. "Sunny!"

She turned back halfway across our sandy front yard. "Yes?"

"Will you be around when I wake up? I . . ." I sighed. *Forget the pride, Luna. If your phase is out of control, the pride won't do you any good while you're ripping up people near and dear to you.* "I need to talk to you about my phase. I think something's off."

Sunny nodded, concern creasing her round face. "Of course, hon. I don't have a class today, so I'll be around. Come find me when you're awake."

Upstairs, scalding my skin under the flimsy shower-head attached to our clawfoot tub, I didn't feel any better. Sunny being a witch didn't automatically make her a were expert. Without a pack to guide me, it was the blind leading the freaking blind.

I put on sweats and a tank top and fell into bed. I think I was asleep before my head was fully on the pillow.

I dreamed about Jane Doe's open, staring eyes and fresh blood running under a street lamp.

I woke up to the sound of Sunny rustling around in her room, humming. Sensitive ears are not a bonus when you have roommates.

My head throbbed, coming to a pinpoint between my eyes. I rolled over, groaned, and looked at my alarm clock. One in the afternoon. For someone who usually didn't hit the mattress until eight in the morning, I was a damn light sleeper lately.

I went to my closet to find an outfit, and my foot caught a pile of jeans. I cursed. Really needed to donate some of this crap to the fashionably challenged poor.

Sunny heard my mumbling and knocked on the bedroom door. I swear that girl has better hearing than I do, and she's not even a were.

"Luna? Are you awake or cursing in your sleep again?"

"Depends on what you mean by *awake.*"

She opened my door and came in, sitting on the edge of the bed in a flurry of velvet. Loose black cotton pants and a flowing purple top with those wide sleeves and a low-cut, lacy neck. On most, the getup would scream *Ren-faire escapee,* but Sunny's small waist and curvaceous top pulled it off. I felt underdressed in my pajamas, and pulled on a robe and boudoir slippers with red satin toes.

"Can we make the talk quick? I'm drying rose hips I picked this morning and I can't leave them too long."

"Promise not to subject me to any more of that tea you brew from them and I'll make it light-speed."

Sunny pursed her lips. "Most people love my teas."

"In case you hadn't noticed, cuz, I'm not most people. Most people don't turn into two-hundred-pound wolves when the moon is full." I threw a pile of T-shirts and underwear off my rocking chair, making just enough room for my butt, and sat.

"You really need to donate some of this stuff," Sunny observed. I handed her a stormy glare in response.

Sunny and I are opposites in a lot of ways, not least of which being the way we dress. When she had moved from our hometown of San Romita to Nocturne City, she practically had to put a gun to my head to convince me that living together was a good idea. Sometimes, like when she was chanting at all hours or cooking a particularly smelly spell, I still wasn't sure of our arrangement.

"So what seems to be wrong with your moonphase?" she asked.

But at times like this, I was damn glad to have her around.

"Well . . ." I sighed. Thinking about beating up Bryson,

in the light of day with a well-rested mind, was embarrassing. What was I, a playground bully? Even if he did have it coming . . . "I had a run-in with Bryson last night."

Sunny raised a curved eyebrow. She knew Bryson. "Go on."

"He touched me. And I grabbed him. I think I broke his finger. He was screaming in pain, literally. And I enjoyed it, Sunny. I practically phased out. I wanted to kill him."

Sunny bit her lip. We look similar, but her face is round where mine is narrow, open and warm where mine has a tendency to make me look like a bitch. She didn't look proud of me right then, which reminded me of all the times I'd faced off against Rhoda and my mother.

"I'm assuming you didn't. Kill him, that is."

"Hex it, Sunny. What do you think? I enjoyed making the SOB squirm more than I've enjoyed anything in a long time, which is a sad comment on my life. But anyway. It's not that."

I picked up and played with one of my pink velvet pumps, purchased for a Valentine's Day date who never showed. I didn't want to say the next part. It was pathetic and stupid. It made me no better than the were thugs who hung around the corner of Kudzu and La Quito.

"The thing that worries me, Sunny, is that I did it in the first place. It just exploded. I've only ever felt were rage when the phase is coming on."

"I can see why you'd worry," Sunny agreed. She stood and pointed to the bed. "Lie down on your stomach. Lift your shirt."

"Oh, come on, Sunny . . ."

"Now, Luna. I don't want a crazed were smashing up my house."

"Our house. I pay half the rent, and as I remember I was the one who found it in the first place."

"And if I hadn't been there to pass a credit check, you'd still be in that horrible studio on Woodmont," she shot back. "Lie on the bed and lift your shirt."

Get past the fairy-princess getup and the touchy-feely caster witch facade, and my cousin can be damn bossy when the mood strikes her. I lay down on my bed and shivered as the purple satin spread touched my bare skin. I pulled my tank up to just under my breasts, exposing the tattoo on my lower back.

"Hmm," said Sunny. "Looks okay. No redness or swelling."

The tattoo ink was infused with wolfsbane and silver. Silver on a chain might offer a were peace of mind, but the only thing that holds back a phase is ink in the skin. And not even ink can stop a were in moonlight.

"I'm not about to phase six and a half days away from a full moon," I reminded Sunny as she prodded the tat. "That would be sort of impossible."

"I don't *know* that," said Sunny. She sat next to me and leaned close to examine my back. "Really, Luna, we don't know anything about this except what we've learned through trial and error. And the fewer errors we experience, the longer my tranquility remains intact."

I blushed thinking about the last "error," and how I'd had to buy Sunny a new sofa. That had been unfair, and cost me two weeks' pay. It wasn't my fault she didn't know how to fasten a kennel door properly.

Sunny finally pulled my shirt down. "It seems fine. Does it feel all right?"

I reached back and rubbed the CD-sized circle of ink.

"It's fine." The skin prickled under my hand, sending itchy fingers up and down my back.

Sunny frowned. "I don't have another explanation for the rage. I don't know enough to even offer an opinion. The only person who does—"

I stopped her. "Forget that. I'll get on the computer and see what I can find out about another charm that negates phase."

Sunny sniffed. "Sure. Tell me if you find anything." She knew I wouldn't. Everything I knew about being a were came from blind experience and dumb luck. Normally, a pack would usher in a were fresh from the bite and teach them the laws and magicks inherent to pack life. Of course, in the grand tradition of my life, I wasn't so lucky.

D eciding to eat breakfast before I started my internet quest, I went to the kitchen. Any way you looked at it, I was screwed from the get-go as far as weres went. Most got the bite at birth, or were born of two were parents and had no need. Weres given the bite after childhood were rare. An adult given the bite was a pain in the ass, all confusion and newly blossomed killer instincts that could get your pack into a lot of trouble.

I checked the icebox, an ancient Frigidaire hulk that looked like it could stop AK-47 fire, to see if Sunny had graced me with any leftovers that weren't made out of soy. She hadn't. Peanut butter and bananas would have to suffice. I assembled all my ingredients and started to chop and spread. "Sunny, where are the plates?" I hollered.

"Sink!" she shouted back from the upstairs.

Sometimes a pack member didn't want the responsibility, and abandoned the human with the bite. Those without a pack, like me, were called Insoli, a Latin term that translated loosely to "lonely ones." I'd heard a lot of other versions. Lowest of the Low. Outcast. Packless. The trifecta of unforgivable were insults.

"Sunny, where are the knives?"

"Left-hand drawer by the sink!"

The kitchen was my favorite room in the cottage, although I'd never admit to knowing what to do in it other than make tasty grilled cheese sandwiches and the occasional batch of brownies. Bundles of herbs hung from the exposed rafters, casting a musty-sweet smell over the whole room. A row of glass crystals dangled from the windows over the old porcelain sink. The floors were weathered wood and covered with rag rugs.

Just like lamenting over my lack of culinary skills didn't mean I had to starve, angsting about my status in the were community didn't make me the unpopular girl with no prom date.

I was a little beyond the prom stage of being a were, anyway. I slapped my sandwich on a plate and carried it to my office.

This was my territory. The desk was real black ebony, bought as a scarred thing with no legs from a flea market. I had a top-of-the-line laptop, flat-panel monitor, and cable modem connection. Useful for case work, but also because I was impatient and prone to hitting machines when they were too slow. I kept a black leather club chair in the corner with a strong reading light. The wall-to-wall bookshelves held the *Death Investigator's Handbook, Diagnostic and Statistical Manual IV,* my criminal justice textbooks from the Cedar Hill Community College, and Sunny's and my senior yearbooks from San Romita High.

My one concession to girliness was the rug—a fake-fur

thing at least two inches thick that I loved to walk barefoot on. I shuffled across it and sank into my chair, waiting for the computer to boot up.

I had taken the first bite of my breakfast when the tinny strains of "Hungry Like the Wolf" startled me into dropping it.

I rooted around the desk and found my cell buried under a stack of rap sheets for suspects in a rape/homicide. Caller ID said it was the medical examiner's office. I flipped the phone open.

"Detective Wilder."

"Luna, it's Dr. Kronen. Tighter than a were pack in a butcher's over here, but I managed to squeeze your Jane Doe in for nine tonight."

That meant I'd have to come on shift three hours early. But then again, the next available autopsy slot would probably be a month from now. Jane Doe had no family clamoring for the body. No one wanted a quick funeral and a chance to cry over her.

"Sounds good, Doc. I'll meet you at the morgue at nine sharp."

"You sound grumpy," he said. "I wake you?"

"I wish," I muttered before I hung up.

THREE

Most cities hide their morgues. It makes good sense to keep them out of sight and not remind the general population of where they're headed when they die.

Nocturne City took no such precautions. The morgue was a sterile granite edifice, nearly as large as the courthouse. Its upper floors housed the NCPD's central crime labs and the medical examiner's administrative offices.

Tonight, though, I was headed for what the detectives only half jokingly called Limbo.

Night shift at the crime labs runs a skeleton crew, and there was no one in the lobby except a bored uniform standing by the metal detector, staring off into space. I dropped my gun, phone, badge, and keys into the plastic basket and walked through.

The basement morgue storage and autopsy bays are cut off from the world of the living by the earth, and require you to take a special elevator down. The car groaned ominously at me as I stepped in, and I vowed to take the stairs next time rather than risk ending up a permanent resident of the building.

The stink hit me as soon as I stepped out—formaldehyde, old blood, dead flesh. If you think a morgue smells bad normally, try having a nose as sensitive as mine and get back to me. I gagged once, swallowed, and held my hand over my face until I got to Kronen's autopsy bay.

He was just starting to wash up and shouted hello at me over the running water. Through the glass I could see Jane Doe's body neatly covered with a paper sheet. Only the rivulets of blood running down the slotted sides of the steel table and draining through the floor grate gave any indication of what had gone on.

Kronen shut off the sink and grabbed a wad of paper towels. "Shall we?"

I followed him through the swinging doors, grabbing a surgical mask as I went and clapping it over my face. The stench in here, much fresher than the rest of the floor, almost knocked me over. Kronen looked concerned as my eyes watered, and handed me some VapoRub.

"Forgot you were the one with the sensitive sniffer," he said. I slathered the ointment under my nose, which brought the smell down from Vomit Inducing to Pretty Terrible. "So, Detective Wilder, what we have here, as I said last night, is your basic sexually motivated homicide."

He yanked back the sheet, sending a fresh scent wave into the air. I saw the raw Y-incision on Jane Doe's chest, the old bruises on her torso, teeth marks on her breasts.

The smell was too much—more than just death. Strong, charred, filling my mouth and nostrils so I couldn't breathe. My vision spun as the smell closed in, so dense and powerful and terrible that I feared it would send me to the floor.

I dropped the mask, crashed through the swinging doors, dropped my head over the steel sink, and vomited until there was nothing left.

Kronen hurried after me, holding my hair out of the way as I retched pathetically. "Oh, dear," he murmured. "Oh, dear. It's all right."

"Damn it," I gasped as I straightened up and wiped my mouth with my hand. My whole body quaked and my stomach felt hollow, the acid burning all the way up to my tongue.

"Are you finished?" Kronen asked. I tried to ignore the flare of shame his shocked expression prompted. I had never pulled a Linda Blair in an autopsy, not even at my very first homicide, when a hit-and-run had nearly split a woman in half.

"I . . . think so," I said, leaning against the wall and breathing. *Breathe. In through the nose, out through the mouth. Don't faint. Don't faint. Don't you dare faint, Luna.*

"I could fax you my findings . . . ," Kronen started.

"No." I straightened up and pushed my sweaty hair out of my face. "I'm fine. Finish."

"Your reaction . . ."

"I ate something bad at dinner, obviously," I snapped. Kronen looked hurt, but led me back into the bay.

I felt like crap for my nasty response to his sympathy. Unfortunately, it was survival. I liked Dr. Kronen a lot, but I couldn't let him think I was weak, because it would get out that Detective Wilder, the little woman, had bailed on an autopsy after puking her guts out while the ME held her head. Then I'd have more like Bryson to worry about, no matter where I went on the force.

I got a fresh mask. Pinched my nose hard enough to hurt. Followed Kronen through the swinging doors.

The smell was still there, pungent, almost sulfuric, but it was bearable. I had the sick, disorienting feeling that I had smelled it before, in different circumstances. It wasn't the scent of were. The sweetish musk was there, faded by death, but this was like rotted flesh raked over hot coals. My eyes watered as I stood opposite Kronen, watching him over Jane Doe's chest.

"Go ahead."

"Your wish is my command," he said, gesturing at the body. "Now, as you can see, there was mutilation to the breasts as well as the throat. No more vaginal trauma than you'd expect to find on a street prostitute, but that doesn't really mean anything."

"It's not the sex that gets them off," I agreed.

"Whoever it was did this, she fought hard," Kronen said. "She sustained multiple fractures to both hands and a broken tibia on her right arm. If she'd survived, I doubt she could ever make a fist again. Surprising for such a frail-looking young woman."

"Cause of death was the throat being torn out?" I asked. The gash had been cleaned and now gaped up at me, black.

"No," said Kronen, surprising the hell out of me.

"What do you mean, no?"

"I mean, of course I thought it was the blood loss and mutilation at first. But when I was doing the rape kit, I noticed this." He slid his hands under Jane Doe's back. "Give me a hand, will you?"

Pick the last thing in the universe I wanted to do right that second, and touching the dead girl was second only to swallowing a handful of silver dollars with a wolfs-bane chaser.

I grabbed Jane Doe's waist, feeling her ribs through

the thin pale skin, and pulled. She flopped over on her stomach with a muffled, wet thud. My stomach was empty, but the jolt of nausea still passed through.

"This," said Kronen, pointing to a tiny red mark in the fold of Jane Doe's buttock, "is your cause of death."

I leaned close. "What the hell is that?"

Kronen got a clipboard and flipped a few pages. "According to the tox screen, high-dosage Percodan with a diazepam chaser."

I stared at him. "Someone *drugged* her?"

"Willingly or unwillingly, is the question," Kronen replied. He covered Jane Doe back up. "Percodan is easy enough to come by, but diazepam is highly controlled."

"Is it a sedative?" I asked, feeling like an idiot and knowing that I'd have to revise my report when I went upstairs. Then McAllister would want to know why I jumped the gun. Again.

"You might call it that," said Kronen. "If you were a rottweiler or a house cat."

"Come again?"

"It's an animal tranquilizer, Detective."

That made my eyebrows go up an inch or three. I trust my instincts, and trusted them enough then to know Jane Doe was more than a trick gone bad. But this—this was beyond anything I had prepared myself for.

"Odd method," Kronen said. "If you are going to mutilate someone."

"No," I said, and felt a tremor start in my hands, radiating inward to my uneasy stomach. Gods damn it, I knew why he'd drugged the girl. "No, he wanted to take his time. He showed her the knife, Bart."

"Her finger was clipped pre- or perimortem," he agreed quietly.

"He made her watch." My blood beat against my head, and the were always lurking in my subconscious howled in rage. "The drugs were there to make sure she stayed docile enough for him to take his time, and didn't scream. But he miscalculated somehow, and she fought him, and he killed her. Gods." I wanted this bastard, now, wanted his blood.

"I have a feeling that They are not at play here," said Kronen. "But perhaps They are, because I also found you DNA." He covered Jane Doe back up with the sheet.

The way this day was shaping up, the only logical thing to say was, "Any idea who contributed?"

"I sent it to be analyzed and they'll run a sample through CODIS to see if it matches any offenders."

In other words, let the wheels grind through the two hundred other DNA samples that came in before mine that day, and then maybe, if I was lucky, I'd get a hit from among the minuscule number of felons whose genetic fingerprint had been entered into the CODIS system.

Plus, Jane Doe was a prostitute. How many DNA "samples" would she have on her, anyway?

"Tell me you at least fixed a time of death," I pleaded with Kronen. He ushered me out of the autopsy bay, and I finally got relief from the pungent stink.

"That, Detective, is far from an exact science, but this might be useful—the rain last night had stopped when she was murdered in the alley. Her body was dry and the blood evidence was intact."

Finally something solid. I could pick up the phone, verify it, and add it to the lines of the case file, slowly painting a picture of Jane Doe's last hours. Did she go somewhere to escape the rain and end up far worse off? Was she a victim of wrong place, wrong time, or was she chosen and stalked by a sadist?

"I have three more identifications tonight," said Kronen. He had shed the paper robe and slippers he wore in the bay and reverted to his usual khakis and crooked tie. This one had a ketchup stain. At least, I hoped it was ketchup. "Call me if you need any more information, Detective Wilder."

The door whispered as he left for the public part of the morgue, where relatives viewed bodies and claimed their own. I looked at Jane Doe once more, leaning my forehead against the glass. The vomit I'd shed because of her still lingered on the air.

Did she gag as the drugs overtook her system, or was it peaceful, like a warm bath? Junkies described the former, suicides usually talked about the worst pain they'd ever experienced, as the body attempted to expel death before time ran out.

I breathed in, out. Why did she smell so strange? Why had she been drugged and mutilated?

Why was the question, and I had that cold. The answer eluded me.

"I'll find out," I promised Jane Doe. "I will." A hollow promise to a dead woman. Nothing I couldn't handle.

Shift change was in full swing at the Twenty-fourth when I got there. Day uniforms and the full complement of detectives that the second shift commanded were walking out in pairs and alone. Rick was conferring with Shelley, the day desk clerk. A few civilians, most of whom I judged to be lawyers by the proliferation of somber ties and expensive suits, were still in the lobby. I went through the metal detector and escaped to my desk.

The squad room was quiet, one second-shift detective hunched over his keyboard, pecking miserably.

No sign of Bryson. No ominous pink While You Were Out slips on my desk. No e-mails flashing in my inbox. I let my breath out slowly.

"Expecting bad news?"

I jumped about a foot in the air. "Crap!"

Lieutenant McAllister took in my reaction with the same placid look that his bony face bestowed on everything from the bodies of ravaged murder victims to an Internal Affairs review board. "Nice to see you're feeling alert tonight, Detective. A word?"

"Crap," I said again.

McAllister nodded in agreement. "Dave Bryson was waiting by my door when I got here this evening. At first I thought the oversize horse's behind was stalking me, but it seems he has a problem with you, Luna."

I sighed, massaging the point between my eyes. "Has Bryson ever not had a problem with me, Mac?"

McAllister's mouth pursed regretfully. "Nothing I couldn't ignore." He gestured for me to sit at my desk, and when I didn't took the chair himself. "Bryson insisted I take a report, which you know I'm obligated to pass to the captain."

"Hey, then I have until about eleven AM tomorrow," I quipped. Roenberg was not known for punctuality.

"Not exactly," Mac said. "Roenberg is waiting for you and me in his office."

Well, hell. Bryson must have raised one heck of a stink if Roenberg had stuck around until close to midnight. Nothing like ego to spur a guy on.

"I don't have time for this," I snapped, deciding to go to the defensive. "I have eight open cases, one of them a rape/murder that could be serial."

"Don't get pissy with me, Luna. I'm not the one who almost snapped off Bryson's finger." McAllister's blue eyes went slaty. His body is long and thin, and he wears a hound dog expression, until the anger rises and you see the depth of the man hiding in the gangly body with bags under the eyes and gray hair.

"Come on, Lieutenant. You and I both know that Bryson deserved a lot more."

"That's immaterial. I can't have my squad running around playing Serpico with each other."

I kicked the linoleum. "Sorry, Mac," I muttered.

"I have no problem with you, Luna," he said. "Not with your gender, or the fact that you're a were. I like you and I think you're a damn good detective. But if you can't control yourself, then I can't have you in my precinct. Ninety-nine-point-nine percent of this city thinks you're a dangerous animal. If you act out on the job, you'll prove them right."

"That is a load of bullshit!" I hissed. I trusted Mac to keep my bite status on the DL, and I resented him holding the secret over me.

"You know it's not, Luna," Mac said. "Now cut the crap before we get to Roenberg's office or *I'll* suspend you." He unfolded himself from my chair and marched away, looking back over his shoulder once to make sure I was following.

His words shook me, went down my throat and formed a cold, hard mass just below my ribs. I couldn't get suspended—I had been a detective for two years and a uniformed officer for five before that, and I'd never had so much as a written warning.

What really stung was that the words had come from Mac. Mac, who had always accepted my being a were as a personal fact, like hair or eye color. I felt like a scolded little girl, and I didn't like it.

And now because of Bryson's macho bullshit I was

looking at lost pay, humiliation, and confirmation for all those whispers. *Wilder can't hack it. Too emotional. What do you expect from a woman?*

McAllister rapped on the wavy glass door with Roenberg's name on it. Roenberg's supercilious voice told us, "Enter."

"Captain," said McAllister, sticking his head in. "We're here."

"Troy," Roenberg nodded in return. "And Detective Wilder. Shut the door."

McAllister had already taken a seat, so the duty fell to me. I shut it gently and stood behind the empty green vinyl chair facing the captain's desk. If he thought I'd sit and be reprimanded like a reticent schoolgirl, he had another thought coming.

Roenberg waved an interoffice memo at me. "Do you have any idea what this is, Detective?"

Already on the offensive. Didn't bode well.

"It's a complaint, sir," I said, knowing what was coming next.

Roenberg turned on Mac. "Is it your habit, Troy, to allow your people to treat my precinct house like some sort of gladiatorial arena?"

Gladiatorial? Oh, he was good. McAllister's neck muscles tensed, but his voice stayed perfectly even. "Luna's informed me that the circumstances were somewhat extenuating."

"I don't give a damn what Detective Wilder has to say," Roenberg informed him while staring at me. His eyes were a watery brown, and the bloodshot irises gave the impression that he was about to cry. Somehow I thought that if anyone cried in the course of this discussion, it wouldn't be the captain.

"Dave Bryson has a history of friction with his partners

and other detectives, no matter what precinct he's been assigned to," McAllister was saying, "as well as two excessive force complaints from civilians."

Roenberg rolled his eyes, picking up an oval silver object from his desk and tossing it from one hand to the other. "Please, Troy. I know all that. What's on the table here is a serious accusation. Detective Bryson had to go to the emergency room with a broken index." The way Roenberg said *broken index* like most people say *massive head trauma* only made me want to slap Bryson harder next time.

"I'm telling you right now, Wilbur," Mac said, some steel creeping into his tone, "I'm willing to go to bat for Detective Wilder in this instance."

I shot Mac a grateful look, but he was staring down Roenberg. The captain set the silver disk aside with a nervous flick, and I realized with a start that it was a caster. Metal casters were rare, and expensive. It took a skilled witch to control the flow of energy through metal, and that was why Sunny and every other caster witch I knew used wood or cloth.

And Roenberg didn't have the blood as far as I could smell.

He snapped the folder holding Bryson's complaint shut and set it on his desk, arranging the edges so they were perfectly even with his blotter.

"Are we done here?" Mac asked him.

Roenberg smiled, close-lipped. "Not even close, Troy. Young lady"—he finally deigned to address me—"how long have you been on the force?"

"Seven years, sir," I said, willing myself not to chafe at the *young lady* part.

"And why did you become a law enforcement officer?"

Did he really expect me to stand up straight, with a

tear in my eye and a quiver in my voice, and say, *To protect and serve, sir*?

Apparently so, because he snapped, "I'm waiting, Detective."

I bored into him. He stared impassively back at me, eyes flat. I was less than nothing to him. The thought of losing my job for good kept me from leaping the desk and trying to wring his turkey neck, but it was an uphill fight.

"I believe that there are evil people in the world, Captain," I said. In the closed room my voice was rough, with a growl underneath it. The rage floating in my animal brain had smelled blood and come out for a closer look. "I believe that there are people who need to be caught, and punished. I became a cop to do just that." And to escape those insistent voices that told me I would never, ever be anything more than another dead end on the Wilder family tree, too stupid to pull herself up and too drunk to realize it.

Roenberg shrugged. "Why not become a social worker? Or a security guard? Something more suited to your temperament? Why bring your issues into my squad?"

"Social workers and security guards have never had the pleasure of interviewing a thirteen-year-old rape victim," I grated. "They've never seen what a .45 automatic can do to a human body. I have. And it is because of this that I will continue to be a cop until I'm either dead or too old to shoot straight."

Mac reached over and touched me on the wrist. I realized my voice was raised, almost shouting. The rage opened its nose and took a deep breath, scenting prey. *Not here,* I prayed. *Please. Not now.*

"Very touching," said Roenberg. He tossed my file at

McAllister. "You're suspended without pay pending the investigation into your conduct with Detective Bryson and a full review of your case log for the past year. Your closure rate is unusually high."

McAllister jumped up. "Excuse me?" Fortunately his yelling covered my muttered "You slimy little . . ."

"Captain," said Mac, face flushed to a bright Irish rouge, "I understand the need to discipline Detective Wilder for the altercation, but she's one of my best detectives. Her closure rate is something to be *proud* of."

"Troy, I'm sure you think Detective Wilder is the most wonderful thing to grace this city since crosswalks and streetlights," said Roenberg. "And I'm sure she's been happy to take advantage of the politically correct attitudes some of our fellow officers have been brainwashed into." He swiveled his chair to face me and pointed a finger. "Detective, you are here to fill a quota, and nothing more. Any success you've had since then is a happy accident."

I moved for him then. Mac's hand clamped down on my upper arm, digging in and hurting me. The were snarled at the back of my head, urging violence and vengeance. I focused on the pain and let it hold me in McAllister's grip.

"We'll be going now, sir," he said to the captain.

"Leave your gun with Lieutenant McAllister," said Roenberg. "And for your future employment, Detective Wilder, may I suggest a career a bit less taxing on your highly emotional personality?" He waved a hand to dismiss us, and I noticed for the first time that Roenberg sported a tattoo on his left palm. I had just enough time to think that the spiked tribal-style circle didn't suit a tightass like him before Mac dragged me out and shut the door.

"That prick!" I exploded as soon as he did.

"Will you shut the hell up?" Mac hustled me down the hall and past Rick, whose moon face wore a deeply concerned expression. "What were you thinking, pulling out that impassioned speech crap in front of Roenberg?"

"I thought maybe I'd appeal to his memory of the time when he was a real cop, but apparently that time was never," I grumbled.

"Roenberg hates mouthy detectives, and he hates mouthy broads more," McAllister said. "Bad luck for you that you're both."

I opened my mouth to spit some more vitriol, but Mac held up his hand. "Luna, I'm truly sorry but I need your gun."

I yanked the Glock out of holster, worked the slide, and slapped it butt-first into Mac's palm. He winced. I didn't apologize.

I shoved my case folder in a drawer and locked it, snapped my badge off my belt, and thrust it at Mac. "Here." I had to fight hard to resist screaming, throwing things, tearing someone's throat out. Or sobbing.

Mac folded his hand around mine, closing my fingers over the badge. "I distinctly remember being ordered to collect your weapon. I've done that. We're finished here."

I grimaced, managing a "Thanks."

"For what? I'm relieving you of duty. You should be pissed off."

"You have no idea how much," I said, collapsing in my desk chair. What I didn't add was at who. Were rage had put me directly in this position. Roenberg had no call to be as big a dickhead as he was, but if I hadn't attacked Bryson for no reason I'd still be sitting around the squad room, drinking iced mochas and avoiding work on my cold cases.

Mac touched my shoulder. "Was it just my imagination, or in Roenberg's office, were you . . . ?"

I shook my head. "Not your imagination. Something's off with my moonphase, and it's driving me freaking insane."

Mac frowned. "Go home, Luna. I'll talk to the chief of detectives in the morning, and we'll get this straightened out."

"Not if Bryson and Roenberg have anything to say. You know they'd throw a party if I got fired. Probably with streamers and little hats."

"Chin up. Tomorrow's another day." McAllister went into his office and shut the door, probably to drag off an illicit cigarette if I knew him. Mac didn't smoke socially, but he always had a pack on him when he worked. A nervous habit, like biting your nails. Most cops who make it out of blues have one to cope with the stress. McAllister had his Camels and I had a dojo near the cottage where I went and pounded the shit out of a black leather punching bag until I was too tired and my limbs were too heavy to think straight. In stressful situations I've caught myself shuffling my feet, moving my arms ever so slightly to punch and block.

I reached the squad room door, hauling my lone spider plant along with my usual book bag of miscellaneous crap I take to work when my desk phone rang. I kept walking. It kept ringing.

I went back and snatched the receiver. "What!"

"Um . . . Detective Wilder?"

"Not at the moment. But hey, I'll humor you. Who's this?"

"Ah, this is Pete Anderson, in the ID lab? I caught the print work for your Jane Doe murder?"

I forced myself to think happy thoughts so I wouldn't scare the guy to death. "Yes, Pete. What is it?"

"You have your computer on?"

I flicked the mouse, and my monitor came back to life. "Yeah."

"Check your e-mail. Your Jane Doe is no more."

I clicked on the file he'd sent me and a screen popped up, created right here in the data banks of the Nocturne City PD. Jane Doe had a name. And a record.

Pete said, "She was born Lilia Desko, one arrest for drugs and two for—"

"Solicitation," I finished for him. "You're sure this is her?"

"Eight-point match," he told me proudly.

So now she was no longer Jane Doe, but Lilia. Just in time for me to no longer be on her case.

"Thanks for all your hard work, Pete. You're a sweetheart."

"Hey, no problem," he said, and I could practically picture his ears turning red on the other end of the line. "Oh, Detective? There is one other thing."

"What's that?"

"Dr. Kronen found more prints on the victim's skin with an ALS." Alternate light source. Kronen had gone above and beyond for an anonymous hooker autopsy. Maybe I should puke on him more often.

"I'm sending you another file," Pete said.

"The person they belong to is in the system?"

"Oh, yeah," he said. "Is he ever. Okay, you should have it now."

I clicked and brought up another face. Male, with hard lines, a broken nose blessed with a devilish crook instead of an ugly bump, shaggy dark red hair, a Fu Manchu biker mustache of the same color, and a look that said, were it an option, he would kill whoever was on the other side of the mug shot camera.

He was kinda sexy.

"Detective? Did you receive the file?"

I cleared my throat. "Dmitri Sandovsky? Yeah." I read. "Says here he was arrested with Lilia for pimping, and a few more times for possession with intent."

"The two P's," Pete agreed cheerily. "Think he might be your guy?"

I looked at Sandovsky's face, the hard mouth and the crazy gleam in his wide, dark eyes. "Oh, yeah," I said.

FOUR

Fog and sharp cold air greeted me as I left the precinct. I started the Fairlane and drove toward Magnolia, aimless.

Dmitri Sandovsky's sheet sat on the passenger seat, taunting me with its orderly list of known aliases—none—and last known address. Surprise surprise. None listed.

Go home. That was the right thing to do. Go home, put in twelve hours of sleep, wait out my moonphase on suspension, and go back to work a new woman.

Instead, a passing street lamp illuminated Sandovsky's snarling face and deep green eyes, burning with the questions I wanted answered—why did you kill Lilia? Why tear her throat and take a trophy? What could she possibly have done to deserve treatment like that?

Could I hurt Sandovsky as badly in return?

I pulled over and looked at the sheet again. Sandovsky's last arrest had been at a shitty tenement block in the Waterfront district. I flipped open the glove compartment and grabbed a map of Nocturne City covered in marker lines. A different color marked the border of known gang territory, known mob territory, and patches of the city known to be controlled by packs. I'd been working on the map since I was in uniform.

Waterfront had a bold border of black, meaning were pack territory. Packs ran their territories with fierce jealousy, and if Dmitri was dealing in Waterfront he either belonged to the pack that ran it or he was one hell of a sweet-talker. He would be known.

I shoved the map back into the glove compartment and debated for just a second before I gunned the engine and took a right onto Leavenworth Boulevard. The quickest way to the Waterfront, and Dmitri Sandovsky's last known address.

As I drove, Leavenworth morphed from crumbling storefronts and beggars to crumbling converted row houses and sleazy club kids wandering along the sidewalk. The road dipped and then crested, laying out the half-moon of Siren Bay below me. At night the freight cranes and containers hid from view; all that reflected were a million lights from the high-rises circling the west shore. If the wind was blowing the right way, you could even ignore the sour salt smell that the polluted bay water spread around Waterfront as a substitute for oxygen.

At one point in Nocturne's history, when lumber and precious metals had passed through the port, Waterfront had been the most desirable address in the city. Overnight millionaires built apartments, hotels, and fabulous wooden mansions, most of which either burned in the Hex Riots or were condemned and demolished by the city as the affluence moved out and the weres moved in during the aftermath.

Humans thought Waterfront was deadly glamorous, a sort of miniature Dodge City hidden within Nocturne's already wildly tangled jungle. I had seen more terrified suburban yokels than I could count come out of Waterfront mugged, beaten, or worse. Every time I had to take a statement from a sniffling middle-class prom queen who thought it would be fun to go slumming with the beasts, I wanted to slap the were population upside the head. I may be Insoli, but they were idiots.

I parked the Fairlane in front of an apartment building where residences would have gone for half a million dollars pre-Hex. Now it was beyond deserted, a squat with no real dwellers, and a smell that could have flattened me from the sidewalk. Two hoboes were asleep on the marble stoop, which had mostly crumbled.

This was a crazy fishing expedition. Sandovsky's most recent arrest was almost a year old. A man like him would keep moving, make himself hard to find. For all I knew he lived on the road and slept only in the beds of the women he visited for a night. In my old life, guys like him were just my type, and they usually came with motorcycles, guns, and outstanding warrants.

I walked down the block a bit, scouting. The sidewalk was full of normal humans, not a were in sight. Good thing, too. I would definitely not be welcomed with open arms. I should go home and go to sleep like a good girl. I was punchy from getting sick and from the awful scene in Roenberg's office. Damn Roenberg. Moonphase or no, the guy was due for a punch in the nose from somebody, preferably me.

Then I smelled them, close and packed together. The scent emanated from a converted wood frame house that was now a bar, replete with tacky neon and a crookedly lettered sign telling me happy hour was from nine to whenever.

I had found the pack that ran the Waterfront. Lot of good it did me, too, because I couldn't go marching in and start the interrogation. Weres had the right to do as they pleased with any Insoli who violated their territory.

I'd learned that one the hard way. Now it really was time to go home.

I had left the Fairlane alone for barely two minutes, but there was already a fat man in a leather jacket and jeans stuffed into steel-toed shitkicker boots eyeballing it. More than eyeballing—he was leaning on the window and practically making out with the door.

"May I help you, sir?" I snipped brightly. He turned on me with unfocused eyes.

"Uhhh . . . hey, honey." The confusion broke into a rheumy smile. "Boy, you're real high-class."

"Thank you. Does that mean you're going to stop breathing on my car?"

"This thing yours? Baby, this piece of shit ain't nothin'."

I took a step closer to him, intending to be imposing and authoritative to make him leave me alone. Then the smell hit me. Shit. He was a were, and had a hell of a lot more right to be here than I did. My stomach churned, the were knowing it was trespassing, the fight-or-flight fear reaching up to clamp my heart.

"Lemme buy you a drink," Sidewalk Warrior slurred. "High-class pussy needs a free drink."

I stared. He misinterpreted. "Oh, we can talk about dough now if ya want. I gots some money. My buddy owes me fifty dollars."

Inhale, exhale. He's too drunk to realize what you are. Relax, this time.

He reached for my arm, and survival instincts kicked in with a scream. I jerked away from him, leather creaking.

"C'mon, honey. I ain't got all night here," my suitor told me. *Run or fight,* the were whispered. *Kill or flee.*

I clenched my fingers against my palm, digging in and reaching for control. He could get me inside. Insoli plaything to a pack member. I could do this.

"Honey," I told him, my voice a silky smooth purr, "I could *die* for a drink."

"Thaasss more like it!" He beamed. "C'mon with me, dollface." He took my arm and dragged me across the street toward the bar. Choppers and road bikes lined the parking spaces in front. I barely registered, letting the drunken were lead me inside. My heart thudded my ribs, and I was more scared than I could remember being in a long, long time. No one walked into a roomful of pack weres uninvited and lived to tell about it.

Yet here I was, blazing the trail. Yay me.

Darkness and blue cigarette smoke caressed me when I came over the threshold. The walls of the place were knocked out, bricks exposed. Scarred hardwood creaked under my feet; a sign above a crude plywood bar proclaimed RIDE OR DIE, a winged and bandanna-clad skull lording over the letters. The skull was a wolf's. Real subtle there, guys.

No one so much as looked at me. The smell of weres was so thick that I couldn't even begin to tell one from the other, and they were all preoccupied with drinks, girls, or both.

"C'mon, honey." The fat man tugged me toward the bar. "You go order yourself a drink, pretty, while I see my buddy about some money for tha party." He winked at me broadly. *Ignore it, Luna, and let him think whatever the Hex he wants about your profession. You're in.*

After the tugging didn't work my pseudo-suitor shoved me in the small of my back. I stumbled up against the bar. The bartender sneered at me.

"What are you drinking?"

My date ambled down the bar until he reached a hulking figure on a stool with his back turned. I couldn't see anything of his "friend" aside from a blue bandanna and a motorcycle jacket emblazoned with a snarling wolf head.

"Lady, much as I'd love to stand here and stare at you until the second coming of Christ, could I get your order now?" the bartender asked. The big guy turned as my errant date tugged at his jacket. I saw his face and choked.

"It's him."

The bartender followed my eyes. "Sorry, lady. I just pour the drinks. Pimping—you're on your own."

I ignored him and strode over to stand behind the fat were, staring directly into Dmitri Sandovsky's eyes. I sniffed deep. Yep, Sandovsky was a were, too.

Fan-freaking-tastic.

"Well hey, pretty," he rumbled at me. "And here I thought Manley was bullshitting when he said he needed the fifty bucks to buy some company." A gravel-scraped voice with just a hint of Eastern Europe in the accent. Green eyes, so dark they were almost black. He'd shaved off the mustache in favor of a red goatee, but otherwise the face matched the mug shot. Complete with crazy smile. In person, he was still kinda sexy.

"C'mon, Dmitri, cough up the bucks!" Manley whined. "Won 'em off you fair an' square at pool."

"Actually," I purred, taking a step toward Sandovsky. "I think your friend here should spend that money on me himself."

Something dark flickered in Dmitri's eyes, and his

smile widened to show shockingly white, straight teeth. "Manley, take a hike," he said without removing his eyes from me.

"Aw, c'mon, Dmitri! She's so hot, man . . ."

Sandovsky turned on Manley and growled. Not just the raspy sound most humans make but an actual growl, deep and rumbling. Manley turned tail and fled to the other side of the room. Sandovsky swiveled back to me. "Where were we?"

"Well." I smiled, giving my shoulders a little shimmy and pushing my chest forward. "You were gonna tell me what you wanted me to do?"

His grin almost split his face apart. *That's right, Sandovsky. This is the luckiest night of your life.*

"Beautiful, what I want is for *you* to tell *me*."

Oh, he was good. I bet those bedroom eyes and that voice made of hard dust alone made girls' panties moisten. It was sure working on me . . .

Focus, Luna. Homicidal sex killer here. Not someone you should find remotely attractive. And you better get him out of here fast, lady, before all his pack buddies realize what you are.

I chuckled low in my throat, placing my hand on his thigh. Hard and muscled. No softness under my palm. "Should we go somewhere?"

Dmitri took another lazy swig of his beer. "You can talk dirty to me right here."

Damn it all.

I leaned into his face and breathed out, lips an inch from his. "Have you heard the one where I take you into bed, push you down, straddle you, and then . . ." I unhooked my cuffs from my waist and let them dangle in Sandovsky's face. ". . . arrest you, handcuff you, and take you in?" I finished.

Sandovsky's eyes popped. "What the fuck is this?"

"Dmitri Sandovsky, you're under arrest for the murder of Lilia Desko," I said crisply. "Turn around and put your hands on the bar."

He laughed at me before I could start in on the Miranda warning, so hard some beer sloshed out of the bottle he was holding. "Sweetie, that's great, but there's such a thing as takin' the fantasy too far. You're not a cop. You're just Insoli trash. And if you *were* a cop in this place, you'd be in deep shit."

"Sweetie," I said, taking my badge off its clip and slapping it on the bar, trying to hide the shock I felt at the fact he had discerned my Insoli standing, "this isn't anyone's fantasy, I am a cop, and the only one here in deep shit is you." Lilia's torn throat came into my head, and my voice hardened as I thought of how Dmitri had been the one to tear it. "Put your hands on the bar. Now."

Sandovsky looked at the shield, at me, at the shield again.

"You said Lilia Desko," he said finally.

"That's right," I agreed.

"Lilia's dead?"

"I don't know, Sandovsky. Why don't you tell me, seeing as you're the one who killed her."

"When?"

"Get your hands up and be quiet," I snapped. "You do have the right to remain silent. Use it."

I expected rage, screaming, Sandovsky putting up a fight. Instead his entire body began to shake, and tears sprouted at the corners of his eyes.

"Lilia's dead," he said again, testing the words.

"Yes, Mr. Sandovsky, she is," I told him, reaching for his arm to restrain him.

He lashed out, sweeping a collection of beer bottles

off the bar. "Fuck!" he screamed, collapsing to his knees, quaking with sobs. "She can't be!"

Real grief is hard to fake. A six-foot-four were biker having a breakdown in full view of his packmates is damn near impossible.

"Mr. Sandovsky?" I said softly. "I need to take you in."

He looked up at me, and I could see the wheels turning in his head, weighing the odds.

Then he slowly got up and placed big, scarred hands flat on the bar. I grabbed his right wrist and pulled it behind his back. Rougher than I needed to be, but he shouldn't have called me trash. The room had gone quiet. Was this Old West or what? I half expected a posse to burst through the front door.

"You're making a mistake," Sandovsky told me as the handcuff locked around his wrist. He wasn't shaking anymore, but he was pale under the goatee and had the shattered look of a man whose entire world had just been rearranged.

"You made a bigger one when you killed Lilia," I told him with a snarl of my own. Being around so many weres was making me cranky.

"I didn't kill Lilia," he muttered. "Didn't even know she was dead." Was it my imagination, or did something stir in his eyes—regret? His mouth tightened. His lips were full and expressive, at odds with his angular cheeks and chin. And *why* was I noticing this?

"What bastard did it?" Sandovsky demanded.

"Why do you care? She was just your whore," I said, reaching for his other arm. The pure hurt in his expression caught me off guard, and it was all the time he needed to rotate his upper body and hit me in the side of my head with his uncuffed hand.

My skull exploded like a flashbulb had gone off inside

it. Sandovsky knocked me sideways into the bar, wrenched his secured arm from my grip, and barreled out the door. I pulled myself upright, ears ringing. My vision skewed distinctly to one side, and the cold, detached part of my brain told me I had a nasty concussion coming.

Were strength. Like meeting a Mack truck head-on.

Manley and his little friends had gathered in a half circle around me, watching with bright eyes to see what I might do for my next trick. Leaning on the bar and willing myself not to fall over again was about all I could manage.

One of the cronies pulled a knife. Big, silver, a fixed-blade hunting job. "Where you goin', *pretty*?" he mocked. All the men had the same snarling wolf head on some part of their clothing. *Thanks, Sandovsky, for running out and leaving me with your chorus line.*

At least he'd also left me his empty beer bottle. I tapped it hard against the bar and then brought the jagged end to Hunting Knife's neck, at the spot where his carotid artery pulsed under the skin.

"Back off or I bleed you." No gun. I had no gun. *Why* had I come into this place with no gun? Curiosity may have it in for the cat, but tonight it had killed the damn werewolf.

The pack circled me, closing in so I could barely move my arms. They were amused by my attempt to protect myself. I was prey.

Only one thing could possibly work in my favor here and that was not being a pack member. No ranking meant no way to judge how much dominance these jerkoffs had over me. Dominance among weres exists mostly to keep the new bites in line, but it can turn ugly fast when folks decide they don't like their place in the pecking order.

"Neil, mebbe you should teach her it ain't nice to play rough," Manley chortled.

I stepped up to Neil's big black boots, leaning in until our noses were less than an inch apart and I could smell the hot dog and relish he'd eaten on his breath. I stared into his eyes, keeping the bottle on his neck. "Move," I growled. The were echoed, telling Neil he was nothing, a simpering pup compared with me. He would be torn apart if he stood against me. I was powerful, he was weak. I dominated, he got the hell out of my way.

I almost *felt* the air go out of Neil. The smell coming off him changed from a musky stink to sour, like stale urine. His jaw quivered, and he dropped his eyes from mine, knife arm falling to his side.

"Shit," Manley muttered in an awed tone. The pack parted.

I had no time to parse that I had successfully dominated a group of weres on their own territory. I was glad to be alive, and out the door faster than Sandovsky, running to close the gap between us.

FIVE

At the street I stopped and sniffed, drawing odd looks from a group of passing clubgoers. Sandovsky was distinctive, his stricken body odor harsh even in the stench that surrounded Cannery Street. He had gone north and I followed suit.

Run hard, remembering the six-minute mile that qualified me for the police academy. Pour my extra-strong heart and enlarged lungs into the chase, feel my muscles work in tandem with my blood and breathing.

Sandovsky's scent trail ended in an alley three blocks up, at a blank brick wall slick with moss and grit. Surrounded by high walls, the alley was pitch-black. I breathed slowly and listened. Nothing. Well, unless Sandovsky could pass through walls, he was still in the alley waiting for the chase to run on by.

A quick scan showed me a rickety fire escape ladder about five feet up. No stretch for a big guy like Sandovsky. I jumped, caught the third rung, and pulled myself up, climbing quickly and wishing harder and harder that McAllister hadn't taken my gun.

The tenement roof was rotten, exposed tar paper flaring from underneath the shingles. It was like every other crumbling building in the city—a flat surface with half a dozen chimneys and an access door labeled CONDEMNED—NOCTURNE CITY HOUSING AUTHORITY in bright orange letters.

I whispered into the night air. "Sandovsky?"

Heavy breathing answered me from behind one of the half-destroyed chimneys, along with growling.

My heartbeat quickened. That definitely hadn't been human. If Sandovsky was some kind of witch in addition to being a were—*Stop it,* I told myself. I reached into my empty holster, brushed leather with my fingers, and cursed silently. I made two fists instead, as if whatever was behind that chimney could be dealt a good hard punch and that would be that.

It growled again. Something like a large dog, only lower and with more bloodthirsty menace creeping along the undertones.

My fear put on rage as a mask. "Whatever you are, get the hell out here!" I ordered.

Heavy treads sounded, and something low and bulky padded into the sickly half-moon light reflecting off the bay. A canine head with pricked ears, yellow eyes that glowed from under heavy brows, and startlingly bright white teeth protruding from under a curled lip.

The red-furred wolf stared at me and growled again.

"Oh . . . crap" was all I mustered as my mind raced at a thousand miles an hour, telling me this was not possible, the full moon was six days away, a werewolf that had been Dmitri Sandovsky was not, not, not looking at me.

Then I saw the handcuffs still locked around the wolf's right paw and I went cold.

He lifted his foot and shook off the offending link. It slipped away easily and landed with a thud on the rotten rooftop. He took a step toward me. Another. Stalking his kill.

I reached out with my foot, bumped a broken brick, picked it up. I might have been about to meet the same end as Lilia, but I would fight just as hard.

Sandovsky continued his measured progress toward me. I gripped the brick and prepared to smash it into his head in the same spot he'd hit me. A grievously injured were would phase back to human. Another bit I'd learned the hard way.

About five feet away Sandovsky stopped and licked his lips, black nostrils flaring to scent the wind. The rooftop creaked under us. As a man, Sandovsky was big but slim, maybe 220. As a wolf he had to weigh close to four hundred pounds.

He bared his fangs, and his back legs tensed. A roar erupted from his throat and then he was airborne, his wide maw coming straight at my face.

I screamed and slammed the brick into him, missing his temple and bouncing it off the back of his skull. I doubt he even noticed. His weight landed on my shoulders, dropping me like a sack of dead Luna. Nothing flashed before my eyes except Sandovsky's wolf face, and pure, unadulterated panic boiled my gut. I thrashed wildly under Sandovsky's weight, adrenaline doing its damndest to keep me breathing.

As Sandovsky reared back his head to tear out my throat and end his hunt, the wood underneath us gave way with a roar and we plummeted through the timbers. Plaster, insulation, and broken brick followed us down, covering me in an oppressive cloud of dust and rubble.

Too much. I blacked out as my body hit solid wood, the last thing I heard the crashing of beams and roof falling on top of me.

There is an iron band across my chest. No, an arm, a human arm, strong and masculine, adorned by a snake tattoo. The snake rears back, fangs reaching for me, and I feel his bite as the man's body presses down on my ribs, cracking me and crushing me and squeezing blood through my pores.

I gasped for air as I came to, roof beam holding me to the floor. The facts presented: I was alive and Sandovsky was gone.

Thrashing and kicking, I threw the beam off me and stood up. My right knee immediately gave out and I sank to the ground again, fighting tears.

I have a horrible phobia of being pinned, ever since I got the bite. It's been fifteen years, but I still wake up fifteen and on my back with Joshua holding me down, straining and panting as he sank pointed canines into my skin when I fought him. My shoulder throbbed where the crescent-shaped bite scar still showed, and I rubbed reflexively. Hiding it from my mother had been a real trick. My father was usually under a car or the influence, and couldn't have cared less.

After a minute I tried to stand up again and sort of managed it. A door-shaped hole led to a balcony, five stories up. My knee would be supporting me again by the time I walked out of this tenement thanks to were DNA, but the pain would take its sweet time to fade.

"Hex you, Sandovsky," I muttered as I started the five-story gauntlet toward the ground. He could turn into a were at will. All were packs had their magicks, passed down from the founder of their Line, but this was beyond anything I had ever witnessed.

Sandovsky was strong, dangerous, and a murderer. And with six days before the full moon, I had to work fast. Headstrong as Sunny and McAllister thought I was, I knew that if I faced Sandovsky at full phase, I would lose. And from what I'd seen of Sandovsky, he wasn't inclined to be merciful.

The waitress's name tag said DORIE. I hobbled through the door of the tiny diner and flopped into the nearest booth, which gave off a sweaty odor. It could have been coated in thumbtacks for all I cared right that second.

"You okay, honey?" DORIE yelled at me from behind the counter. "If yer a drunk, sleep it off someplace else!" She squinted at my face and then announced at the same volume, "Holy cow, you're bleedin'!"

"Among other things," I said. My knee felt like a small, determined dog was chewing on it. I pulled out my cell and started to dial Sunny.

"No cells in here!" Dorie hollered. "The radio waves mess up your brain!"

I yanked my shield off my belt and waved it at her. "Police business. Leave me alone."

She came closer and examined the shield. I prayed she wouldn't bite it to check for gold. "That real?"

"No, I shoplifted it from the toy store."

"I don't need none of your lip, missy," she informed me.

"Then just let me make my gods damn call and I'll be sweet as pie," I told her with a wide, fake smile.

Dorie grumbled but waddled away and let me be. I dialed and Sunny answered with an "Mmmhello?"

"Sunny? It's Luna."

"Luna!" she exclaimed, and I could picture her bolting

up out of her sheets in panic. "Oh, Hex, who died? Are you hurt? Did you shoot someone?"

"Why do you always assume the worst?"

"What happened!"

"Never you mind. Look, Sunny—I'm at the Waterfront, and I can't drive home with my knee, so I need you to grab a cab and take me and the Fairlane home."

"What happened to your knee?"

"Sunny?"

"Yes, Luna?"

"I'm in a lot of pain. Tonight would be nice."

She sounded truly worried, like she might cry. "Why can't you call for backup? Lieutenant McAllister will be worried sick!"

Somehow, I thought now might not be a great moment to tell my hyperemotional cousin I'd gotten suspended. Call it a hunch.

"Sunny, I'm in the . . ." I searched for a sign and saw it reflected in the diner window—STAE ETIN LLA. "All Nite Eats diner on Cannery. Come get me, and we'll take it from there. Hurry, Sunny." I closed the cell gently. Dorie was still staring at me.

"You wanna cuppa?" she finally said.

"From this place?" I said. "I'd have to be suicidal."

After Sunny drove the Fairlane home and I fell into bed, I dreamed about Joshua, who gave me the bite, and his howling screams as I'd escaped and run from his van. These dreams were so real I could feel the warm blood coursing down my shoulder and smell the salty tang of late-night San Romita air.

"You have no idea how bad it will be if you leave, bitch!"

I stumbled over rocks, my bare feet prey to the ground as I scrambled up the beach path. Far below me, Joshua exploded out of the van, yanking on boxers as he gave chase. He had seemed dangerous at the bonfire, but not this—not a man who'd make me bleed and certainly not a rapist.

"Luna! Get your ass back here! It was just a little love bite, baby!"

Crying and half naked, I made it to the coast highway and took off at a run. I'd gotten away in time, while he had his pants tangled around his ankles. I didn't have to look back—I knew what was behind me.

"Luna!"

My mind broke the surface of consciousness.

"Luna!"

I was in my bed, dressed in pajamas I never wore but that were familiar and mine. My entire body felt like it had been disassembled and then put back together by slightly sadistic mad scientists.

"Luna! Phone!"

Sunny's voice carried up the stairs and made my entire head split with pain.

"Luna—"

"I heard you!" I bellowed. "I'm awake! I'm coming!" A wave of dizziness engulfed me. Yelling at Sunny, apparently, was not something the Headache Gods favored.

Standing, either. My knee screamed as I tried to put weight on it, but it wasn't as wobbly as it had been last night. I pulled up the leg of the pajamas—lavender and pink stripes decorated with sprigs of flowers—and examined it. It was swollen, and my thigh was one solid royal blue bruise.

I made it down the stairs with slightly less grace than

Frankenstein's monster. Sunny was holding the cordless phone by its antenna, glaring at me.

"It's McAllister," she sniffed.

"What's your problem?" I demanded, taking the phone when she shoved it at me.

"Oh dear, let's see—we have the frantic phone calls at two AM, me not knowing if you're alive or dead most nights, and oh, don't forget the bitchy attitude that makes everything you put me through *so* much easier to handle."

"Sunny, you're being childish," I told her.

"I'm not the one keeping secrets about why you were even *in* Waterfront last night," she hissed.

"I got suspended," I said calmly.

Sunny's face went bright pink. "What!" she shrieked.

I put the phone to my ear. "Mac?"

"Luna?"

"Hold on a second."

Sunny gave me a glare that would have sent Sandovsky yelping for the hills. "What do you *mean* you got suspended?"

"Bryson's minuscule manhood got bruised and he filed a complaint. Roenberg took it, and suspended me."

"Luna?" McAllister shouted from the phone. "You there?"

I rubbed the point between my eyes. "I went to Waterfront looking for a suspect."

Sunny crossed her arms. "And by the looks of it you found him."

"You can drop that prissy tone," I told her. "You know damn well my job isn't all paperwork and procedure."

"No, apparently it's just a way for you to fight your own little war against people who have more common sense than you," Sunny returned. "Nice to see it's working

out so well." She spun and flounced out of the room before I could think of a comeback. She was being a bitch.
And she was right.

I sat down on the bottom step and raised the phone.
"Sorry, Mac. What is it?"

"Get down to the precinct," he said roughly. "You've
been reinstated."

"What?" I gaped. "How?"

"Don't ask me," he said. "Someone from City Hall
requested you personally to work a missing person
case."

"I'm a homicide detective, Mac. Unless he's missing
and dead—"

"Do you want to come back on duty or not, Wilder?"

"Yes, sir," I said. "I'll be there in half an hour."

S unny was in the kitchen chopping peppers for an
omelet when I found her, shoulders hunched inside a green sweater.

I went on the offensive and smiled. "Planning on
making one for me?"

The knife moved faster, and the cutting board rattled.
"No."

"Aw, why not?"

She stopped chopping and faced me. "You are not
going to sweep this under the rug, Luna."

"Sweep what?" I asked with wide eyes.

"Don't bullshit me," Sunny warned. I played innocent very badly, apparently.

"You're suspended because you're a were," Sunny
said. "No, I take that back. You're suspended because
you can't *control* being a were, and you refuse to figure
out how."

I stopped trying to be nice. "That's not true, and that's a hell of a thing to say. You think I like having to constantly hold on for fear that if I have a bad day, I could kill somebody?"

"Well, I don't know," said Sunny. "You ran from the one person who could have taught you about the bite."

"Joshua seduced me, attacked me, and was well on his way to raping me, Sunny. Should I have stuck around?"

She waved the knife at me and went back to chopping. "The point is, having magicks isn't a gods-given gift that you can run with as you please. It took me a long time to learn how to manipulate the circle and—"

"Hex it, Sunny, I'm not some caster witch who can choose to ignore her powers when they get inconvenient. And I didn't have a wise old mentor to say, *Hey, it's okay if you snap and tear somebody apart when the phase takes you. All part of the package, sweetheart.*"

Sunny stiffened at *wise old mentor*. "She was there for you, too, Luna."

"Don't even start," I spat. "Our grandmother couldn't even look at me when she found out what I was. I'm invisible to her."

Sunny looked away first. Point, me. "She's the most powerful caster witch I know. If you ask her, she'll help you."

"I will *never* ask Rhoda Swann for *anything*."

Sunny sighed. "Do you want an omelet?"

"Forget it," I said. "I'm late for work."

SIX

I n the daylight, the Twenty-fourth looked worn-out and faded, the brick cracked and the windows filmed with grime.

The same city Lexus was in the parking lot, only this time they had taken Bryson's space. I decided the thrill I got from that fact was totally appropriate.

In the squad room McAllister was leaning on my desk. His first words were, "Hex, Wilder. Who gave you that shiner?"

"I walked into some stairs."

"Sure," said Mac. "Roenberg's waiting for us in his office."

The captain opened his door before Mac had a chance to knock. "Troy. And Detective Wilder. Come in, please. We've been waiting." Roenberg's imperious tone had the instant effect of making me feel like I was being summoned to the principal's office for something I hadn't done, but would be blamed for anyway.

Roenberg ushered us in with one limp hand and shut the door. In the clear light of day, the liver spots on his cheeks and the flesh puddling on his neck were even more obvious.

A tall, balding man was talking in whispers with the same snaky jerk who had taken my parking space the night Lilia Desko was killed, seated in the two chairs opposite Roenberg's desk. They looked up in tandem when Mac and I came in.

Mac motioned to me and said to Baldy, "This is the detective you asked for."

"Ah," said Baldy, standing. "It's a pleasure."

Seeing him full-on, I recognized the square jaw and hawk nose immediately. That cleared up the mystery of why I'd been reinstated, but it didn't do a thing to explain why Alistair Duncan, Nocturne City's district attorney, had requested me out of the two hundred detectives roaming the streets.

"Mr. Duncan." I shook his hand. "This is . . . unexpected."

"I've heard great things about you," he said with a smile that looked like it hurt. "This is Regan Lockhart, the chief investigator for my office."

"Detective," Lockhart smirked, offering a hand. My nose twitched. Lockhart really needed to lay off the cologne, expensive or otherwise. When a long second went by without me touching him, he withdrew the hand and dropped the smile.

"You said this was a missing person," I reminded Mac.

"Yes," said Duncan. "I'm afraid it is." He glanced to Lockhart, then to Roenberg before settling back on me. "There's no easy way to say this." He rubbed his knobby hands over his head. The ring of gray hair over his ears stuck up wildly. "My son, Stephen . . . he hasn't been home in two days."

"Is that unusual?" I asked. Lockhart shot me a glare,

like I'd just asked if Stephen Duncan liked to smoke crystal meth and urinate on small dogs. I rolled my eyes and turned my back on him.

"Stephen is a good son, Detective," said Duncan. "He's not answering his phone or his pager. He's never been out of touch for so long."

"Okay," I said, pulling out my notepad and stealing a pen off Roenberg's desk. They wanted a detective, I'd be one. "Any idea where he might have gone?"

"He was going out to dinner with a young woman friend at Mikado's," Duncan said. I scribbled. Mikado's was the kind of trendy restaurant where tiny pieces of food came on white plates and you spent four hundred dollars on a bottle of wine if you wanted to get laid.

"Who's the woman?"

"Her name is Marina. That's all I know." Duncan's affect was flat, almost pleasant. I could have been asking him what he'd eaten for breakfast.

"And did Stephen take a car or was he driven?"

"Mr. Duncan, Junior took his personal Mercedes to the dinner date," Lockhart said. He and Duncan picked up each other's sentences smoothly, like long-term partners on the force did. "We'd like you to focus on this Marina woman, and also trace any credit charges that may have occurred since Stephen fell out of contact. That will be the fastest way to locate him."

I fixed my eyes on his and held them silently until he fidgeted. They were eerie, no color around the pupils except darkness, but I pretended not to notice. "Mr. Lockhart, if you're so sure of how I should do my job, why aren't you heading this investigation?"

"Detective Wilder!" Roenberg shouted.

Lockhart held up a hand to silence him.

"I would like nothing better, Detective," he bit back

at me, "but Mr. Duncan is convinced that my involvement could represent a conflict of interest if prosecution of Stephen's abductors is necessary."

Duncan let out a choked sound. Lockhart grimaced. "Sorry, Al."

I closed my pad. "Mr. Duncan," I said softly, "what make you think Stephen's been kidnapped?"

"Captain, would you please instruct your officer to do as we've asked?" Lockhart broke in before Duncan could speak.

"Everything will be handled to the very best of our abilities," said Roenberg smoothly. He touched the DA's shoulder. "Don't you worry, Al." I fought the urge to hand Duncan the card for my dry cleaner, to get rid of the slime.

Roenberg snapped his fingers at Mac. "Troy, will you please show the DA and Mr. Lockhart out?"

McAllister turned the color of a tomato. Nothing like a game of musical rank pulling to enliven the shift. "Yes, sir," he muttered tightly.

As they walked out I heard Mac say to the DA, "Al, you and I both know your office is above reproach, but the next time one of your lapdogs tells my detectives how to do their job . . ." The glass door slammed shut. I started to follow when Roenberg caught me.

"Detective Wilder, a moment." Goddess on a burning stick, not another one of his "moments."

Roenberg sat back in his leather chair and steepled his fingers. His permanently bloodshot eyes gave me a tired stare. "I suppose you think this is some kind of victory."

"I wouldn't go that far, Captain." When he'd suspended me, Roenberg had lost the privilege of me calling him *sir*.

"Mr. Duncan and I go back a long way, Wilder. I tried to convince him that any other detective on Stephen's case would be more capable, but he would not be swayed. Don't ask me why." He leaned toward me, coming out of his chair, and I could smell his lunch on his breath. Steak and Caesar salad. "That being the way things are, I hope I can trust you to handle this matter discreetly."

I sighed. Here it was, the veiled threat. I knew the moment Lockhart had let the word *abductors* slip this was going to get messy.

"Do you understand me, Detective?" Roenberg demanded.

"I'll handle the case in accordance with departmental media protocol." I smiled at Roenberg. That was the best he was getting out of me.

"That's not what I mean and you know it!" he snapped, surprising me with his ferocity. "You breathe one word of this, Wilder, let one tiny detail slip to the press or your priest or your Hexed mother, and I will have your job and your ass." He stared at me, and the look was desperation writ large. His left hand clenched and unclenched, making the indistinct black tattoo on the palm fluctuate. "You'll be lucky to find work checking IDs in a Waterfront nightclub."

I stood. "I can't tell you how much I enjoy our little chats, Captain. Now if you'll excuse me, I have a missing man to find. Discreetly, of course." I walked out and slammed the door behind me hard.

Roenberg yelled, "I didn't dismiss you!" but I ignored him.

The overweight second-shift detective who occupied the desk across the aisle gave me a startled glance as I sat down and slammed on my keyboard to bring up the police database. I gave him a rude look. "Help you with something, chubby?"

"Bitch," he muttered, dropping his eyes back to the open file on his desk.

I opened the database and searched for Marina, female, between twenty and thirty years old, last name unknown. No arrests, citations, or tickets. Next I accessed the DMV and tried for a driver's license or ID card. Nothing except the maddeningly blinking blue search box and the legend below it—NO RECORDS FOUND.

No arrest record—not unusual. No traffic tickets, maybe, if you were an eighty-year-old white woman who only drove to church and back. But nothing, anywhere in our system, was well on impossible.

I sat back and stared at the ceiling, trying to think of where else to search. There was one person who might be able to help me find Marina. I got my coat and headed for the morgue.

L ocated on the third floor of the city crime labs, the Identification Division was sandwiched into a narrow room overflowing with file cabinets and computers. The tang of ink sat in the air, as well as a thin sheen of fingerprint powder. Three techs were bent over light tables, dusting away.

I sneezed. The one closest to me looked up. "Help you?"

"I'm looking for Pete Anderson," I told him.

"Do you have an appointment?" the tech said deadpan, pushing his black wire-rimmed glasses up his sweaty nose.

"No, but if it would help I could put my foot up your butt and produce one, Mr. . . . ." I glanced at his name tag. ". . . Dellarocco."

"Relax! Jesus!" Dellarocco held up his hands in surrender. "I was joking, Miss . . . uh, Detective, uh . . . ma'am." He pointed into the recesses of the file cabinets. "Pete's back there."

I smiled and patted the lapels of his jacket straight. Dellarocca turned bright red. "Thanks, cutie," I told him with a wink. I'm pretty sure he stopped breathing.

A lone figure bent over a scarred oak table at the back of the identification room, surrounded by musty cardboard boxes labeled with case numbers. Stacks of fingerprint ten-cards stood around him, elbow-high.

"Pete Anderson?" I asked.

He turned quickly. "Who wants to know?"

I showed him my badge. "I'm Luna Wilder. We spoke on the phone a few nights ago about Lilia Desko."

"Oh, right!" he exclaimed, a blinding white smile breaking out in his dark face. A handsome young black man, Pete could just as easily have been grinning at me from a TV screen or holding down a high-powered job in the Mainline district in thousand-dollar suits. Instead his white coat covered a Led Zeppelin T-shirt and a pair of khakis heavily stained around the cuffs. "I remember you," he went on. "To what do I owe the pleasure?"

"Well, it's actually a kidnapping case," I began.

"Thought you were homicide?" He shrugged. "Never mind, who can keep track of that stuff? Mind if I work while we talk?" Without waiting for a reply, he turned back to the ten-cards and picked up a handheld magnifying lens.

"What are you doing?" I asked. "Don't you have AFIS for this?"

"Comparison," said Pete, pointing to a dried tan stick lying in an evidence baggie. "And not if your case is forty years old and was never high-profile to begin with. Most of this unsolved stuff before 1970 never got into AFIS."

I thought at first the stick was some kind of dried plant stalk. After a few seconds I realized it was a finger, the flesh mummified to a brown cocoon.

"Hex me. Where did that come from?"

"A missing woman in 1962," said Pete. "Polish immigrant, did laundry in Waterfront. A nice young woman, by all accounts. She disappeared one night on her way home from work. City was tearing down one of those condemned buildings along the bay last year, found her behind a false wall in the bathroom."

"Sad," I said.

"Not as sad as the fact five other women went missing between the winter of '61 and the spring of '62, all from the same neighborhood, all of a similar age," said Pete.

I raised an eyebrow. "Serial killer?"

"Definitely," said Pete. "Dumb bastard detectives at the time didn't think some missing Polacks were anything to get excited over."

"This happened before Zodiac, before Bundy," I said. "Most cops wouldn't recognize serial murder if it bit them in the behind. Cut them some slack."

"Like this sicko cut her some slack?" Pete pointed at the finger. "He stripped her, cut off her finger with pliers, and posed her like a doll. She died in terror." He caught himself when his voice started to rise and sighed. "I'm just trying to find out who she is. Let the family know, if she had any." He set the ten-card aside and brushed the dust off his hands. "At any rate, as you can see, your kidnapping case is right up my current alley. What's up?"

"White male, late twenties," I said. "Went to dinner at Mikado's with a woman named Marina. Hasn't been heard from since. I'm thinking if we find Marina, we find him. Unfortunately the name is all I have to go on."

"Huh. He take his car?"

"Yes. A Mercedes," I said.

Pete started on a new stack of cards. "Trace the plate. See if it's been reported stolen or abandoned. See if you can access OnStar or LoJack—might work."

"Um, it doesn't quite work like that," I muttered, feeling my face heat. Pete was absolutely right. If I hadn't been effectively gagged, I probably could have found Stephen Duncan already. Damn Roenberg, and damn McAllister for not sticking up for me.

"Any hits on the driver's license?"

"She doesn't appear to have one."

"You try Immigration?" asked Pete. I felt like a fool.

"No."

Pete set down his glass and carefully tucked the finger back into its case file box. "No license and no criminal hits usually means foreigner, legal or illegal. Let's see if she was granted a visa." He led me over to one of the numerous computers, clicked on two icons, and popped up Homeland Security's ICE database of entries into the country via Nocturne City. "Marina," he muttered. "Not a common name. Eastern Europe, maybe."

"Russian?" I said, feeling an uncomfortable sensation in the back of my mind. Lilia Desko, Dmitri Sandovsky, Marina . . .

"Worth a try," Pete agreed. He narrowed the search to

Russian nationals. "Nope, nothing in six months," he said. "If she has no other records, she's probably fairly new."

"Or she's illegal and using a fake name," I said.

"In that case, you're on your own," Pete agreed. "I just ID the crooks. I don't pound the mean streets." He chewed on his lower lip for a second. "Let's try a broad-based search."

"What's that?"

"A search including Russia and all countries that were members of the USSR. Sometimes you can't tell the names and dialects apart."

"Do it," I said. Pete typed in the search box and then hit the blinking icon. The screen went blank, and then a single entry popped up. "Bingo!" he cried. "Marina Narinovich, applied for a temporary work visa two months ago from Ukraine."

I could have kissed Pete Anderson. "Address?"

"Just a minute," said Pete. His face fell. "I don't think this is going to be much help, Detective. It's in Ghost-town."

"Great. Perfect. This is bullshit," I said. "How did she even get away with giving a nonexistent address at customs?"

"People slip through the cracks, Detective," said Pete. "If they didn't, I'd be out of a job."

The meter on my car had run out when I got back behind the wheel, and a pink parking ticket flapped gaily on my windshield. Blue wall, my ass. I grabbed the slip and shoved it into the glove compartment. After I sat and composed myself enough so I wouldn't run anyone down, I started the engine and pulled out into traffic. A dead girl and a missing man behind me at the Twenty-fourth, and the unfinished fight with Sunny at home.

What a fantastic night this was shaping up to be.

The downstairs lights in the cottage were all off when I pulled up, and the moon was just above the horizon over the ocean. I stood in the silver brightness for a minute, feeling the cool prickle as the were responded to the pull.

Five days to the full moon. I shivered, thinking of Sandovsky. What would he be like in full phase? Terrifying. Magnificent. No. I couldn't let myself think of that.

I opened the door gently, stowed my gun in the drawer, and took off my shoes. "Sunny?"

No answer. I climbed the stairs, hearing soft harp music coming from behind her door. I knocked. "Sunny? Can we talk?"

The music shut off, and after a long second Sunny pulled the door open. "What do you want?"

I took a deep breath and resolved to eat crow, humble pie, or whatever else I could ingest. "To say I'm sorry."

"You *should* be sorry, Luna!"

"McAllister reinstated me," I said quietly. Sunny stomped away from me and sat on her bed, holding Mr. Teddy, her ratty bear. "I'm very glad," she snipped. "How long were you planning to keep the suspension a secret?" Mr. Teddy's mismatched eyes glared at me.

"Gods, Sunny! I'm trying to apologize, and you're being a real brat."

"I'm allowed to be any way I please," she said, deliberately not meeting my eyes. "You expect me to help you and keep my mouth shut. I didn't have to leave my mom and Grandma Rhoda to babysit my werewolf cousin, but I did, and you treat me like hired help most of the time."

That's Sunny—sweet, polite, goes for the jugular.

"I'm sorry." I rubbed the spot between my eyes. "I don't think of you that way. I'm sorry that I've been pre-occupied, Sunny. It's . . . it's the phase. It's going to be bad this time, I can feel it. I don't want you to be anywhere near me when it happens."

Her head came up. "Luna, don't pretend that you're doing this to protect me. You're just afraid to admit you have no idea how to protect yourself, and that it scares you."

"Well, excuse the hell out of me if I don't want to mistake you for prey and rip you apart while I'm phased!" I shouted. "And for the record, *Sunflower,* I'm not scared of what's inside me, and I'm not scared of what I can do. I like being a were, and if you don't want to help then get the hell out of my way." I crossed my arms tight beneath my breasts and stood straight, daring Sunny to challenge my lies.

She reached out and took my hand, prying it loose and wrapping her fingers around mine. The strength in her grip surprised me. "Luna, either you let me do this on my terms, or you're on your own and I go back to San Romita," she said. "And if you like being a were so much, then go back to how you were when you first asked me for help."

"Shut up, Sunny," I warned her.

"You can go right back," she went on, talking over me. "Back to phasing every full moon and waking up covered in blood, not knowing if it was a rabbit you killed or someone who was unlucky enough to cross your path. If that's what you want, tell me now."

I wasn't angry with her. I was remembering the first time I'd woken up naked under fragrant rosebushes and sticky with blood that was still warm.

Sunny said, "Eventually Grandma and I are going to find the right working to cast. One that will keep you from phasing altogether."

"That can't be done, Sunny, and you know it. Once you've got the bite it will always come out."

"I can try," she said firmly. "Now, as long as we're being open and truthful and all that, why don't you tell me what happened to your face? You look like you got punched by the Incredible Hulk."

"Incredible werewolf, is more like it," I said.

"That sounds like a horrifying and potentially problematic story," said Sunny. "Tell it to me?"

I told her about Sandovsky, my chasing him onto the roof of the tenement, and what had happened there when I had seen him phase. When I finished her eyes were wide. "He went full-on were and there was no moon? That's . . . that's terrifying."

"No kidding." I muttered. "And when you brought me home, I dreamed about . . . you know." I rubbed my neck. The marks had faded, but the spot still tingled.

"About Joshua," Sunny said.

"And now I have to go to Ghosttown, to find this girl that's involved in my new case."

Sunny shook her head. "Keep playing roulette with the gods if you want. One of these days luck's going to run out and you'll be Hexed."

"Thank you," I said. "Very supportive."

Sunny shrugged. "I do my best."

SEVEN

At midnight I slipped quietly out of bed and dressed to go hunting in Ghosttown. I put on a pair of black jeans that had seen better days, a black cotton jersey over my tank top, and my biker jacket.

I pulled on my steel-toed Cochran boots and laced them. My hair went in a tight bun at the nape of my neck. My Glock went into a waist holster instead of the shoulder rig I usually wore on duty, and to it I added a heavy snub .38 that had been my father's. I didn't even know if the thing still fired, but just having it hanging from my ankle was comforting.

Last, I unclipped my shield from its leather holder and stuffed it deep in my jacket pocket. The last thing I wanted to broadcast in Ghosttown was being a cop.

I tiptoed out the door silently as I could in stiff-soled boots, and started the Fairlane with a rumble. Sunny's light didn't go on, but I saw her bedroom curtains twitch. I waved to her once before I drove away.

The Appleby Expressway took me through the skyscrapers of Mainline, with the sparkling sink of Siren Bay to one side and the black humps of Cedar Hill to the others.

Thirty years ago the Cedar Hill Killer had shared my view, until Nocturne City police gunned him down inside his parents' home in the Hills. Long before that, Jeremiah Chopin, the fugitive from Missouri who had founded a tiny outpost at the coast when he couldn't run anymore, had stood on the ridge above the bay and seen what his city would become.

True to his vision, Nocturne City was a haven for weres and witches and everyone who couldn't go back to somewhere else.

And in the end, in the Hex Riots, they had ripped the city apart. The Appleby soared above apartments on an overpass, and finally faded to factories and do-it-yourself storage, until my headlights lit up a rusty sign painted over with the warning DO NOT ENTER—EXIT CLOSED. I eased the wheel over and felt a bump as the pavement became scarred. Weeds, broken bottles, and other, less identifiable objects were caught in my high beams, and I was sure something small and fast with yellow eyes skittered away from the shoulder of the road.

I stopped and pulled my radio off the hook on the dash. "Seventy-six, Dispatch."

The radio hissed for a long moment. When the voice came back I jumped.

"Dispatch. Go ahead, Seventy-six."

"Investigating a lead at Exit Forty-three off the Appleby Express. Log, please."

The dispatcher had to be new, because she didn't even pause when she rattled back to me, "Ten-four, Seventy-six. Be safe." Anyone raised in Nocturne would know where Exit 43 led.

The radio clicked off and I was left in absolute silence except for the whoosh of cars on the Appleby. I put foot to accelerator and drove off the ramp and into Ghosttown.

Ghosttown had been Appleby Acres, once. Francis Appleby, a forward-thinking postwar mayor, erected the neat rows of homes, hotels, and shops as a miniature income-controlled village at the heart of Nocturne City.

But then the weres and witches moved in. In the small, poor neighborhood there were too many humans who remembered how the packs had once run Nocturne like a hairy, magicked mafia. Fear of witches and the power they controlled spread by viral communication from one block to the next.

In August 1969 Appleby Acres exploded into fire and death. The Hex Riots lasted for fifteen days and demolished Mayor Appleby's carefully crafted haven of progression and a brighter tomorrow. Now, officially, no one lived there.

Unofficially, the weres and witches never left.

A thin ground fog had formed in the night air, dampness leaching from the dark cement blocks that comprised buildings. Ghosttown was above all else a slum, and a terribly dangerous place for anyone without the blood or the bite. Neutral territory for the weres who spread out to run other parts of the city with dealing or pimping; the end of the line for trespassers, who would be lucky if there was enough DNA left to identify them.

All of which begged the question: why was Stephen Duncan, respectable human son of a respectable human DA, slumming with a Ukranian immigrant who listed this dump as her address? If she really lived here, it probably meant she was either a were or a blood witch on the run.

As I drove along what once had been a wide boulevard

with a landscaped median, I saw that the road was pot-holed beyond all recognition. I pulled the Fairlane over, killed the lights, and sat, watching.

Either Ghosttown really was uninhabited like City Hall would have humans believe, or whoever lived here was hiding and waiting. The federal housing blocks made it almost pitch dark, and electrical wires criss-crossed among them like a huge, malevolent insect web. A few dozen yards ahead of me, the burned-out hulk of a Buick sat in state on concrete blocks.

A thin, wavering light materialized from the fog, and a creaking contraption came into view. It was a shopping cart pushed by a man in a ragged raincoat with a flash-light lashed to the front. He saw my car and stopped. I cautiously eased my door open and got out.

He raised a hand. "Evenin'."

"Hello." I nodded.

"Not from Ghosttown, are ya?"

I shut the door and locked it. "You're very astute. I'm not."

"Dunno what that means. Ass-tute."

I walked around the back of my car and stepped onto the sidewalk. With the light in my face, the man's face became nothing but hollow eyes and a flash of teeth, but I could smell him from where I stood. Cheap wine, hu-man dirt, and a distinctive, tangy scent I couldn't place. Not were, nor witch. "It means you're observant," I said.

"Yeah. I sees a lot."

I took a step closer. He flinched.

"Maybe you can help me."

He laughed, which became a phlegmy cough. "Don't think so, lady. Can't help nobody, not even myself."

"But you can," I soothed, giving him one of my trade-mark smiles. "I'm looking for a friend down here."

The hobo laughed again. "Lady, ain't no one lookin' for nothing but a fix or a fuck in Ghosttown."

"Fine," I said, turning to go the other way, down a side street that had once held single-family brick homes. "Maybe you're useless after all."

"Waittaminute!" he yelled, lunging around his cart and grabbing me by the arm. I shook him off. "You don't wanna go that way!" His mouth was a round O, and I finally realized why his eyes were so strange.

They were pure black.

"Don't touch me," I warned. "I really don't like it."

"That way is bad news, lady."

I frowned. "Could you be a little more specific?" How the hell could his eyes be *black*? Like Lockhart's eyes, but these were dead, like glass chips.

The hobo shrugged. "Weres don't go that way no more. Bloods don't go that way no more. Tried to hole up in one of them houses, Meggoth's boys came."

"Meggoth?" How like me to get into deep conversation with a nut job.

"Up the hill and down the dock, comes the callin' of Meggoth . . ."

His eerie singsong sounded familiar, but it could have been because the song was set to the tune of "Mary Had a Little Lamb."

"Okay, enough singing for tonight," I said, changing tacks. "Suppose my friend came here looking for the only things people look for in Ghosttown. Where would he go?"

"Shit, that's easy," he said. "Hotel Raven."

"You people have a real knack for spooky names," I told him.

"Gotta go," he grunted, grabbing his cart by the

curved handles and bumping it over a pothole. Something wet shifted inside. "Feeding time."

As he bumped away I realized that the large wheels and curlicued handles didn't belong to a shopping cart, but to an old-fashioned baby carriage. "Hey!" I shouted. He stopped and looked over his shoulder, head swiveling like an owl.

"Where's the Hotel Raven?"

"Straight that way!" He pointed down the boulevard. "You can't miss it!"

How right the hobo was. The Hotel Raven really had been a hotel at some point, a nice one. It still had the original art deco facade and a marquee filled with burned-out bulbs. Obscene graffiti and symbols I didn't recognize covered the frosted-glass doors leading into the lobby. A pale girl in a white fur coat lounged against them, enticing passersby with a bored look that reeked of sex.

"Hey," she said to me. "Wanna party?"

"Do I look like I came here to party?"

She shrugged. "You never can tell." Her legs were toothpicks poking out of a pink vinyl skirt. I had an unwelcome flash of Lilia Desko, limbs akimbo, as her killer had left her. Sandovsky may think he'd gotten away, but the minute I found Stephen Duncan I was back on his ass.

"Maybe you'll know this girl I'm after," I said. "Name's Marina. She would have been here about two months."

"And why should I know her?" said the girl with a yawn. She was paler than some of the corpses I'd met and about as animated.

"You and she were most likely in the same line of work."

Her eyes flashed. "Hex you, lady. You don't know me."

I had tried to be nice. Now I smiled and said, "You're right. But I bet I could find out everything from your address to your rap sheet if I ran your name through my computer."

Usually when I play the police card people get defensive, or they gain a lot of respect fast. This girl laughed.

"You? Here? A cop in Ghosttown?" She sighed. "Oh, that's rich. Wait until Maven hears."

"And Maven is?"

"Sure are nosy. You won't last long like that."

A fat man in a rumpled white T-shirt, denim jacket, and black trousers interrupted us. "Kindred, honey. I been waitin' all week to see you."

"Baby," she cooed at him, wrapping an arm around his pudgy shoulders. As they walked away she threw a smile back at me, flashing pointy yellow teeth where there should be only straight.

I blinked, and looked again, but she and Baby had driven off in a rusty black sedan.

"I'm losing it," I told myself out loud.

The lobby of Hotel Raven had the same shredded elegance as the outside—here and there carpet still clung to the floors, and chipped marble formed a reception desk. The antique sconces that had lit the place dangled from their sockets like dismembered ears.

The elevators were nothing but gaping holes in the wall, their gates askew and stripped of anything shiny or valuable.

No clerk manned the desk, but a pair of teenagers dozed in chairs with the stuffing pouring out.

I walked the perimeter, looking for any sign that

Stephen Duncan had ever been here. This had been a ridiculous idea from the get-go. I could be sleeping or on my favorite shopping Web site, Feetz.com, combing their listings for a new pair of old Ferragamos.

A shuffle behind me. The two sleeping teenagers weren't sleeping anymore.

One of them flicked a folding knife. "Gimme your wallet."

I reached for the Glock. "Past your bedtime, kiddo. Sorry."

The second robber roared, and in a flash of air he was behind me, clamping my wrist. He smelled like day-old unwashed were. Fast little bastard, too.

"Hey, check it." He grinned at his buddy. "She's one of us, man. 'Nother Insoli."

I kicked out at his instep and he leapt away from me, again faster than the eye could see. Whoever gave him the bite hadn't been stingy with the magicks.

Knife Boy made a move and would have caught me in the ribs if someone hadn't slammed a gym bag into his head.

"Fuck off," said the bag's owner. I spun, jumpy, going for my gun. The petite redhead threw up her hands, dropping the weapon of my salvation to the pavement. "Whoa! Relax! I'm unarmed, Officer. Packless sleaze-balls!" she added as the two punks made a run for it.

I let my hand drop. "Who are you?"

"I'm Olya," she said. Her voice was firmly American, with no trace of an accent. She was also wearing a white buttondown and slacks, and had a folded apron tucked under her arm. The bag was inscribed with a logo and the jagged script CLUB VELVET.

"This is going to sound weird," I said, "but you don't look like you . . ."

"Belong in Ghosttown? I know." She shrugged. "I live here. Work in the city. I bring deliveries from my club's kitchen sometimes, to the ones that can't get out. Wouldn't live anywhere else myself. It's safe." All this recited as if we were talking about the possibility of rain.

"Safe? Are we seeing the same urban war zone, Olya?"

She winked. "I meant safe for people like me. And you, for that matter." She tapped her nose with one manicured finger.

I sniffed. Olya was a were.

"I'm Detective Wilder," I said, to stave off the realization that she had a pack and I didn't. "I'm here looking for a missing guy named Stephen Duncan. I have a photo if you need it." I pulled out the yearbook portrait from Alder Bay Academy that Alistair Duncan had left on my desk at the Twenty-fourth. About ten years old, but still a good face shot of Stephen. Olya took it and held it close to her button nose.

"I'm also looking for a woman named Marina. She lives and/or works in Ghosttown, probably as an escort."

"Her I've never heard of," said Olya. "But this guy is staying in Room Two-Twelve here." She gestured at the Hotel Raven's doors.

"You're absolutely sure?" I said.

"Yeah. He's not from around here—real vanilla, from the 'burbs. Been here a couple of days." She twirled one brilliant red curl around her finger and frowned. "Come to think of it, I've been delivering to his room, and last night he didn't come to the door, so I left his order in the hall. Weird. Usually tips well, too, which is a rarity. I don't risk my job and feed them for kicks, ya know? Ten bucks here and there would be nice."

I was already halfway up the lobby stairs.

"Room Two-Twelve?"

"Two-Twelve," Olya agreed. "So what'd he do?"

"Apparently, nothing," I growled, shoving open the doors to the second floor. I was going to tear Stephen Duncan a new asshole when I found the little prick, sitting pretty in a skuzzy hotel room with his prostitute girlfriend. Wasting my time, letting Dmitri Sandovsky get his act together and skip out of town if he so desired, free to savage more women.

Room 212 was midway down the hall on the left, an innocuous door covered with many coats of deep green paint and cheap brass numerals nailed up crookedly.

"Stephen!" I said loudly, pounding. "Stephen Duncan! Message for you!"

A long silence answered me. The scarred wood floor creaked under my Cochrans. I knocked again, harder.

"Go away." The voice was faint, barely above a whisper. If not for were hearing, I probably would have missed it.

"Nope, sorry," I replied. "I'm waiting until you open this door."

"Just leave me alone."

"Stephen, are you all right?"

"I can't wash off the blood," he whispered. "The sink is broken."

Crap.

"Stand back!" I hollered, and gave the doorjamb the business end of my boot. It was so rotten it didn't even splinter, just caved in with a defeated groan. I came in with my Glock aimed, quickly swept the corners of the tiny single room, and then fixed on the blond figure hunched at the foot of the bed. On the floor below him, bare female legs stuck out, covered in a fine red mist.

I kept the Glock trained. "Stephen?"

He moaned. "Leave me alone, I said!"

"Stephen, what happened?" I came closer and saw what I presumed had once been Marina, supine on her back, left fist extended, her index finger snapped nearly in half. I choked on the smell of old blood and decomposing tissue.

Stephen rocked back and forth, muttering softly to himself.

Marina's throat was gone. A ruin of torn flesh stretched from her larynx to her sternum. Her legs bore deep scratches on the outside of her thighs, and her face was swollen with bruises. The spilled blood had congealed into a sticky pool, and Marina's eyes were open. I took another step, praying that I wouldn't see what I knew to be there, but it was in vain. Marina's left index finger was gone from the knuckle down, neatly clipped.

"Stephen." I turned my back on the body and centered my Glock on his head. "What did you do to her?"

He pulled his hands away from his face and stared up at me, and I realized he was crying. Blood covered his front, but I was in no mood to check him for injuries.

"It wasn't me," he managed to get out. "Wasn't me."

Looking at the anguish playing on his face, I half believed him. "Then who?"

"The were," he whispered. "The were did this to Marina."

EIGHT

The squad car officers that came to collect Stephen when I placed him under arrest stared with wide, disbelieving eyes as they took in the room, Marina, and the residents of Hotel Raven.

I stayed and watched CSU paint the room with blacklight, lift dozens of bloody fingerprints—but not locate the missing finger—and finally zip Marina into a body bag and take her away. Dr. Kronen fiddled with his tie and said yes, the same man had very probably killed Lilia and Marina.

I didn't need his confirmation. If Stephen was a were, the method of murder fit perfectly with both girls.

But it was a hell of a big If. Stephen didn't smell like a were, didn't act like one. He didn't have any scars that I could see, and when you get the bite it's usually in a spot that spreads the were directly into your bloodstream.

Finally, I went to the Twenty-fourth to file a preliminary report. An e-mail from Pete Anderson flashed in my inbox. *So, did you find your Mystery Woman?*

I thought about Pete's finger and the stacks of ten-cards. Six women had gone missing in a four-month span in 1962, he said. All of poor, foreign background. All mutilated. *He tortured her and clipped off her finger with pliers.*

The chill of an unwelcome connection cut me. I pulled up a database search and started typing. *Mutilation Homicide Female 61–62* turned out almost thirty results. Busy season for the psychos, apparently. I narrowed the homicides by address, and the six Waterfront killings glowed from my screen. The case files had never been scanned into the database, so a few lines delineated each woman in the most basic way: *torn throat, no sexual assault, supine positioning of body, left index finger severed at first joint . . .*

Lilia and Marina had both been arranged on their backs. Throats torn. Killings permeated with such rage, it was palpable.

I searched again. *Mutilation Homicide Female, supine, throat cut/torn, finger severed all dates.*

This time, the six murders were from 1907. And there was a photograph.

I clicked and waited. When the grainy scan of a photograph that was never clear in the first place loaded, I nearly gagged. Trade in her bloomers for a thong and her low-slung dress for a halter, and the dead woman could have been Lilia Desko.

No one had ever found out her name. She and six other Irish women working at a sewing shop had disappeared over nearly a year. Each of them found ravaged and dead. Two killers, fifty-seven years apart. Identical.

And impossible.

I pushed away from the computer and turned my back on the haunting photograph. Either I was paranoid and all was coincidence, or I was tracking the world's oldest serial killer.

Stephen Duncan was in the lockup for the night. Tomorrow, I would call his father and interrogate him. I'd catch hell for not informing Duncan and McAllister immediately, but I needed time to process what I'd seen. I couldn't shake the image of Stephen, covered in blood, his terrified eyes begging me to see the horror that had befallen him. *The were. The were did this to Marina.* Either Dmitri Sandovsky had killed the girl, left Stephen alive, and vanished from a locked hotel room . . . or something else was at play.

Either way, Stephen Duncan had answers for me.

W ell, there's no doubt about it," said Mac, dropping a stack of folders on my desk. "Stephen Duncan is absolutely batshit crazy."

"We've had him in custody for twenty hours and you just figured that out?" I asked, paging through the first file. I was cross-referencing old prostitute murders and missing women in Nocturne City while we waited for Alistair Duncan and his son's lawyer to arrive. I separated them by the current year and everything before and started paging through the top folder.

"Christ, Wilder, did you see what he did to that poor woman?" Mac asked, rubbing his eyes. "We're not dealing with an altar boy."

"Mac, I'm not so sure Stephen Duncan killed Marina. Hell, we're not even sure that dead girl *is* Marina."

"Don't start," he told me. "You find a man covered in blood with a dead hooker at his feet, and he tells you some anonymous were did the deed while he watched? And you buy that?"

"What happened to Marina is consistent with the Lilia Desko murder," I said. "It fits that a were did her in. And Stephen Duncan is not a were."

Mac curled his hands into fists. "How can you—oh, right. The smelling."

"Mac, shh. People are staring."

"Get back to work!" Mac bellowed to the squad room at large. "You think this is some sort of goddamn peep show?"

He leaned over my desk. "Work the case, Luna. Don't run around like a chicken with no head chasing wild theories—theories based on, I might add, something that most people don't even want to believe exists anymore, never mind what might hold up in court."

I rubbed my left knuckle, twisting the skin, trying to imagine how it felt. Strong enough to snip through bone and tissue with one squeeze . . .

"What in the name of all things Hexed and holy are you doing?" Mac asked, raising one iron-colored eyebrow like I was crazy.

"He's taking trophies," I said. "Fingers."

"Not very practical," said Mac. "Fingers rot. Most serials take hair or teeth, something easy to preserve."

I stopped rubbing my knuckle. "Or bones."

Mac inclined his head. "Slinneanachd," he said thoughtfully.

"Slim-what?"

"Slinneanachd," said Mac again. "Bone divination. Cast the bones and call a working to see your future."

Oh, gods. He was using magick. "Mac, that is too creepy. How do you know this crap?"

"A Scottish grandmother with a knack for the theatrical," he said. "You look like you swallowed a marble, Wilder. You okay?"

Al Duncan saved me from having to answer that one. He came rushing in, suit coat and gray hair flying, trailed by Regan Lockhart and a middle-aged guy with a briefcase I didn't recognize.

"Al," said McAllister, hurrying over. "I'm afraid we have some bad news."

"Where is my son?" Duncan demanded.

"He's safe," Mac said.

"And you got the bastards that did it?" Duncan twisted his hands together so tightly it was amazing his fingers didn't snap.

"Not exactly," said Mac. "As I told you on the phone, the situation is complicated."

"Then uncomplicate it, Lieutenant," said Lockhart. "Mr. Duncan has waited long enough for his son's return." He and the DA were like a ice-dancing duet—one slipped and the other caught him.

"His son is being charged with second-degree homicide," I told Lockhart. "So unless you're his lawyer—and because you brought this jerk with the shiny briefcase I'm guessing not—shut up and butt out of my investigation."

Lockhart's lips compressed, and his eyes gleamed at me with a hate-filled light. He looked to Duncan.

"Homicide?" Poor Duncan's face had gone beet red. "I don't understand . . . what did Stephen do?"

"Al," said the lawyer, "let's talk to him. We'd like to see Mr. Duncan immediately," he told Mac.

"Of course," said Mac, probably relieved that Lockhart and I hadn't started a deathmatch in his squad room. "Detective Wilder, take Mr. Duncan and his lawyer to the interview room."

I told the DA and Briefcase, "This way." I deliberately ignored Lockhart, but I could feel him watching me until we turned the corner. He had one hell of a stare.

As the two men followed me down the narrow, badly lit hallway to Interrogation, Duncan kept asking me, "Why is he charged with homicide? What happened? How can you have made such a terrible mistake?"

"Sir, you know I can't discuss the details of Stephen's case with anyone but his lawyer," I said. "I'm truly sorry."

"Roenberg was right," he told me as I opened the door to Stephen. "You were a bad idea." The way he said it, I thought he was almost pissed at me for doing my job. Well, Hex him. It wasn't my fault he'd raised Ted Bundy, Junior.

I slammed it after them a little harder than necessary, and watched through the mirror as Al Duncan's face lost all color when he got a look at his blood-covered son.

"Good God, Stephen!" he cried. "What have you done now?"

Stephen started bawling again. "I'm sorry, Dad. I'm sorry . . ."

I went back to my desk and waited for the lawyer to finish telling Stephen to lie so I could interview him.

The photos of all missing women between twenty and thirty-five for the past year were spread out before me when Bryson barreled in, knocking the back of my chair and sending the glossies flying.

"Hear you blew the DA to let you back on the force, Wilder! Can't say I'm happy to see you."

"My sentiments exactly," I replied, picking up the photos. "Glad to see you're still the biggest dickhead with the smallest dick in the Twenty-fourth, David."

"Watch it or I'll sue you for sex harassment next." He grinned.

"If I thought you knew the definition of the word *ironic,* I'd use it now," I said. My blood pressure was rising even being in the same room as Bryson. I commanded the were in me to be silent. I was not getting suspended again over a limp noodle like him.

"So where's this mama's-boy hooker killer I'm supposed to interview?" he demanded.

"Excuse me?" I said loudly. "I'm sure you don't mean Stephen Duncan."

"Yeah, him. *Stephen.*" Bryson made his voice high and lisping, and flipped his wrist.

"That's my case," I told him, quiet and angry.

"Nope. McAllister paged me special. Looks like he can't take any more of your feminist affirmative action shit, either."

"We'll see about that," I said. I went to knock on Mac's door, but he opened it before I could and shrugged apologetically.

"I know what you're going to say, Luna, and it isn't my call. The DA requested another investigator."

"So you get *Bryson?*" I hissed. "That asshole couldn't find his balls with a compass and a Sherpa, never mind handle this murder case. And I know he may be Roenberg's favorite ass kisser, but he is far from discreet."

"He's the only one who can do it," said Mac. He sighed and rubbed his face with one palm. His eyes were baggy, and he looked rumpled and exhausted. "Everyone else is working something."

"And what exactly am I supposed to do while Bryson takes over my investigation?"

"Damn it, Wilder, I don't know. Don't you have any other cases to work?"

"Not since you suspended me! They all got reassigned." I let my tone soften. Maybe this could still be salvaged. "Mac, please. At least let me observe the interview."

He sighed. "Fine. Go. Let me see if I can damage my career a little more before the shift ends."

B ryson had thrown Alistair Duncan out of the interview room when I got there. The DA leaned his forehead against the one-way glass, eyes closed, as Bryson and Stephen's conversation filtered through the tinny wall speaker.

"So who was this broad?" Bryson asked, rocking his chair back on its hind legs. I asked whatever charitable gods were listening to topple it and give him a concussion.

"Her name was Marina," said Stephen softly. He hadn't been allowed to clean up, and the blood on his buttondown had dried to a deep purplish red.

"Okay. So you met her, took her to Ghosttown, fucked her brains out, and then did her. I got the chronology right here?"

"I told you," said Stephen. "It wasn't me."

"Then why you got her blood all over you, Junior?" Bryson bellowed. "You're guilty as hell, and you're just lucky it was some stray tail that you got your yayas out with and not a society skirt, because then not even your daddy could save your sorry ass."

"Detective!" the lawyer snapped. "Is there a question somewhere in all this vitriol?"

I snuck a look at Duncan Senior. He stared blankly, head still resting on his hand. That same flat look was on his face as when I'd first met him and he'd told me with an offhand cheerfulness his son had mostly likely been kidnapped and might be dead.

"Let's start over," Bryson said. "Where'd you meet her?"

Stephen stared down at the tabletop and mumbled in a monotone, "This place . . . called Club Velvet. It's a . . . well . . . some of my friends dared me to go there and I . . . we just connected."

A circuit clicked on in my memory and I saw the logo on Olya's gym bag.

Sunny believes in fate and coincidence. I believe in instinct and intuition. I'll buy that things happen for a purpose. And as long as Bryson and McAllister were occupied with the Duncans, I was free to find out what that was.

NINE

Club Velvet was not hard to find. Hard to miss would be more like it. An art nouveau nude, covered only by her hair, was writ large in neon above pink script seven feet high that faded from pastel to neon and back again.

For such an ostentatious establishment, just west of the Mainline district in a neighborhood filled with trendy restaurants and boutiques that sold fake designer bags and real Rolex watches, the club had a pathetic amount of security. No one checked my ID at the door. There were no bouncers or red velvet ropes, just well-dressed, mostly middle-aged women coming and going. In pairs.

I laughed. Stephen Duncan had picked up Marina in a high-end lesbian nightclub. That explained the *my friends dared me* line.

The lobby was done in the same spectrum of light and dark pinks, nude pictures hanging on the silk-covered walls. I saw recent repairs to the covering as well as some ugly stains that hadn't quite washed out. "What happened there?" I asked the hostess.

"A break-in a few months ago. Some of our neighbors don't approve of our ... flaunting ourselves, is how the last letter put it. They think we make too big of a target." She smiled dazzlingly. "Name?"

"I'm looking for Olya."

"Olya is off tonight," she said icily. "If you're a friend of hers I must tell you waitstaff are not permitted to have guests during business hours."

I showed my shield. "I'm no guest. She's a witness in a homicide."

Her lips pursed. "In that case I will call our owner and manager, Ms. Carlisle. Please wait in the bar." She took my elbow and guided me to a brass-bound ebony monstrosity lining the back wall of the club. After I had been sat on a plush stool, she glided back to her stand and picked up the phone.

"Something to wet your whistle?" asked the butch bartender, who had cornflower-blue eyes and didn't look old enough to drink, never mind dispense.

"Just a sparkling water for now."

"You a narc?" she asked. I raised one eyebrow.

"Is it that obvious?"

"I saw you flash the Icicle Queen when you came in. That's what we call Henriette. Icicle Queen."

"And what's your name?"

"Kyle," she said. "I know, I know—weird for a chick. Options are limited for unisex names—you'll never see more Alexes and Jamies than in this place."

"Well, Kyle," I said, accepting the sparkling water with a twist, "I'm not with Narcotics. I'm Homicide, and I'm looking for Olya."

"No shit. Olya Sandovsky? I thought that girl was straight. As in no record."

I choked on the water. "What did you say her last name was?"

"Sandovsky." She pointed to the far end of the bar, at a large figure in shadow. "That big biker dude down there is her brother."

The ambient music's low bass beat died out and my pounding heart became the only thing I heard. Dmitri Sandovsky leaned forward into the light and took a pull from a tumbler full of dark liquid. His eyes were glazed, and he slumped on his stool with no swagger.

I left my water and a puzzled Kyle and approached. My entire body shook, remembering the punishment it had received at his hands. The gleam of night lights off his yellow wolf eyes and his growl were still vivid in my memory.

"This," I said to him, "does not seem like your kind of place."

Sandovsky swiveled his head slowly to look at me. "Took your time," he grunted. "Way you chased me up on that roof, I thought for sure you'd be back for round two before now."

"Sorry to disappoint," I replied. This time, I had the upper hand. I had a gun, and a club full of people for Sandovsky to worry about.

"If you think a pack of humans is gonna stop me from phasing, you're wrong," he said.

Well, at least I still had a gun. "Why did you kill Lilia?" I asked. I wasn't convinced he'd killed Marina. Hell, I wasn't convinced he was good for the first murder. Sandovsky was a bundle of were impulses. My killer was a kind that cut off women's fingers and made ritual objects from their bones. But I went where fact dictated, and the fact was Sandovsky *could* have killed both women.

He took another drink, draining the glass and slamming it down hard, almost missing the edge of the bar. The smell rolled off him in waves. Sandovsky was very, very drunk. "Why would I kill Lilia? Ya dumb bitch."

"Gee, maybe because you were her pimp and she pissed you off?" I unsnapped my holster. "And it's Detective Dumb Bitch to you."

"I'm *not* Lilia's pimp no more, and I *didn't* kill her," he snarled, eyes flickering with gold in their depths.

Lies stink. They smell wet and coppery, like nervous sweat coming to a boil. Dmitri smelled like nothing but expensive bourbon, cheap cigarettes, and weariness.

"Your DNA and your fingerprints were all over her dead body," I reminded him. Kyle watched us from down the bar, her left hand on the phone. I blocked her view with my back and whispered in Sandovsky's ear, "Lilia fought hard for her life. She was drugged and brutalized, but she still fought."

The ice in Sandovsky's glass rattled. His hands were quivering.

"She had something to live for," I continued, making my decision: Sandovsky wasn't my killer. "The way things are looking, that was you. So you can either keep trying to outrun me, or you can help me find the freak that mutilated and killed her. But if you run, I'll change my mind, Sandovsky, and I'll believe that you were the one to torture her to death. And then we'll hunt."

Sandovsky bellowed and swept his arms out, sending a spray of broken glass to the floor. *"Fuck you!"* he screamed.

I drew my Glock and aimed. "Calm down, Sandovsky." Around us, Club Velvet's patrons took flight like linen-and-silk-wrapped birds, some overturning their chairs as they ran from the gun and Dmitri Sandovsky's angry, twisted face.

"Lilia fought him?" he demanded. "She didn't go easy?"

"No," I said, keeping my sights on the center of his forehead. "And for that she died slow and hard."

"Damn it. God damn it." Sandovsky's chest was heaving, and his hands shook. The sheen of a tear appeared on his cheek and worked its way down.

"Dmitri," I said, keeping my voice soothing and low. "Calm down and put your hands behind your head."

"Bastard!" he roared. "I'll fuckin' kill him! Slow and hard. Just like her." His eyes flashed to yellow then back to their human emerald green, and I tightened my grip on the Glock.

"No one is killing anyone tonight, except maybe me," I said. "Hands. Head. Now."

Sandovsky's body tensed and I saw the spring, the tackle, me going down under his weight, him wrestling my gun from me and taking aim.

Then he shuddered and let out a sob, collapsing. "Hex me," he choked. "Gods. It's my fault."

I slowly lowered my weapon. "What do you mean, Sandovsky?"

"She wanted out," he told me. "I took her to eat at this diner and go back to our pack house and we . . . she was going to come with me, out of Nocturne. Be my mate. I got out of the skin trade and she wanted out, too. Wasn't for her . . . in Ukraine she was going to be a teacher . . ." His shoulders shook, and he turned his face away from me. For someone like Sandovsky, crying in front of a woman cop was probably worse than torture with hot pokers.

"I didn't even know she was dead until you showed up at the Waterfront joint."

"And you decided to resist arrest and almost kill me because of your deep and unimaginable grief?" I asked.

Sandovsky sat hard on a bar stool. "She was one of us. From the pack. And she's dead. *You* wouldn't understand."

The alcohol and the shock had finally gotten to him, and he slumped glassy-eyed, staring at me without really seeing.

I bristled at the veiled insult but sat on the stool next to him. "Why did you run if you didn't kill her?"

"Pack law says I gotta do it," he muttered. "I gotta be the one to send the killer down. Think I was gonna let an outcast like you cut in line? No way."

I got out my handcuffs. "Let's go, Dmitri. We can go to my precinct and clear this mess up."

"He's not going anywhere." Olya walked out from the back room and put an arm around her brother. Except for the red hair I would have pegged them as distant cousins, at most.

"You're going to stop me?" I inquired.

"An Insoli with a gun against two Redbacks. The odds are not in your favor, Detective Wilder."

Kyle came from behind the bar holding a baseball bat.

"And here I was going to tip you, too," I told her.

"Dmitri didn't murder Lilia," said Olya with feeling. "But you should be finding out who did, and fast. Because when the pack finds out, the fucker is dead. And I don't mean *as good as*. I mean dead. Painfully."

"I'm not going to leave your brother alone and skip merrily home," I said. "He's a material witness, at the very least." Lawyer-speak was what I resorted to when I was absolutely out of options. It didn't seem to ruffle Olya in the least. No one else remained in Club Velvet to wonder why if a waitress and a scruffy biker suddenly turned into two large red wolves. Olya was right—definitely not in my favor.

"Leave me alone, Detective," said Sandovsky. "Just turn your back and walk away."

"Don't you know it's stupid to turn your back on a wild dog?" I asked. "You never know when he might bite."

Sandovsky took a deep breath through his nose with a soft growl. I felt a tingle and blushed. He was scenting me. Male weres use it to decide on potential mates—or rivals.

Silence reigned until Dmitri exhaled and blinked those deep greens at me. "For an Insoli, you're not bad," he said with a crooked half smile that was as forced as steam from a subway grate. Heat washed my face. My cheeks had to be crimson. Great, because nothing enhances a badass image like a schoolgirl blush.

"Leave and come tomorrow to the old Crown Theater in Ghosttown," Dmitri said, his face settled into a stone mask. I knew I'd never again see him show the side I'd seen when he realized that Lilia was gone.

Olya's eyes snapped to him. "Dmitri!"

"Shut your mouth," he growled. Olya dipped her head meekly, just like Manley had when I'd pulled a dominate. Dmitri was not only a pack member, then. He was a high-up, maybe even close to an alpha. I filed that tidbit away and asked, "What's at the Crown Theater?"

He smiled a little. "It's my pack house. We'll talk then."

My pack house? Seriously high up in the ranks.

"Forgive me if walking into the home territory of a rival pack does not sound like a fun night out," I told Dmitri. "Can't we meet somewhere public?"

"Get over yourself, Detective," said Olya, laughing

without any humor. "You're not a threat to the Red-backs. You're not even a blip."

"Does that arrogance ever get in the way of your big mouth?" I snapped. "Or do they have a custody arrangement?"

"Feisty," said Olya. "No wonder the one who gave you the bite didn't keep you."

"Olya, quiet," said Dmitri in the same tone. She shut up, but I still ached to slap the knowing smirk off her face.

"Tomorrow night," Sandovsky said. "Dark." He sniffed once and tossed his head. "Come on, sis. You're off early." They left through the curtained-off entrance to the back room.

Kyle hopped back over the bar and put her bat away. "Sorry about that. Amanda Carlisle, the owner—she lets the pack members use this place as a crash pad if they're in a bad way. Even gave Olya a job."

"And you have no problem with any of this?" I asked her.

She shrugged. "I'm human, but I got nothing against people with the blood. Anyhow, I've seen what Dmitri can do. Before the letters and the vandalism, there were these college guys from Nocturne University who would come around and hassle us. They pulled Ms. Carlisle out of her Mercedes one night and were tearing her clothes off in the employee parking lot. Sandovsky showed up. One look at those teeth and the fratholes were pissing themselves. They didn't know *what* they saw, but it scared the crap out of them."

"How noble," I muttered.

"He isn't a knight in shining armor," said Kyle. "But he's all right. And believe me, he's not a killer."

"I know," I told her. "But something is going on

with Dmitri, so do me a favor and don't tell me what to believe."

I got home as the pink edge of daylight peeked over the ocean, and the pale waxing moon was a ghost against the graying sky. I fell into bed and woke up at some ungodly early-evening hour with Sunny shaking my shoulder.

"Luna!" she cried. "I may have found something!" Her eyes were painted with dark rings, and she was pale.

"How long have you been up at a stretch, Sunny?"

She shrugged. "All night. Small price to pay. Look at this!" She handed me a blue leather-bound volume I recognized as my one of my grandmother's old spellbooks. Caster witches worked largely from memory, these little books memorized and burned.

"Sunny, how did you get this?" I demanded.

She bit her lip. "You don't want to hear how."

"Damn right I don't, but you're going to tell me anyway."

Sunny sighed and worried the little tassel hanging from the book's spine. "I may have . . . well . . . borrowed it. The last time I saw Grandma."

I put the book back in Sunny's hands with more force than was strictly necessary.

"So how often have you two little circle-scribblers been visiting behind my back?"

Sunny didn't rise to the bait. "You're the one who declared war on your mother's entire side of the family, not me. Grandma's a great caster witch and I can see her if I please."

"Sunny, the woman is evil. She'd as soon stab me with the good silver as look at me."

"You know that's not—" Sunny started.

"Oh, you bet it is. I disgust her. What other reason would she have for leaving her fifteen-year-old grand-daughter on the streets?"

She threw up her hands. "You don't want my help, fine. I'll be outside."

I gave her about fifteen seconds after she flounced away, and then followed her. She was in our backyard, where the roses grew thick up a trellis below my window and a bare patch of earth with a pit at the center served as the focus for most of Sunny's workings.

She had her wood caster and scriber and was drawing a practiced circle into the dirt. She etched a symbol at each of the corners and moved to the center.

"What's that for?" I asked, pointing at the circle. Caster witches channeled their power and usually didn't need visual markers for workings.

"I'm binding," said Sunny. "Now go away. You're breaking my concentration."

"Binding what?"

She let her arms fall and glared at me. "All that wonderful negativity you've been spewing lately, if you must know. The auras around here are so black, I can't even work up a simple finding spell, and I've lost my spare set of house keys. Again."

"I thought you needed a double circle for a binding," I said. I picked up Rhoda's spellbook and leafed through it. Page after page was filled with spidery handwriting and artful drawings of sigils, plants, and caster runes.

"Double circle? No." Sunny shook her head. "That's only for binding the really nasty ones. Entities and dae-mons."

"Ew," I said. "Thought daemon summoning went out with the iron maiden."

"No one ever accused blood witches of being smart," Sunny said.

I found the folded-down page corner that marked the working Sunny wanted to try on me. The title was "Tincture of Wolfsbane." Underneath in my grand-mother's precise handwriting it said, *for the reversal of shapeshifting curses, to prevent transmutation.*

"It was meant for a human," said Sunny, raising her caster again. "Someone who's been afflicted with a transmutation curse like boils or something. If I tweak the recipe, I bet it could suppress your phase until the moon wanes."

"Tweak it how, exactly? It's not a brownie mix." I read down the list of ingredients, herb names I didn't recognize plus such appetizing items as *charcoal* and *silver nitrate.*

"Well," said Sunny, "if I were to give you the tincture the exact way it is now, when I did the working it would, um . . ."

"It would what?" I demanded suspiciously.

Sunny bit her lip. "As a were and not a human, that combination could kill you."

"Oh, that's great, Sunny! The cure to the moonphase is death?"

Her caster gave off that distinctive crackling smell that meant her working was starting to draw energy. I backed up to the stoop. Magicks make my skin crawl when I get close.

"Don't get all hysterical," she told me. "You have to have an open mind about this if you ever want to control your phase."

"Sunny, I appreciate what you're trying to do here, but I'd rather turn into a slavering hell beast every full moon than swallow a bunch of poisonous herbs and hope for the best. Really."

"Then I guess you're on your own, because I don't see you running out to get help from anyone else." The caster gave off an ever-so-soft hum, and Sunny's eyes flickered as the power coursed through her.

"I'll just be going, then," I said, and beat it into the cottage. After spending most of my childhood with either Rhoda or Aunt Delia, I had seen enough workings to know I didn't like watching. I rinsed quickly in the shower and got dressed again, going to the kitchen to scavenge for fatty leftovers.

Sunny came in a few moments later and washed up in the sink. "That feels better!" she exclaimed. "Not so dark in here now. You really need to lighten up, Luna."

"Yeah, because perky is *so* me." I had changed into a tight white T-shirt and my lowest-riding jeans to meet Sandovsky, and Sunny looked me over with a critical eye.

"Date? You? Really?"

I rolled my eyes. "Much as I would love to shock you, cousin, no. I'm meeting someone. A were."

Her eyes went wide. "Who?"

"Dmitri Sandovsky."

She gave me the cocked eyebrow that said I had clearly already gone insane, and now it was just a question of whether or not to call the mental ward. "The man who beat you up so badly? And killed that poor girl?"

"He's not the murderer . . . at least I don't think he is," I said. "Although he does pack a mean tackle." And a set of drop-dead-deep green eyes. Nice red hair, too. Good shoulders.

"Come on back to Planet Earth when you have a

minute," said Sunny, snapping her fingers in my face. "You can't seriously being going to meet this psychotic, Luna."

"I have to," I said. I wouldn't admit I wasn't entirely against seeing Sandovsky again. Nothing wrong with looking, even if he did kick my ass.

More importantly, Sandovsky was so twitchy that he had to know more than he told about Lilia's murder. Lilia and Marina had been killed by the same man—or whatever—I was sure. And the more I thought about him, the more Sandovsky didn't fit the profile of an organized, ritualistic killer. Why go in for drugging and torture when he could phase and probably literally bite someone's head off?

He wouldn't, because I was looking for another type of predator, smaller and quieter but no less venomous. I needed to put a face to the theory, see the savage in the flesh. Not knowing made me jumpy, and my skin itch, as if the two murders were a physical affliction.

"I'm still going to prepare the tincture," Sunny told me with that unflappable Swann stubbornness. "In case you change your mind. Full moon coming up fast, you know."

"Why not?" I said. "All it can do is kill me." I stood and grabbed the keys to the Fairlane. "I have to interview Sandovsky at sundown." In the soft predusk sunlight it sounded ridiculously melodramatic. But then again, I was riding into an outlaw city to interview the leader of a were pack. If my night didn't contain a little drama, I'd feel almost let down.

TEN

After the bloody scene in the Hotel Raven and my encounter with enough creepy shit to last me a lifetime, the last thing I wanted was to go back to Ghosttown.

But I went, leaving the Fairlane on the same rotted boulevard, and walked until the row houses became high, narrow storefronts and the Crown Theater dominated the corner.

The Crown was built modern in the 1950s, with a lighted marquee and a sleek white brick front accented with steel chevrons that had rusted and cut across the face of the place like gangrenous veins. One of the last buildings to go up in Ghosttown before the packs and the bloods moved in, I would guess, and one of the few to escape the Hex fires unscathed.

A row of road bikes sat proudly at the curb, all of them shined to a blinding intensity, most of them classics worth more than the Fairlane and Sunny's convertible combined. A few burly Redback weres, obviously chosen for their ability to hulk and glower, were working the theater doors.

One of them scented me openly, smirking, and I couldn't have felt more insulted if he'd copped a feel. "Sniff this," I told him, extending a middle finger.

He turned to the other member of the Easy Rider Fan Society and proclaimed, "Yeah, it's her."

"Sandovsky said you'd be comin'," the other one grunted.

"Although if you don't wanna come with him, cutie, you can come with me," the first one added.

"Points for originality," I told him, "but the only place I'd come with you is to the downtown lockup, where I would proceed to throw you in a cell with the baddest homeboy I could find, sit back, and laugh my ass off." I went between them and shoved open a door.

I heard the second were say, "I like her, man."

"Go bang a blood witch," the first replied.

The lobby was all peeling plaster and painted facade, looking like every seedy adult movie theater I'd ever been in. The cheap gilt molding was flaking like golden snow, and soggy wine-colored carpet stank of fifty years of slow rot.

Olya appeared from the back of the concession stand, a toolbox and a roll of electrical wire in her hands. "Oh. You came," she said. "I bet Dmitri you wouldn't show."

I grinned. "How much did you lose?"

"Enough," she grumbled. "Follow me."

I followed Olya down a narrow hallway lit with corroded copper sconces that flickered and sparked ominously. Good thing the Crown was too damp to go up in an electrical fire. "Doing some home improvement?" I asked Olya, pointing to the roll of wire.

"This damn place hasn't been rewired since it went

up," she said. "And since the city cut the power, forget this jury-rigged shit. We're lucky if we can run a hot plate."

I smelled the mold and the must and decades of bodies crammed together. "Why live here?"

She turned and glared at me. "You go where your pack goes. This is home."

"Sounds fun, just like summer camp," I commented.

Olya stopped and gave me a look that was equal parts pain and pissed off. "I suppose I could live alone in a gutter somewhere like you, Insoli. Or better yet, in a Russian work camp like my brother." She poked her finger into my chest. "We didn't have to let you leave the Velvet in one piece, bitch. When you're in another pack's den you show some respect."

I met and held her anguished look. "I'm not a member of your pack, Olya. I'm here to find out who *murdered* a member of your pack. And I may have to put up with shit from your brother to get the information I need but I do *not* have to take a damn thing from you. Back off."

She growled. I growled. We stood there in mutual dislike for a few seconds more before she pointed across the theater. "Dmitri's behind the big screen. Do what you have to do and get the hell out." She turned and flounced away from me, managing to look like a spoiled princess even in jeans and a dirty cotton shirt, lugging a toolbox.

"Thank you," I said to no one.

The seats of the Crown had been mostly ripped up and stacked in corners. A few had gotten converted into beds, and held snoring weres in stages of undress I didn't glance too closely at. A sharp smell of old celluloid and older dust drifted through the air. I followed the path picked out to the edge of the torn projection screen, and went behind.

Someone had made an attempt to turn the space into a sort of lounge, ancient plaid sofas and a console television with the screen kicked in arranged in no order, like cast-off oracle bones. Manley the Cowardly Werewolf was splayed on one of the sofas, smoking. He saw me and said, "Shit."

"Relax, Manley," I told him. "Didn't you get the memo? I'm invited."

"Oh yeah?" he said, stubbing out his butt and standing. "Who by?"

" 'By whom,' and Sandovsky."

"Quit bein' a bitch or I might take it into my head to school you across the mouth," he said.

I stared him down to see if the dominate still worked.

Manley started to quiver all over. "Stop doin' that!"

I grinned. Still worked. Like a charm.

Manley growled. "Knock it off I said!"

"Wayne, give it a rest," boomed Sandovsky's familiar voice from above us. I turned and saw a tiny flight of stairs leading up. Sandovsky was midway down, arms crossed.

Manley took a quick leap away from me and back onto the sofa. "Sorry, Dmitri," he muttered. "Didn't know you was bringin' the fuzz around to our pack house."

"The fuzz?" I laughed. "What crappy B movie did you grow up in?"

"Knock it off," Sandovsky told me in the same tone he used with Manley, Olya, and the other Redbacks. "I didn't bring you here to stir shit."

"Talk to me like that again and you'll wish I hadn't come, period," I warned.

He rolled his eyes. "Upstairs." He turned and went back up, the treads creaking under him. I followed. Sandovsky was wearing ratty jeans that grabbed his ass in all the right ways, and I couldn't help but notice. I looked down at my feet.

The mysterious *upstairs* turned out to be a long storage room that ran the length of the building above the seating floor. It was full of cardboard cutouts of movie stars last popular thirty years past, nibbled by mice. Pieces of arcane machinery from the projector and the concession stand crouched like formless nightmares in the low light. Sandovsky wound his way through the wreckage and opened a small door at the opposite end. I followed in the near dark and tried not to break my ankle on the stray pieces of trash underfoot.

Once, the space had been the projection room, and the tiny window still looked down on the theater. Now it housed a bed made with military corners, a ratty armchair, and a huge, battered bookcase full of odds, ends, and, surprisingly, books.

Sandovsky shut the door and indicated the chair. "Sit if you want."

"No thank you. I haven't been sprayed for fleas and ticks recently."

His lip curled. "You always such a bitch?" He was back to being Mr. Big Scary Were Man, but judging by the ruin of bottles and cigarette butts on the floor by the bed he'd had a rough time of it after we parted ways at Club Velvet.

"You bring out the bitch in me," I told him.

"Ain't that the truth," he muttered. He grabbed a pack from his shelf and tapped out a black cigarette, lighting it with a Zippo from his back pocket. He sucked on the clove and exhaled bluish smoke before extending the pack to me. "Want one?"

"I don't smoke."

"You should. You're wound tight enough to pop."

I crossed my arms. "Sandovsky, did you bring me here to jerk my choke chain or did you really want to talk about Lilia?"

His face hardened and he mimicked my gesture, crossing his bare arms and causing pectorals to pop out under his Indian Motorcycles T-shirt. He wasn't sculpted by any stretch, but the muscles were there, rocky and lean, the kind of body built by a lifetime of forced labor and hard, dirty fights.

I dug my nails into my own arm. *Focus, Luna. So what if he has an incredible chest?*

Sandovsky was watching me, a thin trail of smoke escaping from his nose. His anger had been replaced with plastic amusement. It was his default, I was starting to realize. Everybody has a mask that they pull on when they're hiding vulnerability, with varying degrees of success. Mine is Bitch. Sandovsky's seemed to be Sardonic.

"Okay, lady cop." He smirked. "Let's talk about Lilia." He turned his back to me and went over to the projection window, flicking ash down into the theater. "Lilia was a good girl," he said. "She came from the same town in Ukraine as I did. Hardworking family, father died in the fallout from Chernobyl when she was just a baby. I liked her."

"Let me guess. High school sweethearts?"

"Hey." Sandovsky turned and jabbed his cigarette at me. "I'm doin' you a favor, so you can cut the fuckin' sarcasm. Just because Lilia was a whore and I pimped doesn't make us shit to be scraped off your shiny cop shoes. We weren't always like this."

"I thought you said you weren't her pimp," I reminded him.

"I wasn't. Not anymore. When Lilia first came over to the States she was scared, had just phased for the first time and needed someone to help her settle in. When you have to hide inside for three or four days of every month there ain't a lot of respectable nine-to-five jobs that'll take you."

I got close to him so I could watch his eyes. They remained placid green oceans, with only the barest hint of turbulence. "And I suppose being stronger than the average pro wrestler, able to see in the dark, and prone to fits of rage doesn't help, either." His body radiated warmth, like a banked fire, and I regretted closing the distance. Well, not really, but I probably should have.

He dragged, exhaled. "Heh. You're not as ignorant about the bite as Olya thought." He turned his head and looked at me full-on. "You feel it. Oh, yeah. You feel it when the moon's getting full, like it is tonight." He threw away his butt and asked me, "So, you ever kill anyone while you were phased?"

I gritted my teeth so he wouldn't see how the question rattled me. "We're talking about you. Do you know who killed Lilia?"

"No," he said. "No, I don't. But I would dearly love to find the bastard."

"Lilia had drugs in her blood," I told him. I could get fired for this, and rightly so. You don't go around blabbing confidential case details to a witness just because he's hot as all get-out.

"What drugs?" he wanted to know.

"That's what I'm going to ask you." I looked him in the eye, giving the stare I was getting so good at. "I saw your arrest record. I know you moved up from pimping to dealing, Sandovsky. Lots more lucrative and less hassle than screwing around with whores all day, I imagine."

He got close to me, getting in my space so I'd have to back up. I didn't move. Forced to look up to make eye contact, I asked, "Did you give Lilia the drugs that knocked her out? If you did, you could be charged with manslaughter." I paced to his bed so I could get out from under his tall frame. "She couldn't defend herself when that creep jumped her until it was too late. Did you make it possible for her to be murdered? Is that why you're playing the guilt-racked card?"

Sandovsky clenched his fists; I could see the effort in the cords of his neck. He was about one microfiber away from hauling off and hitting me across the face. I shifted my feet to equalize my weight and dared him, in silence, to try it.

"All I did to Lilia that night was fuck her brains out," he said roughly. His tone was nasty and disinterested but the way it scraped out of his throat belied the grief that was still in him. "Since I know that's what you wanna hear. She was good, free pussy, so I took it. So what? I'm an animal anyway, right? I don't feel one way or the other. Right?" He closed the gap between us and gripped my arm, hard.

I let my kickboxing stance go and looked away from him. Sandovsky unsettled me with his mere presence, and I had let that rattle me. Now I was officially a jerk.

"Sandovsky, I'm sorry," I said after a minute. He grunted and let go, rooting through the pockets of his jacket until he came up with a joint.

"Lilia *was* a good girl. Too good for this, and she used to cope. My future mate was a fucking junkie—is that what I need to say? I didn't give her drugs, but I'm sure she had some. She was sweet and she wasn't smart and I didn't stop her from using like I should have. There. Now get the hell out of my bedroom."

Instead I reached out and put a hand on one of his ropy shoulders. He tensed like a coiled spring. "You can help me put the brakes on whoever killed Lilia. If you do that, I'd appreciate it. Enough to get off you and your pack's back."

"What makes you think one little packless were is anything to me?"

"Maybe because you can't sit still when you're in the same room as me?" I offered. He gave me that smirk-mask again. I longed to know what he was really thinking under there.

"Don't flatter yourself, baby. So what if you rev my motor a little?"

Oh, gods. Don't you dare blush, Luna. And really don't dare to think about how long it's been since you revved anyone's motor.

"That's not it, Sandovsky, and you know it." Sounding like a total puritan should steer the conversation back on track.

After a long minute of lighting up and inhaling, holding, and releasing the pungent pot smoke, he said, "I'm only tellin' you this as courtesy, because maybe I like you a little more than I should. This ain't your business to take care of. It's pack business, and there will be pack justice."

We could argue later. "I accept that. Tell me."

Sandovsky exhaled again. "Lilia had a rich john. I told her to get out of it but she wanted some money stashed for when we got the hell out of Nocturne." He laughed once. "'Cause I'm such a hard case, I can't even buy my woman a burger and a Coke. Lilia did like finer things."

"What was the rich john's name? Would *he* give her drugs?" Was he the type to rape and cut throats?

"That came later." Sandovsky's jaw twitched. "I never let her do that stuff when she worked for me, and I let myself think I'd finally get her clean when we went away. She'd never tell me the john's name. Probably because she knew I'd wring the sleazy bastard's neck."

I frowned. "Was he violent with her?"

"Not so you could see. But whenever she came back from bein' with him, she'd have this look, like she was a million miles away. Real spacey, and she'd get so jumpy I couldn't go near her."

Perhaps stating the obvious, I said, "That sounds like drugs."

"Detective, I've seen what every drug known to man can do to F you up. This wasn't drugs. She'd look like she'd just seen something so horrible she couldn't bring herself to say it."

"Did she tell you *anything* about him?" I asked.

"Just that he was some rich prick living off Daddy and hadn't done shit since high school except ride around in his Benz and piss on people like Lilia and me. She said he couldn't go an hour without mentioning what a big-shot lacrosse player he'd been at his little preppy school. Lacrosse. Pussy." He snorted.

The ice in my gut was not imagined this time. "Did she say which prep school?"

"Shit, how am I supposed to remember? I think it was Alder Bay or Cedar Heights . . . definitely a tree name."

I swallowed to quell my furious heartbeat and told Sandovsky, "Thank you. That helps."

He lay down on his cot and took another pull off the joint. "Sure. Whatever. Now unless you'd like to join me, get out and leave us alone."

Not even going to *touch* that one.

I opened his door. "I'll find him, Sandovsky," I said.

"Dmitri," he replied.

"Excuse me?"

"That's my name. You can call me Dmitri."

"All right. Good-bye, Dmitri." I shut the door and left him lying there, leaving the Crown in a cloud of my own frenetic thoughts.

O n the street I walked for my car at a fast clip, my shoes hitting pavement too hard for me to make out the footsteps at first. *Clip, clop.*

I stopped and turned around. All the streetlights were burned out, and the marquee of the Crown cast scant light into alleys and jagged open spaces where anything could be hiding. I took a step backward and said, "Whoever you are, play out the horrorshow scene with somebody else, okay?"

After a few seconds of walking I heard it again. Footfalls of something heavy and sharp almost perfectly in cadence with my own. *Step, step. Clip, clop.*

The corner of the boulevard yawned ahead. I picked up the pace in tiny increments, trying not to make it look like I was running. A smell of cordite and rotted things had overpowered the stench of Ghosttown, and my were instincts screamed at me to break and flee.

The boulevard was fifty yards . . . forty . . . I made it to a light trot. *Clip clop clip clop clip clop.*

Hex *that.* I ran. Now there were more of them and I swore I heard whispers and cries and fluttering wings . . .

At the mouth of the street I pulled my Glock, thumbed the safety, spun, and aimed. "Hex off!" I screamed, more panic making itself evident in the words than I was happy with. My heart beat a thousand miles an hour, and I fought not to gag at the burning-trash smell.

Nothing was behind me except old lampposts, wrecked cars, and piles of trash that rustled in the wind. A breath I hadn't meant to hold rushed out of me.

Wings. Jesus. *Nothing* had wings. Those rumors about blood witches being able to fly around as giant man-bats were definitely exaggerated.

Still, if I had stumbled onto a blood working, good sense dictated I would get the hell away. Blood witches used their own bodies to draw the magicks, and their power was so unadulterated it could open doorways to the dead. And to worse places. Rhoda had told Sunny and me bedtime stories of daemons unleashed on the world by idiotic blood witches whose power got away from them. Sunny would hide under her covers, but I was the one who always ended up with nightmares. Probably just my animal brain's good sense. No one wanted to meet a daemon face-to-face. Blood witches who tried to summon them routinely went insane.

They couldn't be called, or pulled, with workings. They couldn't exist here at all.

So there was nothing behind me, and never had been.

I believed that until the sidewalk in front of me started to burn.

It started with the crackle of a working, and grew into a whooshing roar that liquefied and then became solid again in a glowing orange sigil that seemed to change and bend as I watched. My eyes ached and feed-back screamed in my ears, until I realized that it was me screaming.

Voices hissed up at me, that same fluttering and whispering of wings and tiny scraped throats.

I turned tail and hauled ass out of there, sprinting

down the boulevard and hitting the side of the Fairlane with a smack. My keys slid to the ground and I groped desperately, knowing that if I looked behind me I would see something that should never have eyes laid on it, something so terrible that it charred the very air, because I could smell it and it was coming—

I slammed the key home and jerked open my car door, throwing myself inside as the cacophony passed overhead with a scream of defeat. The Fairlane rocked from side to side as I cowered in the driver's seat, holding myself like the little girl hearing the ghost story all over again.

When it had been silent for a good ten minutes, and my hands had stopped trembling enough to fit the key into the Fairlane's ignition, I started the car and hung a U-turn on the boulevard with a screech, merging onto the Appleby and driving way too fast toward downtown.

ELEVEN

Alistair Duncan's elegant Victorian bungalow sat on a side street in the type of neighborhood where the homeowners' association regulates the height of your bushes and has a hissy fit if you paint your shutters the wrong color. I parked illegally by a hydrant and jumped the stairs two at a time to his front door, pounding hard enough to rattle the leaded panes.

"Open this door, Mr. Duncan!" I pounded again. "Don't make it my official business to open it for you!"

His harried face appeared behind the milky glass, and after unlocking a series of deadbolts he cracked the door. "Yes, Detective Wilder? May I help you?"

How dare he sound so damn calm after the night I'd had? I stuck an arm out and shoved the door wide, forcing him to get out of the way or be trampled. "You didn't tell me Stephen was involved with Lilia Desko."

He blinked. "Who?" Dressed in plaid pajamas and an expensive wool cardigan with leather patches on the elbows, Duncan was every inch the absentminded DA. Reading glasses dangled from his neck.

"Lilia Desko," I said, separating each syllable. "A dead prostitute that you oh-so-conveniently forgot to mention Stephen was involved with before she died."

"Detective, I have no idea what you're talking about and it's very late," he said, ruffling his hair. "I'm sorry, but Detective Bryson is working Stephen's case now. I'm going to have to ask you to leave."

"Bryson is working your case, not Lilia's," I snarled. "And your spoiled prick of a son is no longer my responsibility. So you can either tell me what you know or I go down to the jail where dear little Stephen is waiting for arraignment and I roust him out of bed for an interrogation. And by the way, when a judge denies the son of the DA bail, that means they think he's guilty."

His eyes narrowed and he leaned toward me, craning down from his lanky height. "Get out of here, Detective Wilder. Your accusations are baseless and I won't have this kind of behavior from a member of the force in my home." He held his fingers beside my face and snapped. "I could have you suspended like that." Snap. "Your pension like that." Snap. "Or your professional reputation, so you will never work in law enforcement again." Snap.

I upped the ante and got even closer to him. "And when I tie Stephen to Lilia's *and* Marina's murders I will bury him as the sadistic freak that he is. Regardless of what happens to my *professional reputation*. Or yours. Sir."

"You're threatening me?" Duncan hissed.

"I believe so."

"You bitch," said Duncan, his voice rising. "You're exactly what's wrong with the force."

"Al? Everything all right in here?" Regan Lockhart, in the same all-black suit, appeared from the archway leading into Duncan's dining room. He had materialized out of shadow without making a sound.

Lockhart saw me and his right hand dropped inside his open jacket. Mine went to my waist rig. We stared at each other until Duncan spoke.

"Everything is fine, Regan."

"Everything is *not* fine, Regan," I countered. "What in the name of the Hex Riots are you even doing here? Are you two secret lovers or something?"

Lockhart smiled, and something glinted in the depths of his eyes that looked almost human, like I'd amused him in a secret way. "It's not what you think, Detective. I assure you of that."

Al Duncan's cheeks turned the color of cheap red lipstick. "Get out of my house, Detective Wilder," he snarled. "You're finished in Nocturne City."

"You don't get it, Mr. Duncan," I said. "Your son ripped two women apart, and all you're worried about is yourself."

"Leave," Duncan said. Lockhart moved between us, holding up a hand to keep me away from Duncan. He still stank, but not of cologne this time. Something smoky, unidentifiable.

"We have a witness now who will testify that Lilia and Stephen had a long-term and often abusive relationship," I said. "So go ahead and can me, Mr. Duncan. We can stand on the unemployment line together. Reminisce about the good old days before you were a corrupt son of a bitch."

Lockhart started. "You have a witness?"

"Yes," I said, meeting his eyes. "A very reliable witness."

"Who is this witness?" Duncan demanded.

"His identity is confidential," I shot back, keeping my real attention on Lockhart, "so it looks like all you and Sonny-boy will be doing is cooling your heels until arraignment."

Duncan's jaw worked for a moment until he ground out, "You have no idea how badly you have screwed yourself, Detective Wilder. I look forward to your payment for interference."

What melodramatic crap.

"Good night, sir. Mr. Lockhart."

Duncan turned on his heel and stormed off. Lockhart blinked at me as I shut the door. His eyes, when they opened again, were pure black.

I n the Fairlane, I took a minute to breathe. What I had done was insane and potentially damaging to my case, but the threat of Dmitri testifying had bought me a little time. And I had seen Al Duncan before he got angry, the panic that had washed over him. The revelation about Stephen and Lilia had struck him. And let's not even start on Freaky-Freak Lockhart and his eerie eyes. Sometimes you can see the madness under the surface of a person, and I'd seen it in Lockhart, him and his secretive smiles. Al Duncan was playing Russian roulette keeping that guy employed in his office.

I pulled out and started for home. I was exhausted and tomorrow I would be interviewing Stephen Duncan again, no longer a likely suspect but a sure killer, brutal and vicious. Never mind that he wasn't a were. I'd been wrong, it'd happened before, and I should just be glad I'd keyed in to his pathology before he was released and cut off someone else's finger. Men like Stephen didn't need a were inside them to drive their bloody urges. They were monsters, stalkers in the night jungle.

The moon had swollen into a silver orb, and it cast light on the street ahead of me. I felt its cold light cut through me, and shivered.

I got home close to midnight, far earlier than I'd landed in months. Sunny was standing by the kitchen stove watching our red teakettle intently, as if by biting her lip and frowning she could make the water boil faster. I opened the FrigiTank and looked for an alcoholic beverage or ten. Of course, there was nothing.

"Jasmine tea?" Sunny offered when I banged the door shut. "Help you sleep."

"The only thing that will put me to sleep tonight is a brick to the head," I told her.

"Oh, gee, did the interview not go well or something?" Sunny inquired with wide eyes.

I flipped a hand at her, too tired for a rebound. The energy needed to tell the whole story of Dmitri, Duncan, and Lockhart's creepy smile was not forthcoming, either.

The kettle screeched and Sunny poured the steaming water into her mug, took down another one, and made me a cup as well. "Try to rest, Luna. Every time I see you those bags keep getting bigger."

I glanced at my reflection in the kitchen window. "I do not have bags," I muttered, pushing at the skin under my eyes.

Upstairs, I found an old packet of allergy medication that one of us had taken for some ailment long forgotten. The package instructed me to take one tablet every six hours. I took three, washing them down with the jasmine tea.

A lot more effective than a brick to the head.

The first thing I saw when I woke up was the glowing blue display on my alarm clock, placidly telling me it was 3:23 AM. I registered that the wind had picked up and the trellis roses were lashing back and forth outside my window, casting kinky shadow patterns across the bar of moonlight streaming in.

Over the face of the man standing above my bed. He pressed a hand across my mouth before I could breathe, strong as a steel plate.

I kicked up and out, struggling to free my arms, but my heavy quilt effectively had me pinned. I stared up at his face, a plain black stocking mask with two shiny dark eyes. That charred smell rolled out from him and choked my nostrils.

Oh, this is good, Luna. You drug yourself insensible and totally miss the fact that some wacko pervert has snuck into your bedroom until he's right on top of you.

"Don't make a sound," he whispered. His voice was high and smooth.

I tried to say, *Kind of impossible with your hand across my face, jackass,* but what came out was "Kurmph!"

He reached behind him with his free hand and took out a knife in sheath—a blade with a matte-black handle designed not to reflect light. He thumbed the sheath off and touched the point to my cheek. I was shivering now, hard, my body racked of its own accord.

"If you have anything more to do with the weres, Stephen Duncan, or any other aspect of your current case," the masked man hissed at me, "I will turn you into a pretty little doll, with no tongue." The blade skated over my lips. "And no voice." It caressed down my throat and pricked the hollow. "And no heart." He drew the blade down with force and cut my T-shirt open, leaving a thin scratch in my chest that stopped just over my left breast.

"Do we understand each other, Officer?" he breathed.

Fear is not something that you will ever meet face-to-face. It will sneak up on you and grab you, wrap arms around your chest, put ice in your blood, and freeze you still. I lay there, cold, as he ripped my bedding back and sat astride me, keeping the point of that horrible knife twisting in the soft flesh over my heart.

"Just to be sure you won't do anything foolish, like tell someone we had this interlude," he said, lifting my left hand to his mouth. My arm was stiff as a corpse in rigor, and he jerked at it. "There's a good girl." He smeared my own hand in the blood from my cut, and then unzipped the black nylon jacket he wore, revealing a bare chest covered with brandings that showed up as dark veins in the moonlight.

He took my saturated palm and pressed it to his flesh, and I felt a *pop* like I had connected with static electricity. The charred smell came back tenfold and my stomach bucked. Touching magicks is like touching heat lightning, and his were black as a moonless storm.

A tiny light flamed on in the recesses of my mind, and with remarkable clarity I realized that if he had only intended to scare me, he would be gone already, leaving a job well done. He wasn't a blood witch—otherwise he'd be using his *own* blood. Something else was going on here, and it was dark and ancient and filled up with the most primitive kind of fear.

"Now you're marked," he told me in that same whistling hiss. "And we see everything you do."

My right arm, creeping across my mattress and up over the edge of the nightstand, finally closed around the prize, a now-cold cup of jasmine tea.

"I guarantee you didn't see this," I whispered back and smashed the mug into the side of his skull with all the force of my fear. With my desire to get out of this alive, it was a considerable blow. The cup pulverized into shards of ceramic sand, and he went over the side of the bed and down to the floor, howling.

I was up and over him before I'd had time to blink, racing out of my room, bare feet tangling in the hallway runner and pitching me down the stairs at an angle that made my ankle sag and give under my weight.

At the bottom in a heap, I heard him screaming in another language. Pain always sounds the same.

Across the living room even though my ankle cried out, to clutch a hand around the drawer where I kept my gun, rattling it desperately for a full three seconds before I remembered it was locked. I reached for the key on my neck chain.

It wasn't there.

His heavy panting finally caught up with me and he laughed, thickly. "Looking for this?"

I saw the key dangling from his fist and lowered my hands to my sides. He had a Glock, too, a .44 that looked like a slim black cannon in the low light.

"Don't run, Detective Wilder. You'll just make things worse on yourself."

With the gun and all, he made a certain amount of sense. But when did I ever do what anyone told me, never mind masked creeps breaking into my cottage? This son of a bitch didn't know me at all.

I bolted for the kitchen. He snarled and tossed the key aside, reaching for me as I passed. I kicked over a chair to block his way and didn't look back to see if he fell. If I could just get outside, to the working circle, I could stand inside it and be safe . . .

I heard and felt it all—the trigger clinking, the slow-motion boom as the gun fired, and burning cold-hot pain pass through the meat of my right arm.

The bullet spanged away somewhere into the wall and I was left with the worst agony I've ever felt, worse than any bullet had a right to inflict. It spread through my arm and my chest and clenched around my lungs and heart, a horrible full-body spasm that almost dropped me. I looked and saw a shiny liquid like mercury bleeding from the wound.

Silver. The Hexed bastard had used a silver bullet. And it had *worked*.

Crap.

"I warned you," he called, examining me with a critical eye on his handiwork.

I staggered to the cutlery drawer and grabbed the first sharp things I saw, a handful of cheap steak knives we'd never used because Sunny wouldn't let meat in the house.

"Not advisable, Detective!" he shouted at me, taking aim again.

"Go to hell!" I replied, and hurled a knife at his head.

It stuck in his leg because I'm not a circus performer or a ninja, and he fired. A cluster of herbs next to my head shattered in a puff of sweet-smelling dust. I needed cover. I was in a gods damn kitchen. Never mind details, I needed cover.

I whipped open the door to the FrigiTank and ducked

behind it just as he unloaded a volley on me, apparently tired of the *you throw, I shoot* game we were playing. The bullets impacted with the door, and the plastic in front of my eyes cracked.

He ejected his clip and loaded a fresh one. "Cute." He was back to hissing. "Now I suppose I'll just shoot you in the head for my trouble. You know, if you hadn't hit me—"

"Freeze!" a quavering voice screamed from behind him. Sunny stood in the kitchen doorway with my Glock trained. "Drop it!" she yelled at him when he didn't freeze, but turned to stare at her.

"Oh, witch," he said. "What are you doing with that?"

I hit him from behind and locked his gun arm behind his back, squeezing on his knuckles until he let the weapon go. I made his knees buckle and he went to the floor.

"Sunny, get my handcuffs."

"Luna!" she cried, her eyes quarter-size with panic. "Are you . . . ?"

I smelled that smell again and with a moan that sounded like ribs breaking he heaved himself up and sent me sprawling, going at a dead run straight for my cousin, who dropped the Glock in alarm and backed up so fast she fell. Hex it, he was stronger than Sandovsky.

"Forget the gun, he's got a working on him!" I screamed as she sat there with her mouth in an O, letting him bear down on her.

She blinked and held out her right palm. "Blood to dust!" she shouted. It was a standard dispel for blood witches, and did nothing. He kept coming.

"Blood to dust!" Sunny screamed. He grabbed her outstretched arm and I *felt* the impact of their two magicks hitting each other.

"Forget that! He's not a blood witch!"

Sunny jerked against him, tears coursing down her face with pure helpless terror as he held her close.

"Are you going to take me seriously now?" he asked.

I picked up his gun and it was heavy, so heavy I could barely hold it steady, but I did, raised and aimed. "Let go of her."

"You think that will kill me?" he sneered.

"No," I said honestly, "but I think it will hurt a whole hell of a lot."

I lowered my aim to clear Sunny's quaking body and squeezed the trigger.

A fountain of flesh erupted from the same thigh where I'd planted the steak knife, and he howled, shoved Sunny aside, and barreled through the front door and out into the night. The screen door flapped on its hinges and then everything was quiet except for the whoosh of the waves and Sunny's soft mewling sobs.

I dropped the gun and went to her, wrapping my arms around her while she cried and shook. "I'm s-sorry," she hiccupped. "I didn't wake up until I heard the screaming, and then I waited too long to get the gun . . ."

"Sunny," I told her. "Your timing was perfect. You're my gods damn hero."

She sniffed hard. "Who was he? Something bad . . . he made my skin creep . . ."

"He was bad, all right," I agreed. "Freaky-deaky blood-licking bad." I helped her up and sat her on the one chair that hadn't been knocked over. "You stay put. I'll call Mac and the crime scene unit."

"I was so frightened . . . ," Sunny whispered. I picked up the phone and punched 911. I would never admit to Sunny that I had been terrified, too.

TWELVE

Mac showed up within fifteen minutes, the strobe on top of his personal car going a thousand miles an hour and filling our still-dark living room with bloody flashes.

"Oh, Hex," he said when he burst through the door and saw the wreckage.

"We're all right, Mac," I said. "We're fine."

"You're not fine, Luna," Sunny piped up. I shot her a look.

"I'm fine," I repeated to McAllister.

He had taken hold of my arm and was examining it. "Sweet merciful gods, what happened to you? It's . . . burned. Does it hurt?"

"What do you—ow! Let go of me, Mac!—think?"

He didn't get a chance to tell me, because the blue crime scene van pulled up, followed by an unmarked car containing a detective I didn't recognize.

"Estevez, from the Forty-third," Mac said by way of introductions. "Wilder, from Twenty-fourth Homicide. This is Estevez's jurisdiction."

"Hell of a thing to happen, Detective Wilder," said Estevez, who was tall and broad with chubby cheeks, sort of like a cuddly tank. "Do you need medical attention?"

"I called the paramedics," said Mac. "She'll get all the help she needs."

I pulled McAllister aside. "I should show the crime scene unit where the bullets went, and where he was in my bedroom. Could you stay with Sunny?"

He nodded and took a seat next to her. "You okay?" he asked by way of greeting.

"No, Lieutenant McAllister," she said. "I'm not." Her hands were still shaking as they clutched the tissues.

Mac said, "Call me Troy. What can you tell me about the break-in?"

"Ma'am," called a CSU tech from the head of the stairs, "could you come take a look at this please?"

I climbed up to meet him, aware of the twinge every time I tried to put weight on my left ankle. Okay, it wasn't just a twinge, it was excruciating, but I wasn't about to let anyone know.

"You said you woke up and saw the perp standing over you?" said the tech as he went into my bedroom. Flashes popped and the lights were on, yellow marker tags hovering over the knife on the floor and the shards of mug.

"Yes," I said. "And he put his hand over my mouth to keep me quiet, but he was wearing cotton gloves."

"We'll check for fibers," said the tech, "but to be honest, Detective, I doubt we'll find anything. This guy was a professional—not only did he manage to get into your house, he relocked the window so we have no way of knowing which one he used."

"We found footprints in your rosebushes under the

trellis," said the second tech, stowing her camera and producing a field print kit, "so we assume it was your bedroom window. He might have hidden in your closet."

Then why hadn't I scented him? He'd smelled of char and death—not something I'd be likely to miss.

I looked over at the bedroom window, an old wooden thing with wavy glass that wouldn't stay open if your life depended on it. A man, climbing on a rickety trellis from the outside and attempting to jimmy a heavy window . . . he'd have to be a Hexed ghost.

The techs had opened my closet and were examining my shoes. "Do you notice anything missing, Detective?" asked the female tech.

"No, but when you're finished my Dior pumps better not be," I said. The fragrant roses peered back at me when I looked out the window, not a petal out of place.

Then I saw something that chilled me. The metal latch at the top of the window frame was covered in a thick layer of white paint. Intact and pristine, matched with the rest of the frame.

"Did you find forced entry anywhere else?" I asked the techs behind me, "like the kitchen door, or a downstairs window?"

"No, ma'am," said the male tech. "Just the footprints outside."

"Thank you," I murmured. I backed out of the room and then hobbled downstairs as quickly as I could. I felt the frissons up my spine and crackling over my scalp, the were—and human—reaction when something is Not Right.

Mac met me. "Tech dug the bullet that hit you out of the wall. He can't figure it out. Some kind of soft metal?"

"Silver," I whispered.

Mac's eyes widened. "Silver bullets? Are you shitting me?"

"Does this arm look I'm shitting you?"

Mac whistled. "Really works, doesn't it?"

"Yeah, unfortunately. I'm just lucky he has lousy aim."

McAllister grabbed my unwounded arm and guided me into our bathroom, shutting and locking the door. "Tell me what really happened, Luna."

"I woke up, and there was a nutcase in my bedroom who attacked me with a knife and told me to leave Stephen Duncan and another witness in the case alone."

He frowned. "Why would he tell you that?"

I looked down. "I, um, I've sort of been investigating him. And his father."

"For what?" Mac shouted. "Stephen likes to murder prostitutes! Al Duncan is the district attorney, for God's sake! Hex, Luna, please tell me you didn't go to his house."

He knew me too well.

"Shit!" he exclaimed when he saw my expression. "There's no way I'm going to be able to spin this, Luna—you're through."

All the tension boiled over and I snapped, "Thanks for the prognosis, Mac. Now would you like to hear about the witch who tried to murder me, or shall we continue the lecture?"

Mac sat on the toilet lid and gestured me to the lip of the tub. "Witch?" he said with a sigh. "Keep going. I knew it could only get worse."

"After he had me subdued, he . . ." I shivered at the memory. "He rubbed my hand in my own blood, and then he opened his jacket and made me touch his chest. It had markings . . . like tattoos, only they were skin. Brands."

The electrical spark that had hit me when I touched him now caused my chest wound to throb and made my hands shake.

"Did he say anything else?" Mac asked.

"He said, 'Now you're marked, and we see everything you do.'" I didn't *believe* him, necessarily, but telling Mac after the witch had ordered me to be silent made my heart flutter arrythmatically.

Mac rubbed his chin. "Marked for what? And who's *we*?"

"Hexed if I know, Lieutenant. After that, I hit him and got away, and he chased me downstairs, shot me in the hallway with the silver, and I was hiding behind the refrigerator when Sunny got the drop on him with my gun."

"And after that?"

"After that, he got away," I told Mac, looking him in the eye, "and I was glad to see him go."

"He knew you're a were," said Mac. "Why bring the silver otherwise?"

"And he's a witch," I reminded him. "He had to have magicked his way in here, and using my own blood, and his markings . . ."

"Well, if he's not a blood or a caster, what the hell is he?" said Mac.

If I closed my eyes I could still see those brands on his chest, black and swirling like a monstrous tentacled creature.

"Strong," I finally said. "And he's after me for something."

"Estevez has the investigation under control," said Mac. "So what can I do for you, Luna?"

I stood up. "You can go home, Mac, and let Sunny and me get some rest."

"What if the witch comes back?"

I thought of that shadow over me as I swam up from sleep. "He won't. He got what he wanted."

Mac sighed. "I'm staying the night, Detective, whether you like it or not. You may be able to take on anything this side of a called daemon, but your cousin is only human, and a traumatized one, too." He opened the door. "Show me what couch I'll be sleeping on."

A fter I got my arm stitched and bandaged by paramedics, who thankfully didn't ask how a graze wound had gotten burned, they gave me painkillers and I slept dreamlessly for the first time in weeks.

Mac had left when I woke up and Sunny was sweeping broken glass in the kitchen. I came as far as the door in my bare feet. "Sorry about your herbs."

She waved me off. "I can always get more from Grandma."

"Sorry you had to be here when this all happened."

Sunny stopped sweeping and came into the living room. "I'm the one who should be sorry."

I blinked. "Why?"

She sat on the edge of the sofa and chewed on the end of her index finger, a habit I'd teased her about mercilessly when we were younger.

"My dispel didn't work," she said finally.

"He wasn't a blood witch, Sunny," I said. "You're not responsible, trust me."

"And that's another thing—if he's not a blood witch, then what is he?"

I sat next to her. "We'll figure it out."

"Maybe Grandma . . ."

"*Without* Grandma."

Sunny hugged a throw pillow. "Who, then?"

I patted her on the leg. "I'll find somebody."

I turned on my laptop and surfed to Google. The first search term I tried was *occult experts*. A bunch of "psychic" readers and right-wing sites warning about the dangers of associating with weres and those of the blood were all I got.

Occult knowledge was more of the same. Strings for combinations of the words *werewolf*, *were*, *occult*, *supernatural*, and *paranormal* turned up fantasy art sites, a meeting forum for "vampires"—which held a lot of photos of humans dressed in black and blood red with pasty white makeup—and some local ghost-hunting sites, one of which advertised a tour of "Nocturne City's Most Haunted!" in bright flashing letters. Ghosttown was at the top of the attraction list. I hoped the happy hunters liked getting eaten by creatures.

My fingers paused.

Meggoth. Search.

A lone link popped up, a PDF file attached to Nocturne University Library. Graduate thesis, written in 1970. "Faces of Meggoth: Daemon Invasion in the Modern World." Jacob Hoskins was the author. Maybe he could give me some answers, like why the name *Meggoth* sounded so damn familiar.

I clicked to an alumni directory and dialed the main number.

"Alumni Affairs."

"Yes, hi. My name is Luna Wilder. I'm trying to get some information on a former graduate student of yours. Jacob Hoskins?"

There was a pause and the perky voice breathed for a few seconds.

"Hello?"

"Information about alumni is confidential," she stated, "but in this case Hoskins is still attached to the university. What is the nature of your inquiry?"

"I'm a detective with the city. I need to talk to him about a paper he wrote in graduate school. 'Faces of Meggoth'?"

I could almost feel the frost that fell when I said the words.

"I'm sorry," she snapped. "No more information is being released at this time." The dial tone buzzed in my ear. Rude bitch. She might as well have given me an invitation to come snoop.

I went upstairs, did fifty round kicks, fifty push-ups, and a hundred sit-ups to take my mind off the complications that seemed to be piling into my life with alarming frequency, and then went back to sleep until noon.

B uilt on the grounds of the former Blackburn estate, Nocturne University had been educating the metropolis and the surrounding coast since Theodore Blackburn had turned his enormous mansion over to the city in 1870. The double homicide that occurred shortly before, involving Mrs. Blackburn and a female servant, had been a great motivator. Students dared one another to go into the cupola at the top of the now-library, and the police were still called to pull them out with a fireman's ladder.

Blackburn Hall had been built later, a long brick building resembling England's Parliament. It housed three floors of faculty, and after consulting a directory I found Hoskins on the second, in a tiny office with a casement window and floor-to-ceiling bookcases.

I knocked on the open door. Hoskins jumped and slid his glasses up his nose. He was very thin, with pulled cheeks and wispy close-cut hair. Milky gray eyes stared at me from behind the plain wire-rims.

"Mr. Hoskins," I said, holding out my hand. "I'm Detective Wilder. I tried to find you through the Alumni Office, but—"

Hoskins shot out of his chair and pointed with a long scarecrow finger. "Get out! This is harassment!"

"Whoa!" I held up a hand. "Mr. Hoskins, I just want to talk."

"It's *Professor*, no thanks to you people. Now leave my office!" He reached for the phone on his desk. "Right this instant, or I'll call Security!"

I shut the door behind me and approached Hoskins. His eyes got big and his breathing got fast. Sharp copper teased my nostrils.

"Professor, you don't have to be afraid of me," I said. "I just need to ask you some questions."

He slammed the phone back into its cradle. "I have had enough *questions* to last me a lifetime, miss, and I don't care to answer any more." He pointed at my shield. "You may be young and pretty but that still marks you as a thug."

Just my luck that the one guy who might know something hated cops. "I'm not here in an official capacity," I told Hoskins, keeping my voice low and soothing. "If it will make you feel better . . ." I unclipped my shield and tucked it away. "There. Now we're just two people. Talking."

He regarded me for a long moment. I stood in the center of his carpet feeling very exposed.

"I suppose you're too young to remember," he said finally. "I apologize for my previous behavior. To you. Never to the police." The word wasn't so much spoken as spat.

I gestured to the leather sofa facing his desk. "May I sit?"

"No," said Hoskins stiffly. "Tell me what it is you want." He sat abruptly in his chair and began squaring off file folders with the edge of the desk.

"Um . . . okay." I shifted my feet. Between the severe expression and the prissy accent, Hoskins must be a master of humiliation with his students. I certainly felt on the spot.

Hoskins flipped open the top folder and marked a grade with a fountain pen. "Get on with it."

"You wrote a research article called 'Faces of Meggoth' when you were a graduate student," I blurted. "I need to know what Meggoth is."

"You mean whom," said Hoskins, not looking up.

"Fine, yes, who?"

He sighed and closed the folder. "I am going to regret this, Detective Wilder. I can feel it already."

I sat down so I could look him in the eye. Hoskins immediately stood again. "You can call me Luna," I offered.

"*Meggoth* is one name for an entity that has bewitched blood witches and bedeviled the rest of us for many thousands of years."

Entity . . .

The circuit clicked on. Meggoth. Entities. Rituals. Headlines thirty years old splashed across the front page, along with a picture of two bodies, one the killer's and one the sacrifice.

"Cedar Hill," I breathed.

Hoskins's lips compressed to invisibility. "Now you see why I resent intrusion."

I stared, seeing the mousy professor before me thirty years younger but with the same glasses, holding a mug slate as the camera flashed in his eyes.

"What happened to you, with Cedar Hill . . . ," I started.

"You have no conception of what I went through," said Hoskins. "So don't spread your sympathy here. The only reason I still hold this job is because I had already achieved tenure. I lost countless speaking engagements, my book deal. My entire life was tainted. And it was all your department's fault."

I couldn't meet his eyes, because he was right. In the early 1970s, anyone accused of being a blood witch met with Salem-level furor. Hoskins had been arrested prematurely, on the flimsiest of evidence, and was only released after weeks, when a primitive lab found that his blood type didn't match what the Cedar Hill Killer had spilled at the last awful scene. By the time the Nocturne PD caught Marcus Levinson, it was too late and he'd murdered more women.

Hoskins had retreated to his desk. "Get out. This time I mean it."

I sucked in a breath and started to talk instead. "Professor, I know I have no right to ask for your help now. You had your life ruined because Marcus Levinson was rich and protected, and that was a terrible mistake. But there's going to be another one made if you don't tell me what I need."

He dropped his pen and buried his face in his hands. "I can't help you!"

So much for sweet-talking. I leaned down so I was right in his line of sight when he looked up. "Tell me who Meggoth is."

Hoskins quivered and his eyes glistened. "He's the shadow of rage, Detective. He's the wanderer between worlds. *Meggoth* is just one name for something that is older and more terrible than anyone knows."

My gut twisted. "A daemon."

"*The* daemon," said Hoskins. "One of only three to survive the Descent. If you believe legend."

Ask me a week ago, and I would have laughed in his face. Now I wavered between incredulity and just plain fear.

"But he can't be here," I said. "Uncalled daemons don't exist. Daemons don't exist *at all,* if you listen to most witches."

"A few hundred years ago bacteria didn't exist, if you listened to most men of medicine," said Hoskins. "Daemons exist, Detective, as power. That's what Marcus Levinson wanted." He ran a hand through light, thinning hair. "Daemons can be channeled like any other energy. Levinson knew this, and he kept trying. Failing to call a daemon through and killing again and again with his rage mounting each time, reaching so desperately for something he could not comprehend."

"Levinson was insane," I told Hoskins gently. "Even if he hadn't been an amateur witch, he would have killed those women for some other equally flimsy reason."

"You are so very sure, Detective," said Hoskins. "Why is this?"

I debated with myself for just a moment, then pulled down my collar and turned so Hoskins could see the four circular bite scars along my shoulder where Joshua's double fangs had pierced me.

He didn't shy, just took off his glasses and breathed on them, then leaned in for a closer look. "I see," he said finally. "In that case, Detective, may I advise you to be cautious. The Cedar Hill Killer may have failed in his workings, but there is no reason to believe the next witch will."

"Little late for that," I said. "I've already had someone attack me over this mess. Maybe you could you tell me what sort of witch uses a victim's blood instead of their own?"

Hoskins rolled his eyes upward. "In some tomes there are accounts of witches channeling energy directly through their bodies without the use of blood ritual. I assume your assailant was versed in this sort of magick."

"That sounds bad."

"Oh, it is," he agreed. "Extremely so. To gain power that way, your witch would have to feed his body almost constantly with energy—have a working circle cast on him at all times."

"Branding," I said.

Hoskins nodded. "Skin branding would certainly be effective. I am sorry I can be of no further assistance."

I opened the door and let the late-afternoon sunlight stream into Hoskins's cramped little office. "Trust me, Professor, you were a bigger help than you imagined."

He shuffled his feet a bit and almost smiled. "I wonder to this day what Levinson was really trying to accomplish with those rituals."

I wondered that, too. The time line of Cedar Hill was all wrong for the killer I was tracking, but in a lot of ways Marcus and Lilia's killer were the same—insane, sadistic, and with an eye toward black magick.

"If I find out," I told him, "you'll be the first to know."

THIRTEEN

The next day found me angry and sore from the impending phase, stalking down a side street near the university. A fine rain, mist really, fluttered around me and landed on my eyelashes, blurring the neon signs in the shop windows.

Devere Street was pure Old Nocturne: tall brick buildings, iron fences encircling the trees, and lampposts that still burned gas. Basement businesses peered out from behind burglary grates.

Second Skin was one of them, a door and a tiny storefront painted black with snarling Chinese dragons rampant around the innocuous hand-carved sign. Neon advertised body piercing; a tiny pentacle was painted in the corner of the window, a nod to the old practice of signaling witches and weres that they were welcome. I pushed open the door, and discordant chimes jangled.

Below-ground dimness and the smell of murky incense washed over me. I squinted against the smoky half-light. "Perry?"

"Back here," he rasped. I stepped around the counter,

a hunk of black wood plastered with flash, and entered the tiny back room. Contrastingly bright, the walls were covered in flash and a few oil paintings, the only pieces of furniture a black leather dentist's chair and a drafting table. Perry sat with his back to me, skinny body hunched, his ponytail lying across his shoulders like a sleek black snake.

"How's it going?" I asked cautiously.

He grunted. "Can't complain." One hand moved, and I saw the edge of an ink drawing. A woman's arm, engulfed in flames.

"I need to ask you a question, Perry," I said.

He spun on his stool to face me. "Well, isn't that special, Detective." He grinned.

Most people who see Perry for the first time can't manage to not look shocked, or in some cases genuinely terrified. Half of his face is rippled white scar tissue, with a milky eye rolled to the side and a streak of pure white running through his hair. The other half is normal—a thin, ratty face, bad teeth, and icy blue eye. Then they see the tattoos covering him from neck to who knows where, and the bluish clawlike nails of the hand on the scar side. When he talks, you can catch a flash of serpentine tongue.

"I met someone who has some interesting ink," I said. "Well, not ink. Brands, carved right into him. I was hoping you'd know about that."

"Branding? Nah," Perry snorted. "Don't go in for that body-mod stuff. The ink speaks to me. The flesh is just so much canvas."

"Be that as it may. You know anyone who *is* into it?"

Perry nibbled on the end of his pen, rolling his bad eye toward me. I took a step back. Not because he disgusted me, but because when the mangled, white eye stared at you, it wasn't Perry looking out.

"You might try Cassandra LaVey," he said. "Seen her ads?"

I shook my head. Perry huffed. He turned the scarred side of his face away from me and added another curlicue to the drawing of a gowned woman being burned at the stake. "Let me have a look at you," he said, putting his pen down and standing up. He rubbed his leg on the scarred side. A metal brace peeked out from under his jeans. "Sit."

"I really don't have time," I lied. "I'm working and all . . ."

"This'll just take a minute," he said, jerking the dentist's chair upright. I knew I didn't have a choice and straddled it backward, pulling up my shirt to expose my back.

Perry grunted softly as his fingers grazed my skin. "The *lady* Cassandra refers to herself as the body-mod goddess. She does it live at a watering hole around the corner on Saturday nights. Theatrical bitch. Cheapens the art."

"Branding is her specialty?"

"If you can call something that requires a dull knife and the hands of a longshoreman a specialty," said Perry. "This tat is hot to the touch. You been putting it through a workout."

I sighed. "You could say that."

Perry had given me the tattoo, a pentacle surrounded by the phases of the moon, when I moved to Nocturne City. The ink concoction was supposed to keep the were in me at bay, at least long enough for innocent bystanders to run away. Results were mixed.

"So are you going to tell me why you're so interested in branding all of a sudden?" Perry asked.

"No," I said. With his unique condition, I trusted Perry

about as far as I could toss the Fairlane. "But thanks for your help."

"Hell," said Perry. "If that tat ain't working, I'm no help at all."

I pulled my shirt down and dismounted the chair. "It's been working. I've just had a lot of stuff making me want to phase lately."

Perry cocked his head and looked at me with his good eye.

"I met another were," I continued. "Two, in fact. Him and his sister."

"Him? He your type?" Perry asked.

"That's debatable," I said, trying to ignore the memory of Dmitri's eyes.

"Well, tell him if he hurts you I'll kick his furry ass back to the Dark Ages," Perry grunted, picking up his pen again.

I smiled and patted his nonscarred shoulder. "What would I do without you to look out for me?"

"Hah!" he barked. "Since the Hex Riots I can barely hobble to the can. But thanks for pretending to care."

I looked down. "Seriously, Perry. You're the only one who never gave me crap about helping me."

The milky eye swiveled to look at me. "What was I supposed to do? Let you keep killing people?"

My heart plummeted, and I tried to remember it wasn't Perry saying those things. He had a condition, just like me. He wasn't to blame. I wasn't to blame. If anyone was, it was Joshua.

"You okay?" Perry barked, the human-shaped side of his face frowning. I nodded shakily, and his face went hurt. "Shit. I say something I shouldn't have?"

"It's fine," I said. "Just the unpleasant truth." I started back to the front of the shop.

"Hey, Wilder," Perry called.

I stopped. "Yeah?"

"If you see Cassandra," he said, "tell the bitch I said hello."

The passenger's side of the Fairlane was a ruin of paper and old cartons. It's a sad fact that when I'm hungry there's almost nothing I won't eat. Lately I'd been on a ChickenHut jones and had the empty nugget boxes to prove it. Plus I got a perverse pleasure out of eating there, since they had made my life so miserable when I'd been an employee.

I had to pay for community college somehow.

Stephen Duncan's face peeked at me from his case file. I had to give that back to McAllister. It was Bryson's to screw up now. Much as I would posture to anyone who asked, the witch had done his job. I was scared, and I couldn't shake the back-of-the-neck tickle of being watched. I rubbed the cut on my chest. It still stung.

I shuffled the Duncan file into a semblance of order while I thought about Professor Hoskins some more. He seemed to know what he was talking about, but he also seemed a few cashews short of a nut assortment.

I scribbled *county records* on my hand so I wouldn't forget to go look over the Cedar Hill files at some point and stuck the key into the Fairlane's ignition, placing Stephen's picture neatly in the clip on the front of the file.

It was then that I saw it: a shadow on his neck, peeking out of his Alder Bay jersey. A tattoo or a birthmark, something spidery and maleficent. As I squinted to make it out, my mind conjured images of the burning Ghosttown sidewalk.

County records could wait, and the branded witch be damned. Quickly as it ebbed and flowed over me, the fear was gone and replaced by my aroused predatory instincts. I stepped on the accelerator and drove toward the jail.

S tephen had been transferred from the central holding cells to the county jail, and the booking officer there barely glanced at my credentials before shoving a sign-in sheet at me and going back to her magazine.

I went through the metal detector and got wanded by an equally surly female guard before getting buzzed through two gates and a door to the interrogation room. Stephen was led in a moment later, scraggly and miserable in a bright yellow DOC jumpsuit.

"What do *you* want?" he said, flopping in a chair across from me.

I had brought props and shoved a glossy of Lilia's crime scene at him. He glanced at it and then sat back.

"Don't know her."

I held the photo no more than an inch from his face. "Look again. You do."

He reached up and slapped the picture away. "I said I don't, so I don't. What is it with you people? I didn't kill Marina, either." He looked down and away from me. "Why won't you believe me?"

"When I find someone covered in blood next to a dead body, I guess I'm just naturally suspicious. Especially when he fucks two women in a row who are murdered. That's a piss-poor track record, kid."

"I don't have anything else to say," said Stephen, and kept his word by shutting up and staring at the center of the steel table between us. I let a silence stretch as I mentally roved over the pathetic list that I had assembled. Dmitri, who could have done it but didn't, and I knew that just like I knew what blood tasted like. Stephen, a spoiled, sexually dysfunctional torture junkie if all the evidence was to be believed. And out there somewhere, the faceless murderer who drifted through decades with a wake of mutilated women behind him. There was muscle tissue and tendon connecting all of them, but I couldn't see it yet and it was driving me crazy.

"At the Raven, you told me that the were had killed Marina," I said finally. "Did the were kill this girl, too?" I took a deep breath and prepared to lie my ass off. "I have a witness who saw you with her multiple times, Stephen, and compelling evidence that you are a killer. You of all people should know that lying to me now is just going to hurt you at trial."

Stephen didn't have to know that Dmitri had never actually followed Lilia to any of her trysts. Interrogation is the equivalent of poking an alligator with a sharp stick—anything for a reaction.

He twitched when I mentioned someone had been watching him. Lawyer street-smarts didn't seem to be genetic in the Duncan family.

"I don't have anything to say," he repeated. He took a deep breath and said in a truly nasty tone, "I didn't know the bitch."

I grabbed Stephen by the back of his neck and slammed his face into the table, pressing his cheek on top of the scene photo. "Her name was Lilia Desko," I said. "She was drugged, mutilated, and left in an alley to bleed to death. *Look* at her," I demanded as Stephen struggled. "Because she wasn't just a body. She was a girl with a future, and someone loved her. You did this to her, and there is nothing you can do to hide from me."

I let him go. He jerked away from me, shaking. "I didn't do it!" he shouted. The spoiled-little-boy facade cracked, and his eyes had the same wild desperation as when I'd first seen him at the Hotel Raven.

"Then tell me who did, Stephen," I said.

His head shook wildly before the words were even out. "I can't!"

"Then what *can* you say? Because at this point I'm still seeing you ripping those girls open."

He sniffed hard. "We went out. Lilia and I."

Finally. "How long did you patronize her?"

He shrugged. "I don't know. Six months? Since I moved back to the city to live with my dad." He rubbed his wrists under the shackles. "She was kinda sweet and dumb . . . trusting for a hook—I mean, a working girl."

Trusting enough to take a needle from a stranger? "Did Lilia have a habit?"

He nodded. "She shot some meth, I think. We did coke together." Stephen bit his lip and looked stricken. "God, don't tell my father that."

"I'm not wearing a collar with a little bell, Stephen, so it's safe to assume I'm not the DA's lapdog."

"She was trying to clean up, though," he said, his face going soft. "She'd been going to rehab through the city's free program, outpatient. It was tough. They made her quit cold turkey and then she'd get frustrated and shoot up again, and then she'd cry and whine about it. Honestly, Detective, it was irritating as hell."

If Duncan the elder was so flat you could have spread him over toast, Stephen was all over the place, leaping from hostile to nostalgic to irritable in the space of a sentence. He wanted to talk about *irritating as hell,* he should look in a mirror.

"Well, she had at least one man standing behind her efforts," I said, thinking of Sandovsky.

"Oh, yeah, the boyfriend," said Stephen with a snort. "Some winner he must have been."

I decided it wouldn't help my cause to say that from where I sat, Dmitri was more of a man than Stephen could imagine on a good day. I just asked, "When did you see Lilia last?"

He shrugged. "Three weeks ago, I think. Marina started getting jealous."

"Wrong, Stephen," I told him. "My witness tells me you saw her the night she died."

"Your witness is full of crap," he told me, trying to cross his arms indignantly. For the first time I saw a resemblance to Alistair.

"Right now, I trust him a whole hell of a lot more than I do you," I said. "So why don't you be straight with me? Think of it as a refreshing change from being a weasly little prick."

Stephen drummed his fingers on the table. He either couldn't sit still or stared off into space. I wondered if it was lack of sleep and stress, or if he'd found a friend in jail with more cocaine.

"I didn't want Marina to know. We were getting pretty serious. But Lilia and I got together sometimes. Marina may have been on the game but she was very traditional. Wanted kids, wanted to meet my dad. All that mail-order-bride shit."

"And Lilia wasn't traditional?"

He snorted. "Hell no. She was a wild child. She said my old man could go screw himself if he didn't approve."

The drumming abruptly stopped and he went back to staring. "I liked that about her."

I tried to imagine Stephen showing up at the Duncan manse with Marina in tow, introducing her to Alistair as the love of his life. I couldn't see it. Senior seemed like the type who would rather eat rat poison than accept anyone who had even a hint of low class.

"I didn't kill them," he told me again.

I sighed. "Stephen, at this point it doesn't matter. They're still dead."

"Then maybe you should be out doing, oh, I don't know, your *job* instead of storming in here and harassing me."

He just had to get indignant, didn't he?

I grabbed him again, and this time he struggled. He was strong, but not any stronger than an ex–lacrosse player should be. I jerked down the collar of his jumpsuit and got a look at the mark on his neck, inky tentacles seeming to spill off his skin. A sigil, one that pulsated with magicks that gave it life.

I felt a shock as my hand came in contact and jumped back. The same burned-ozone smell that had caught me when I'd been attacked rifled the air in the interrogation room.

Stephen was looking at me warily, rubbing his cheek where I'd planted it in the tabletop.

"What's your problem?"

I sat down, rubbing my raw palm. "How long have you had that tattoo?"

He blinked stupidly at me. "What tattoo?"

There was such a thing as playing innocent, but this was taking it too far. "The one on your neck, Stephen. The sigil."

"Detective Wilder," he said, edging his chair back. "I don't have any tattoos. Now I think you should leave, and not come back unless my lawyer is here."

"You don't see it . . . ," I murmured. The sigil on Stephen's skin squirmed under my eyes and made the point between them pound. I could accept that he couldn't see it. Even the most novice caster witch knew how to glamour. But not to feel the oily slippage of a working scribed into his very skin?

Stephen stamped his shackled feet on the floor. "Quit staring at me with your mouth open! I told you to get out!"

Now he *sounded* like Alistair, too.

"Just a word of advice before I go," I told him. "Even if you didn't kill those women—which I doubt—you're involved. The less you tell me, the harder I will nail your pampered ass to the wall as an accessory."

"That's it then," said Stephen. "You had a bum time growing up and you're taking it out on me?"

I stood up and buzzed for the guard before answering him.

"I'm trying my Hexed hardest to make sure you go to the gas chamber before you kill anyone else." The door lock clicked and I stood aside for the jail guard.

"And by the way," I said as he walked past me, "I did have it rough, but the day I am jealous of you is the day hell opens a hockey rink. You're worse than pathetic. You're trash."

"You think you know what's going on? Think you'll figure it all out?" Stephen hissed, jerking against his shackles. "Never! You're just a stupid Insoli whose bite should have poisoned her!"

"Move, Duncan!" the guard ordered, putting him back in line. I watched them go, mouth open again.

Where had a human boy like Stephen learned old
were curses like that? If I could figure that one out, I
had a feeling I'd be a good deal less confused about
this case.

FOURTEEN

At the Twenty-fourth, I stopped in to check my messages and update the status of my other open cases. A few of the day-shift detectives nodded or waved at me. I hung around so much I was becoming familiar, which was funny because with the blending of night and day that comes with stress and no sleep, I felt like I hadn't been to work in weeks.

Detectives with tough cases are easy to spot—we're the ones with circles under our eyes, mussed hair, clothes that have been slept in, on our fifth cup of coffee. We don't stop, though, because we've become consumed by the victims and the mechanics of the crime, and the only escape is to assign guilt to someone.

Sometimes we can't handle it, and we beat suspects like Bryson; or we drink, smoke, start taking cash to look the other way. Or we turn it inward and eat our service weapons.

I had eight messages, none of them from Captain Roenberg. Al Duncan had taken my threat seriously.

My phone trilled as soon as I set it back in the cradle, a blocked number with a Nocturne City prefix.

I figured the worst it could be was a mouth-breathing death threat and picked up. "Yes?"

"Hey, Detective," said Dmitri easily. "I was hoping to catch you before you went home. You got a minute?"

I must have held the phone, stone silent, for a good thirty seconds because he said, "Luna?"

"I'm here. How did you get this number?"

"Called the main police line and asked for you, like everyone else." He chuckled. I could hear rock music and hubbub in the background on his end and someone shouted, muffled, "Dmitri, you want another beer?"

He must have nodded affirmative because I heard him swig before he said, "You don't talk much, do you, Detective?"

"I talk plenty! Most of the time people wish I'd stop talking!" I snapped with more vigor than I intended.

"If you say so." He chuckled again.

"Why are you calling me?" I demanded.

"Listen, if you don't want to talk . . ."

"No!" I cried when I heard him start to hang up. "Actually, I'm glad you did call. I have something I need to ask you, as a fellow were."

He swigged again. "Sure, you could do that. But how about asking in person?"

Another incoherent moment for Luna. Was he saying what it sounded like he was saying? No. Couldn't be. *Could* be. What to say? Be professional. Be cool.

"I suppose that wouldn't be too awful." My voice came out a purr. Too cool. Way too cool. Verging on sexy. Gods, what was I doing? Every time I met Dmitri I ended up either injured or pissed off. Sometimes both.

"Glad to hear it," Dmitri said. "Want to come over to the Crown?"

"No offense, Sandovsky, but if I never step foot in your pack house again, I'll be a happy woman."

"Well, anything that makes you happy, Detective," he said with a low rumbly laugh. Skin all up and down my back and arms tingled.

When you're a police officer, a suspect making you tingle is a bad sign.

"How about Maven's, the bar on Devere. By the university?"

Sandovsky snorted. "Why the hell are we going to that freak joint?"

"Because I have to interview a potential witness," I told him, "and I thought you'd appreciate the fact they have lots and lots of beer."

"You know me too well," he said, and I could almost picture the smirk on the other end of the line.

"Seven sharp," I told him.

"I wouldn't dare stand you up, Detective," he said. "I'd be in fear for my manhood."

"What did you mean, Maven's is a freak joint?" I asked before he could hang up.

Sandovsky laughed again, and I tingled again. Damn it. "You'll see," he told me. "Meet you there at seven."

S unny found me just as I hit the wall in the back of my closet and uttered a growl that would have done Lon Chaney proud.

"Let me guess," she said, surveying the ruin of vintage shoes, dresses, and lingerie that concealed my bedroom floor, "you've decided to give away your prized possessions to the Shiny Master of Sparkly Overpriced Accessories and join his cult."

"If the Shiny Master of Whatever can help me put together a decent outfit, he is *welcome* to the rest," I told her, puffing a strand of hair out of my eyes.

"What's the big occasion?" Sunny asked, automatically beginning to refold everything I had thrown out of my closet.

"You know that were I didn't have a date with before?"

"Sandovsky?"

"Yeah. I sort of have a date with him now."

Sunny blinked, looked down at the Gaultier heel she was holding, and then looked at me again.

"You're going out."

"Yes."

"On a date."

"Yes."

"With a murder suspect?"

I grimaced. "He's not *really* a suspect anymore. Now I think the DA's son did it." *Proof* was another matter . . . but that's what this date was for. Who says you can't multitask at love?

Sunny flopped on my bed. "Oh, Luna, why can't you use Match.com like everyone else?"

I grinned at her. "Because if I was everyone else, I couldn't give my caring and concerned cousin a heart attack, now could I?"

Sunny rolled her eyes. "Wear whatever you want. I guarantee Sandovsky's not interested in your clothes, just what's under them."

"Why, Sunny," I told her, "your cynicism is shocking."

She got up and left at that point, and I went on

obsessing until I realized it was time for me to take a bath and get ready to meet Dmitri at Maven's.

M aven's was a perfect example of interior design gone horribly Goth. With satin-draped walls in red and black, reproductions of oil paintings hanging in black frames, and furniture that had enough feet for a herd of wooden cows, it resembled more than anything a high-end Victorian brothel.

Lamps with colored shades hung over the tables and velvet-covered chairs, bathing the entire place in red. I felt like I was inside a beating heart.

Most of Maven's patrons didn't display any more taste than the decorator. Pasty bodies strapped with spikes, lace, and leather to an androgynous man, accompanied by approximately eighteen pounds of black eyeliner per face.

Even though I was all in black—knee-length satin skirt, tight tank, my jacket, and my Chippewas—if we had been playing that *one of these things is not like the others* game I would have lost badly. Every single eye I met on the way in glared at me with overt hostility.

Dmitri was hunched in a corner near the bar, clutching his bottle of Rolling Rock like a shield. I waved at him over the elaborately coiffed head of a plump girl sausage-wrapped into a corset and PVC mini skirt and made my way through the suffocating brocade space to his table.

"I told you," he greeted me.

"It's not so bad," I said. "Although I feel a little out of place without my bleeding soul exposed for an uncaring world to see."

Dmitri cracked a smile and then flicked his hand at the bartender. "Drink?"

"Theoretically, I'm on duty."

He shrugged. "Suit yourself." After another pull from his bottle he said, "So what's this big question you want to ask me?"

I sighed. "Is there any way that someone can be a were and not know it?"

Dmitri cocked an eyebrow at me. "That's an odd damn question, Detective."

"Humor me?" I pleaded.

Dmitri shook his head. "Nope. Sometimes you hear that phasing makes you lose your memory, but it ain't true." He smiled without any humor. "Trust me, Luna—when you're turning into a giant wolf, you tend to remember."

I don't know why I'd expected him to offer some revelation on were lore that I, as a lowly Insoli, was not privy to. Stephen Duncan was just a lying psychopath trying to throw me off, and all the parts of my brain hollering that Stephen as Suspect didn't quite fit needed to shut the hell up. The logic train had pulled into the station and all passengers were getting off.

Anyway, I had come here for reasons other than a Q&A with Nocturne City's sexiest pack leader. And damn it, why did my traitorous brain insist on using that adjective to describe Dmitri?

"Okay, well, it's been fun. And informative," I said, standing a little too quickly and banging my knee on the table leg. "Gotta blast." Time to put Dmitri, Stephen, and weres period aside and go find Cassandra LaVey, the body-mod goddess. If I couldn't prove that Stephen had attacked Marina and Lilia, I could at least find who'd attacked me.

"Hey, wait just a minute." Dmitri took my arm, not ungently. "You got your answer, now I got a question for you."

I turned back to him, and he stared into my eyes with such intensity it felt as if the floor had evaporated under me and I was rocketing upward at the speed of light.

"What are you doin' to solve Lilia's murder?" he asked.

I crashed into the ceiling as my ride halted abruptly. It would have to be that question.

"Weres who mate are packbonded," said Dmitri. "Until her death is reckoned with I'm bound to make that my first duty."

"Make what your first duty?" I asked, though I already knew. The special were brand of justice, administered with tooth and claw.

"Making the doer pay." Dmitri glared and drank his beer, straight-ahead stare indicating the topic was closed for discussion.

I sat down again, and felt as torn up as if a blood witch's athame had ripped me open. I had a sworn duty to be dead-set against things like street justice and revenge killing, but at the same time I liked Dmitri, and I knew him now. If he went on with his pack duty, he would be hurt.

Could I handle that? I wasn't sure, and it chilled me more than the overcirculated air in Maven's.

"Dmitri," I said after a long moment, "you're a smart guy, and the reason I'm telling you is that you're going to figure it out eventually."

I bit my lip as he put down the drink and leaned in, now intent on me. Discussing an open case with anyone except other cops is an automatic termination, and revealing evidence or suspect lists to anyone outside law enforcement pretty much guaranteed whatever you had would be thrown out at trial. Then again, I doubted Stephen Duncan would ever make it that far. Daddy's boy would plead out and get to spend his summer vacation in a criminal psychiatric hospital.

"I'm looking at someone," I admitted. "But he's claiming that a were killed the woman he was found with."

"A were?" said Dmitri. "Good. I can find him quicker."

"Wait!" I snapped. "I'm not finished, damn it." I glanced across the club again. No sign of anyone who could be Cassandra, unless she was under twenty-five and favored Day-Old Corpse as her foundation shade. "There was no were scent on the second body. And the only one on Lilia was her own. The guy is not a were, Dmitri—but he keeps saying the were did it like a freaking mantra."

"So he's a crazy motherfucker. Doesn't mean he couldn't kill Lilia," Dmitri said.

I put my hand on his forearm. "You have got to let me handle this. I'm equipped. You're not."

"You're a cop—big Hexed deal!" Dmitri snarled. A few of the leather-and-lace crowd looked over at us. "So what if you can flash a badge?" he went on. "You won't do what's necessary of a were whose packmate got killed by an outsider."

That stung, but I shrugged it off and kept my voice level. "I'm not a member of your pack," I reminded him. "And had I known you were going to be an asshole about the whole thing, I would never have asked you here to try and help me get some real punishment for the Hexed creep who did this."

Dmitri put a hand over his face and breathed in. His wide shoulders, encased in another T-shirt—Black Sabbath, this time—shivered for a moment before he got control.

"Sorry," he said roughly. "I just . . . I miss her. You wouldn't know what it's like, being mated and then having that other person ripped away with no god damn warning."

"How do you know I don't?" I asked quietly.

Dmitri snorted a laugh. "I know, Detective."

I wasn't sure whether to be flattered Dmitri had finally let down his guard or insulted that he wouldn't give up harping on the Insoli thing. As if I didn't understand what it meant to be a mate. I understood. I had been one, and the loss of abandoning Joshua after the bite had sat deep in the pit of my stomach for years, a physical need I didn't understand until I stopped drinking and went to school and the police academy.

The appearance of Cassandra LaVey saved me from having to think that one over anymore. A spotlight hit the tiny stage at the far end of the room, and illuminated a woman with black hair, black makeup, a black dress, and black boots with spike heels at least five inches tall. From a distance, Cassandra looked as if she were pulling the light into her, and her pale triangular face floated above her high lace collar.

She raised her arms above her head, gypsy sleeves falling back to reveal arms so scarred they shone.

"Good evening, children."

The fashionably challenged assembled cheered when they caught sight of her.

"Freak show," Dmitri muttered. I was inclined to agree.

"Tonight we draw the flesh and spill the blood," Cassandra proclaimed, arms still raised. "Who will be the first?"

A chorus of the crowd rushed the stage, and Cassandra performed a twirl before telling her followers, "Let the flesh-changing begin!"

The lights in the bar went down and that music with no words and a pulsating beat that was popular when I was still wearing more than the standard number of rings in my ears and going to all-night parties started to throb. In the dimness I saw Cassandra slip offstage through a plain black door suspiciously devoid of any filigree or lacquer.

I nudged Dmitri. "I need to talk to Cassandra! Wait here!"

He yelled something back over the music, which with heightened hearing ranged on painful, and went to the bar to procure more booze.

I wound my way through the dancing bodies, careful not to get impaled on anyone's jewelry, and knocked at the stage door. On closer inspection the letters VIP were painted black-on-black in large curly script. Oh, scandal. Wonder what went on back there.

The door opened a slit and a blue eye in a sallow face peered out, topped by scraggly blond hair in pigtails. "Kindred?" I said in shock.

Her visible eye went wide. "You!"

I shoved my way in before her shock could give way to remembering who I was, and the door—heavier than it looked—clicked shut and locked behind me.

"Oh, crap," Kindred said with a heavy sigh. "You're really not supposed to be in here. Cassandra and Maven'r gonna kill me." She wore a variation on the white latex Come-Pay-To-Screw-Me outfit I'd first seen her in, but the disaffected speech and flat face were the same.

"Relax," I told Kindred. "I know how to behave in the VIP room. I promise not to spill my drink or arrest anyone."

The gentle bubble of speech died down as I moved past a despondent Kindred and toward Cassandra, who held court with a large cluster of Maven's less tacky patrons. A quick scent made me nearly choke on copper and sweat. Cassandra liked to keep herself surrounded by blood witches.

She raised her glass. "As we are all children of the darker gods here, on this dawning of a most auspicious twilight I toast you all as blood and brethren, bonded by the dark flesh. To flesh!"

"To flesh!" the witches around her chorused.

I giggled. It was just a tiny sound, no more than a short peep before I bit the insides of my cheeks to stop it. Wouldn't do to be cackling at Cassandra's act if I wanted her cooperation.

Every single head in the room turned my way. The closest glared. Cassandra lowered her glass and stepped free of her cadre, eyeing me up and down.

"Who are you, unbeliever?" she asked in a tone so far from the theatrical I wondered if I was talking to the same woman.

I slid my fingers into my jacket pocket and touched my shield, then took them out again.

"I'm a friend of Perry's," I said. A rush of hisses and expletives ran through the crowd.

"Perry's *friends* aren't welcome here!" Kindred shouted. "Cassandra, she forced me to let her in! I didn't disobey you!"

"Yes, and you did a bang-up job of being guard dog, what with the whining and the pouting," I told her.

"Perry sent her to spy on me," Cassandra said definitively. "How unmannerly of him."

I put up my hands. "Listen, Cassandra. I just came to talk to you." I was going to kill Perry for this.

"Talk is not what we do here," Cassandra told me. Her irises expanded, and in the brighter light I saw the inkiness spill across her entire eye. She smiled. "What we do here is sculpt flesh."

It all happened so fast that even now I can't really say how the three men closest to me managed to pin my arms behind my back, holding me with my shoulders twisted painfully as I struggled with blind fury.

I screamed the only invective my frenzied mind could form. *"Dmitri!"*

More of the crowd moved toward me, a tide of angry-eyed people reaching out. The man who had my arms ripped off my leather jacket and tossed it aside. I breathed a silent thanks as my badge went with it. Being a cop in this situation would not help me. The other two hissed when they caught sight of my Glock.

"Cassandra!" one shouted. "She's armed herself."

Cassandra smiled. "A lot of good it does her now." She pointed her finger, also painted black, at me. "What did you hope to accomplish with that crude instrument?"

"Not what's happening obviously. *Dmitri!*" I screamed again, thanking whatever deity was watching over me that the Evil Dead weren't smart enough to recognize a police rig.

An impact hit the door from the outside. A size twelve steel-toed boot, at a guess.

"Luna!"

I had guessed right.

I struggled to turn my head and saw the door explode open, Kindred jumping back with a yelp. Dmitri barreled in, stopping when he saw me pinned. He cursed in Ukrainian.

"Bring her here to me," said Cassandra, not even ruffled by the appearance of a large, pissed-off were in her club. "It's time we had a true demonstration subject."

"Touch her and I'll rip your fucking hands off,"

Dmitri warned. He hissed as a flick knife appeared at his throat. The bartender from the main room kicked the door shut behind him and nodded at Cassandra.

"Sorry about the disturbance, ma'am. He went for the door before I even realized someone was screaming."

So screaming was dandy and normal in this place. Hex, this was seventeen kinds of not good.

"Let me go," Dmitri warned. The bartender laughed and tightened the knife, nocking skin and bleeding a thin ribbon down Dmitri's throat.

I thrashed and struggled as hard as I could, but against three determined blood witches even my were strength wasn't making a difference. They ripped off my shoulder holster and gave it to Cassandra, who set it aside with an expression of distaste. I was shoved to face her and released, panting and enraged.

Cassandra grabbed my chin. I yanked out of her grasp and put up my hands in a combat posture.

"Oh, my," she said. "You are so agitated. Please." She reached toward me ever so slowly, like I might bite. I would, if it came to that. She placed both hands on my shoulders and fixed me with her black-on-black eyes. "Rest, child," she told me.

I felt lead creep into my limbs, and the sounds of the club faded as Cassandra's face grew to cover my entire field of vision. I felt remarkably pleasant, like I had just slipped into a warm bath and could stay there for a good long time.

A shudder ripped through my abdomen, a terrible cramp that was usually the first sign of phase. With it came the panic and the rush of adrenaline, and I looked back up at Cassandra and saw her waver with confusion.

My first impulse was to tackle her, rip her to pieces, make her hurt for thinking I could be laid low with a cheap glamour. I smelled the close press of bodies, most of them laden with hostility, and thought better of that plan. I tried to keep the dopey, obedient look on my face while Cassandra's worry vanished and she smiled.

"That's right, child. Come here to me." She motioned me to a heavy wooden chair with a plush cushion and sat me in it, arranging my bare inner arms outward. Across the room, Dmitri stood stock-still and bleeding, breath coming fast.

A man in a velvet smoking jacket and obscenely tight leather pants presented Cassandra with a black leather zipper case the size of a dictionary. He was albino, with white hair and pink-rimmed eyes.

"Thank you, Maven," Cassandra told him. Maven grinned at her and went back to Kindred. He put a hand on her white-leather-clad ass and watched me like I might juggle fire or pull a rabbit out of somewhere.

Cassandra unzipped the case and revealed a row of surgical-steel knives and scalpels, as well as a set of tiny pliers and piercing needles. She selected a scalpel with a curved end, like a boning knife, twirling it between her fingers as she leaned in and touched the very tip of the blade to my skin. *That's right, bitch.* I smiled inwardly. *Get nice and close so it hurts.*

I looked past her shoulder and found Dmitri's eyes with mine. I tried to telegraph that everything was all right, but I must've done a lousy job because he just bared his teeth, which were looking pointier by the second, and growled.

"After we have used you up," Cassandra purred in my ear as she produced silk scarves—black, of course—from her left sleeve and lashed one of my hands to the arm of the chair, "we will begin on your partner. He is extremely virile. His blood will be saccharine."

She left my other arm exposed, touching it with the pads of her fingers and scraping with her blackened nails. When our flesh met, I felt the same electric *pop* I had when the man who attacked me forced me to rub my blood on him.

I jerked involuntarily. Cassandra hissed. "Liar!"

Hey, at least now I knew I was in the right place to find the guy.

"Filthy liar!" Cassandra screamed again, pinning my wrist as I tried to yank away and plunging the scalpel into the soft underportion of my forearm. Just like my attacker, she was far stronger than she should be.

I tore the scarf free and swung at her with my other hand, connecting with her nose. It fountained blood as her falling jerked the scalpel across my skin, flaying it open. Hot red pain traveled up my arm into my chest, the mingled blood and torn nerves exciting all my were senses to the bursting point.

Cassandra opened her mouth and howled, which served as a rallying cry for her onlookers. I tried to back away from them and at the same time stanch the free-flowing blood from my arm with the black scarf, but I felt a thousand hands on me and before I knew it I was on the ground, boots and hands and heels pressing into me as the faces milled above.

"Shame on you for insulting Cassandra," said Maven. He crouched next to me and I thrashed once, feebly, as he touched my cheek. His hand was like icy paper. "Now I guess we'll just have to dispose of you, flawed and worthless as you are." He lifted my cut arm and let it flop back. "Someone get me the straight blade."

The crowd rushed to do as he said. To my ears it sounded like the rustling silk wings of faraway birds. The red light started to drip down out of my vision as black crawled over it, and Maven's bony overstretched face was at the center of my universe.

"Interesting," he was muttering, patting down my body. "How did you resist Cassandra, hmm? Tell me your secrets, plain human." His hands searched over my waistband and under my tank, pushing it up until I could feel cool air seeping through my bra.

Maven hissed as my upper chest came to his view, and I knew he saw the long scratch left by the masked attacker's knife. "Dark ones . . . ," Maven murmured in a tone that anyone, no matter what persuasion, uses to invoke the gods when seriously screwed.

"Cassandra!" he shouted. "Get yourself up off your arse, woman! Come see!"

"I am with blood, Maven!" came her nasal reply. I was so tired. I just wanted them to stop talking, wanted all the people pressing so close to go away and let me go to sleep.

"I don't care about your nose!" Maven snapped, losing the British accent as his anger came out. "Come the Hex over and see what you've done!"

Cassandra appeared next to him, two pale moon faces orbiting gently overhead. She sucked in a breath. "Oh, no."

"Feel it," Maven grated. "It sings of another's mark."

"I . . . I had no idea," Cassandra gulped, sounding frightened. "The brands . . . a watchman must have found her and she came here looking for him because of my brands . . ."

"It doesn't matter," said Maven. "What matters now is that you have trespassed on her flesh and they will see."

For a shining second, I thought he was going to let me go. Whatever my attacker had done to me, it had been enough to scare the ever-living crap out of Maven and Cassandra.

Then Cassandra said, "Kill her. Kill her quickly."

So much for that rosy scenario.

"Everyone go! Leave us!" Maven said. "We must dispose of her before this violation is discovered."

The crowd drew back with a flurry of distressed whispers, and before I had time to ponder what about my healing cut scared the pair so badly, Maven was straddling me with a long blade to my throat. Through my blood-loss-induced haze I saw his arm tense to draw it across my windpipe and permanently end this nightmare of blood and ceremony I was trapped in.

A gunshot boomed out, and you could tell the normal humans from the others because they all screamed and broke into a run.

I rolled my head to the side and saw Dmitri brandishing my service weapon. A roll in the other direction showed the bartender slumped unconscious but breathing with a trail of blood running out from under his head.

Dmitri racked the Glock's slide with a practiced motion and aimed at Maven and Cassandra. "Don't you fuckin' twitch," he ordered.

Maven held up his hands in a placating gesture. "If we don't erase this trespass, we are all in dire trouble. You have no idea what you're interfering with, were."

"And I don't give a witch's ass, either," Dmitri snapped. "Back away from the detective!"

"You stupid animal," said Cassandra, moving disdainfully away from me. "Reap what you sow, then." I felt a brush of silk skirt over my cheek, and she was gone.

The relief of knowing that I wasn't going to die pushed me over the edge into unconsciousness, and I was only

faintly aware of Dmitri gathering me into his arms and
carrying me out of Maven's and into the cool night.

W hile I slept I saw Joshua again and I begged
him not to leave me. Cried for him not to.
Unaware of the sticky blood running down
my shoulder or my nakedness in the back of his beat-up
van, I clung to his hand and begged because I could *feel*
him, under my skin, a need that burned me up. I didn't
understand it, but it hurt and I couldn't bear to have him
leave me with this pain.

Of course, when he turned back in the dream I remembered the reality of the night—the suffocation of
him on top of me, clawing at the zipper of my jeans,
pressing me into the stinking carpet and forcing my
blood out through my pores. I saw the rampant snake
tattoo on his wrist as he covered my mouth to muffle the
screams. And it wasn't Joshua who had run crying and
battered down the beach road after starting the evening
with stolen beer and the promise of a hookup.

I ran from Joshua and from the bite, and only later
did I realize the horrible ache of being Insoli, and that
the choice between being a slave or an outcast was the
most painful one I would ever make.

FIFTEEN

When my eyes opened the first thing I saw was Sunny's face hovering over me, brows almost touching.

"What's up?" I croaked. "You look like somebody died."

"With good reason, because you almost did," she said severely. I hoisted myself onto my elbows.

"Oh lighten up, Sunny. I just got a scratch." My forearm was wrapped in gauze and surgical tape. No hospital bracelet. Sunny must have done the job herself. "Nice work, by the way."

"You need stitches." She still didn't smile. "The cut is deep and you lost a lot of blood. You need to see a doctor."

I waved my hand. Pain shot up my arm, lighting up the wound like Vegas. "I don't need a doctor," I gritted. "This close to the phase I'll heal up before we even make it to the ER, seeing how traffic is this time of day." That was a good question—what time of day *was* it? My alarm clock said 10:30 AM. Considering the last time I'd checked my watch it had been a little after seven the night before, I had been out for a while.

Begging a far more interesting question: how had I gotten home, anyway?

"Sunny, how did I get here?"

She shot a glance toward my door. "Your, um, friend brought you."

Oh, crap. "Friend?"

"Yes," she nodded. "The very large, very attractive Mr. Sandovsky that you've gotten all crushed on lately."

"I am *not* crushed," I warned her.

So Sandovsky had not only carried me out of the club but all the way back to the cottage, too? No matter how much crazy, weird, wacked-out shit I saw in a day, life just kept pulling new and delightfully mutated rabbits out of its hat. "Did Dmitri say why he brought me?"

"Ask him yourself," said Sunny. "He's sitting in the living room."

I bolted upright. My wound protested, and I told it with a forceful bound out of my bed to shut up. "He's here? Now?"

"Was when I came up here to check on you, so unless he's turned into a pumpkin and vanished he should still be," said Sunny. "He wouldn't leave until he was sure you'd be all right. He mumbled something about owing you."

"Hex me now," I moaned, covering my eyes. Just what I needed—my very own guardian were angel.

Sunny pulled my silk lounging robe out of my closet and tossed it to me. "Put this on before you see him. It brings out your eyes." She walked out and slammed the door, calling down the stairs, "Would you like a refill, Mr. Sandovsky? Or another bagel?"

Hexed fire, Sunny was feeding him. I yanked on the

robe and tiptoed down the hall cautiously, trying to catch a glimpse of Dmitri before he saw me in my ultimate morning-after hair and ratty sweatpants peeking out from under the robe. As soon as my foot touched the first stair step, though, his head snapped up and his nostrils flared.

I gave up trying to be coy. "Morning, Dmitri."

"Morning yourself, Detective," he said. He put the teacup on the coffee table and stood. "Nice place you got here."

It was the first time I had seen Dmitri by the light of day. Lit by the sun his skin was translucent along his sharp cheekbones and aggressive chin, and the hair was darker than I realized, more of a copper than a red. The eyes were the same bottomless green. In my girly, fluffy living room with its overstuffed couches and worn braided rugs, he looked hopelessly out of place. He shifted his feet and left black boot prints on the hardwood floor.

"I see you've gotten some refreshments," I said, indicating the mug and the plate holding the remains of a wheat bagel. I suck at small talk, but what do you say to a gorgeous alpha were who's gone all heroic on you?

"Yeah," said Sandovsky. "Rose hip tea your cousin made. Pretty good, actually."

"If you're telling the truth, you'd be the first one," I told him. Time to figure out what the hell he was still doing here. Liking a girl and bringing her home injured in the dead of night are two very different countries, and I wasn't sure I was comfortable with him crossing the border. "Why did you bring me home? How do you know where I live?"

"Relax, Detective," he said, holding up a hand. "I got

your address from your ID. You were bleeding bad, and I didn't think you'd want a bunch of questions at a hospital. I wrapped your arm up in some bar towels and drove like a bat out of hell." He pointed out the window at the low black bike sitting next to Sunny's car. I groaned.

"Please don't tell me you drove me home, bleeding and unconscious, on the back of your motorcycle."

Dmitri shrugged. "I didn't know where you parked your car." He picked up his wolf head jacket and slipped it on. "I can see you're not overwhelmed with gratitude, so I'm gonna go."

"Wait, wait," I commanded as he headed for the door. He turned back, one copper eyebrow cocked. If the night made him seem sexy, in sunlight he was full-on mating material.

Bad thoughts, Luna. Bad! No Internet shoe shopping for you!

"You saved my life," I told him. "I don't know how to thank you for that. But that doesn't change the fact you haven't been exactly cooperative from the get-go."

"At the get-go you were in my face, embarrassing me in front of my pack and trying to arrest me," he tossed back.

"I was doing my job," I snapped. "Arresting is what I do to suspects."

"You know, I save your Hexed life and you're still a bitch," he said.

"Maybe instead of standing here insulting me, you should take what I said last night to heart and stop trying to vigilante out on the man who killed Lilia."

He swept the cup and plate to the floor, where they shattered in a puddle of lukewarm tea and crumbs. "Don't you dare think that because I talk to you, you can order me around, Insoli bitch!" he screamed. "You'll never even be *capable* of feeling what I am right now!"

I reached up and slapped him across the cheek hard, punctuating the blow with a growl. Dmitri growled back and grabbed my wrist, pulling it tight to my side and me against him.

"I should knock you senseless for that," he whispered to me. He was shaking with the effort of keeping himself under control, and his eyes flashed yellow.

"Then do it," I said calmly. After last night, and the nightmares that came with it, Dmitri was last on the list of things that scared me.

He let out a long trembling sigh and loosened his grip, shoulders slumping.

"I know exactly what you are feeling right now," I whispered, putting an arm around his neck and my mouth close to his ear. He didn't pull away. "Lilia didn't have to die for nothing. Don't throw away a chance to really punish this guy because you have to exact some cockeyed pack revenge."

He released my wrist and stepped back, not able to meet my eyes.

"I didn't mean that. The Insoli thing," he muttered.

"I know, but you're still a son of a bitch for saying it," I told him.

"I'll make it up to you, I promise." He smirked and I saw the flash of devil in his eyes that must have been present a lot more before Lilia's death snuffed it.

"Oh, really? How?"

Dmitri shook his head. "Don't tease me, Detective. You'll regret it."

"Not very secure, are you?" I prodded. "Aren't you supposed to say I'd like it?"

Maybe I just wanted to poke him once more for the

Insoli comment, but I was totally unprepared for Dmitri to grab my shoulders and push me against the living room wall. His eyes were hooded, and he leaned close and scented me as I squirmed.

"You would like it," he rasped. "But then you'd regret it. I'm not what you want, Luna."

He was right, of course. Absolutely. The totally wrong kind of man for me, a repeat of almost every one I'd been with up till this moment.

"You're exactly what I want," I purred. *Way to stay strong, Luna. Bravo.*

Dmitri shuddered as he scented my arousal and then his mouth was against mine, tasting me and sliding down my neck, his hands tugging my shirt upward to expose the fact that I spent way too much money on lingerie.

"Sunny . . . ," I hissed as Dmitri's hand moved the waistband of my sweats. "Sunny might come back . . ."

"Shut up," he muttered against the pulse point in my neck. His fingers brushed over my Brazilian wax, and he rumbled approval deep in his throat as his two longest fingers found wet and slid inside. His other hand pulled my bra cup aside and twisted my nipple painfully as his teeth closed on my neck.

My tee slipped down to expose four round bite scars and Dmitri sucked in a breath, pulling back like I was red-hot iron. His expression caused humiliation to flame up instantly.

I slid down the wall, readjusting my clothes. "I guess you were right. I do regret it."

"The hell didn't you tell me a Serpent Eye gave you the bite?" Dmitri demanded. He jerked at his belt buckle with irritation, trying to accommodate a newly appeared bulge.

"What in Hex are you talking about?" I said, brushing myself off. My wound throbbed again and my limbs felt heavy.

"The four-fang scar. Serpent Eyes. Pack that doesn't have pack magick." Dmitri was standing on the opposite side of the room, like I had sprouted a small mutant head out of my shoulder. "They never know what the bite will do."

"Well, all it's done for me is cause a lot of grief and gotten disgusted looks from you." I sighed.

Dmitri shuffled his feet. "Sorry. Just wasn't expecting to see that."

"Forget it," I muttered, hoping that the free-flowing font of embarrassment welling inside me wasn't telegraphed in my voice. I had forgotten for two minutes that Dmitri and I were different, but now he had hammered it home and soldered it shut.

Sunny stuck her head into the room. "Everything all right? I heard some yelling. And thumping." She used the same kind of tone orderlies use on the lunatics.

"Fine," I said calmly. "Dmitri and I were just discussing some of the finer points of the case."

And before anyone could say anything else, I turned calmly and walked through the kitchen and out the back door. Once I hit the fence I broke into a run, practically falling over myself to reach the tiny falling-down boathouse that rested on the beach below the cottage.

I would never be like Dmitri. I would never call a pack my own. I had thrown away the one chance at a normal were life when I threw Joshua's sweaty body off me and ran away from him, bleeding out my last seconds of plain humanity into the sand.

The boathouse was dim and smelled like old fish. Previous tenants had left nets and one dilapidated kayak that

Sunny always talked about using during the summer but never got brave enough to take out on the waves.

I ignored it all and ripped the tarp off the kennel in the corner, large enough for me to crawl inside as a human and strong enough to hold me as a were. I hoped.

My pulse pounded in my ears and all I could see was Dmitri's flat look of disgust when he laid eyes on my bite. Days of holding in the phase made my tattoo flame with pain, and the pentacle on my neck hissed when my fingers brushed against it.

I crawled inside the cage and wrapped my arms around my knees, muttering "No, no, no." Denial was my last line of defense against the phase.

The door clicked shut after me, and as if a secret signal had been sent, my hands spasmed and a cramp doubled me over, digging wire mesh into my cheek and side.

"Hex!" I ground out, a scream waiting behind my teeth. My skin prickled with a thousand pins as hair began to sprout and my jaw creaked, making room for my were fangs.

I lost the battle and screamed, not with pain but with unadulterated were rage. I saw Dmitri again, black and white, and this time my desire was purely to kill him. Him, Joshua, and anyone else who would deny me this, this painful release that made my fingers bleed and my skull crack and my body fold in on itself.

Sunny knocked, of course. She would know the only reason I ever came down here. "Luna? You okay in there?"

Far from okay, body seizing, skin searing off as muscle rippled underneath. Dimly, I realized the pain wasn't dissipating, because I wasn't under a moon and couldn't fully phase.

I looked down at my still-human hands, black were nails dripping blood onto the sandy floor.

"Luna?" Sunny rattled the handle once.

"I'm fine!" I shouted thickly, fighting against my underslung jaw. I breathed in once, twice, and grabbed my pentacle necklace, forcing the burn of silver to haul me back to the daytime world.

The door rattled again, harder. Dmitri had joined the party. "Hey, Luna. Listen, if I did something . . ."

Oh, he knew damn well what he'd done. And didn't he sound contrite, too? Maybe I should give him a few more bite scars . . .

My hands reverted to normal, bitten and with a scar across my left knuckles from a knife-wielding gang punk. Long canines withdrew with a sting and when I closed my eyes and opened them again, my vision was in color.

I breathed again, still holding the silver in my palm, and opened the door. "I said I'm fine."

"Okay," said Sunny, holding out my cell phone. "McAllister's calling."

"Boyfriend?" Dmitri smirked as I took it.

"My lieutenant. What is it, Mac?"

"We've got another one. Strip club off Magnolia," he said without bothering to give a *hello*. "A dancer mutilated in the dressing room after the last shift."

My throat tightened and I had to swallow before I could talk. "The same as Marina and Lilia?"

Dmitri's head snapped up.

"Worse," said McAllister. "Roenberg is on his way to the scene. I suggest you get there before he does."

"Roenberg won't let me touch it, Mac." He'd probably give Bryson the case with a big bow, Hex it.

And then I felt the niggling *wrong* that had dogged me throughout the case come painfully clear. "Mac, Stephen Duncan is still in jail."

"Not since this morning, eight AM," said Mac icily. "As you can imagine, another, identical killing sort of crosses his name off the shortlist for psychosexual mudering perverts. His lawyer was very eloquent."

"How did they get him a hearing so quickly?"

"Luna, he's Alistair's son. How do you think?"

"Wonderful."

Mac hung up, and I kicked the side of the shed so hard a piece fell off. "Gods damn it!" I might as well have still been standing over Lilia's body. Everything that I had built up was shot to hell.

I turned on Dmitri. "You have something I need."

He raised an eyebrow. "Oh? I can think of a few things, what's yours?"

I pointed out the window at his bike. "How fast can you get me to Magnolia Boulevard?"

Double Trouble—LIVE XXX DANCERS EVERY NIGHT!—defined *hole-in-the-wall*. It was built into a storefront longer than it was narrow; the plate-glass windows had been blacked over and the door replaced with a high-security gate and a bouncer. Currently, said bouncer was giving a statement to two uniforms. All three stared when Dmitri stopped his bike at the curb with a roar that could shake fillings loose.

I hopped off and he followed me. "You'll have to wait out here," I said. "I can't have you running around a crime scene."

"I'm not all that interested," he said, although I could

see by the way he craned his neck and flared his nostrils that he was. "I don't particularly enjoy bloodshed unless I'm involved in it."

"Good to know you have a hobby." I flashed my shield at the uniforms, who were eyeing me circumspectly. One raised an eyebrow. I didn't blame him. Right now, bandaged and bedraggled as I was, I didn't look much like a cop. Maybe a really sleazy undercover narcotics officer. Definitely not a homicide detective.

"Hey!" said the other. "Detective Wilder! I remember you! The dead streetwalker from a few days ago."

"The same," I agreed. Officer Thorpe's eyes were still tired, but I smiled again and he smiled back. At my shoulder Dmitri stiffened.

"Sorry I can't let you in," said Thorpe. "Strict orders to wait for Captain Roenberg."

"He's not days, either," I reminded the pair.

"No, ma'am, but he is a captain." Thorpe chuckled.

I rolled my eyes. "Has the ME shown up at least?"

"No ME until the captain surveys the scene," said Thorpe. His partner jabbed him and he turned red. Obviously I wasn't supposed to have that tidbit.

"Really," I said, smiling still. "And why would that be, exactly?"

"We are not at liberty to reveal that information," said the partner, who seemed immune to my feminine wiles.

"In other words, you don't know shit," I told him. "You're just being a good little choirboy and doing what you're told."

He walked off in a huff, but Thorpe started to respond when the bouncer stepped up. "Excuse me, but are y'all going to be finished with this statement soon? I could really stand to get home and take a shower."

I shifted my attention to him, took his elbow, and led him away from Thorpe and Dmitri. "I'm Detective Wilder, and I'll be handling the investigation," I said. "Why don't you tell me what you know?"

"Ernest Copperfield, ma'am. I'd shake hands, but . . ." He extended them, and I saw that the palms were stained with blood. I had an unpleasant flash of my trauma-induced dream, stickiness coating my palm when I reached for my neck and touched the jagged bite.

"You found her," I said. Copperfield averted his eyes and nodded once.

"Yes, ma'am. I was a trauma nurse for five years but I never saw anything like this."

"Trauma nurse? Pardon my asking, but what the hell are you doing bouncing drunks in a crappy strip bar?"

"I had a little problem with the pharmacy," Copperfield said. "Lost my license."

"Clean now?"

He nodded his blond-thatched head. "Yes, ma'am. My parole officer piss-tests me once a month, so I got to be."

Great. An ex-druggie ex-con finds the body. By all plain human standards, I'd be an idiot if I didn't shoot him straight to the top of the suspect list.

"Okay, Ernest," I said. "I'm going to take you inside and we're going to walk through exactly what happened up until the time you found the victim."

"Katya," he said. I turned back to him.

"What did you say?"

"That's her name. Katya something. One of those *ski* names, like Polanski. But not Polanski."

I snapped my fingers at Thorpe, standing worriedly just out of earshot. "Call Immigration and find out if the dead girl was here legally."

She wouldn't be, of course. Why else would she work in a place like this and become the perfect target for murder?

I turned back to Ernest. "Do you happen to know where she was from?"

He shrugged. "Sorry, ma'am . . . I just make sure the customers don't get frisky and the girls aren't skimming tips or stealing the booze. Not supposed to have personal conversations."

"And you, of course, are a model employee," I said. "All right. Let's go in."

He shuffled his feet. "Do I have to, ma'am? Don't really care to see that sight again."

I studied his complacent brown cow eyes and the country-boy handsome face. "Ernest," I said. "I would really appreciate it if you could do this for me. And I'm sure Katya would, too."

He flinched, and I confirmed what I suspected about the *no personal conversations* line being bullshit.

"Lead the way, Detective," he whispered.

The interior of Double Trouble was spare, with clunky wooden booths that looked like they belonged in a bowling alley arranged around a skinny stage with a pole at the lip. Pink strings of lights had been nailed along the base of the stage and they blinked gaily, oblivious to the uniformed officer who guarded the door to the dressing room. Otherwise, the club was empty. CSU should have been swarming, paramedics should have been called. Instead, Double Trouble had the air of nothing so much as a gaudy funeral parlor.

"I started in here," said Ernest. "I'm on lockup duty, so I'm the last one to leave. Close up the bar, check the back door and the kitchen, and lock up the front. Turn off lights. Ya know."

"What time was this?" I asked.

"About six AM," he said. I checked my watch. It was almost eleven.

"Ernest," I said. "How long did you wait to report this?"

He couldn't look at me. "I saw that the light was still on in the dressing room and I went in to check. That's when I saw Katya, all sprawled out on the floor."

"Mr. Copperfield," I said icily. "Answer my question."

"I saw the blood and I knew right away she was dead. I still tried to feel for a pulse and stop the bleeding. I know that sounds real stupid but I was a nurse, ma'am. It's still instinct."

I unhooked my handcuffs and slapped them on the nearest table. "These are going on you unless you tell me the truth," I warned. "Do it now and you might not be charged as an accessory."

He sniffled. I sighed. Another dead girl and another man left behind with scars. I glanced outside. Dmitri was leaning on the motorcycle with his arms crossed, trading black looks with the uniforms.

"When I saw her lying there I panicked," said Ernest. "May I sit down, ma'am?"

I indicated a booth and stood in front of it, poised to perform a flying tackle if Ernest bolted. "You tried to revive her. Sure you weren't already in the room when whatever happened went down?"

"No!" he almost shouted. "I did *not* do this thing!"

"Okay, okay," I said. Thorpe was at the door giving us a look. I wished there were somewhere we could talk without open ears listening in, but it wasn't like I could whisk him away to my convenient Fortress of Solitude. "Calm down, Ernest. You saw the body, you checked her. See anything else?"

He leaned forward and put his head in his hands, bent almost double. Barely audible, he said, "I saw . . . things . . . on her changing table."

"What sort of things?"

He sighed. "Katya had been entertaining."

There it was, the grain of truth that everyone will hold like a diamond until you pry it out. A lot of strippers did after-hours hooking to subsidize what they made dancing. In a place this scummy, it also made sense that she'd be coked to the gills while doing it.

"I get it," I told Ernest. "This place closes at four—it has to by city ordnance, right?"

A nod and another searching look from the big cow eyes.

"So you all go away for a few discreet hours to let Katya and whoever else is tricking do their business, and then come back to lock up."

"Yes, ma'am," he said. "That's correct."

"And when you do, Katya is dead and you notice some unsavory items on her dressing table, which you, being a complete gentleman, clean up before calling the police."

"Yes," he said, leaving off the *ma'am* and sounding miserable.

"You stupid son of a bitch," I told him. "You destroyed probably the only evidence we'll ever have of who Katya was last with. Way to go. Really." Damn it, he'd slipped by me again. I could not wait to latch my metaphorical teeth around this bastard's jugular.

"I had to!" Copperfield shouted. "Y'all would have found out my history and looked at me! And I never did it!"

I hauled him up by the shoulder of his jacket and breathed in his nervous, blood-tinged body odor deeply.

The tangy scent hit me immediately. Before Ernest could get out a peep I reached into his inside pocket and pulled out the bag of off-white power.

"You may be clean, but I'm betting the meth is a nice bonus to your paycheck each month, isn't it?" I said.

He was already shaking his head. "It ain't mine."

"You're under arrest, moron," I said. "Turn around, hands on the table." I rattled off his Miranda warning while I handcuffed him.

"You're makin' a mistake!" he hollered at me. "I didn't give my stuff to Katya! This was different! Vials and needles!"

I closed the cuffs around his wrists and turned him around. "Needles?"

"Yeah!" he said, perhaps seeing a ray of light in a crappy day that had just gotten much worse. "Not the reusable shooting needles, either. Surgical ones, disposable. Had a stamp."

I closed my eyes and breathed. When Dr. Kronen or whoever did the autopsy tested Katya's blood, they would find diazepam, the animal tranquilizer that my killer used to keep his victims quiet and compliant as he tore them to shreds.

"Did you see her john, Earnest?"

His chin was on his chest and he looked utterly defeated. "No. I stay far, far away from that side of the business, ma'am."

"Katya have anyone bothering her over the last few days? Maybe a younger guy, blond like you?" Worth a shot. Stephen might not be the doer, but he knew things. Maybe watching got him off.

"No, ma'am."

Wasn't Earnest just a font of usefulness. "The officer will take you to booking," I told him. "You're being charged with possession with intent, and you're damn lucky it's just that."

"Yes, ma'am," he said as I handed him off to Thorpe.

"Oh, cut it out," I told him. "You're not fooling anyone."

Thorpe hustled Copperfield out, and that left me alone with the body. I felt around for the rolled-up pair of rubber gloves I carry on duty and slipped them over my hands before pushing open the dressing room door.

A riot of cheap glamour greeted me, spangled and lacy and PVC costumes made in a variety of stripper clichés like schoolgirl, maid, and naughty cop. Personal effects were strewn everywhere, and a cot in one corner was made up with cheap nylon sheets that imitated satin. An illicit brothel with taste. How touching.

Katya lay on her back like the other girls, throat slit and legs folded under. Unlike Lilia, no defensive wounds marked her arms and hands, just the neatly sectioned missing finger. He was getting better at drugging the victims.

The air around the body felt electric, like a malevolence had stood where I did not long ago. I sniffed, trying to find anything unusual beneath blood, death, and perfume. The air itself was slightly burned, like after a lightning strike. Not like the alley, not like the stinking room at Hotel Raven. This time, the killer had come into his own. The rage was gone, and a coldness far more terrifying had replaced it.

I touched Katya's corpse, the naked torso and the small rough hands that belied a former life not spent wrapped around a pole. The cuts on her neck and chest were fewer this time, with less blood, smooth. I frowned at them. They looked almost surgical, nothing like the frenzied gashes of the other girls. Less blood, too. If it weren't for the missing finger, I would doubt that this murder had the same perpetrator. But it did. I could smell him here, feel him just over my shoulder.

My fingers grazed Katya's belly, and I saw a small pink gash that hadn't immediately been apparent in the light cast by the bare bulbs of the makeup mirrors. It was the start of a cut to mimic what had happened to Marina and Lilia, ripped from neck to stomach. Unfinished.

He had been interrupted.

For just a moment, the temperature in the room dropped to absolute zero as my latex-clad fingers rested on the dead girl's skin and I realized I was crouched exactly where the killer had been a few hours before. And I had to make a run for it. Copperfield had come back to lock up, and I had to flee. Where?

I saw it from my stolen viewpoint next to Katya, the edge of a metal door hidden behind a rack of fluffy lingerie. I was up and over the body and into a cement alley before I had time to think, leaping outside like I could grab him by the back of the coat.

Nothing rattled in the alley except scraps of newspaper and a few stray garbage bags. I let out my air and leaned against the back wall of the strip club, heart thudding like a subwoofer.

"Detective?" said Officer Thorpe.

I stripped off my gloves and tossed them in the nearest Dumpster before turning to him. My hands shook. I was becoming one of them, the cops who turn inward and suck on the barrel of their nine-millimeter. *Did you hear about Wilder? Yeah, went postal. Couldn't handle the pressure.*

"Detective?" he said again.

"What is it?"

"We kinda got lucky," he admitted. "This place has a camera they installed a few years ago."

"Security?"

"Um, not exactly," he admitted, blushing. "They were taping the dancers to sell the footage on their Web site. It's pointed at the stage but it might catch who was in the club right before closing. Assuming the perp was in here. Ma'am."

"What is it with the *ma'am* business?" I asked no one in particular.

"Sorry, ma'am," said Thorpe, and then bit his lip in the cutest way.

"You can send a copy of the footage to the Twenty-fourth Precinct, Officer. And thank you."

He held the door open for me but I shook my head. "I need some air." And to walk the rest of the alley, hoping against hope that he had left some trace of himself for me.

Thorpe muttered something into his radio and let the door slam shut. And I saw it. The sidewalk sigil and Stephen's invisible tattoo, gouged now into metal. It glowed silver in the morning sun.

Looking directly at it was like taking a power drill to my forehead. The hisses and whispers rushed to my ears, and I wondered if this was what Stephen's world sounded like. My head panicked, and my gut felt the cold clench of knowing I was wrong, yet again.

I shut my eyes against the glare of the sigil and pulled out my phone, aiming the camera at the door. The phone chirped with a new photo and I slapped it shut before I had to look at the sigil again.

Time to go around the corner and tell Dmitri what I knew, and then call McAllister to do the same. Before I could spread the news, Roenberg's scraggly little shadow loomed up behind me. As a greeting he demanded, "Detective Wilder, what on the Hexed black earth are you doing in my crime scene?"

I tried to stop myself, I swear I did. "I'm sorry, sir, this crime scene? The body right inside the door here? If this crime scene is yours, I do apologize because when I didn't see any uniforms or a medical examiner or CSU processing, I just sort of assumed it was free and clear for me to stroll right in."

Roenberg went from pasty to bright red in the space of maybe half a second. I saw a vein at his temple. "Get out," he grated. "Get the hell out of here."

I dropped a curtsy. "My pleasure, Captain."

"And if you think you can stroll back to work think again!" he shouted. "You're fired and you can take your mick lieutenant with you!"

I froze, shoulders hunched. It was one thing to threaten me—with my pathological inability to take people's shit I had always half-expected a scene like this—but it was another entirely to go after Mac.

"Did you hear me, Detective?" Roenberg bleated. "Both of you, out on your rear ends!"

I turned around. "Screw you, sir. Go ahead and fire me. I'll scream so loud to the chief of detectives, her ears will bleed. And you can try as hard as you like, but you can't protect Stephen Duncan anymore. I know he's working with a partner, a magick user who just tortured that girl in there to give him a gods damn alibi." I jabbed a finger at his flushed pug-dog face. "If you do anything to Troy McAllister, I will be forced to make all of this very public. I'm sure the many taxpaying citizens of Nocturne City will be just *thrilled* to find out they have a police captain consorting with weres and blood witches and Hex knows what else. And I'm sure Alistair Duncan will be *especially* thrilled."

Roenberg shook his head slowly, eyes wide like Bigfoot had showed up dancing the Macarena.

"Put that up your ass and smoke it," I said before he could profess ignorance, then turned on my heel and stormed out the mouth of the alley.

SIXTEEN

Dmitri was waiting in the street, and stood up when he saw how pissed I looked.

"What happened?"

Roenberg came hurrying after me and said loudly to Thorpe and his partner, "Officer, you will send the footage to no one but me, do I make myself perfectly clear? The lid on this situation shuts now!"

"Yessir, Captain," the partner said.

Dmitri touched my shoulder. "What happened? Who's the suit?"

I sagged. "My captain. He fired me."

Dmitri blinked. "What? That cocksucker. Want me to go kick his ass?"

I waved a hand, turning my back on the club and the whole mess. "Right now, what I want is for you to take me home."

"What about the girl?" he asked as he kicked the bike's starter. "Same as the others?"

"The same," I agreed, "except this time he didn't get to finish. And he's started leaving me presents."

Dmitri looked over his shoulder as I climbed on and latched my hands around his waist, pressing my cheek into the broad leather expanse of his back.

"What sort of presents, Luna?"

I felt the weight of my phone in my jacket pocket. "That's what I'm going to find out."

S unny bit her lip as she examined the grainy photo. "This is a very unusual mark."

I rubbed my wound under the bandage. It was healing and starting to itch. "I was looking for something a little bit more specific than *unusual*. I've never seen a sigil that looked anything like it before." Granted, I usually tried to avoid looking at them. Safer that way.

"That's because this isn't a sigil," said Sunny. "Like I said, it's a mark."

"Translation?" said Dmitri, who was on our sofa again. Sunny sat in her armchair and pulled her legs under her, still squinting at the screen.

"A mark is made to control," she told him. "Given from a caster witch to a familiar or a blood witch to a golem to compel or enslave. They're nasty and evil, all of them, but this one . . ." She blinked and handed the phone back.

"Hurts your head, doesn't it?" I said.

Sunny nodded, lip still firmly planted between her teeth. "Whoever drew this, Luna . . . they aren't working from a spellbook. Something had to show them."

Dmitri raised an eyebrow. "Something?"

Great, we were back to the daemons, the White Whale of magick. Call me Ahab.

"Theoretically," said Sunny, "this mark shouldn't exist."

"Well, it does," I snapped, waving the phone at her. "And now you're telling me it's being used to *control* someone." Someone being Stephen Duncan. Stephen as Spree Killer didn't fit, but Stephen as Marionette did. The kid was about as sharp as a lead pipe and might as well have had I'M STUPID AND ARROGANT, PLEASE USE ME FOR NEFARIOUS ENDS tattooed on his ass.

"We need to know who set the mark, Sunny."

She was already shaking her head. "I can't, Luna. Calling a mark that's not your own is beyond most caster witches. And besides, calling it wouldn't get you the person who set the mark, just who he marked it with."

"I know who he marked," I said grimly. "What I want is him."

Sunny touched the back of my hand. "Don't ask me to do this," she whispered. "If I try to call the mark and I touch the will of the enslaved, you know what could happen."

"What?" demanded Dmitri. "What happens?"

"Sunny could lose her ability to cast," I said. "If she touches the magick too closely, her ability to set a circle and call a working will burn out."

"It's the whole reason we use casters," Sunny told him. "To buffer ourselves and keep safe."

"Shit," Dmitri muttered. He stood, stretching and rolling his shoulders like the indolent wolf he was. I tried hard not to stare, but he caught me and flashed a quick smile. "Thanks for your help, Ms. Swann."

"Call me Sunny," she said distractedly, staring at the shelf that held her spellbook and the pilfered ones from my grandmother. "We can't call the mark," she said.

"You told us that already," I reminded her, feeling

defeated and suddenly very tired. My normal reaction would be to settle myself in the office with a few case files and a large amount of junk food, and do paperwork until something clicked in my brain. But now I had no more paperwork to do.

I decided I could hold off on telling Sunny that bit.

"We can't call the mark," Sunny said again, "but I can find who made it. Originally, I mean. What sort of thing is its maker."

I turned to look at her. "You mean find the *something* that the mark belongs to?"

Sunny nodded. "Simple, kind of like dialing a reverse directory. When the witch texts at Alexandria were burned, a great consortium of witches banded together and keycalled all the spells back from their origins, so none were lost. Magick always leaves a signature, and I should be able to trace it."

"Is it dangerous?" Dmitri asked.

Sunny's mouth set. "Not if you know what you're doing." She got up and went into the kitchen, calling, "I just need a few minutes to set the circle! Can you get me my birch wood caster out of the lockbox?"

I pulled the black lacquered box from the top of the bookcase and opened it with the hidden latch, taking out the flexible pale wood caster.

"What's the difference?" said Dmitri, picking up the ebony one Sunny used for ceremonies and gatherings where she had to impress people.

"Birch wood is pure," I said. "They give it to novice caster witches because it helps keep them safe. Excuse me."

I carried the caster into the kitchen and held it out to Sunny, who was mixing herbs briskly in her censer.

"You don't have to do this for me."

She stopped mixing. "Will it keep more girls from dying?"

I nodded silently.

"Then of course I have to."

"I suppose you don't need to hear that using a spell from one of *her* books is the worst idea since building Pompeii?"

Sunny shook the censer to settle the herbs and struck a match. "I knew you'd feel that way."

"She doesn't have your or my best interests in mind, Sunny, and if she knew you had that book . . ."

"Oh, I'm sure she knows," said Sunny calmly. "And I'm sure she's furious with me. But it's not about you and her now, Luna, so will you please help me?"

She lit the herbs and set the censer at the center of the table, arranging her four corners with an expert hand. I grabbed the edge of the braided throw rug and whipped it back, revealing the circle carved into the kitchen floor. While a circle set in earth was good, one carved into wood was best. Sunny only used it when she absolutely had to, because a working circle in wood, like a caster made of wood, wears and rots over time, fraying the magick.

"Could you call Dmitri?" she asked me when I'd gotten the circle uncovered. "I need him, too."

"Anything you want," Dmitri said from the doorway. Sunny looked startled, and he grinned. "Were hearing."

"Take a seat," said Sunny, pointing to a chair. We all three made a circle around the censer. Sunny put her hands on her caster and shut her eyes. The prickle worked its way up my spine, and I tried not to think about the times Rhoda had tried to teach me workings, and how every single time I had been a complete and utter disappointment.

I tried not to think about the name *mutt* and whispers about my blood being diluted. Or the time I'd wandered into one of Rhoda's circles alone and nearly had my hair singed off.

Sunny had grabbed me then, but Dmitri gripped my hand now.

"She said to hold hands," he explained when I shot him a startled look.

"Luna, are you all right?" Sunny asked sharply, her eyes still closed. The air around us began to whine as the circle rose and snapped over the table like a slap.

I gripped Dmitri's hand tightly. "I'm fine," I said. "Get this over with."

Dmitri watched Sunny intently, but without fear, as her fingers went limp on the caster. Every inch of my skin vibrated as the working started to rise. The censer, which up until now had been trailing wisps placidly, began to roil and puff smoke across the kitchen.

"Take the picture and put it in the censer," said Sunny in the flat please-leave-a-message tone working witches get.

I decided that now was not the time to argue about the hassle of replacing a department-issue cell phone and dropped it inside, still displaying the sigil picture.

Sparks shot as soon as the phone touched the censer, and Sunny's caster began to crackle like an entire forest was burning.

"What the hell's happening now?" Dmitri hissed. The smoke from the censer was bruise blue and smelled like burning hair. The caster twisted and bent under Sunny's fingers like new wood over an open flame. I glanced away from the spectacle at my cousin's face. Her eyes were rolled back in her head, and the corners of her mouth were tight. Her entire body held itself like a high-tension wire.

"Reveal to me . . . your maker," she stuttered, and her voice came out very small. Sunny was scared. I dug my nails into Dmitri's palm.

"Reveal to me your maker!" Sunny demanded again. The smoke was choking, nearly obscuring her, and my phone jumped around the censer like a hot plastic coal. The whine rose again, and this one I knew from experience. It was a badly strained working ready to snap.

Sunny choked before she could chant again, and began wheezing, her hands rigid and locked on the steaming caster. I looked back at the phone, its screen shining brightly with the sigil.

"Let her go!" I screamed. "Reveal to me your maker!"

The sigil glowed and lifted off the screen, hovering above the censer in the riot of smoke. It pulsed once with a gold gleam, and a voice sighed, "Release me."

I stared, frozen. All that my brain came up with was the oh-so-clever, "What?"

A report sounded and the censer shot across the kitchen, embedding itself in the far wall. My half-melted phone slid to the floor with a *plunk*. The whine cut off and Sunny fell forward, sucking in air as I rushed to help her, not caring that my movement broke the circle.

This particular working was done, anyway.

S unny accepted the cup of tea Dmitri offered her gratefully and laid her head on my shoulder when I sat next to her, the way she would when we were kids. "I'm sorry."

"For what?" Dmitri demanded. He paced the living room and stopped in front of us. "You don't have a god-damn thing to be sorry for."

"The keycalling didn't work," Sunny said dejectedly. "I was sure we'd at least find who worked the mark . . ."

"It did talk," I told her. "The mark."

Sunny sat bolt upright. "It talked? What did it say?"

"*Release me.* Kinda sounded like Darth Vader with a cold."

Sunny set down her teacup. "Hex me."

"It was pretty fuckin' freaky," Dmitri agreed.

"Did it say anything else?" Sunny asked.

"No, that was when the censer exploded."

"Hearing the voice of the enslaved through the mark is impossible," Sunny said flatly.

I took her word for it, except that hadn't been the voice of Stephen, the only enslaved I knew about. Something else had been speaking to me out of the smoke.

I got off the sofa and put on my gun and jacket.

"Where are you going?" Sunny asked.

"*We.* We are going to the university to ask someone about this."

"And what am I?" Dmitri demanded.

"You are my attractive but intimidating companion, and this guy we're seeing does not do well with intimidating."

He didn't smile.

"I'll call you as soon as we figure this out, I promise," I said. Dmitri grabbed my hand, but let me pull away after the flip of a second.

"You better," he whispered, and I remembered his breath on my neck, covering the bite. From freaked to horny in sixty seconds.

Once we were out the door Sunny grabbed my elbow

and demanded, "How does someone from the university know so much about magick?"

"Maybe not magick," I said as we crossed the crushed seashells to her convertible, "but he knows an awful lot about daemons."

SEVENTEEN

Professor Hoskins's office was as creepily organized as I remembered, with a stack of bright blue test folders replacing the stack of papers on the corner of his desk. The professor himself was nowhere to be seen.

"Should we just barge in like this?" said Sunny nervously, glancing at the paintings, masks, and imposing bookshelves.

"I'm sure he won't mind. Too much," I amended after she gave me a look.

"He's got an impressive collection of books, I'll say that." She reached for one with a pentacle on the spine.

"Don't touch," I warned her. "He gets a little twitchy."

"Who's there?" Hoskins demanded from outside the door. "My office is strictly off limits. Who's in there breathing?"

"It's me, Professor Hoskins," I said, opening the door fully. "Detective Wilder."

"Oh," he said, heaving a sigh. "Detective. I apologize. I have warned my students time and time again but they simply cannot resist barging in and putting their hands all over everything." He paced inside with hurried steps and then caught sight of Sunny. "Oh, dear. Who is this?"

"This is my cousin, Sun—Rhoda," I told him, shooting Sunny an apologetic look when she glared. I had a feeling Hoskins's head might pop off if he had to deal with a girl dressed like a ye olde peasant wenche and named Sunflower.

"A pleasure to meet you, Miss Rhoda," he told her, sitting at his desk. Sunny looked relieved and sat as well. Hoskins jumped back to his feet. "I am terribly sorry, Detective Wilder, but I am busy. How may I be of quick assistance?"

Sunny started to stand up as well and I shot her a death glance to keep her in her seat. I was not up to playing musical seating with the professor.

"Tell me about Meggoth, Professor. Tell me about daemons."

Hoskins pursed his lips and I saw a wall of disdain clamp over his eyes like the slamming of a cell door. "I cannot help you," he said brusquely. "As I told you the first time you came here seeking things that don't bear any of your concern."

"Women are being *killed,* Professor," I told him quietly, leaning on his desk and deliberately shoving the stack of folders out of alignment. "Their murderer is leaving behind a daemon mark. What part of that is not sinking in?"

Hoskins twisted his fingers together as he backed away from me.

"Whatever your issues are with the Nocturne PD, this doesn't involve them. The witch leaving the mark? He's after *me*." I pulled back the bandage on my forearm. I was practically healed so close to phase, but the wound was still red and a little bloody. More than enough for a lightweight like Hoskins. "This happened when I tried to find him myself," I said. "You know more than you told me, and I let it slide."

"Then continue to do so, for all of our sakes!" Hoskins pleaded.

I shook my head. "Sorry. I've seen the error of my ways and I've come to repent."

"You should leave, I think," Hoskins started, reaching for the damn phone again.

My hand snaked out and clamped around his wrist. He let out a decidedly unmanly yelp.

"I think that you are going to sit down and tell me everything you know about Marcus Levinson and the daemon he tried to summon. I think you will be thorough and complete in your recounting, this time. After that, I promise I'll walk out of your life and you'll never have to think about Cedar Hill again."

"You're *that* Jacob Hoskins?" Sunny exclaimed. "Wow. Thought you looked familiar."

"Thank you for that timely icebreaker, Sunny," I sighed.

She threw up her hands and mouthed, *What?*

Hoskins took off his glasses and rubbed his eyes with thumb and forefinger. "I apologize," he said finally. "I must seem terribly irrational to you, Detective."

"Just a little, yeah." I scratched my arm and took a seat next to Sunny. "Now. Tell me the story of a boy and his daemon."

"Marcus's daemon has a name, you know. Meggoth. 'Lost beauty.'" Hoskins tapped his fingers against his blotter and then sat back. "On the provision that you breathe not a word of this to anyone else, I will relay the truth."

"Should I leave?" Sunny asked.

"I see no reason for you to, unless you're a member of the university tenure board," said Hoskins. "Ms. Wilder, do you know why I was considered a suspect in the first place?"

Sunny and I both waited for him to enlighten us. Hoskins swiveled in his seat and stared out the tiny casement window toward the Blackburn mansion.

"Marcus Levinson was one of my students," he said finally. "Several years before the killings. Not a gifted or even particularly bright student, but one with an insatiable lust for knowledge of blood workings."

"What did you teach him?" Sunny asked.

"Not what he wanted, I can assure you," said Hoskins. "Marcus became disgusted that my classes taught only the theory of magick, not the practice. No blood witch in the city would take him as an apprentice, and caster witches would have spit on him."

With good reason, on both parts. No blood witches in their right minds would want someone as high-profile as the richest rich kid in Nocturne City organizing their spellbooks and carving up stray cats for workings.

"In the end Marcus was expelled from the university, although his parents made sure to have the records altered so it appeared he merely dropped out," Hoskins said.

Scandal. I was interested now. "What got him the boot?"

A smile turned Hoskins's lips upward for a moment. "He broke into my office and stole a very rare volume, one of the only instructional texts ever written by a blood witch."

"Is the book here now?"

"No," said Hoskins. "Levinson copied what he

wanted into his spellbook and burned the original text. I was distraught."

"I'll bet it was worth quite a bit," Sunny commiserated.

"You misunderstand." Hoskins tilted his glasses down his nose. "When you are a teacher you learn to quickly recognize which students are worth spending time on versus which are a waste of time. Marcus was neither. He was a natural witch, and utterly insane. That boy scared me, and when I learned he had the text, I was in fear for my life." He sighed. "As it turned out, he had something far worse in store for me, because Marcus gave them my name when he was questioned about the murders. You know the rest."

"How awful for you," said Sunny.

"Awful, yes, but not why your cousin is here. She wants to know what happened after Marcus stole my book. The daemon."

I flipped open my notepad and jotted down what Hoskins had told me before nodding at him to go on.

"Detective Wilder, do you remember how many victims Marcus took in the end?"

I did a quick count in my head. They taught Cedar Hill at the academy as an example of what weres and witches could do to your investigation. How evil/bad/nasty/insert scary word here we could be.

"Six."

Hoskins raised one finger. "There should have been seven."

"Why?"

"Seven is the imperfect circle," Sunny murmured. "The blood witch summoning cast."

"Ridiculous and useless to Marcus, because daemons cannot be called like dogs," said Hoskins. "He never grasped that. The time, the place of the moon and stars in the sky, the tides—any infinite number of details must present for the blood witch calling the working. Everything must fit together. No witch can call a daemon at will."

"There are stories," I muttered. Like the one about how at one time, daemons had walked around just like people, and had humans as slaves. The blood witches liked that one.

"You can only call something that exists already," said Sunny, rolling her eyes. "That's why you can't call up the dead. Or daemons. They're not of our world."

"And yet Levinson was convinced he could do it." I looked to the professor. "Why?"

Hoskins spread his hands. "That, Detective, I will never know. You would be better served to examine Marcus than ask me."

"Well, unfortunately a patrol officer put four rounds through his chest and head when they found him with pieces of the Levinson family maid," I said. "Unless you know a handy medium, we're out of luck." I looked to Sunny.

She shook her head. "Don't even think about it."

"Marcus needed seven," I said. "Assuming for a moment they're trying to summon the same nasty, my guy's gotten three. If the working is completed and the daemon is called through, then what?"

"Theoretically, you make an offering and swear your services to the called daemon and in return he grants you a particular reward," said Sunny. My expression must haven given away my shock to hear that from her, because she spread her hands.

"Grandma told me."

"Why am I not surprised?"

"If your murderer is indeed attempting to call Meggoth through, the offering will be flesh," said Hoskins. "Meggoth worships it." He hopped up and went to his wall of books, opening a cloth-bound portfolio and removing a musty drawing.

A daemon reached upward to a row of naked women who extended their arms in welcome, but he was fixed on the image above. The eighth woman was alive and looking toward an angry, roiling sky. She didn't appear to notice his existence. I touched the drawing when Hoskins presented it and felt no pop of power, just an overwhelming sense of loss.

"*Meggoth, Descended*," Hoskins told us. "When the caster witches purged the daemons from the world, he was the only one of his kind left. Alone, and imprisoned on a plane that was no longer his own."

Sunny wrapped her arms around herself. "He loved someone."

"Serah," said Hoskins. "The caster witches executed her for consorting with him."

"Sucks to be Meggoth," I said. Sunny jabbed me in the ribs.

"Oh come on," I said. "He was a daemon, a force of pure evil. Am I supposed to believe that all he needed was a hug?"

"Many people in this city feel the same way about you, Detective," said Hoskins severely. "At any rate, we will never know the details of Meggoth's ritual, only the theories. Marcus's records of his attempts are in his spellbook, and that was confiscated by the police when he died."

"Luna could get it!" Sunny exclaimed, grabbing my knee. "She has access to all that stuff!"

I looked at the floor. Sunny would find out soon, but she wasn't going to do it in front of Hoskins.

"Did you ever see anything like this?" I changed the subject, sketching the mark from memory. I left several details out purposely. Who knew what completing the thing in my own hand would do?

Hoskins squinted. "The mark," he murmured. "Yes. They showed me pictures of that. From before."

My heart accelerated. "You've seen it?"

"None other, though you've gotten it wrong," said Hoskins. "If you're considering magick working as a hobby, take up something else."

"Don't be cute," I growled. "Unless you want me to get up and de-alphabetize your books."

Hoskins harrumphed while Sunny shot me a death glance and said, "She really doesn't mean most of what she says around the phase."

"Marcus left this with each of his unfortunate conquests," Hoskins said. "He didn't get it right, either."

I stared at the mark, no longer twistingly alive but benign scratches of ink. Marcus had used it. Stephen wore it. They were calling the same damn daemon.

"Looks like I'm right. Meggoth rises again." I slapped the notebook closed and stood. "Let's go, Sunny." My mind was racing faster than a runaway teenager with Daddy's gold card.

"Nice to meet you!" she called as I dragged her out. Hoskins jumped up as I was about to shut his door and came to me.

"Detective. Meggoth offers what is beyond a human being's most depraved fantasy. The promise is too much for his avatars. They will give their lives for him."

"Good," I told Hoskins. "After seeing those women, I will gladly give this avatar a fast kick toward the afterlife."

"Before the Descent, an uncalled daemon could pass his power to a blood witch to complete the working," said Hoskins. "If that is still true, you will be in a very bad way."

I thought about finally getting to meet the man who had done this face-to-face, and felt my eyes begin to shift toward yellow. Hoskins hissed and took a step back.

"I'm not helpless," I told him.

"I can see," he squeaked.

I smiled. "Just so we're clear."

"One last thing," said Hoskins as I was walking away. "I wish you good luck. Maybe now Marcus and I can finally have some peace."

"We're way beyond luck," I said, "but thanks anyway."

O utside the faculty offices, I pulled out my cell phone and speed-dialed Mac at home. "They're sacrifices," I said when he answered groggily.

"What now?"

"Lilia, Marina, and Katya. Sacrificed by a blood witch for a working."

"Who the hell's Katya?"

"The latest victim."

"Okay. What are the girls being sacrificed to?" McAllister asked.

"He has many names."

Mac heaved a sigh. "What the hell have you been doing with your free time?"

"Will you let me finish? A blood witch is trying to call a daemon in this city, and the experts agree it would be possible for him to succeed."

"Who's the blood witch?"

"No idea, sir, although he's using the Duncan kid for something."

"Nice work, Detective."

"I could do without the sarcasm right now, sir."

"Well, hell, Luna," said Mac. "I could do without getting screamed at about you for one damn day. I've already gotten a shrill phone call from the captain this morning."

I changed course abruptly so Sunny wouldn't hear. She looked over her shoulder, annoyed, but kept walking to the car. I took refuge behind one of the stately oak trees that Nocturne University did so well.

"Mac, he needs four more. He'll keep going. He's driven." And if the blood witch controlling Stephen *did* manage the impossible and summon up a daemon, I didn't want to think about what would happen. Not rainbows and a unicorn parade, for sure.

I heard Mac exhale. "I know you've got something here, Luna, it's not that."

"Of course I do," I said. "I don't go flying off on mad hunches nearly as often as you'd think."

"You'd better meet me at the precinct," Mac said. "We need to talk."

EIGHTEEN

"What happened?" was the first thing Sunny said when I got in the car.

"Don't ask."

She examined my face closely. I knew I was pale and twanging like a plucked violin string, eyes bloodshot from no sleep. Sunny had the grace not to mention any of this.

"You better believe we'll talk later," she said. "Where to?"

"The Twenty-fourth," I said quietly. McAllister knew about Roenberg firing me. He had to be cutting me loose.

I pressed my lips together and tried not to think about just how much that hurt.

Sunny parked in front of the precinct house and opened her door.

"You don't have to come," I said quickly.

"And yet, I am." She shut her door and beeped the convertible's lock.

"Suit yourself." Shift was changing, and my fellow

officers from third watch were arriving in ones and twos. I didn't see Bryson yet. Good thing, considering how my day had gone so far. I would probably kick Bryson in the groin first and ask questions later.

"Hi Luna—Sunny!" Rick exclaimed when we came into the lobby. He grinned widely and turned an adorable shade of pink.

"Hi, Rick," said Sunny, also blushing.

"I'll leave you two alone," I said, going through the metal detector.

The squad room had that silently rushed air of 5 PM, day workers anxious to get home and us night people shuffling in reluctantly to take up the reins through the dark hours.

My desk was exactly how I had left it, minus the case files of missing women I'd been cross-referencing. "Where the hell are my files?" I asked the squad room at large.

"These case files?" Bryson grinned at me from his desk, waving the stack of mellowed manila folders. "These right here?"

I took a step toward him. "Those are mine."

"Wrong, sweetheart," he told me. "They're mine now. Captain Roenberg brought 'em to me special this morning. Hear you chewed on his balls at that titty club crime scene and got canned."

I held out my hand to Bryson. "Give me back the case files, David, before I do something I really regret." My ignoring his attempts to piss me off should have been a warning, but Bryson was never one for subtlety.

"You see, your problem is you don't get laid enough,

Wilder," he told me. " 'Cause if you did you'd be home with your man wearin' nothing but a cute little apron instead of tromping around here like Bitchzilla, tryin' to pin something on Stephen Duncan. Nice kid, by the way."

Inside my head, the were opened its eyes and took a cautious breath. It smelled the rage building in me and stuck its head out to look. "You hide your good opinion of Stephen very well," I whispered.

My hands shook. My body shook. The blood roared inside my head, and the were took a step outside the tiny cave where it hibernated twenty-eight days a month.

Bryson shrugged. "That was just an act. Real cop would know that, Wilder." He tossed the case files aside and laced his fingers behind his head, looking up at me with the same wide shit-eating grin I'd come to hate in my two years at the Twenty-fourth. "See, here's your issue with the Duncan kid: smart, great looking, wouldn't jump an alleged woman like you if ya got down naked on your knees and begged. And you're over here in your bitch boots with your bitch badge takin' it out on him, trying to make yourself feel better." He shook his head and turned away from me. "Sad, Wilder. Very sad."

Turning his back on me was the mistake. The final insult the were could not ignore.

I growled. Not the frustrated huff of air that usually made itself into a nasal sound of annoyance, or the edge my voice took on when I was trying to sound intimidating. A were growl, an animal sound that ripped itself deep from within my diaphragm and rattled around the squad room. Dmitri would be proud.

Bryson started to say something else, probably tearing me down so that in his small mind he was clearly the victor, but I spun his chair around and backed him against the desk, pinning an arm on either side and boxing him in. I got close enough to smell the pricey aftershave covering up the cheap shampoo and stared into his eyes.

"Bryson," I said. "I pride myself on self-control. I know that I can ignore your adolescent baiting with ease."

He didn't even try to push me off, just looked back at me with a wide-eyed fish expression. Terror masked the other scents, musty and enticing at the same time, and I purred low in my throat, feeling the sting that meant my pupils were slowly but surely changing from human black to animal gold and the gray around them had taken on a glow. Bryson squeaked. He sounded a lot like Professor Hoskins.

"I have to tell you, though," I continued. "If you send so much as a funny-eyed look in my direction, if you ever feel the need to stare at and comment on my chest and my ass, or if you ever again tell me how much and why I need to get laid—in other words, David, if you continue to be yourself—I am going to *lose my temper*." The last delivered in a low snarl that made the hairs on Bryson's ropy neck stand at attention.

"Jesus!" he stammered, grabbing at the case files. His hand quivered, and they slid to the floor with loud plops. He thrust a handful at me. "Take them, you crazy bitch, and get the hell away from me!"

"Thanks," I said with a sweet smile, snatching the files from his hands with a snap. My teeth must have fanged out more than I thought because Bryson gave another squeak and bolted from his chair, disappearing into the men's room.

My victory was short-lived. McAllister opened his office door and beckoned to me. "Did I hear Bryson?" he asked when I walked over.

"Haven't seen him all night," I said.

"We have problems," Mac said, shutting his office door behind me. "I told you to go to the club and work the crime scene. I specifically did not say show up, cause a ruckus, and call Roenberg incompetent." He fished in his desk drawer and brought out a cigarette. It dangled from his lip, unlit. "Luna, you're probably one of the best cops I've ever commanded, but sometimes I just have to sit back and wonder what goes on in that head of yours."

"Mac, Roenberg's covering for Stephen Duncan to protect the DA's rep and you know it. The captain had no ME, no CSU, just a giant freaking broom to smooth the whole thing over with." Talk enough and maybe Mac would forget about the whole letting-me-go part.

"Luna, I know Wilbur is dirty as gym socks, but you are not going to prove that by pissing off everyone who can throw up an obstacle to your case."

I wanted to hit something, but I settled for my palm. "I don't care, Mac. Fire me. I promised these women."

"You *promised* them?" Mac demanded. "Jesus. You know not to get attached, Luna. You know damn well. You can't work the case if you're in a body bag next to the victim."

How did I explain to him that it was more than a case, generic and numbered inside a brown folder? Lilia was a were, a member of my own blood. Marina was a poor, dumb, trusting girl who just wanted the man of her dreams. All three of them were vulnerable and dead because I hadn't caught the killer fast enough. The thought twisted in my stomach.

"I can't see a way around this," said Mac finally when I didn't come up with a retort. "I have to put you on administrative leave, Luna. Roenberg has already instigated procedures to fire you."

"Fine," I said softly, already unhooking my shield.

Mac took the little piece of gold and turned it over once in his hand before sliding it into the drawer next to his flattened pack of smokes. I took out my Glock, checked the chamber, and took my two extra clips out of my jacket pocket. "You'd better take this, too."

Mac looked up at me with worry writ large in his face.

"It's not what I might do to myself," I said, opening his door. "It's what I'll do to Stephen Duncan and his blood witch puppeteer when I catch them."

Mac took that in stride, just saying, "Don't put yourself in jail over this piece of shit."

I smiled. I wanted to scream, but what the Hex would that accomplish? "What choice do I have?" I asked Mac.

"You're the other, Luna. You scare people like Roenberg. They don't *want* your help."

I sagged. Mac's words hit me like a club to the gut. "And what about you?" I whispered.

Mac clicked his lighter against the end of the cigarette and exhaled. "Me? This tears me up, Luna. You're like my gods damn little sister."

"Yeah. Some brother you turned out to be."

"Don't take it out on me," said Mac. "And not on yourself, either. You fought a good fight, kid, but now it's time to go home and reboot your life. I know you're right about the murders, but you can't make this case. Roenberg has already cleaned out the club, and what little evidence was probably there is long gone. Duncan won this one."

"I have to go," I whispered so he wouldn't hear I was trying not to cry.

Mac dragged. "Where, Luna?"

"None of your business. Why do you care where someone like me goes, anyway?"

"I'm not the one you should be angry at," he said again.

"You'll do for now," I snarled. "Good-bye."

I slammed the door on his wounded expression, digging my nails into my palm so I wouldn't have to let out my tears.

I tore Sunny away from trading smiles and stammered small talk with Rick and led her out to the car, ignoring her protests.

"City archives," I said when we were inside.

"You have that look," she said. "What happened?"

"Archives, now," I said.

Sunny threw up her hands. "Fine! Don't want to talk to me, go ahead. Just build that nice big wall you have higher." She jerked the car into gear and sped into traffic.

"Sorry," I muttered after we'd driven for a few minutes in silence.

She glared. "Forget it."

"Fine," I mimicked her. "Don't let me be sorry."

"Why are we going to archives?" She changed the subject, but not the icy tone.

"Case files from before 1980 are stored there," I said. "I need to take a look at Cedar Hill."

"For what?" She looked suspicious.

"For clues to the whereabouts of Jimmy Hoffa. To figure out who's controlling Stephen Duncan, Sunny. What do you think?"

"With you, I never know. So who do you think this blood witch is?"

"Don't know."

"So we're flying blind against someone who tortures women for pleasure? I'm reassured."

"Why is it only with *me* that you automatically assume the most morbid, terrible scenario you can imagine?" I snapped.

Sunny gave me a somber look. "Years of experience."

"Very funny. Watch the traffic." I was glad she seemed to let the spat go. I had enjoyed tormenting her when we were girls, but girls do that. Sunny, for all her trappings of witchiness, was saner than I'd ever be. I needed her to stay just that way.

"So are you going to answer my question?"

"I did!" I said irritably. "I'm looking for anything that can tell me who we're dealing with. Photos, murder weapons, autopsy reports. They're bloody. You'll probably have to shield your eyes from the graphic violence."

"I meant about what happened at the station," she said.

"That I am not talking about," I said tightly. Let Sunny stew—I wasn't about to tell anyone I had just been fired. I wasn't even admitting it to myself. If I wasn't a detective, what was I? The wannabe druggie kid who had hopped off the express bus in Nocturne City? The fry cook, then night clerk, then cocktail waitress who drank too much and felt sorry for herself a lot? Without the job I was no better than a piece of seaweed washed through the dirty currents in Siren Bay.

"We're here," said Sunny, pulling up to a meter in front of the shiny glass-and-steel archive complex. She handed me a quarter for parking. I almost told her to save it; no one would ticket a cop's cousin. Then I felt the absence of weight from my gun and the empty spot on my waist where my shield would sit.

I put the quarter in the meter before going inside.

The evidence depot held endless metal shelves piled high with endless cardboard boxes that held the bits and pieces of evidence making up cases cold, unsolved, and simply buried. Filing something into the depot was as good as shoving it into a black hole and wishing it gods-speed.

A sign on the wall by the check-in desk warned me that no unauthorized personnel were permitted beyond this point.

The little plastic window, akin to a ticket booth with a big slot below it for passing items, was occupied by a clerk who resembled a mountain troll in business casual more than anything. The troll's name tag read BRENT. He wore a well-concealed waist rig under his cotton shirt.

"Yeah?" he said, crossing his arms over a chest that could have served as a battering ram.

"Detective Wilder," I said in the most officious voice I could muster. "I need to check out the evidence from the Cedar Hill killings." I rattled off the case number and fixed King Kong Clerk with my most bitchy, impatient stare.

"Let's see some ID," he rumbled.

You have got to be kidding me. An evidence clerk who follows procedure. What next, a vegetarian were?

"My badge number is—" I started.

"The number won't do you any good without the badge, missy," he said. Missy? *Begging* to have his head smacked against something hard.

"Look, Brad, just give me the box and then you can go back to pumping iron or working your glutes or whatever it is a gentleman of your size does to kill time."

"It's Brent," he said. "No ID, no box."

"You're a real credit to your job," I informed him.

"Golly gee, thanks, miss. When you grow some charm, feel free to try again."

He was *so* lucky I was wearing my veryold-veryexpensive Yves Saint Laurent blouse today.

Foiled, I stormed back down the hall to the open doors. Down the wide steps Sunny sat in the convertible fiddling with the radio. I could kick and scream and hit Brent in the face, which would be therapeutic but not terribly productive, or I could take a deep breath and find a new strategy.

Maybe I really was getting a handle on this were rage thing. And maybe someday soon, a blood witch would jump on a broom and do a lap around the city limits.

I bounded down the steps and knocked on the car window. "Sunny!"

She bolted upright and blinked at me in alarm. "You scared the crap out of me," she declared, rolling down the window.

"I need your talents," I said.

Sunny stared at me in silence for a second and came back with a predictable "Excuse me?"

"I need you to make some sort of scene to distract the Manthing watching the door while I sneak in and get the Cedar Hill boxes."

"And why can't you just make him give it to you?" said Sunny. "You're a police officer. You have authority."

"About that . . . ," I said, looking at the black patent-leather toes of my shoes.

Sunny closed her eyes. "Oh, no. Not again."

"It's not suspension this time," I said quietly. "Roenberg fired me."

I expected Sunny to get that disappointed look she always wore when I did something typically boneheaded, the one that I hated because it made her look like my grandmother.

Instead she snapped off the radio and got out of the car. "This isn't right."

"You're telling me," I muttered. "But hey, who needs a city job with benefits and retirement, right? I'm sure the ChickenHut will be thrilled to have me back on the fryer."

Sunny started up the steps to the archives.

"Sunny?"

"Come on," she called over her shoulder. "We're wasting time."

I took the steps two at a time and caught up with her. "Where are you going?"

She went through the door and took a hard left, stopping about twenty feet from the plastic window where Brent lurked. I quickly ducked back into the main lobby before he saw me. "Sunny!" I hissed. "Get out of there."

She looked over her shoulder at me. "You wanted a scene."

Sunny opened her mouth and screamed. It was a piercing, panicked sound that made my head vibrate. Brent jumped straight up like a ferret had bitten his rear end. Sunny stood in place, mouth open and eyes wide, shrieking at the top of her lungs.

Brent banged open the partition and ran over to her. "What? What?"

Sunny took a deep breath in and then shouted at the top of her lungs, "Rats!"

"Rats?" Brent looked confused, surprisingly natural on him. "What rats?"

"Right there in the lobby!" Sunny shrilled. "Two nasty foul rats running right across my feet!" She grabbed Brent's arm and jerked him away from the depot door with force. I slipped behind his back as they went by and edged toward it.

"Look, lady, we don't have rats in here," said Brent. "I think you're imaginin' things."

"I most certainly am *not*!" Sunny shouted. "And I take exception to your attitude!" She grabbed Brent's chin. "*Look* at me when I am talking to you, you . . . civil servant!"

Brent locked eyes with her, and Sunny said calmly, "So my will becomes yours, yours becomes mine," and released him. Brent kept staring, glassy-eyed, seeing Hex-knew-what because Sunny had glamoured him. Like a dominate, only with hallucinations. Since my run-in with Cassandra, I knew all too well the kind of warm-bath stupor he was in.

"He'll be out for a few minutes at least," she whispered, making the *go* signal with her hands.

"You're turning positively evil," I told her.

"Yes, waiter, more key lime pie would be divine," said Brent.

The half-plastic door creaked with disuse as I stepped inside and pulled the shade to shield me from anyone who happened to be curious.

Just to the left were tall filing cabinets full of evidence logs indexed by case number. A single sheet of paper inside noted the name of the victim, the nature of the crime, and the row, shelf, and box number where the evidence linked to them could be found.

CEDAR HILL sat between CAESARO, PETER and CENTER DRIVE ALL-NIGHT DINER, a browned folder with the case number and name typed crookedly at the top. The folder itself was empty.

I tucked it under my arm and walked down the spotless white hallway past a series of metal doors marked with case numbers and years.

The door to 1975–80/LGF was locked, of course. I fished in my jacket pocket for my wallet and took out my gold card. With all the abuse I put the poor thing through via the Internet, this seemed only fitting.

I knew how to jimmy a lock before I joined the department, but seven years had refined my technique. I slipped the latch in under thirty seconds.

Good thing, too, because I heard footsteps and bass voices coming up fast. I jumped inside the dark file room and shut the door except for a tiny slit to peer out.

Two shadows passed in the hall, and I shrank against the cool plastic, holding my breath.

"You take that stuff to the burn pile yet, Leo?" said one voice.

A grunt, then, "I'm workin' on it."

"What the hell do I pay you for, you big dumb ox?" demanded the other voice, nasal and very managerial. Leo sounded more like a disgruntled longshoreman.

"I said I'm workin' on it."

"No excuses," said Boss. "Discarded evidence, incinerator, now."

A tap of men's shoes walking away. Leo muttered under his breath. "Dick."

He grunted away and I cracked the door. The hallway was deserted except for a broad, retreating back encased in a white muscle shirt and khaki work pants pushing a cart of evidence boxes stamped with the red legend DISCARD.

I would never make it as a thief. My heart was hammering and the door handle was slick from my sweat when I touched it again.

My tiny penlight flashed on row after row of boxes stacked to the ceiling. Dust tickled my nose as I found the right aisle and shelf for the Cedar Hill records.

I was not entirely surprised when the spot was empty. My shoulders slumped as the tension of the hunt ran out of me. That was it, then. Another dead end, another spot I'd been beaten to by the witch and his seemingly endless influence.

Before I stepped out into the hall I picked up the wall phone, dialed Sunny's cell, and told her, "I'm done, start the car."

"You know, out of all the jobs in the world, 'wheel man' was one I never considered. You've opened up so many new worlds to me, cousin."

I rolled my eyes and hung up on her. The proverbial coast was clear, until I heard Leo coming back and whipped the door shut again.

He stopped and looked right at me, eye-to-eye. *Don't check the door,* I prayed. *For everything Hexed and holy, just keep walking.*

Leo blinked and continued pushing the now empty cart toward the front office.

"I have more boxes for the ovens, Leo!" his boss shrilled. "Back you go."

"Put you in the oven," Leo grumbled.

The incinerator was at the end of a long hall, and I could feel the heat from ten feet away. Boxes were piled to the ceiling in the glow from the door of the oven.

"Great," I muttered. This would take hours.

I dove in, tossing files and evidence bags aside as I rooted for my particular Ark of the Covenant.

Finally, under a stack of faxes from some long-forgotten day-trading fraud, I saw a plain lidded box with the handwritten case number on the side. I grabbed it, then yanked my hand back with a yelp as a sizzling pain shot through it.

I risked turning on the lights and saw why. The Cedar Hill box was covered in wards, inked on the top and bottom and each of the four sides. If anyone *not* the witch who placed the wards attempted to mess with the box, they would get the surprise of a lifetime.

I kicked the pile of old evidence and cursed. I don't know what made me madder—not being able to look at the file after all I'd gone through to get it or being outsmarted by the nameless blood witch yet again.

I took off my jacket and wrapped it around my hands, driven now. If I could just upend the box and see what was inside . . .

"Who the hell are you?"

I spun, box in hand, to see Leo in the doorway with his cart and an expression of bovine surprise.

"Um." Not my most eloquent lie, to be sure.

Leo shoved the cart out of the way and started for me. "You made a big mistake coming in here, lady."

"I just needed this, I'll be going now!" I chirped, holding the box between me and the evidence thug. The wards hissed as they singed hand-shaped holes through my jacket.

I really liked this jacket, too.

Leo rolled his shoulders as he loomed up to block my route to the door. "Stealin' from the depository is a crime. I'm here to make sure it doesn't happen, and I'm already having a royally bad day, so you're pretty much screwed, you little thief." He pointed to the floor. "Get rid of the box and put up your hands."

As the smell of expensive leather on fire grew stronger, I did exactly what Leo asked. I shoved the box hard into his gut and darted around him to the door.

Leo screamed as the wards crackled across his unprotected flesh, fronds of blue fire racing up both arms. He flung the box away and fell into a pile of other evidence, raining it on his own head.

The Cedar Hill file slid to a stop just shy of my toes, the wards sparking angrily but already fading. The witch hadn't taken the time to make them stick, and their batteries were out.

I picked up the box again, wincing as it burned my palms, and told Leo, "Play with someone your own size, although for you, that would be Sasquatch."

Leo roared an unintelligible curse and got to his feet swinging. I kicked the door shut in his face and took off down the hall for parts unknown.

"Hey you!"

Crap.

Brent and the manager of the depository were advancing on me down the narrow hallway. "You're not authorized to be in here!" Boss sniped at me, pointing a hostile little finger.

"Drop the box," Brent said, aiming the contents of his shoulder rig at me.

My survival instinct whispered *fight or flight*. Since I'd already had a go-round with Leo, I turned tail and hauled ass down the hallway toward the red sign that blinked EXIT.

A bullet pulverized the wall behind me. Brent wasn't kidding. He was also a lousy shot.

"Stop her!" Boss screamed. "Do your job!"

The EXIT sign led me to a tiny stairwell—a stairwell that was boarded up and chained with a NO ENTRY sign. How ironic was that?

A door to the outside was boarded over with two-by-fours and a flimsy lock. I threw my shoulder against it with all my were strength as Brent came barreling up behind me.

It cracked only a little. I cursed loudly and hit it again, because I hadn't come this far to end up dead in a crummy stairwell. Especially not at the hands of a hired goon named Brent.

I slammed into the door again and this time the timbers gave with a groan.

The exit led me to a loading dock connected to the street by an alley. I have no idea what kind of image I made, racing for freedom carrying a blackened, smoking cardboard box, chased by a man who could be an extra in a Steven Seagal movie, but I'll bet it was pretty damn hilarious.

"Stop or I'll shoot, lady! Again!"

Yes, definitely hilarious.

I poured on more speed, hearing Brent's heavy panting behind me, and then I was at the mouth of the alley, dodging between startled pedestrians, Sunny's convertible blessedly idling at the curb.

I screamed at her. "Sunny!"

She whipped her head around, eyes wide when she saw Brent and his pistol emerge onto the sidewalk behind me.

"Sunny, open the door!" I dove into the passenger's side, flung the burning box into the backseat, and looked at my cousin. "What the hell are you waiting for? Drive!"

She was watching Brent. "Is he really an employee in the archives? I remember them being a lot less gun-toting."

Brent landed on the trunk of the car with a crash and pressed his gun against the window. "I'll blow your fucking brains all over this little girly ride, lady!"

"Sunny, I don't want to die."

"Okay, okay!" she shrieked. "Hex me, I didn't think he was actually going to shoot us!"

"In the real world, Sunny, people with guns usually wave them around with that exact thing in mind."

"Don't get snippy with me! I'm driving!"

Her foot hit the accelerator and we left Brent in the dust, sprawled in a thirty-minute parking space in front of the city building. Sunny's hands were bloodless as she gripped the wheel and she stared at me with wide eyes.

"What on the Hexed earth have you gotten me into, Luna Wilder?"

I sat back and took a deep breath, expunging the smell of burning wards for cool, blessed air. "I wonder that myself most of the time, Sunny."

"That is not funny," she said quietly.

"I know," I muttered. Sunny took the turn onto Heron too fast and changed lanes before she said anything else.

"We're in danger."

"When have I not been in danger, Sunny? Walking the streets as an Insoli were is like having a giant sign on your back that says, HELLO, I'M INFERIOR AND WOULD LIKE THE CRAP KICKED OUT OF ME."

"I didn't mean you," she said quietly. "I meant the rest of us."

I sighed. "I'm sorry."

"What are you going to do about it?"

I pointed over my shoulder. "Find a quiet place where I can look through this file and find some answers."

Sunny nodded and put her blinker on. "I know a place."

NINETEEN

The placed turned out to be Faery Food, a tearoom and bookshop run by a caster witch in Sunny's loose circle of friends. The owner greeted Sunny warmly—I don't think I've ever heard so many "bless you within the circles" at once—but looked at me with suspicion.

"You're the cousin?" she asked me.

"Luna, this is Genevieve. Gene, Luna."

I held out my hand. "Can't say I've heard a lot about you, but hi."

"It's nothing personal, but I don't shake hands with weres," said Genevieve. "Their energy is too unpredictable."

"Gene is a touchseer," Sunny explained. "She can read people by touch."

"I know what a touchseer is," I snapped. "We grew up with the same grandmother."

"Rhoda's a lovely woman," said Genevieve, endearing herself to me even more.

"Tell you what." I dropped the Cedar Hill box on a table and got a hit of satisfaction when Genevieve recoiled. "Bring Sunny whatever it is she wants to eat or drink or call the corners with and you two can chat while I sit over here with my icky were energy and go through this file."

Genevieve wrinkled her nose but swept away in a swirl of green-and-blue robe with matching slippers.

"And while you're at it, shake hands with twenty-first-century fashion trends," I muttered.

Sunny shot me her *grow up* look. "She's just being cautious."

"I know damn well what she's being, Sunny. It's not news to me that most caster witches hate us."

"I don't hate you." She sighed. "Neither does Rhoda or Genevieve or anyone else with the blood."

"The witch who tried to kill me being the exception, of course."

Genevieve returned with a tray and two steaming cups. The witches sat on a sofa overfilled with pillows and I turned to the Cedar Hill box, flicking the lid off with a snap of wards.

The contents inside were singed but intact, mostly copious amounts of paper shoved willy-nilly into file folders. The case detective's notebooks were shoved into the bottom along with a leather-bound ledger.

I went for the notebooks first and discovered that the case detective liked to make lists of women he was dating, eat at restaurants featuring gravy (and made notes while doing it); and that under the page related to Marcus Levinson he had written a single word, *FREAK*, underlined several times.

That was the sum total of the case detective's personal opinion. The papers in the files were autopsy report copies and a bunch of transcripts from Marcus Levinson's bail hearing that had been misfiled. Useless.

Finally I picked up the ledger and saw that it was a really a book with a sigil scratched into the front cover. The first page was crammed with tiny penmanship. Initials in the upper corner read M. L.

I dropped the book. "Sunny?" It couldn't be. Surely the thing Marcus valued most in the world, that he had gotten expelled from the University and finally died over, couldn't be sitting in front of me.

Sunny leaned over my shoulder. "What's going on?"

I opened the book again. "Is this what I think it is?"

She ruffled the pages, wide-eyed. "Unbelievable."

I agreed. Marcus Levinson's stolen spellbook looked, on the surface, benign. The spidery, precise text was not only microscopic but also written in another language, seemingly a random arrangement of letters.

"There's a lock working on the book," said Sunny. "A scrambling spell. There will be a chant to reverse it and make the text readable again."

"Great. Why don't you ask your friend to cop a feel and divine what it is?"

"Her gift doesn't work like that," said Sunny prissily. Her phone rang and she jabbed at it in irritation. "Hello?" She frowned and after a moment handed it to me. "They want to talk to Detective Wilder."

"Who is it?"

Sunny shrugged. I took the phone and a male voice asked, "Detective?"

"Yeah, sure, whatever. Who's this?"

"Officer Thorpe, ma'am. You know me from those two homicides." Thorpe. Calling me on Sunny's cell phone. Weird, but weird barely registered with me these days so I let it go on by.

"What do you want, Officer?"

"I have something you need to see, ma'am." His voice sounded creaky and tense, like he was straining to sound normal. "Something from the club killing. That girl . . . Katrina. You'll be very interested."

"Katya," I murmured. "Her name was Katya." Sunny questioned me with raised palms. I didn't have the miming skills to convey *this is the strangest phone call I have ever gotten,* so I just shrugged back.

"Katya. Whatever," Thorpe agreed. "Lieutenant McAllister told me to get you over here. He said you'd know how to deal with it." Thorpe's recitation was almost practiced, and I got that hinky sensation that had nothing to do with were instincts—just a cop's bad feeling. Still, if it could lead me to the witch, I was damn well going to show up.

"Where is here, Officer Thorpe?"

He rattled off the address, a condoplex in Mainline, and added "Hurry, Detective. Please."

I started to ask what the big Hexed hurry was, but he hung up with a clatter. I dialed another number from memory and waited through about fifteen rings before Dmitri's groggy voice answered.

"Yeah?"

"It's me," I said.

"Well, Me, hearing your voice was almost worth rolling out of bed for." Flush crept up my cheeks and I quickly turned my back on Sunny and Genevieve.

"I need a favor, Dmitri."

"Your wish is my command and all that crap. What is it?"

I lowered my voice. "A gun." I may be curious, but I'm not dumb. Whatever Mac thought Officer Thorpe should show me, he could show me when I was armed.

Not that a gun would really help against most things that had tried to kill me lately, but it made me feel secure, so screw what anyone else thought.

Dmitri, to his credit, didn't even change his tone when he said, "Any particular kind of gun?"

"Something that puts holes in bad people. Beyond that, use your judgment."

"Meet you in half an hour. Where?"

I gave him the address of Faery Food and rang off. Sunny took her phone back and asked, "Was that who I think it was?"

"None other than your favorite were biker tea enthusiast," I told her. I turned to Genevieve. "If you think I'm bad, wait until you meet my friend. His energy would sneak up and cut you for your wallet."

Genevieve sniffed. "I'm glad you find my gift so amusing."

"Sometimes," I quoted Dr. Kronen, "humor is all we have to keep the wolves of insanity at bay."

"I think it's a little late for you," Genevieve told me, and retreated into the kitchen with the now empty tea tray. Bitch.

I went to the curb to wait for Dmitri, sitting with my feet in the gutter and my chin in my hands. When he rumbled up on the bike, he grinned and said, "Need a ride, hot stuff?"

"You've got a book of those somewhere, don't you?" I greeted him.

He shrugged. "I used to tease Lilia with corny pet names. Drove her up the wall." My expression must have turned, because he stopped smiling and held out a plastic shopping bag. "Big holes, just as the lady requested."

The gun Dmitri brought was a Colt 1911, the big

army .45 developed to stop enemy soldiers injected with methamphetamines. Worked nicely, thank you.

"When you go all-out . . . ," I said, working the slide on the monstrosity and finding a full clip.

"Nothing but the best for my favorite member of the pigs." Dmitri nudged me when I didn't laugh. "I'm kidding. If you're a pig I'm a dachshund."

"You're absolutely right," I agreed, tucking the Colt into my waistband. "I am officially no longer a pig."

Sunny came out the tearoom door, and I leaned in to Dmitri. "And if you get my cousin started on her rant again, I'll beat you senseless."

Dmitri's nostrils quivered. "Maybe I'd enjoy that a little."

Sunny held up the case file. "You forgot your box. Hello, Mr. Sandovsky."

He flashed her a polite smile. "Sunny." Lewd to cute in thirty seconds flat. What a catch.

I gestured her over. "You go with Dmitri." She opened her mouth to protest but I said, "Someone has to keep the spellbook safe until I find the blood witch. And keep Sandovsky here on good behavior."

"I don't have 'good' behavior," he grumbled.

Sunny patted his arm. "I'm sure we'll find it somewhere."

Dmitri shot me a look as she got into her convertible with the box. "If she's this perky the entire time, I'm not responsible for the consequences."

"You get used to it, trust me."

He touched my hand. "Where are you going with that big gun on your hip, Luna?"

I squeezed it in return. "Nowhere I can't handle." He got on the bike and followed Sunny into traffic, and I walked in the opposite direction and didn't think about how down-deep guilty lying to Dmitri made me feel.

T he condo that Officer Thorpe's address matched was one of the soulless new complexes that sprang up as the city backed away from Waterfront and Highland Park like you back away from a snarling chained-up dog, and declared Mainline fashionable. I buzzed the number on the address. The intercom clicked open, and static hissed at me for a few seconds.

"Hello? This is Detective Wilder—Thorpe, is that you?"

Nothing. After a long second, the door buzzed and I stepped into the vestibule.

A row of mailboxes sat next to another door that led to a courtyard and the homes inside the pristine walls. I checked the number Thorpe had given me and started when I saw W. ROENBERG on the nameplate.

Why the Hex had I been summoned to my ex-captain's condo?

The door swished, and I snapped my head up to meet Regan Lockhart's eyes. He smiled and nodded, looking not surprised in the least to see me.

"Ms. Wilder. How nice to see you again. We keep meeting under a confrontation. I'm relieved that won't be happening any longer."

Enough bombshells in a short enough time, and eventually your brain throws up its hands and says, *Okay!* Because of this, I managed to just stand there staring at Lockhart while he said, "If you've come to see the captain, I'm afraid he's not available."

My danger instinct began pinging off the charts. "He

buzzed me in," I managed in what to me sounded like a remarkably neutral tone.

"No, I did," said Lockhart. "Captain Roenberg has vacated, I'm afraid. But please do investigate for yourself. A police presence really is called for." He pulled out his cell phone and dialed 911.

The only thing I could think to say was, "What did you do, Lockhart?"

"What was necessary. Good-bye, Detective Wilder." He tipped his head and left the lobby in a swirl of black coat and self-satisfaction.

I was really glad I had gotten the gun as I ran through the short expanse of garden and cleared Roenberg's steps in a jump.

His doorknob turned at my touch and I kept my back against the frame, covering his foyer until I was sure by scent and sight that I was alone. When I was inside, I locked the door after me.

The condo was sterile and humorless, sort of like Roenberg himself. Dishes were neatly stacked in the drainer; a tan sofa and chair matched the walls.

I peered into a dining room with a thick layer of dust and saw three brown boxes on their sides, with the contents spilling out. Small plastic bags marked EVIDENCE and a few file folders marked PETROFF, K. An empty DVD case sat next to the files, open. The evidence Roenberg had commandeered from the club.

And on the table, scribed in fingerprints, there was blood.

I whipped around, gun arm swinging out. Behind me was a door into Roenberg's bedroom. I nudged it open with my toe and found my own reflection in a floor-to-ceiling mirror. Posed just to my left, in a chair, was Officer Thorpe.

"Hex me," I muttered, lowering my arm and slumping against the wall. Thorpe's throat had been sliced neatly just under his chin, and a fan of blood covered the front of his blue uniform shirt. Roenberg's cordless phone dangled from one limp fist. Thorpe's eyes were open, and I shut them.

"Sorry, Officer," I whispered. His blood was fresh and my stomach roiled. There had been no reason for his death, and the fact enraged me. I don't know how long I would have stood there, staring at the body, if someone hadn't pounded on the front door.

"Nocturne City police! Open the door, Detective Wilder!"

Crap didn't even *begin* to cover that.

"Detective!" They pounded again.

"This is Detective Wilder!" I shouted. "What's the problem?"

"We need to take you into custody, Detective! Open this door or we'll come in and get your cop-killing ass!"

Gods DAMN it. Lockhart had called the cavalry on me. Vindictive little bastard. Were hearing picked up the cops outside saying, "Break it down."

"We're coming in, Detective!" another one shouted. I frantically searched the bedroom for anything useful.

An open travel case and pile of Roenberg's socks and underwear were on the bed. He was long-fled. A television cabinet stood open across from Thorpe's body with a DVD in the player. It blinked at me. The disc was unlabeled and silvery—the kind of thing someone might use to record illicit porn videos. Roenberg must have been interrupted jerking off. I ripped the DVD out of the player and shoved it into a pocket, then ran back through the kitchen and out the rear door just as the cops kicked in the front.

TWENTY

Later, I sat on the smelly plaid sofa in the Crown, with Sunny across from me, ankles crossed primly as she watched the Redbacks mill in the larger part of the theater.

Olya Sandovsky climbed the steps from the seating pit and stopped dead, staring at me. "What the hell are you doing back here?"

"Phase and bite me," I snapped, not looking at her.

"Watch your mouth, Insoli," Olya said. "Come moonrise, you're going to have a house full of very territorial weres on your hands."

"Olya, what leads you to believe that *anything* about you intimidates me?"

She growled, and I knew if I met her eyes she would pull a dominate, and she would win. I was an intruder in her pack as much as I had ever been.

"We appreciate your brother letting us stay here very much," Sunny interjected, standing and putting herself between Olya and me. Olya scented her and then curled her lip in disgust.

"Great. First the Insoli and now one with the blood," she said, stepping back like Sunny might taint her.

"Yeah. Watch it or she'll put a curse on you," I said. "You'll never fit into skinny jeans again."

Sunny crossed her arms and tried to glare menacingly, succeeding in looking like she had just sucked a lemon.

"You two are a joke," said Olya. She flipped her hair in my face and flounced upstairs to the projection room.

I sank down on the sofa again, and Sunny slumped beside me. "Luna, if I have to spend one more hour here with these weres, I am going to lose it."

"We can't go home," I said.

"Why not?"

"Because Roenberg knows where I live, as does anyone else with access to my personnel file." Like Lockhart.

Sunny worried the hem of her skirt. "Do you think Lockhart will try to hurt you?"

"It's more like *when* will he," I said.

"So he's the blood witch, then," Sunny sighed. "At least now we know."

"You know," I murmured, giving voice to the sensation that had been bothering me ever since I'd fled Roenberg's condo, "I'm not so sure about that. If he was a blood witch, he could have killed me when I met him in the lobby. He goes to this elaborate length to set me up as a cop killer and yet doesn't remove crucial evidence of his crime from Roenberg's place."

"He likes to play games," said Sunny, shrugging.

"Or he's not the blood witch," I said. "Just another crony. Either way, if I ever see him again I'm going to kick his balls so hard he vomits them. He got me fired and he slit Officer Thorpe's throat."

"Yes, and we still haven't had a discussion about the *fired* part of that sentence," Sunny muttered.

I had never been more glad to see Dmitri. He came down the stairs, Olya yapping at his heels, and rolled his eyes. "Can't you women ever play nice?"

"I want them gone," said Olya. "Why are they even here in the first place?"

Dmitri turned on his sister. "They're here because I invited them to be here, because Luna is helping me with Lilia, and because *you* don't get to say a damn word about the way I run this house."

Olya whimpered and looked at her shoes. Dmitri swiveled back to me, eyes smoky. "You okay?"

"Fine," I whispered. The aura of the dominate still rolled off him, and I got weak in all the right places.

He fingered my shirt. "You got some blood there."

I looked down at the spot. "Some of Thorpe's. Must be."

Dmitri jerked a thumb toward the stairs. "I'm sure Olya has something you can borrow. Then you can come back downstairs and tell me who the hell Thorpe is and why you're so spooked." He whispered in my ear as I passed him, "I'll help you, but keep the pack out of it or so Hex me, you'll be sorry."

Damn it, he smelled good.

"I won't," I promised before I followed a glaring Olya up the stairs.

"You know, you're nothing like Lilia," she told me. "I have no clue why he likes you so much."

"You obviously don't know your brother very well," I said, pointing to my chest. Olya snorted.

"Don't flatter yourself, Ex-Detective. Dmitri never went this far for a piece of ass."

"Lucky me," I muttered.

"All Lilia wanted was to be by his side," said Olya.

"To be his mate. And that's all Dmitri wanted her to be."
She opened a door to what had obviously once been a
storage closet but was now stuffed with clothes, a cot,
and Olya's uniforms from Club Velvet. "I didn't like
Lilia, but I wanted my brother to be happy. After everything he's endured, he deserves it."

She shoved a plain black T-shirt and a cotton jacket
at me and crossed her arms. "The last thing you will
make Dmitri is happy. If you keep after him, Insoli, I'll
make sure you regret it."

I stripped off my bloody shirt and threw it back at
her. "Olya, after the day I've had your misplaced protec-
tiveness isn't even cute." I re-dressed and matched her
glare. "And for your information, your brother isn't interested in me. At all." I thought of Dmitri pressing
against me, his shockingly soft lips on my neck, his
pulling back when he saw my bite scars. I boiled.

"Just get out of my pack house," said Olya, opening
her door and ushering me out. "You smell like gutter."

"And you smell like a spoiled puppy who I've only
refrained from smacking across the mouth because her
brother is keeping my cousin and me safe."

She just gave me an infuriating smirk. "Like I said,
Detective—don't flatter yourself."

D mitri had the concession stand set up like a tiny
café, and he tossed me a beer before sitting at
the single table. "Okay. Spill. What the Hex
happened to you?"

I put the DVD on the table between us. "I got this
from my former captain's condo. It's the recording from
the night Katya was murdered. The blood witch who's
controlling Stephen and Regan Lockhart is on it."

Dmitri flicked the cap off my beer with his thumb and handed it back. I took a long pull, letting the cold, bitter tang slide down my throat.

"I take it complications ensued."

I nodded, watching the water bead on the curves of my bottle. "Unfortunately, I got a little too trusting and now I think I may have a murder pinned on me." I sighed. "At least now I know who got Stephen involved with the witch."

Dmitri leaned forward. "Who? Did he kill Lilia? Tell me."

"Regan Lockhart, the chief investigator from the DA's office. He was at the condo, and he makes sense. Control Stephen and by extension control Alistair. Leave your blood master free to bathe the whole city in blood. And yes, it's probable he killed Lilia."

"Lockhart," said Dmitri slowly. He let out a slow breath and slumped back in his chair. "You don't know how long I've waited to hear that name." He picked up the bottle. "You mind?" I shook my head and he said, "It's kinda anticlimactic. You know?"

"All that's left is the dying," I agreed quietly. "Me, Lockhart. Probably you. You don't stand a chance against Lockhart and the witch."

"Your faith is touching," he said, finishing off the bottle. "But I ain't alone."

"Excuse me?"

Dmitri covered my hand with his. "I've got you, don't I? Fearless lady cop. If you'd chase me up onto a roof with no gun, this Lockhart asshole should be a walk in the park."

I swallowed so he wouldn't see the frenzy of loathing and anxiety and fear Lockhart's name conjured. "Yeah, Dmitri. You've got me."

He threw the bottle into a plastic garbage can and picked up the DVD, twirling it around one finger. "Let's see what's on this disc."

I don't know," said Pete Anderson when I called him from Sunny's cell. "Video isn't really my area of expertise."

"Come on, Pete," I pleaded. "You'd be doing me a service. I need a handsome man with a laptop and a brain."

He sighed. "You know I would like nothing better than to rush to your rescue, Luna. There's a problem, though."

I growled. "What now?"

"You're barred from the labs," he said. "Some tool named Wilbur Roenberg sent around an all-staff e-mail with your picture, explaining that you'd been fired and were banned from the premises."

I gripped the phone so hard the plastic creaked. *Tool* didn't even begin to describe Roenberg.

"Is it true?" said Pete, sounding hurt that I hadn't called him before anyone else to relay the news. "Are you really axed?"

"Afraid so," I said.

"So . . . who's handling these three murders now?" he asked.

"David Bryson," I said. The name tasted bad.

"Oh, gods," Anderson groaned. "That guy. Wouldn't know trace evidence from his own ass if it bit him. He contaminates the scene and then raises hell with me for not finding anything."

"If you want to really turn the screws on Bryson, help me look at this tape," I said. "If we could get a positive

ID, I can give it to my lieutenant, and he'll make the arrest. Not only will a dangerous, er, murderer be off the streets, but you can make Bryson look like a horse's ass." And stop a witch bent on Hex-knew-what evil, but I didn't spread that info to Pete. He was plain human, after all.

"Where can we work on the video?" he asked.

Dmitri was going to kill me for this. "Take the expressway to the old Appleby Acres exit, and go until you hit the Crown Theater."

Pete went silent. "That's Ghosttown, Detective."

"I'm aware, Pete."

"Okay," he said after a moment. "But if something in there eats me, I'm blaming it all on you."

I went to the front of the Crown and stood on the curb, watching the empty boulevard for Pete's headlights and wishing I smoked or knitted or did anything to occupy my mind other than rock on the balls of my feet.

The moon, a circle with one edge just slightly flat, hung over the dim lights of Ghosttown like a pale, bald eye peering over the horizon. I looked up and felt my skin prickle and the stab in my lower back as my breathing slowed and the power of the phase overtook me. Not yet moonrise, but coming too fast for comfort. The night sounds of the city flowed away and there was nothing but me and the blessed, bright moon.

"Not so bad, is it?"

I nearly leapt out of my rapidly phasing skin. "Dmitri!"

He lit a clove and blew smoke into the black sky. "When you don't fight it, it can be wonderful. Something you never learn unless you're part of a pack."

My hands and face stung as the phase retreated and I blinked to clear the yellow from my eyes.

"I don't think *wonderful* is ever the adjective I would use for the phase."

Dmitri dragged and jerked his chin at my shoulder. "He worked you over good."

I was glad there were no streetlights so he couldn't see my shamed flush. "Who?"

"You know who. That Serpent Eye cocksucker who gave you the bite and decided he didn't want you."

"His name was Joshua," I whispered. "And he did want me. He wanted me badly. I was the one who ran." Only a half-truth, but I couldn't admit that Joshua had been so bad that even knowing what I knew now about how it feels to be severed from your pack, I would still be racing up that beach road in the dark.

Dmitri dropped his butt and stamped it out. "You don't have to suffer for him, Luna."

I slid a glance to his profile. "Come again?" I said.

Dmitri took a deep breath. "I could give you the bite and make you a Redback like me," he let out in a rush.

My heart did a rapid slam-dance against my rib cage before settling somewhere in the region of my belt buckle.

"How?" I whispered.

"It's easy," Dmitri shrugged. "Another pack leader gives an Insoli the bite and claims her as his own."

"Claims me. Like a slave."

Dmitri shook his head violently. "Never. Some pack leaders work like that, but never me. I wouldn't make the mistake Joshua obviously did." He looked me in the eye. "You deserve a pack, Luna. Think about it."

I had never been more relieved to see a plain white sedan pull up to the curb and Pete Anderson emerge.

Dmitri scented plain human and snarled. "Who the fuck is this?"

"Holy shit," Pete squeaked, holding his laptop case in front of him like a shield. He pointed a quivering finger at me. "I'm with the detective!"

"You invited this human here?" Dmitri spat.

"He's going to help us with the disc," I soothed. "It's fine."

"You know, Luna, just when I start liking you, you pull something like this," Dmitri snapped, throwing open the Crown's door and storming inside.

I kicked the pavement. "Hex you, Dmitri."

"Listen, if this is a bad time . . . ," Pete started.

"No," I snapped, opening the door and jerking Pete inside the theater by the arm. "This is the perfect time and he is just going to have to *get over it*!" No one heard me but a pair of Redbacks disassembling a motorcycle block in the lobby. I sighed and led Pete through the seating pit and into the makeshift rec room where Sunny was glaring at me with what could only be described as an evil eye.

"Sunny, Pete and Pete, Sunny," I introduced, handing the DVD to Pete.

"Pleasure," he said as he plugged in his laptop. I saw Dmitri sulk into the doorway and watch the three of us cluster around the monitor, but I ignored him. He couldn't run steaming hot and snarly and then expect me to beg for more.

"Okay," said Pete, popping the DVD into the laptop's drive. He opened the editing suite and watched as a progress bar lit up the screen. "So this is your basic E and C."

"E and C?" I said, feeling like the only caster in a roomful of bloods. Normally, I was good with computers—I could make them sit up and do a trick or two where protected files and passwords were concerned—but digital tape was beyond me.

"Enhance and capture," said Pete patiently. "Look, why don't you just sit back and watch, okay?"

"She will not," said Sunny. "You may be smart but that doesn't exempt you from manners."

"Listen, I didn't have to come to this hellhole," said Pete, grimly pressing buttons. "Being around people with the blood makes me tense, so give me some space."

"Sunny." I held up a hand to ease her. "Let him work, okay? We need this footage."

"Call my house a hellhole again and I'll tear out your tongue for an appetizer," said Dmitri from the doorway. Pete's breathing hitched. Dmitri grinned, showing fanged-out teeth. "No pressure, Petey."

I shot Dmitri a glare that would Hex a daemon. He flipped a hand like we weren't worth his time and strode off to Hex knew where. Fine. Who needed his sexy ass anyway?

Pete rapidly saved and moved a series of files to the desktop. After a moment he clicked on the one named VIDEO and a player opened, showing a grainy moving image in which I could barely make out a stripper on the tiny stage of Double Trouble. Her face and the crowd were lost in a haze of pixels.

"This is a shitty Web cam that was transferred to DV," Pete said. "I don't know how much better I can make the image quality."

I leaned forward and squinted at the upturned faces of the men. Somewhere, the witch was in there. Lockhart, too. "Try."

Pete heaved a sigh. "Fine." He stopped the footage and began selecting tools from the bar at the bottom of the screen. "I'll equalize the levels as much as I can. Filter out the noise, the unnecessary pixels in the image field."

I pointed at the crowd. "Let's isolate the frames where the guys at the stage are facing the camera."

"Do you have any idea how long that will take?" Pete asked me.

"We're looking for the man who killed a member of this house's pack," I said. "It would behoove you to do it."

Pete blinked. "Wow. You didn't tell me that."

"Moonrise is in a couple of hours," I said. "Get to work." I didn't add the obvious—that when the moon came up I would be just as phased as everyone else in the pack house and Pete would be screwed—but from the ferocity of his typing I think he got the message.

He fast-forwarded the footage, filters working on the bad lighting and low quality to bring a slightly blurry but well-lit picture to life on the screen. Every time the camera caught the flash of a patron's face turned toward it, Pete captured the frame and saved it as an image file.

After almost forty-five minutes, the tape was over and Pete's desktop was full of images. He closed the video, cutting Katya off in midgrind. She hadn't been a terribly attractive girl in life, but she moved with the sensuous confidence of a trained dancer.

"Okay," said Pete. "I'm done." He stood up and rubbed his eyes. "You guys go on playing Dick Tracy. I'm headed home."

"Thanks for your help," Sunny called after him. Pete's cell phone trilled and he answered it, walking out without a word to us.

"Your friend isn't socially retarded or anything, no, sir," said Dmitri with sarcasm that could blister paint. He flopped himself on the sofa, a fresh drink in hand.

I shrugged. "It comes with the skills."

"So, can we look?" asked Sunny eagerly. I took Pete's chair and began opening the image files. A lot of them were useless half profiles caught in low light or men looking at their feet and showing us the tops of a lot of bald heads.

We clicked through at least sixty pictures and with each one my hope that Stephen, the witch, or Regan Lockhart had been in Double Trouble before he tore Katya's throat faded, and my potential arrest warrant with it.

"Just a few more," said Sunny, and yawned. "If I'm sleeping here, I have a feeling I'll need to get a head start on the night."

"We'll finish after this one," I said. I was tired, too, the day from hell starting to catch up with me. All I really wanted to do was sleep for about two years, wake up, and realize this had all been a sadistic and extremely vivid dream.

I opened the next file and stared at the pale face caught full on camera. My breath caught. Dmitri leaned over my shoulder. "What? You got something?"

"Him," I said matter-of-factly. I felt like the floor had dropped out from under me and I was plummeting.

The face on the tape was familiar to me, hawk nose and hard eyes catching mine. But it wasn't Regan Lockhart or a nameless blood witch.

The face staring back at me from the screen was Alistair Duncan's.

TWENTY-ONE

S hock is a funny thing. You think you're fine, sitting there and watching something too hideous to comprehend unfold before your eyes, and it's only later that you come to realize that you're comfortably outside your body, watching it react and seeing the horror grow on your own face. You don't really feel your head go light as the blood drops out of it or the numbness in your shaking hands until someone brings you back to yourself, as Sunny did to me.

"Alistair Duncan," she said quietly. "He's the district attorney, isn't he?"

We were sitting by ourselves on a loading dock at the rear of the Crown. I'd been silent the entire time, thoughts rushing and tripping through my head in a maelstrom too quick to comprehend.

I just nodded at Sunny's question.

"He killed those women?"

"How could I be so stupid?" I asked no one. How, indeed? A smart cop would have long ago recognized Duncan's machinations for what they were. I was blind.

Oblivious. I'd let Alistair Duncan slide away from me as easily as his knife slipped through the three women's flesh.

"You're scaring me," said Sunny, sparing a glance away from the pavement in front of us. "Your face . . ."

"I'm fine," I whispered. "I'm fine."

"What do we do now?" said Sunny.

I knew I had to tell Sunny the truth—she was my cousin, she was in the crossfire, she had to know. Still, it was the most difficult thing to open my mouth and start talking. "If Al Duncan murdered three women, we're not safe, even here. By now Lockhart knows that I'm not in custody, and that means Duncan knows."

Sunny said nothing, just stared ahead into the black alley that faced us, her face grimmer than I could ever remember it being. "So what you're saying is, we're dead."

"I am so sorry, Sunny . . ."

She held up a palm. "Don't, Luna. You're not sorry. It's your nature to hound things until you catch them or drop dead."

I pulled my knees to my chest, stung. "That was such a shitty thing to say."

Sunny pinched the point between her eyes. "I'm sorry."

"Me, too."

"So what do we do now?"

What a truly excellent question from my ever-practical cousin. Every bone in my body screamed *Action!*—go to Duncan's place, kick his door in, hunt him down, and make him feel terror for once in his entirely too-long life.

But the real answer was, there was nothing I could do. I no longer had the authority to as much as look at Al Duncan cross-eyed. I wasn't a cop anymore.

I was just Insoli.

"Luna?" Sunny crossed her arms expectantly.

"How should I know?" I threw up my hands. "We sit here and wait for Duncan to kill more women, and finish whatever the Hex he's trying to do just like the rest of the city."

Sunny gave me the look, with the one cocked eyebrow. The one that said I had let her down in some unimaginable way. It stung, not because it was undeserved. I had let her down. I had let down Dmitri and Lilia, Katya and Marina, McAllister and everyone who thought I was capable of not screwing up. Just another inept human who ran against a blood witch and lost badly.

"Where's the box with the Cedar Hill files?" I demanded, jogging inside the Crown, Sunny at my heels.

"What are you doing?" she asked as I began to rip papers from their folders, tossing Levinson's spellbook aside.

"Alistair is after the same daemon as Marcus. There's got to be a thread." The top page of the transcript from Marcus's bail hearing caught my eye. Marcus had been released into his parents' custody at that hearing, been taken to their home, and promptly savaged another woman. The system had done a bang-up job.

The smudged and many-times-xeroxed copy listed basic information like name of defendant, judge, docket number, date. In the box for legal counsel for the defense, the name *Alistair L. Duncan* was typed neatly on the line. She looked over my shoulder.

"Hex me."

Alistair had been Marcus Levinson's attorney thirty years ago. He had learned all of Marcus's secrets, and now Marcus was dead and Alistair had them all to himself.

"We have to find Stephen."

"Why, and who's Stephen?" Sunny asked.

"Stephen Duncan, Alistair's son. He disappeared after Duncan bailed him out. He's the one with the mark." I tossed the spellbook to Sunny. "Figure out how to read this. Dmitri and I are going out."

"Where are you going?" Sunny yelled as I jumped the stairs and jogged up the aisle toward the door. I didn't reply, because the answer would provide Sunny with entirely too much satisfaction. There was only one person I knew who could attempt to call a mark, and much as the thought of seeing her sent heat and anger racing along my spine, if I didn't find Stephen soon we were all screwed.

The light in my grandmother's small cottage, perched on a dead-end road at the dead end of the cliffs at Battery Beach, was still on when we pulled up. As a worthy witch whose magick rose and fell with the moon, she would probably be staying up until it set.

I was just glad it hadn't risen yet. My tattoo and the pentacle were holding back the phase, but the back spasms were getting closer and closer together, sharper and more persistent. Merely a friendly reminder from my body of what I was about to give birth to.

Grandma Rhoda opened before my first knock fell. "Luna," she said, blue-white eyes flicking up and down me once before settling on Dmitri. "And I don't believe I know you."

"This is Dmitri, Grandma," I said with a forced smile. "We need your help with something."

She considered that for a minute. My grandmother

was the consummate woman of few words, unless she was scolding Sunny and me. Finally she sighed. The verdict was in my favor.

"You'd better come inside, then."

Dmitri had to duck to make it through the narrow front door, but he did it gracefully and wiped his boots once we were in. "This is a nice place, Mrs. Wilder."

"My name is Swann," she told him curtly. "*Wilder* was the unfortunate surname of the animal my daughter married."

"She means *animal* figuratively, right?" Dmitri whispered.

I glared. "Don't be an ass."

Grandma walked to the exact center of her small living room and then turned to us, arms folded. "So, Luna. What have you gotten yourself into this time?"

I ordered my inner fifteen-year-old not to chafe at the tone and posture that even now I associated with the worst contempt. I only partially succeeded, because when I gestured to her denim love seat and asked, "Should we all sit down?" it came out sounding like I was being punished and had just been grounded from my boyfriend.

"The moon rises at eight twenty-one tonight, Luna. It is currently seven thirty-eight. Get on with it."

"Damn it, Grandma. Sit down," I ordered. "This is going to take a minute."

She glared at me, as only a hardened caster witch can glare, but she folded her shawl more tightly around her body and sat. I took Dmitri's wrist and pulled him down next to me.

Then I told my grandmother everything, starting with Lilia and working my way toward Stephen Duncan and my burning need to find him.

"And we have to do it before his father finds him. He's the only lead we have to Alistair."

Grandma rubbed her chin with a smooth hand, and then chuckled. Dmitri grunted. "Something funny?"

"Not really," my grandmother said. "Just that for someone who strives for normalcy, Luna, you certainly have been keeping some strange company."

"It's not by choice," I told her tightly. Her and her damn smug after-the-fact pronouncements.

"Of course not," she said with a solicitous nod. Standing, she went to a mellowed oak armoire in the corner and opened it wide, revealing rows of jars and bundles of herbs so neat they'd make Professor Hoskins proud.

"I can do my best to find this Duncan boy," she said. "But calling a mark is not the same as scrying for lost car keys."

She spread a blue cloth marked with her circle across the table and got out a censer similar to Sunny's, only older and crackling with a lot more power.

"You might wanna watch out with that," Dmitri told her. "Last time Sunny used one of those things it ended up planted in a wall."

"Oh, really," said Grandma, turning her eye on me. I cursed silently.

"When were you going to inform me of the mark being warded, Luna?" she asked, putting a stick of sage into the censer and taking a birch caster out of her casting box.

"Just do your best, Grandma, please," I begged. "This could be a matter of life and death."

"You know it is traditional for caster witches to demand payment in advance of a working that could compromise their safety," Rhoda said, pausing with the matches to light the censer in her hands.

I felt my face go crimson. "You have got to be joking."

Rhoda crossed her arms. "Luna, you of all people should know that this is not a joking matter. A warded mark could cause serious harm, kill me even." She smiled. It wasn't a happy smile. "But then again, you never cared much for the safety of others, did you?"

Red rage clamped down over my good sense and I was on my feet, finger jabbing in her face before I knew it. "Listen, you miserable old bat! I had enough of you when I lived here, and I don't have to put up with your shit anymore!"

"I believe you do," said Rhoda in that infuriating tone that she used with nonwitches and small children, "if you want me to call this mark."

Hex it, she was right and she knew it. I clenched my hands hard enough to bruise my palms, and took deep breaths until I lost count. "What's your payment?"

"If I find this person for you," said Rhoda, lighting the censer and fanning the smoke with her hand until it boiled over the edges, "you will release Sunflower from her obligation to you and allow her to return to live with me."

"Sunny doesn't *want* to live with you! She thinks you're out of your nuts-to-begin-with mind as much as I do!"

Rhoda sat at the table and placed one hand on her caster. To Dmitri she said, "Be a dear and get me that crystal on the leather thong from my cabinet."

Dmitri handed it to her with distaste and stepped away from the circle. I felt the magick stir as the working coiled and readied itself.

"Sunny is *not* leaving," I said again.

"Perhaps, but she will be allowed to make that choice for herself and not out of any cockeyed obligation to her stupidly unfortunate relatives." Rhoda folded her hands over her caster and smiled placidly at me. And why shouldn't she? She had won.

I started to sit in the circle, and she pushed me off. "Ah-ah. No weres in the circle. The energy becomes unforgivably tainted."

"What *is* it with you caster snobs?" I muttered. Dmitri favored my grandmother with a soft growl.

"Try it and I'll fix you so fast you'll never even be able to contemplate having pups" was her response. Dmitri raised an eyebrow at me.

"Charming, isn't she?" I said.

"Luna, spread out the city map on the table inside the circle," she ordered, "and step back."

I did as she asked and wriggled as Rhoda's working slid over my skin. Sunny's magick always made me feel like I had a bad case of gooseflesh, but Rhoda's was a firm cold pressure on the skin, one that you itched to brush off as soon as it touched you.

The birch caster began to crackle while Rhoda stayed stock-still with her eyes rolled back in her head, humming softly.

I had forgotten how freaky it can be watching someone in a trance state—she's there but she's not, just a sham body standing in front of you while the person you know gets replaced by something other.

My grandmother took the crystal between her fingers robotically. It began to describe a small circle over the neat pink-blue-green grid of the Nocturne City Chamber of Commerce map. Rhoda's humming rose in tone until it began to grate on my ears, and her eyelids fluttered like butterflies in the throes of a hurricane.

I saw her arm tense and knew the mark had been touched by her working. Rhoda gasped, and then strangled as she fought for breath, the crystal falling to the floor.

"Shit," Dmitri muttered.

I won't lie and say I was filled with shock and concern, but I did reach into the circle and shake her shoulder once.

Rhoda choked, rigid as rigor, blue beginning to creep around the outside edges of her lips. When our skin made contact I felt the sick prick of blood magick, and I knew she'd found Alistair Duncan.

"Let go!" I screamed, grabbing Rhoda by the collar and trying to shake her out of her trance.

Dmitri pulled my hands off her. "Move," he demanded, and took hold of the caster, which was rippling like wax over an open flame, pressing it down to the table with a slam.

Flames popped from the table and Dmitri was flung backward into the nearest wall, leaving a burned replica of Stephen's mark etched into the center of the map. A polite warning to anyone else stupid enough to try to see past the wards.

Grandma slumped over in her chair, her eyes coming back into focus. "Luna," she said, surprised. She rubbed her throat. "I felt hands. Around my neck."

"I am so sorry," I whispered. Seeing the blue handprints around Rhoda's throat, I hated Alistair Duncan for thinking I could be flicked away so easily.

"It's not the first time I've encountered something unsavory on the other side," said Rhoda raspily. "Don't you worry, although I know you never do."

She gave a small sigh and then slumped against me, out cold. "Hex me," I muttered as I propped her up.

Dmitri pulled himself to his feet. "She okay?" His eyes were saucer-wide and dark with near panic.

I hauled Rhoda up and supported her with one of my shoulders. "Fine. It takes a lot out of you."

Dmitri half carried Rhoda to one of the sofas and laid her down. "So now what?"

I looked down at the map of the city. Somewhere amid five million people a monster was looking back at me, and laughing.

It was a crazy idea, even more so because despite my tendency to shapeshift at inopportune times and attract absolutely the wrong kind of witchly attention, I had absolutely no aptitude for magick. Sunny and Rhoda were the ones in the family with all the witch genes. I was just the boring one who got an unlucky bite on the neck.

I went to the cabinet and looked at the ordered jars, none of which held what I needed. My hands shook as I felt far back for the locked black lacquered box I knew was there. I found it and took it out, turning to Dmitri. "Help me?"

"With what?"

I gently pulled aside Rhoda's shawl and found the small square key to the box. I unlocked it and found a plastic baggie of gray herbs, resembling burned tobacco.

"Go into the kitchen," I instructed, trying to keep my voice strong. "Find me a bowl—glass or ceramic—and some more matches."

I set the box on the table and went to the bottom drawer of the armoire. Out came a round flat mirror, which I set to the left of the city map. Visions came unbidden, of a smaller, more curious Luna who dared to peek into her grandmother's private room when she heard strange noises and who saw white eyes, a rigid face, and putrid poison smoke rising from a burning bowl. A flat mirror with faces reflected in it, faces that screamed and clawed and tried to break free.

Dmitri came back with a brown bowl and a box of kitchen matches. "This okay?"

"Fine," I said distractedly. Better than telling him the truth—that the flat mirror sitting innocuously on the table scared the hell out of me.

"Now, what in all the fires of the Hex Riots are we doing?" he asked.

I dumped the herbs into the bowl, realizing I had no clue what the correct proportion was.

"We're going to catch ourselves a spider," I said, lighting a match. "Stand back. The fumes are toxic."

"Whoa," said Dmitri, grabbing the match from me and pinching it out. "Toxic? What *is* it?"

I sighed. "Nightshade. Nightshade and a scrying mirror. This is how we find Stephen."

Dmitri was already shaking his head. "No way. No way am I going to let you do that when your gran was almost popped just for holding a piece of wood." He frowned. "Besides, don't you have to be a medium or a witch or something to scry with a mirror? Less control than a caster."

"Sure you're not a witch?" I threw back.

He crossed his arms. "Dated a few in my time."

"Either you shut up and hold my hands, or get out," I said. "I'm the only one here to do it, so I'm doing it. If I can't call Stephen's mark I'll just have to find him the old-fashioned way. With or without you, knight in shining biker leathers."

"You," Dmitri informed me, "are a pain in the ass." He sat across the table from me and extended his hands palms-up.

I lit the match and dropped it into the nightshade. Immediately blue-gray smoke began to roil as the leaves curled and burned.

"Bright Lady of the Moon," I whispered, the only prayer I knew. "Bright Lady of the Moon, please let me see." I reached across the table for and gripped Dmitri tightly. I held on to the warmth and the rough palms, letting it anchor me to the world of the visible and bright and living.

Then I lowered my head and breathed.

TWENTY-TWO

At first, I saw nothing. My vision swam with black haze and caustic smoke. A breeze ruffled my hair, and cleared the smoke to reveal a plain room with a bank of windows looking into nothing.

Alistair Duncan faced away from me, standing. An aura moved around him, slimy and silver-gray like oil. I supposed it had always been there. It would explain why my skin crawled whenever he got close to me.

"I'm very disappointed in you." His voice came from down a long tunnel, lips not quite moving in sync.

Beyond Duncan, through my skewed viewing of the room, I detected another presence. Duncan was speaking to a tall, indistinct figure whose skin was fairly bathed in gold. His aura, however, was so black that it sucked the magick from the very air, like a collapsed star vibrating around his form.

"You are nothing but a puppet," Duncan was saying, "A puppet I've spent a great deal of time and energy on, and you *will* obey me."

The golden figure looked into my eyes, and I felt like

someone had wrapped my heart in ice. He smiled, and I *felt* the words. "Release me, Luna."

How in Hex did he know me? I didn't want this strange figure with his inhumanly blank aura to know me. His eyes felt like they pierced flesh and saw secrets. They hurt.

"Alistair." A voice broke into the rush of the nightshade vision, and Duncan whipped his head to the right.

"What in the name of all things Hexed could be important enough to interrupt this?"

"Stephen's gone, Alistair."

Duncan cursed and walked out of my line of sight. He returned dragging one of the thugs who had held me down in Maven's while Cassandra cut me. Duncan shoved the thug to his knees and pointed at something on the floor I couldn't see. The overdressed muscle hissed as he touched the floor, and I could only imagine what kind of calling circle Alistair had drawn. Black and writhing and headache-inducing. That seemed to be his style.

"If you don't find him," Duncan was saying, "you will be joining the imperfect circle for good. Am I clear?"

The thug squirmed. "Clear! But he's gone home!"

Duncan released him. The golden figure watched these proceedings with a lazy grin and I realized why the thug wasn't freaking out. Only Duncan and I could see what was in the circle.

The haze began to gather again, and I had the feeling of the floor spinning and falling out from underneath me. The voices of Duncan and his thug grew warbly. The nightshade was wearing off.

I spun around in the vision, a move that made me more than a little likely to throw up, and cast about for any sign of a landmark I could use.

"Why did he go home?" Duncan asked as my eyes lit on the intertwined AA writ large on the wall behind the thug's head. Appleby Acres. Ghosttown.

"He said he had to visit them," said the thug. "He wasn't making any sense, Alistair."

Duncan released the thug with a kick and turned back to the circle, but the golden daemon was a faded aural memory. "No! Hex it!" Duncan screamed, kicking the circle open with a foot across the markings. He turned on the thug. "Find him, or it's you we'll be feeding Meggoth with."

The thug scrambled out of the room, and my vision went black.

I came back to myself slumped over the table, choking with the scent of burned nightshade in my nose. I felt weak and roiled and my stomach lurched when I lifted my head.

"Luna." Dmitri lifted my chin with his hand. "There you are."

I coughed again and managed to nod. "I saw him."

"Where?"

I reached for my notebook and pen. "I don't know. Somewhere in Ghosttown. Old Acres symbol on the wall, pre-Riots." I sketched the symbol quickly and held it out to Dmitri.

"Only place I know of that the packs haven't picked over is the old housing authority. Nothin' up there except a bunch of office furniture and rotary phones."

"Was it burned during the Riots?"

"Part of it," said Dmitri, helping me up. "Some of the offices didn't get it too bad."

I carefully locked my grandmother's door behind us as he helped me out to the bike. "Then that's where Alistair Duncan is."

"Duncan is the one who murdered Lilia?" Dmitri asked. I nodded.

"I'll kill him," said Dmitri.

"Be serious," I said. "The man is a district attorney. If you kill him as payback for Lilia, you'll be in Los Altos breathing in cyanide gas before you can say *vigilante*."

Dmitri's face turned a hard, ugly kind of determined that frightened me. I knew the look of violence, and when the look came on so fast and furious the only thing you could hope to do was get out of the way. "I don't care," he said. "I haven't cared since Lilia died. I knew I wasn't coming out alive, but I'll be damned if I let the bastard get away free."

"He's a blood witch, Dmitri, one who's been practicing for almost thirty years. You won't be able to kill him. We find Stephen, make sure he's safe. Alistair is too much for you alone."

"He's a man. He bleeds," said Dmitri.

I bit my lip as he got on the bike and glared until I joined him.

"I don't know if Duncan is a man, anymore," I said quietly as Dmitri hit the accelerator and we roared away from the cliffs, back toward Nocturne City.

He didn't have a response for that.

The lamps along Alistair Duncan's street flickered as Dmitri pulled the bike to the curb. The old gas lights cast an orange glow over the pavement and blurred the edges of everything, making the entire street into a dream scene.

I whispered to Dmitri, "Wait here for me."

"No way," he rumbled. "I'm not leaving you alone in that house."

"If you go in then I will have contaminated the crime scene," I said. "I can't risk it."

Dmitri growled and made a move to follow me. I put my hand flat against his chest. "I'll be fine. Really."

"The minute I hear anything, I'm coming after you," he promised.

I didn't answer. Dmitri had been kind and bought my ridiculous excuse. Even now I entertained the fantasy that if I could just catch Duncan in the act, a spontaneous working would ensue and I would have my job and my reputation magicked back to me.

Duncan's house was dark, a pile of newspapers on the lowest step. His clay urns of flowers were wilted, and two package notices from the postal service flapped on his front door.

I took the Colt out of my waistband and eased the storm door open. The knocker fell once, twice. Only silence answered me.

Up and down the street, only a few lamps burned behind the leaded-glass windows of the old homes. A wind ruffled the spring leaves in the trees along the street and my hair.

I took off my borrowed jacket and wrapped it around my hand. I prayed Alistair Duncan didn't have a fancy alarm system to go with his fancy house, and punched the glass in the door.

It shattered, fragments tinkling into the house, small thuds as they hit the carpet runner in the foyer. I examined the jacket and found a large and irreparable tear up the back. Great. Another reason for Olya to bitch at me.

I glanced over my shoulder at the street. Dmitri leaned against his bike, the glow from his cigarette making his face a black hollow behind it.

He stood at my look, but I waved him back and worked my hand through the jagged hole in the glass, sliding the old-fashioned bolt lock on Duncan's door free. I pulled my hand back, too fast. It caught the glass, and an L-shaped cut blossomed on my palm. I bit my lip and held in the pain. If Stephen or Duncan's little vampire brigade or any combination thereof was inside, it wouldn't do any good to let them know I was here before I was good and ready to do some butt kicking.

The door shut behind me with a creak of old springs. The air inside Duncan's house was close, with an unpleasant undertone that was sharp and overwhelming at the same time. The thickness coated my throat, and I tried not to choke.

A ruin of charred logs, but no fire in the sitting room fireplace. Piles of dishes in the kitchen sink and used paper plates filling the garbage. A soft buzzing of flies. I didn't check the downstairs bathroom but assumed the worst.

Duncan's study, by contrast, was immaculate and covered with dust. The only paper on top of his enormous, mellow-varnished editor's desk was a copy of Stephen's arrest report. My signature sat at the bottom of the first page as the arresting officer, black and spindly.

The circuit of downstairs led me back to the foyer and up a wide staircase. The air was warmer on the second floor, and even closer. Patches of dampness blossomed on the back of my shirt.

A narrow hallway revealed three doors leading off. I pushed the first open and stepped back quickly, aiming the Colt in and covering all the corners. A guest bedroom. I couldn't imagine Alistair and Stephen going in for lavender prints, so Duncan's wife must have designed it before she died.

The next door was Stephen's room, still decorated in the cranberry-and-gold Alder Bay Academy colors, with plaid wallpaper to match. A posed portrait of Stephen in his lacrosse uniform, poster-size, dominated the wall over the bed. Trophies marched across a bookcase that held few books. No wonder the kid was screwed up.

The last door was at the end of the hall, leading to a large room that spanned the back half of the house. The smell was worse here, and when I touched the doorknob it was sticky.

Something dark twisted in my gut. I did not, did not want to open that door.

I closed my eyes, breathed out, and pushed the door open, aiming in blind with my gun. Nothing. No daemons and no monsters reaching out to grab at me.

I opened my eyes. Then I screamed. I screamed for Dmitri and for the panic roiling itself upward to the forefront of my mind as I saw the three women's bodies spread-eagled on Alistair's bedroom floor, all of them mutilated, all of them dead.

It seemed like hours but it was probably less than ten seconds before Dmitri kicked open the front door, bounded up the stairs, and grabbed me, pulling me away from the open door. "Hex me," he muttered when he looked inside.

"Hoskins," I managed. "Hoskins said he needed seven."

"This is fucked," Dmitri was muttering. "Just fucked."

I pulled away from him and back into the room. Sigils were painted on all four walls, huge ones. They bore little resemblance to Stephen's, but they were still hideous, twisted images that made my forehead ache and my skin heat to look at them. Stare for too long and they seemed to twist and come alive, reaching out millions of bloody arms for me.

The three women were lined up neatly on the floor, like logs. The cheap single mattress and bed frame, the only pieces of furniture in the room, were soaked in their blood.

"Stay outside," I told Dmitri. "I just want to check the bodies." The women had no throats to feel, but I picked up each of their hands and found the squishy limpness of the several days' dead. Rigor mortis passes and the body become pliable, like a doll. Their faces were frozen, mostly in grimaces of bloody terror: three of the missing girls from the past year's unsolved cases.

"I'm sorry," I whispered to each of them, closing their eyes. I searched the room for anything else I could use, but Duncan had removed all tools of his ritual and there was nothing left except dead girls.

I sat on the edge of the blood-spattered mattress and put my head in my hands. I was too late. Stephen had been taken, Alistair—or whatever he was—had gotten away free and clear and with six sacrifices to his name, and all I had to show for it was a lost job, another crime scene, and Dmitri, who was watching me from the doorway with that penetrating green stare.

"I've seen some things," he said. "But not like this."

You and me both, I wanted to say, but that old Hardened Cop Pride wouldn't let me. "With Lilia, Marina, and Katya this is six."

Dmitri frowned. "I'm not going to like what happens when he gets to lucky number seven, am I?"

"Meggoth will be free to do whatever the Hex he wants."

Dmitri passed a hand over his face. "Meggoth?"

"One of the names of a daemon Alistair Duncan is after."

He sighed. "Okay. How do we kill the fucker?"

"You had to ask that, didn't you?" I sighed. The closed bedroom had to be close to eighty degrees, and the smell was awful. I was exhausted and shaking, but I stood up and put my gun in my waistband. I had to see it through, for Sunny and the dead girls, and maybe, if I was honest, for Dmitri and his blood debt to Lilia.

From above my head, a ticking sounded.

Dmitri's slouched frame snapped upright. "The hell was that?"

I shushed him with a hand and redrew my gun. The small attic door across the room from me was firmly shut but not bolted. I carefully sidestepped the dead girls and drew it open.

"Careful . . . ," Dmitri whispered. I waved him off and flicked the light switch at the foot of the stairs. Nothing blazed to life. Heading alone into the darkened attic of a blood witch. Just what I live for.

Unlike the rest of the comfortably antique house, the attic stairs were narrow and uncarpeted, with old square nails sticking out at odd angles, ready to snag the unwary foot.

I felt around for my penlight, flashing on cobwebs and cardboard boxes labeled X-MAS, STEPHEN'S STUFF, and DIANE PROJECTS. Diane Duncan had been the wife. I wondered if she knew what Alistair had been up to. Some women found that sort of thing irresistible. Like being a rock groupie, with the slight chance you could be devoured by a summoned entity or used as a conduit in your witch's spells. Nice, innocent nonmagick blood was best for that sort of thing. Even better if you were a virgin.

I sneezed hard into my sleeve. The attic was dark,

dusty, and seemed utterly deserted. But I had not imagined the sound. I forced myself to take a quick sniff before the dust overwhelmed me again.

A whimper came from the far corner. I smelled live human, and stepped closer. My light caught pale blond hair and a face smeared with blood.

"Well, Stephen," I said, keeping my gun aimed. "You know how they say, *We really have to stop meeting like this*? In our case it should be, *We really have to stop meeting with you covered in blood and me pointing a gun at you*."

"Go away," he rasped at me.

"There's an original one," I said. "Got any more for me? Like *the were did it*? 'Cause that one was classic. Had me going for a good long time."

"I told you," he whispered. "I told you it wasn't me."

"And I believe you," I said, trying to be placating. I've never been very good at humoring people. I'd be terrible with suicides and hostage negotiation. Probably why I did so well in Homicide. The upset people were already dead.

Stephen's wild eyes roved over me, and he drew himself into a tighter ball. "Get away from me!" he screamed. "He sees everything I do!"

"If you're talking about Lockhart, he's not here right now. Nor is that escapee from the Cure's reunion tour Alistair sent to collect you. Just you and me, a couple of people talking."

"You don't understand," said Stephen.

"Then enlighten me," I said quietly. Behind me, the stairs creaked, and Dmitri made his presence known. He caught sight of Stephen and sucked in a breath.

"Hex me."

"The phase . . . ," Stephen said. "I can't control it. *He*

makes it come over me. *He* uses me. My *father.* He *compelled me.* I killed those girls down there. The hooker in the alley. Marina . . ." He shuddered. "I can't . . . be this thing anymore. I won't."

"Relax," I said. "Really. I promise that Alistair is not going to bother you again."

Stephen laughed. It was a creepy sound, dry and strangled. "You can't protect me, Detective. But you're welcome to try." He uncurled his body and sat up, staring straight into the light. His pupils contracted until his eyes looked pure white. "It'll come. I feel it. You wait."

"When did you find out your father was, er, magickally inclined?" I asked. As long as Stephen was up for crazy ramblings I could play along.

"We're wasting our Hexed time," Dmitri murmured.

"Shut up," I hissed.

"A long time," said Stephen. "I went away up north, to school, and then he couldn't call my mark as easily. But my mother died, and he got me back. You know what he said to me, after the funeral? He gave that bitch what she had coming . . . coming . . ." His back arched and his features rippled, like a miniature earthquake on his skin. I took a step back.

"Tried to warn you," Stephen moaned. "I tried, but he put it inside me and now I can never leave, I can never ever get it out . . ." His face twisted again and he screamed, a spasm passing through his body.

"Get out," Stephen suddenly said, his eyes snapping back into focus. His voice was clear and scared, but human. I imagined this was how he had sounded before Alistair got the claws into him. "He needs one more. Get out now—!"

It came before he could finish the sentence. I've phased countless times, but never seen it happen to another. Even so, I knew every muscle's pull, every agonizing stab of pain, the horrible, ecstatic molding and twisting of human into a were.

Stephen's face elongated in the jaws and he dropped to all fours, twitching and bunching until hair sprouted and his bloody shirt and pants fell away.

Dmitri grabbed my arm. "We need to get the Hex out of here."

"Wait!" I demanded. I couldn't tear my eyes away from Stephen. He was fully phased now, but like no were I had ever seen. He resembled more the image of a were from the mind of someone who had never seen the real thing. A lantern jaw, short stubby ears, patchy gray coat, and a misshapen body with a bloated stomach. The one thing that stood out vividly were rows of pointed, two-inch teeth jutting from his jaw. A red tongue with no place to go lolled on one side of the mouth.

The were raised its pinky-yellow eyes to mine and snarled, a wet sound. Black saliva oozed from between its misshapen teeth.

"Luna," Dmitri hissed in my ear. "Back away. Don't make any sudden movements. You'll just piss it off."

I was too scared to make the comment about Dmitri having a real talent for stating the obvious. He pulled hard on my arm and I slid backward a step, then another, feeling the cooler air from the downstairs tickle the back of my neck.

In front of us, Stephen padded forward on feet with malformed toes and curling black claws that scraped the naked wood. "Keep going," Dmitri muttered. "Don't you dare stop, lady."

The were-Stephen opened its mouth and roared. I jumped a yard out of my skin at the sound rattling around the small attic. Looking at its runny eyes, I saw an intelligence that while not human was far greater than any were I had encountered.

Something *other* was watching us out of Stephen's eyes, and it didn't appreciate the fact that we were trying to skip out on it.

I turned to Dmitri and met his eyes. "Run."

To give him credit, Dmitri didn't argue with me. He just dropped my arm and bolted, clearing the stairs as I dove down behind him and slammed the attic door shut, fingers slippery with other people's blood fighting the deadbolt. Dmitri shoved me aside and rammed it home as the were-Stephen hit it from the other side. Wood shook and splinters popped out around the door frame.

"Everything Hexed and holy," Dmitri panted as he braced his back against the door. "You ever see anything like that?"

"Nothing I want to remember," I said. "Come on!"

He shook his head. "You go. I'll hold it as long as I can."

I reached out and grabbed Dmitri by the front of his jacket. "Don't be noble. This is *really* not the time."

He tried to shake me off, snarling. Stephen hit the door again. "I'll take care of myself. Get away while you can."

Men.

I took a firmer hold on Dmitri and pulled him down to my level. "I am not a damsel in distress," I said. "And you are not my knight in shiny freaking armor. Got it?"

He nodded after a long moment. "Got it."

"Good. Run for your life."

Even as Dmitri let go of the door and Stephen crashed through it, he still had the thoughtfulness to grab my hand.

And they say chivalry is dead.

We only made it to the hall before Stephen caught us, still snarling that wet, unnatural sound. I turned to face him, drawing the Colt out of reflex. Stephen tensed and sprang in a fluid motion surprising for his malformed body. He hit me square in the chest and I caromed into Dmitri, both of us going down in a heap. The Colt went over the banister and slid off to parts unknown.

When my air came back and my vision resolved into something other than two spinning black circles, I was surprised not to see Stephen crouched over me, putting his huge teeth to good use.

He went right over me, stepping on my chest with all four feet before he bounded down the stairs and out the door Dmitri had kicked in. Tires squealed as he crossed the street.

I detangled myself from Dmitri and went after the were, arriving on the porch in time to see him disappear into the darkened park opposite the Duncans' house, yellow-pink eyes flashing before the trees swallowed him up.

The front porch seemed as good a place as any to lean on my knees and suck in precious air, so I did. Dmitri joined me a few seconds later.

"Shit!" he said, hitting the wall. "We lost him!"

"And you're upset by this?" I asked. "Did you see the size of those teeth?"

From a remote pocket in Dmitri's coat, a cell phone tone trilled. He and I both jumped. I smirked. "Never pegged you for a Barry Manilow fan."

"Shut it," he told me before answering. He handed the phone over almost immediately. "It's your cousin."

"You really need to get a new phone," said Sunny as soon as I said hello.

"It's going to be a little hard to turn in a claim to my former department that says, under reason, *Phone was melted by pure evil.*"

"The lock to Marcus's spellbook is pretty elementary," said Sunny. "He really wasn't a very skillful witch. And his handwriting sucks."

"How long before we know what it says?" I asked.

"Not long," said Sunny. "I just need you to stop by the cottage and pick up a few things for the working."

She rattled off a list. I kept my eyes to the shadows and watched for Stephen's return, but who was I kidding? He would run straight back to Alistair. Stephen was given no choice, just like I had no options. We were both driven by the phase, but as we pulled away from the Duncans' abattoir I hoped against hope that our destinations were different.

TWENTY-THREE

Whena we pulled up at the cottage, I smelled it on the gentle wind coming off the ocean, that burned, crisp smell that I had come to associate with pain and blood.

I stopped Dmitri with a hand from opening the door. "Someone's here."

He growled, shoulders rolling inside his jacket.

"Shh!" I hissed, wishing with all my heart that I had the Colt in my hand. Not that it would do any good, but I had been trained to feel secure with a weapon. It would at least stop me from trembling.

The door was still locked, and I gently turned the deadbolt and pushed it wide, springing back and peering into the dark sliver the door revealed. Dmitri, less than an inch away from me, sniffed. He smelled it, too.

I looked back at him and jerked my head, indicating we were going inside. He nodded, knotty hands going into fists, as I eased the door open with my shoulder and rapidly swept the living room.

The shadows were empty pools of blackness as far as my were eyes could tell, and I relaxed a fraction, letting out a tiny breath. I took another step inside, Dmitri still just behind me.

My attacker hit me from the side, where he'd been waiting behind the front door. It felt like a pipe, or a wrench, cold metal that burned where it impacted with my skull.

As I went to my knees and lost my grip on the gun I placed the shocky, short-breathed feeling from when I had been shot. Silver.

Over the throbbing in the back of my head, I rolled over to see my attacker, attired in the same mask and Windbreaker he'd worn days earlier, step in front of Dmitri. From my wonderful vantage point flat on the floor, I saw that I had landed in the center of a chalk circle.

I'd been inside plenty of circles. The pentacle and the four corners of power are not pleasant, but at least symmetrical and ordinary. This was a circle inscribed with crude letters around the edge and ugly, curlicue wards of power radiating from the center. It made me itch just being inside, and when I tried to roll out I found I couldn't move. The edges of the circle flared as the wards took hold and pinned me prone.

Dmitri made a move for the man in black, but he moved fluidly to the side and tossed a flat silver disk in Dmitri's path. The disk flashed and evaporated. Dmitri howled in pain as the light burned his sensitive eyes, dilated from the darkness, and lunged for my attacker once more before going to his knees, choking and spitting out blood.

My attacker laughed. "Don't worry, Sandovsky. No permanent damage, just a simple talisman to prevent you from getting too upset." Dmitri folded on his side, breathing labored.

He turned on me and removed his ski mask. "As for you, Detective Wilder . . . I'm afraid things are not so simple." He dropped the mask and smiled at me. "You shouldn't have come back here," Lockhart said. "I told you we see everything you do."

He opened his jacket to reveal the brands I had seen so closely the night he came into my bedroom.

"I knew it," I snarled. "I knew it since I saw you at Alistair's that night, when you let your glamour slip."

"Very observant, Officer. And it did you such a service in the end, eh?" He got a chair from the dining room and set it inside the circle next to me, hauling me up by my T-shirt to face Dmitri. Setting me in the chair almost gently, he left the circle and ripped the phone out of the wall to tie Dmitri's hands.

The wards had me functionally paralyzed. My mind was beyond panic, and saw the entire thing from the cool, detached viewpoint of "Oh."

"You killed Thorpe," I said.

Lockhart carefully skirted the edge of the binding he had imprisoned me in and brought out a small case that held soldering iron and a roll of shiny wire. "Why, yes, Detective, I did, after the flaming sidewalk failed to do the trick."

"You really thought you could scare me off from your master?" I snarled. "Your games don't impress me, you bastard."

Lockhart, closed the case and tossed it aside, smiling grimly. "Your problem," he said, plugging in the solder-ing iron and setting it on the table, "is that you don't take a hint." He tested the temperature against his finger, frowned, and turned the power up. "I told you to leave

Alistair Duncan alone. I shot you in the arm with a Hexed silver bullet—listen to me, I'm starting to talk like a plain human. My point being, any sane woman would have given it up. But not you. You just kept hunting him, like a wolf and a wounded deer, and frankly I'm at the end of my chain with your interference."

"What did Duncan do to you?" I sneered. "Torture? Threats? Or did he just dangle a big fat wad of cash and the chance to be a sick son of a bitch in front of you? You seem like you'd enjoy that."

Lockhart shook his head. "Not even close to it. You fail to understand, Detective—"

"I understand," I cut him off with a snarl. "I understand that you chose to become right hand to a man who murders innocent women—sacrifices them. And I understand you probably enjoy it as much as he does."

"Detective," said Lockhart impatiently as he took the iron off its stand and held it to the end of the wire, "what part of this are you not hearing? I do not work for Alistair Duncan. I mean to *dispose* of Alistair Duncan."

Nothing like having your righteous indignation cut off in midspeech to grab your attention. Even when I thought it couldn't get any worse, Lockhart kept right on rolling.

"What in the name of all things Hexed are you babbling about?" Dmitri demanded from the floor. The hot wire came close to him and he winced.

"Let me guess," I said flippantly, hoping it would distract Lockhart for a few more seconds. "Our friend here is a rogue daemon hunter wandering the night seeking revenge on all things magickally naughty."

"Wrong," Lockhart said with a thin smile, "except for one thing." He held the melting wire over Dmitri's arm and let it drip onto skin. It sizzled and Dmitri screamed. I could almost feel it on my own arm—hot, searing, nerve-burning silver. "I *am* a sick son of a bitch."

"Hex you!" I shouted at him. "You want me, then deal with me!"

"I've been Regan Lockhart for some time," he continued conversationally, ignoring my screams. "Only a bit less than the time Alistair Duncan made the mistake of thinking that he could be the one to call the daemon known as Meggoth. Thirty years, to be precise, waiting for Duncan to learn and for the circumstances and dates and times and tides and Inferno knows what else to be right for a calling. I've lived in this stinking world for too long to let Meggoth escape me again, Detective, and I won't have a pathetic Insoli were stand in the way of my hunt."

I stared at him, wanting to tear his throat out, which he interpreted as, *What?*

"Make no mistake," said Lockhart as he started to melt the wire again, "you've put up a very good fight. Between your interfering and those freaks Duncan has under his thumb, I almost lost the daemon. Fifty-seven years is enough time in this realm. I *won't* lose him."

The wire came close to Dmitri again and I screamed, "Don't!"

"No, no," Lockhart chastised. "You haven't learned your lesson quite yet."

"Leave him alone or I will rip your throat out," I snarled. "I swear on the moon."

Lockhart turned one eye on me.

"Detective Wilder, an Insoli were does not threaten a watchman. Shut your mouth."

I bared my teeth at him but kept quiet. Lockhart had all the aces. My only hope was to figure out what the Hex he wanted.

"Duncan mistook Meggoth for a true daemon, a resident of my jurisdiction, not one of the Abandoned. Meggoth has wandered your world since the Descent, hiding in the spaces between magick and mortality, waiting and watching and trying to find *her* since his exile."

The third time he came at Dmitri with the wire, Dmitri lashed out with his feet, trying to bite, kick, knee— anything to hurt Lockhart. Lockhart jumped out of the way, and the only thing Dmitri accomplished was falling forward into a prone position.

"The Abandoned are fugitives," said Lockhart. "Refuse. I was dispensed to bring Meggoth to our empire for punishment, and I have become very short on patience." He came to the edge of the circle and caressed the dancing wards with his fingers, making them crackle. "We are both hunters, Luna, relentlessly pursuing a target." He stood up again and took out the gun I remembered from the night he had shot me. "Unfortunately, you hold something that I must possess in order to subdue mine."

He bent over Dmitri with the wire again, this time touching it directly on to the skin.

"I'll tell you!" I jerked desperately against the binding. "Just stop! What do you want?"

Dmitri panted against the pain, bent almost into a fetal position. "Luna, don't . . . worry . . . about me."

"Touching," said Lockhart, reheating the wire and turning to me. "I seek Marcus Levinson's spellbook, the one he copied from the original tome written by the blood witch who sealed Meggoth in your world, safe from the Descent. Where's this book? Speak."

To tell would be to set Lockhart on Sunny. I looked to Dmitri's paper-white face and then down. "I can't tell you that."

Lockhart pulled out the gun, the one I remembered from the night he shot me. "Then we move to the next step." He chambered a round and held it against Dmitri's kneecap. "I mean you no disrespect," he told Dmitri. "Weres are a low form, but nonetheless you are one of us. Unfortunately, your companion and I are at cross purposes. We both want Duncan and Meggoth. I have—what do your plain humans call it—privilege of seniority?"

"She'll never tell you," Dmitri promised him. "She's stubborn as a phased were with a rare steak."

"Detective Wilder does not have a lot of options," Lockhart told him with that damn smug grin. "Either she refuses to tell me, ensures your death, and lives the rest of her life as a cop killer, or she speaks up like a sensible person and takes her chances on my goodwill." He ground the gun barrel deeper into Dmitri's knee and cocked his head at me. "Which is it, Detective?"

I have never begged for my life. Even in situations when I probably should have, I've never broken down, never given in to that deeper than deep belly-shaking fear that imminent death brings over a person.

But this wasn't another person. This was Dmitri. When Lockhart put his finger on the trigger I thought about Olya first. She would take losing her brother hard and badly. Sunny would cry for Dmitri. He would have to die knowing that he'd never fulfilled his pack duty to Lilia. According to weres, that meant he would never walk in an afterlife that held any kind of happiness.

Lockhart flicked off the Glock's safety.

"It's upstairs!" I blurted. "In Sunny's room."

I tried not to show that I had been holding my breath when Lockhart took the gun away from Dmitri's leg and holstered it. He reached into the circle and clamped his hand around my wrist. "Show me."

It was a horrible gamble, foolish and desperate, but I remembered the scream that had come from him when I smashed his face in with my tea mug. Lockhart felt pain, and he felt it when I swept up the hot soldering iron with my free hand and jammed it against his cheek. He threw me away from him, and my arm hit the outside of the warding circle. Pain raced across my entire frame like 220 volts lighting up a Christmas tree. I yanked my arm out of the binding wards and saw a neat circle of flesh seared away.

Lockhart doubled over, breathing hard through his nose but making no sound. "Bitch," he ground out.

I crawled to Dmitri and untied him with my good hand. "Nothing personal, Regan. After all, it's not even your face."

"You have no idea what you've landed in the middle of," he whispered. "Meggoth will kill you, and he will enjoy it. His sacrifices are finished and he can finally get what he wants. Why do you think I tried so desperately to bring him back?"

"I don't care, Lockhart," I said. "Alistair tried to kill me. You tried to kill me. At this point, I'm not differentiating. Take your holy daemon hunt and go Hex yourself."

Lockhart's smile was becoming decidedly creepy.

"You stupid were," he said. "Someone should have put you down at the beginning." Most of the skin on one of his cheeks had peeled away and the muscles twitched when he spoke. He picked up his gun and aimed one-handed, covering his burned face with the other. "But it doesn't matter now, Officer. You told me what I needed."

"Oh, I totally did not," I scoffed, mustering up a laugh. "You think I'd really tell you where the spellbook is? Get real."

Lockhart's face twisted and he chambered the gun, leaving smears of his own blood on the barrel. "Where is it?"

Behind me, Dmitri spoke up. "Leave her alone."

Lockhart swung the gun to Dmitri. "You are in no position to give orders, Mr. Sandovsky."

Dmitri got to his knees, shoulders hunched. With a roar, red fur erupted along his backbone and he fanged out, eyes going gold.

I took that as my cue to do something diversionlike and slammed a boot into Lockhart's kneecap, sending him to the ground. He screamed for a change, and the sound was almost musical.

I disarmed him, twisting his wrist almost completely around and applying pressure. When our eyes met the gun was against his forehead.

"You're not going to kill me," he rasped. "You don't have it in you."

I pressed the barrel of that gun against his skin hard enough to leave a mark, wanting so badly to pull the trigger and pay him back for the misery he caused. I wanted Regan Lockhart to hurt as I had hurt, I wanted him to feel pain and terror and helplessness.

The were commanded me to kill and take my dominance back.

"You're right," I finally said, swallowing hard to keep my voice even. My hand shook, but I thumbed the hammer down slowly, deliberately removed my finger from the gun's trigger guard. "You're right, Regan. I won't kill you."

I dropped the gun from his forehead and stared into his black, expressionless eyes, the eyes of someone faking human emotion and not doing a very good job. The glamour rolled back and his skin became waxy and hair-stiff, the barest shade of human.

"Don't you think for a second I don't have it in me," I hissed at him. "The only reason you're still alive is that you're not worth my fucking time."

He started to speak, but I stepped away and let Dmitri come forward.

The sounds Lockhart made when he saw Dmitri as a were, when Dmitri landed on him and put teeth to his throat, were indelible. I will hear them until I die.

Screams grated from his ruined throat until he had no more air or blood in his borrowed body. When Lockhart had bled out on my living room floor, Dmitri de-phased, naked and blood-covered.

"For Lilia, bastard," he said, and gave the body a kick.

"Pants?" I offered. It was the only coherent sentence I could think of. Pretend everything is normal and it will be. If I gave in to the building panic I would very likely spend the rest of my life in a padded room, wearing pajamas with Velcro fasteners.

Dmitri pulled his jeans back on and started threading his belt. "God damn," he said. "That was uncomfortable." He cast one last look at Lockhart. "He should have known better than to fuck with us, right?" The nervous musky smell coming off him told me he was as freaked out as I was, but he hid it a hell of a lot better. I decided if Dmitri could play it cool, so could I.

"You did good, Luna," he said, putting a hand on my shoulder. I ducked out from under it.

"Tell me that when we find Alistair and lock him in a deep dark hole until the Rapture."

"And if we don't?"

I closed my eyes. "Then we have a much bigger problem and all of this will just be an amusing footnote."

Dmitri said, "You're bleeding."

The spot where my arm had touched the binding wards hurt a lot now, and the circle of seared flesh was bleeding freely.

"You are, too," I said, trying to stanch the flow with the hem of my shirt.

"Who cares about me?" said Dmitri. "Get your ass upstairs so I can have a look at you."

I started to object to the continuation of the damsel treatment, but Dmitri pointed up the stairs. "Go."

"Only if you let me look at you, too," I relented, touching the silver burn on his forearm. He hissed and yanked it away.

"Fine. Let's just stop you from dribbling all over the floor before your cousin has heart failure."

"Makes sense, because she'll totally ignore the dead daemon bounty hunter on the floor and focus right on a few blood droplets from me."

Dmitri growled, showing teeth that were still fanged. Oddly attractive, on him, I decided. I also decided he made a good point about the blood after all and let him hustle me upstairs.

TWENTY-FOUR

I n the bathroom I fetched bandages, antiseptic, and peroxide and laid them out on the edge of the tub, then held out my hand. "Arm."

"No way," said Dmitri. "You first."

"Are we really going to argue about who gets to play doctor?" I must have flushed brighter than a sunburn at high noon, because Dmitri smirked.

"Maybe I just want to touch you first," he told me in that gravel-laced voice that spoke of sheets wrinkled and stockings torn.

I swallowed hard so I wouldn't squeak. "Why?"

"Maybe I like it," he murmured. A full-body chill danced over me. Whether or not my brain allowed me to acknowledge the smoking-hot man that was Dmitri Sandovsky and what he did to me, my were and his were responding like two wildfires feeding off each other.

"You made a mistake with me, Luna," he whispered into my neck, one hand sliding up the nape and tangling in my hair.

"What?" I managed, although to this day I'll never know how I spoke.

Dmitri purred low in his throat. "You left me wanting more."

I pushed away a few inches and looked him in the eyes. His were cloudy, like old emeralds, and his cheeks were as flushed as mine. "Why do you want this so badly, Dmitri?"

He flashed me that grin that I'd seen the first time I ever met him, the one that was a perfect and impenetrable mask. "I figured if I sweet-talked you a little, you'd be more inclined to let me do what our laws demand where Lilia is concerned."

I jumped up, scattering first-aid supplies over the bathroom floor. "Damn you, Dmitri!" I yelled. "Is that what I am? A Hexed *replacement*?"

He at least had the grace to look ashamed. I was hot all over, and not just from what had almost happened. I had a flash of Joshua positioned over me, snake tattoo in my face, smirking like I was all his.

"Get out!" I snarled, throwing open the bathroom door. "I don't need you to clean up my scars."

Just when the night couldn't get any worse, Luna and Dmitri find an entirely new way to Hex everything. I was beyond pissed at Dmitri—this was twice he had shoved me away and twice I had felt the burning shame of rejection by an alpha. It made me feel small, vulnerable, and young.

I hated it.

Dmitri had his head in his hands, still on the edge of the tub. "Luna . . . I didn't mean that."

"Then stop being so gods damn selfish and listen to yourself!" I was breathing hard, and my heartbeat thundered in my ears. A border of black appeared around my vision and tunneled on Sandovsky, the object of my rage. "Lilia is *dead*!" I screamed, thrusting my finger at him. "And it's horrible and sad and it hurts and it's not fair! But you're wasting yourself chasing after the man who did it, because you can't touch him! I can't touch him! No one can unless you put aside your asinine pack law and help me!"

Dmitri picked up the bottle of peroxide and flung it against the wall. It shattered and spread a crisp-smelling pool across the tiles. "You think I like being this way?" he thundered. "Knowing I got to die to keep the pack honorable?"

"Why?" I spread my hands. "Dmitri, why do you have to die with her?" I sagged against the door frame, too exhausted and too short on plasma to hold myself up. "Pack law is Hexed and stupid. Pack law doesn't take into account that there are people still on this earth who need you." Tears pricked and I tried to fight them, but that battle was over before it started. "I need you," I whispered, and started to sob.

Dmitri stared at me for a long second, the mixture of pain and helpless rage on his face heartbreaking. Then he took my face in his rough hands and kissed me, hard.

Our mouths met and my lips were wet from crying and screaming. His were dry and warm, soft like worn velvet. He pushed into my mouth with a warm tongue, covering mine, and we kissed for what seemed like an hour, my hands claiming the skin on his back and clinging, his tangling my hair with long thin fingers. I felt something inside of me break and burst as Dmitri pulled me flush against him, never letting go of the kiss.

"I'm sorry," he mumbled against my lips.

"Bastard," I hissed as I reached for his belt. He grinned as I freed him from his pants and stripped off my own T-shirt.

"You love it." He unzipped my jeans and slid them down to my knees, lifting me onto the edge of the sink and catching me in another kiss.

We didn't speak as Dmitri pushed himself into me and touched his hips to mine in a steady, insistent rhythm, my thighs sliding on the cold porcelain. In fact, the first sound I made was an involuntary shriek when he slid his hands under my ass and lifted me to him, sending a stab through me that tingled to the tips of my toenails.

I braced my arms against the wall, letting Dmitri hold me up as sweat broke out up and down my back and he groaned with each stroke. This was different from Joshua and from the men in the bar where I waitressed and from anything, ever. The were let go and raked her nails across Dmitri's shoulders and he howled and dropped me. I slammed the porcelain hard and slid to the floor, caring only that Dmitri and I were separated. I sprang to my feet and he instantly pinned me against the sink again, but I pushed him away hard and turned, gripped the edges of the basin, and watched in the mirror as he came up and grabbed my hipbones, leaving fingerprints.

"You made me bleed," he rumbled, pressing into me again. I groaned and leaned forward, my nipples swelling where they touched cold porcelain.

"Make me," I begged, and meant it. Dmitri's hand snaked up into my hair and whipped my head back, exposing my shoulder and neck. He entered me again with a force that made the mirror rattle on the wall.

"Dmitri . . . ," I warned him in a half moan as the lights started to spin in front of my eyes. He snarled.

"Not yet." Abruptly the pumping stopped and Dmitri licked slowly across my trapezius and up my neck, tasting my sweat and my scars. I watched his eyes as he bared his teeth and sank them into the juncture of my shoulder, drawing two fine droplets of blood. It wasn't the bite, and it hurt a lot. I screamed as he latched on to me, half pleasure and half fear.

Dmitri snarled and yanked back on my hair again, holding me totally vulnerable. The stroke of him inside me was harder, and he reached around to grab my swollen tits, twisting the nipples to the point that they swelled to blood-red buds and I screamed again.

This time it was all pleasure.

Dmitri responded to my cries and growled, shuddering against me and in me. His hands sprouted talons and I felt a soft pelt grow against my back as we moved. I met his eyes in the mirror and they were gold, his teeth fanging out as his lips pulled back. I pushed into him, all sense gone as the scent of him hit me and the phase swelled his cock into something that pierced me like I was a virgin again.

"Dmitri," I whispered again.

He pushed me down, my cheek against the porcelain, his talons raking along my hips and ass. I gasped incoherently as he mated with me, until he threw back his head and snarled, then pumped twice and came, the hand curled in my hair tightening until I moaned because it hurt.

Dmitri stood, naked and erect again, watching me splayed across the vanity. I couldn't move, not if Alistair Duncan himself suddenly jumped out of the shower.

The were growled softly, a human grin splitting his

fanged mouth, then he picked me up and laid me on my back, the cool tiles slicking with sweat. "Don't . . . please," I moaned. I hurt so much that I'd probably faint if he entered me again.

Dmitri moved my legs open and lifted my hips, inhaling deeply and then closing his mouth and rough tongue over the soaked patch between my thighs. He licked me, repeated and insistent, and my orgasm ripped through me after only a few strokes. Dmitri dropped me back to the tiles and let me scream until I was spent, then rolled his shoulders and let the phase retreat until he was completely human again. He grinned at me, reached over, and cupped my cheek without a word.

After we could stand upright, I wrapped myself in a huge fluffy bath towel and sat on the edge of the tub. Dmitri felt in his jeans and lit a cigarette, staring at me. I squirmed.

"What?"

"Nothing," said Dmitri with a smirk. "Just, most women would have something to say after that."

"Now is not the time, Dmitri."

"Okay, Luna. You just let me know when it is the time." More smirking. What a self-satisfied alpha male.

"You know," I commented, "you're acting very smug. It wasn't *that* kinky."

He grinned, tongue flicking his teeth once. "That comes later."

I couldn't think about just how delicious that sounded because Dmitri's phone shrilled from somewhere in his blood-soaked clothes. He checked the number and flipped it open. "Yeah. Sunny? Sunny, calm down. *Who's* gone?"

He listened for another second and then shut the phone, looking at me with saucer-eyed panic. "Something came to the pack house. They're all dead."

I jumped up, towel falling away and me not even noticing. "Is Sunny okay?"

"She's the one who called me . . ." Dmitri trailed off, the phone dropping from his hands with a clatter. It took me a clock tick to realize why he was in shock.

"Hex me. Olya."

W e took a different way into Ghosttown, an abandoned on-ramp that had once connected with downtown. The road was much smoother and showed signs of patching. Dmitri reached the main intersection, Hotel Raven glowing above us like a neon juggernaut, and swung a hard right toward the Crown.

He stopped the bike in the center of the street without a kickstand and let it drop as he sprinted into the theater. "Olya!"

The doors of the Crown had been unceremoniously knocked in, glass crunching under our feet. One of the Redback door guards who'd hassled me the first time I showed up lay on his back, blood streaming from every opening including his eyes. I checked for a pulse, but it was long gone.

Dmitri had already pelted through the seating pit and up to the projection booth, and he shouted, "Get your ass up here!"

I ran, picking my way through the bodies of every Redback who had been in residence when Alistair's apprentices came through. Most of them had similar wounds to the first; a few bore silver burns in the shape of clubs and crosses.

Sunny was in Olya's closet, crouched behind a row of designer boots. In happier times I would be envious, but now I noticed the cut on Sunny's head way more than I noticed Olya's impeccable taste in footwear.

"Dmitri, I tried," she was sobbing. "These people in black came and just . . . started killing weres."

"Duncan's thugs," I murmured.

Dmitri gripped her shoulders. "Where's my sister?"

Sunny disintegrated again. "They took her with them."

"But she's alive?" He shook Sunny when she only choked out another apology. "Sunflower! Is Olya alive?"

She nodded once. "She was when they left. She was screaming . . . I couldn't do anything . . ."

I nudged Dmitri gently aside and gathered my cousin into my arms, where she heaved out her tears and clung to my jacket. Olya's jacket. I gripped Sunny tighter. "It's not your fault." Magick words she had soothed me when we were kids, even though I was older and taller and tougher. When Rhoda made me cry, Sunny always knew that it wasn't my fault.

"They died," Sunny sniffled. "How is that not my fault?"

"No one could have stopped them," I whispered, rubbing her back like she would have when I couldn't sleep. "Now, do you think you can help Olya and Dmitri for me?"

She managed to stop sobbing hysterically, always a good sign. Either that or she was going into shock. Please gods, don't let it be option number two.

"Did you bring the things I asked for? To read the spellbook?"

Thank the moon for my stubborn, bossy, tough-as-an-old-leather-purse cousin. She accepted the plastic shopping bag I handed over and checked inside, rubbing tears off on her cuffs. Dmitri passed her a bandanna, slightly greasy.

"Thank you." She blew her nose into it. "This is all I need." She pulled the spellbook from where she'd been sitting on it and stood up. "It will be a few minutes."

She took her caster and chalk out of the bag and began drawing on the cover of the book, a simple pentagram and circle. "I've never unlocked someone else's spellbook, so if it explodes it's not my fault," she warned us, setting the book on the floor and stepping back. She lit a taper out of the bag and touched it to the chalk, which absorbed the flame and spread a soft glow up the walls of the closet.

The cops showed up just as Sunny touched her caster and began to chant.

TWENTY-FIVE

A dozen squad cars screeched to a stop in front of the Crown with flashers spinning crazily against the facade. A SWAT van and an unmarked followed them, also with full lights and sirens.

"Well, now we know how Bonnie and Clyde felt," I told Dmitri as we watched them from the second floor. "Not as exciting as I imagined."

"How the fuck did they find this place?" Dmitri shouted, slamming his hand against the sill.

A portable spotlight caught us in its gaze. "Luna Wilder!" a robotic voice bellowed over a megaphone. "You are wanted for the murder of Thomas Thorpe! Exit the building with your hands up!"

The door of the unmarked swung wide, and Captain Roenberg exited with a handcuffed figure in tow. Pete Anderson. I pointed for Dmitri's benefit. "That's how he found us."

"Give me that!" Roenberg demanded, yanking the megaphone away from the SWAT officer. "Wilder! Get your cop-slashing ass out here or Anderson goes to jail in your place!"

"Hex you, tool," Pete snapped before Roenberg could hold the megaphone away.

"Sunny," I said, not moving from my spot in the window. Across the street, on the roof of a tenement, two black shadows moved as snipers set up a firing position on Dmitri and me.

"Luna, what in the name of all things Hexed and holy is going on?" she asked. Her caster was enveloped in the same soft orange light, which pulsed softly in counterpart to the spinning lights outside.

"I need you to get the spellbook readable," I said. "And I need you to do it now."

"No pressure," said Dmitri, who also hadn't twitched a hair.

"I have what you want!" I shouted down to Roenberg. "Let Pete go and we'll talk!"

"No negotiations!" he shrilled back. "You surrender this moment or I'll send in SWAT!"

Roenberg was a small fly in Duncan's web, but I'd be Hexed if I let a blood-witch-blowing slimeball like him push me around ever again. He wouldn't be so superior when I put his boss in jail.

"You think you've got it all figured out!" I yelled out loud. "Well, Hex you, Roenberg, and the broom you rode in on!" An insult rolling off my lips had never felt so good.

"Have it your way, Wilder!" Roenberg hollered and threw the megaphone aside, gesticulating wildly at the SWAT squad.

The moon came out and for a moment the spotlight wasn't the brightest thing on the block. The spasm of phase almost doubled me over, and Dmitri ducked below the window, cursing.

Shit. Phase was the last thing on the gods' good earth I needed right then. Dmitri's hair was already a little bushier, and he was fanging out.

"Sunny, *hurry up!*" I yelled at her.

"Last warning!" Roenberg screeched from the street. "I'm sending men in!"

There was a *pop* of truly vile-smelling magick and the spellbook leapt off the floor, landing splayed on its spine. Sunny blinked and then grinned. "Kid stuff. Here, the lock's broken. Take the Hexed thing away from me." Now that it was readable, the sigils on the wrinkled pages were definitely giving off pulses of something icky.

I grabbed up the book anyway, cradling it like the gold it was. "We gotta split."

"I'll stay," said Sunny. I heard the SWAT team kick in what was left of the Crown's door and start up the stairs.

"No!" I told Sunny, the way you tell small naughty dogs no. "We're all leaving, right this second."

Sunny shook her head. "I've had some practice being a diversion lately."

"Sunny, I said no!"

SWAT boots landed in the hallway outside, and Dmitri practically ripped my arm off as he pulled me into the next room.

"Call Mac!" I screamed to Sunny. "I'm sorry!"

She waved me off. "Don't be sorry, get running!"

As Dmitri and I hauled ass down the projection room stairs, I heard the SWAT leader shout "Freeze!" at Sunny. I dug in my heels and tried to go back, but Dmitri practically carried me through the loading dock entrance and onto the next street. We didn't stop running until we could no longer hear sirens.

The streets had petered out to roadblocks at the opposite end of Ghosttown before either of us spoke. "The housing authority is where he'll have Olya," I said. "I know that it's your obligation to see this thing through, so I hope you don't hate me when I say I really don't want to go there, Dmitri." The absolute truth. Alistair Duncan and everything about him scared me. The girl who hates magick, compelled straight into the lair of a blood witch.

Dmitri stopped and cocked his head. "Well, fuck it, Luna, I don't, either. But that butcher has my sister, so I don't exactly have a big Hexed choice here, do I?"

"No," I whispered. Dmitri stopped walking.

"You don't have to come."

I saw all of the staring eyes in turn: Lilia, Marina, Katya, and the three women in the Duncans' house. I started walking again. "Yes, I do."

"Why?" Dmitri demanded, jogging to keep up with me.

Alistair had left them abandoned in death, like trash. They had no one. "Pack duty," I told Dmitri. He gripped my hand and matched my pace.

"I understand."

The housing authority was a half-burned hulk, one side all glass and steel boasting of an atomic age and the other collapsed and charred. A single light glowed from the floor-to-ceiling windows on the still-standing side.

"He's in there," Dmitri said. "I smell him."

I did, too, not so much a smell as a feeling in the back of my head, a frequency that I couldn't quite make out.

The clouds that had sprung up were scudding briskly across the sky in a high wind. A flash of silver appeared now and then.

I walked faster.

Dmitri stopped me just before I crossed the line from clouded moonlight to pure shadow.

"Whatever happens in there, I kill Duncan."

I yanked my arm away from him. "No."

"Luna . . ."

"No!" I faced him, furious. "Give it up, Dmitri! Duncan will lay you out without a second thought!"

"What makes you think you're so much better?" he demanded as I pulled open the rusty double doors. "What makes you think he won't kill you, too?"

"Because he wants me," I whispered. "He wants to kill me and claim dominance." I stepped into a universe of steam and red light.

I remembered Lilia, and the neon sign that had marked her burial spot.

Dmitri was beside me again by the time I had stepped through the steam and saw the body hanging from the hook.

Stephen had chains around his wrists and was naked, his body flayed at the ribs and the face and torso beaten almost unrecognizable.

He moaned when I came close. "Get . . . out . . ."

I tugged at the chains until they released and he tumbled into my arms. "I am so sorry," I said. "So sorry . . ." I didn't realize I was repeating myself until Dmitri pulled him away from me and brought him into the light.

"Shit," he exclaimed. Stephen's face was already halfway through the phase, his impossibly long teeth sprouting from a human jaw too small to contain them. His body fought the phase with every shred of will it had left, but it wasn't much.

Stephen stared at me, with those unbearable human eyes. "Run," he rasped.

The were face erupted, and he went down on all fours. The wounds were still there. Forcing him to phase was just the final part of Alistair's torture.

Stephen growled and advanced on me, one front paw tucked to his chest. Now it wouldn't matter whether he became the were willingly or not. He was a predator, wounded and in pain and very, very dangerous.

Dmitri made a move and Stephen turned on him, snapping jaws on flesh. Dmitri yelped and yanked his arm away. Blood from the bite sprayed Stephen's snout. Aroused, he tensed to spring and knocked Dmitri to the ground, aiming teeth for his jugular.

I swung the only thing in my grip, the spellbook, at his head. Stephen latched on to it and I yanked in return, pulling him off Dmitri.

"Yeah, that's right," I ground out as his terrible head swung to face me. "You want me, don't you?"

He did, and he advanced, as inexorable as a black blood clot on the face of the heart.

Just before he sprang, he faltered. I'll never know if it was his wounds, or if he saw me trying to save Dmitri, but whatever it was, Alistair had enough of his game. Stephen choked, his big head lolling from side to side, twitching on the floor as his windpipe contracted millimeter by millimeter.

"Leave him alone!" I screamed into the steam.

Stephen mewled, one twisted foot knocking against

mine. His tongue was beginning to turn blue, but according to Alistair his suffering was far from over. I decided then that I didn't care whether Dmitri or I or the gods themselves disposed of Alistair Duncan, but he sure didn't have much longer in this world.

"I'm sorry," I whispered once more to Stephen, and then reared back and slammed my boot as hard as I could into his skull.

He went still without a sound. His corpse didn't revert to human. Same jaws, same leaking yellow eyes.

"You don't get him," I told Duncan as I closed them. "You lose."

I turned my back on the grotesque carcass and went to help Dmitri. He groaned as he pulled himself up. "Son of a bitch. I'm bitten." The bite was black around the edges, and blood was oozing steadily from one of the big veins in Dmitri's forearm. I took off my jacket and tore a sleeve.

"Here." I tied it off in silence, just us and the swirling steam. Dmitri touched my cheek.

"You okay?"

"No," I started, "I'm not—"

A scream rocketed around the open lobby, echoing off the smooth walls and scarred vinyl. Dmitri's head snapped up and he took off. I had to jump over Stephen's body to keep up. How I was going to explain this body to McAllister and CSU, I didn't know.

Then I realized that no one besides Dmitri, Duncan, and I would ever know what happened tonight, and at least one of us was going to be dead come sunrise.

Dmitri bounded up metal stairs, the screams louder and more frequent. I recognized the office from my nightshade dream and yelled, "Dmitri, wait!"

He went through the door anyway, and I came in

behind, almost slamming into his back. He was stopped short, nostrils flared, dark pupils fixed on the two figures across the room.

Alistair Duncan smiled at me from sunken cheeks and said, "So good of you to come, Detective Wilder."

Olya Sandovsky struggled against the bonds that held her in the center of the calling circle and screamed for her brother. She was tied to the floor in the center of seven points, all but one holding the polished finger bones of the dead girls. The sacrifice.

Candles at the edge of the circle lit the room, and tinted skylights allowed cloudy silver to illuminate the wounds seeping Olya's blood into the working around her.

Dmitri went for Alistair, faster than I'd ever seen anyone move. Alistair seemed to breathe out slowly, and Dmitri was knocked aside, slamming face-first into the wall and falling back.

"I see my son didn't fail me in the end," said Alistair, standing over Dmitri like a shade. He motioned, and Dmitri's bitten arm jerked. He screamed, and the sound rattled glass and my back teeth.

Alistair clenched his fist, and with a rending of flesh a were paw appeared from the wound in Dmitri's arm.

Alistair grinned. "Don't know when to leave well enough alone. I love that about you weres. It makes you very apt subjects for my enjoyment." In the courtroom cadence that hypnotized juries for seventeen years, he asked, "How does it feel having the beast within ripped without, Mr. Sandovsky?"

With one final twist, Dmitri became half were, half man, the bloody union between the two leaking out of him. I screamed, too, long and devastated, as wolf legs and human body twitched and went still.

Alistair brushed his hands together as if they'd been

soiled and then turned back to Olya's gasps. "Shut your mouth," he snapped. "You'll be all out of breath soon enough, no sense wasting it."

"Mr. Duncan," I said.

Alistair inclined his head to me. "Yes?"

I held up the spellbook. "You know, it really pays to do your research *before* you start the calling."

Duncan went even whiter than he already was. "Give me the book, Detective."

"Hex you, Alistair. Let Olya go and we'll talk."

Alistair hissed. "Bitch!"

"Likewise," I said. "So what's in this book anyway, Alistair?" I thumbed a few pages at random. They were definitely in English now. "Is it like a manual? Care and feeding of your human slave, by Meggoth?"

Duncan laughed. "If you knew what that book said, you wouldn't be standing here making a pathetic attempt to bargain with me." His eyes narrowed, and the blackness of the iris spilled out like an inkstain to cover the rest. "Now give it to me."

I rolled my eyes. "Here, take the Hexed thing." I cocked my arm and flung it into the far corner of the room, and ran for Olya as Duncan dove. I didn't care if I had to rip her arms out of their sockets to get her free.

Too late, I felt the prickle of a working circle snapping into place. I'd never experienced a calling before. It felt like running into a wall of concrete. Magickal concrete. I flew backward and smacked a real wall of concrete, sliding down it until I was in a heap, breathless, every inch of my body on fire.

Duncan went for the book again, but I was faster and gripped it the same time as he did. His lip curled. "Let go."

"You reconsider sacrificing Dmitri's sister and we'll

talk," I told him. Our hands were almost touching on the cover of the spellbook, and this close Alistair was musty and burnt with blood workings.

He tried to yank the book away from me and I snarled, letting myself fang out.

"All right, all right." He held up his free hand. "Let go and I'll release her."

"Unh-unh. Release and I let go."

Alistair glared. "You really were a mistake, Detective."

I smirked. "That's what you get for believing Roenberg."

Duncan's mouth twitched once, and then he sighed and Olya's ropes went slack. She sat up, massaging her wrists. "She's free to go," Alistair said.

I took my hand off the book. "Hope your daemon master chokes on it."

Duncan didn't hear me as he turned and strode back to the circle, drawing a silver athame from under his coat and raising it above Olya's head.

"Gods!" she screamed.

I tried to stand, but I'd put myself through too much abuse and my legs went out from under me. I couldn't get to Olya. I was weak.

The were howled in despair as Duncan lowered the knife and cut a clean line across Olya's throat.

"Seven souls for seven sins, seven's blood and seven's pain." Alistair used the athame to cut off Olya's left index finger and placed the bloody stump on the last point of the circle. He read from the spellbook, "Heed my call, and make the wanderer between worlds whole!" Gold smoke began to roil across the circle he had chalked. The smoke drew to him, entered his throat and nose.

Alistair choked and fell to his knees. "Yes . . ." He grinned. "Yes . . . take me . . ."

The smoke coalesced in the center of the circle and formed a shape, first a silhouette and then rapidly a body and finally a man, olive-gold-skinned with a lion's legs and tail and a crocodile's pointed teeth. A serpent's tongue flicked from between black lips as he looked upon the human world.

TWENTY-SIX

Meggoth regarded his body and the surroundings for a moment.

"Finally!" Alistair cried. "Thirty years and I have you!"

"Alistair Duncan, why have you not fallen before me?" Meggoth cocked his head. He had a thick accent and his words were muddled, like it had been a long time since he'd used a human voice.

"You bastard." Alistair grinned. "I spit on you. You really think I waited all of these years to become your *servant*?"

"You have no choice!" Meggoth rumbled.

Alistair got to his feet. "Look at where you are, wanderer."

From my excellent vantage on the floor, I saw the calling circle was doubled, and Sunny's words came back. *Only for binding the really nasty ones.*

Because it wasn't a calling circle at all. It was a binding.

"Traitor!" Meggoth bellowed.

Alistair held up his casting chalk and broke it in half. "By wards worked in blood, I bind you in eternity, Meggoth, to serve *my* will."

Meggoth's eyes flamed gold and he let out a scream of pure rage. Alistair just smiled. Who wouldn't, when you were a blood who had just managed to enslave the most powerful daemon known to witchkind?

"You will suffer like no other," Meggoth promised Duncan. Alistair shook his head.

"That attitude will never work. Say, *What do you command of me, Master?*"

Meggoth threw himself against the binding circle. "I did not bow to the Descent and I do not bow to a blood-wielding maggot like you!"

Right at that second, I liked Meggoth a lot.

Alistair shook the spellbook at him. "That's very impolite. Would you like me to compel you with your true name, wanderer?"

Meggoth glared silently at Duncan. I was surprised, considering the look, that Alistair didn't burst into flames.

"What do you command of me, Master?"

"For a start." Alistair tossed the chalk away. "Dispose of this Insoli trash lying around."

Meggoth met my eyes as I crouched in the corner and I felt the chill at the very core of my soul. His mind was touching mine, and I was cold.

Such a pitiful creature, he echoed in my head. *Hardly worth my trouble.*

"*Not really your choice anymore,*" I answered him without thinking. "*You've got a* master *now.*"

Your death will be quick, Insoli, he spoke. *Do not tempt me to make it slow.*

I looked into those golden eyes, so icy and barren,

not like a were's. I wasn't cold anymore. A soft glow permeated the edges of my vision.

I realized I wasn't afraid. Of Meggoth, of Alistair, of dying.

Not the phase. Not anymore.

"Do as I say!" Alistair screeched. "Before I send you back and find another more suitable to my needs!"

Meggoth didn't break his gaze with me as he crouched and caressed Olya's face once.

All I wanted was her. My Serah, he told me sadly. *She offered me a place when all others had vanished into the dark. The caster witches took her for it.*

"Kill the were," Alistair warned. "Or I won't let you have any more fun."

The demon slowly turned toward him, and I got the impression that Alistair's circle, powerful as it may be, was little more than a flimsy fence for Meggoth's vast power.

"Are you under the impression, Master, that the offerings we procure are for *pleasure*?"

Offerings. Not sacrifices. The daemon had reduced Alistair's pleasure in the calling to what it really was— disgusting.

"I took pleasure in them," said Duncan. "I don't really care what you think about all that." The binding circle sparked and Duncan leapt back. "Careful! That would have been unfortunate."

Meggoth regarded the lines at his feet pulsing with power. "I should not be here."

"Of course you shouldn't!" Duncan shouted. "According to humans and weres and those stupid scared caster witches, you don't even exist." He kept well clear of the circle as it began to vibrate on a high-pitched note. "Yet here you are."

Meggoth's eyes stilled pinned me to the wall, the same scene from my nightshade dream, with him looking past my skin and into my thoughts. I winced as the working holding the circle in place strained and bent, sending a shriek through the ether only I and the daemon could hear.

I never wanted to break this world, he said. *I seek only to regain what was mine and exact swift vengeance on those who commissioned it. I am not Meggoth the destroyer. I do not seek death for death's sake. My name is truly Asmodeus, the lonely walker of worlds.*

I tried sending another echo back to him. *"My true name is Luna Wilder, and I am a protector of this one. You must help me."*

I cannot. I must do as the mortal commands.

"Duncan doesn't know his binding is failing. He'll kill everyone in Ghosttown if it snaps."

Asmodeus's gaze grew heavy. "Good-bye, Insoli."

"Finally!" said Duncan. "Good boy. And after you kill Detective Wilder, I believe I will find you a woman. I will watch."

"Don't be a fool," I echoed to Asmodeus. *"Alistair is one of the ones who harmed you. Just a blood witch too smart for his own good."*

Why do I trust a were? Your kind bears me no good feeling.

I shot a glance at Duncan, grinning away over Olya's body and chuckling as his binding sparked and popped, weakening with every passing second. The wards, worked in blood, would never give way, but the circle transforming their power was about to.

I didn't really want to think about what happened when wards strong enough to bind a daemon had no conduit for their energy. *"Maybe you should trust me because I'm the only one alive in this room who hasn't tried to Hex you over.*"

I am sorry, Asmodeus echoed. *This must end.*

Crap.

Asmodeus held out his hand toward me, and I kept my eyes open. I would face my death head-on, like the warrior-wolf that had spawned my kind on dark hilltops millennia ago.

Out of the corner of my eye, silver flashed in the candlelight. I sent one last, probably futile echo to Asmodeus.

End it.

I kicked the discarded athame hard as I could, sending it skidding toward the circle. Soaked in Olya's blood, it passed within the binding wards. Within the daemon's power, the knife came to rest in his palm.

"What are you doing!" Duncan screamed.

Asmodeus smiled at him, a perfect mimic of Duncan's expression. "Ridding this world of you."

He sent the athame straight up like a bullet, shattering the blackened skylights over the circle. Moonlight flooded the sacrificial pyre, washing over Asmodeus and Duncan and filling every corner of the room.

It touched my skin, and I burned.

It touched my soul, and I phased.

I saw everything tinged in silver, clear and crisp as sunlight. Release into the phase was the purest euphoria I had ever known. A tingle raced over my skin as fur sprouted and I instinctively curled on all fours.

No pain as claws sprouted from my hands, as my jaw elongated and my eyes sank and expanded and glowed as golden as Asmodeus's skin.

He echoed, *Do what you must.*

Phased, I could hear everything—a dull thrum of power from Alistair, the screeching of his broken circle, and the terrifying void of quiet from Asmodeus, the vacuum from a power so vast it covered everything.

Asmodeus told me to do what I must. I knew he meant break the circle, and that was death for me. Binding wards could only be dispelled by the witch who cast them, their power drawn back to his blood.

You understand me, Asmodeus echoed. *And that is why I am sorry for you, Insoli.*

I echoed back. *"I do."*

I advanced on Alistair Duncan step by step, claws clacking against the cement. I let the cold bloodlust in my eyes fill him with the fear of every victim whose life he had destroyed. Visceral memories flashed by, not so much sights but sounds and smells. Joshua, my own screams, the volcanic pain of the first phase, and the metal-tainted blood in my mouth that I recognized instinctively as human.

I kept walking, on four black paws, feeling the hot wind from the breaking circle ruffle the fur on my spine. None of it mattered anymore. I was a were, and we *did* kill and we *did* hunt and we enjoyed it, because it was part of us.

I bared my teeth at Duncan and snarled, scenting his musty, used blood and marking him as prey.

Duncan screamed over and over again, stumbling and tripping over his own feet, backing away from me toward the circle, which shot blue sparks as the working gave way.

As Alistair's foot slipped over the binding wards, I leapt on him and tore his throat out.

His blood was hot, tainted, and bitter over my tongue,

and it released the wards with a flood of misplaced magick that tore across my body like a lightning strike. That was the last sensation I remembered before the circle broke with a fierce snap and I found myself de-phased, staring up into a full, silver moon blessing me with its light.

When I could move I crawled across the floor to Dmitri, cradling his head against my naked body. "Please," I whispered. I didn't know who I was praying to, and it didn't do any good. Dmitri's ravaged form remained just as lifeless.

Bare feet whispered behind me and I looked up into Asmodeus's face.

"You released me," he spoke aloud.

"Yeah, well, you might as well get it over with and kill me now." I stroked Dmitri's cheek once before releasing his body and covering myself under the daemon's eyes.

"I am not a monster," said Asmodeus.

"Could have fooled me," I snapped bitterly. Argue with a daemon, I didn't care. Dmitri was dead. Dead because of me. My fault. The hole in my gut that had opened when I ran from Joshua widened and deepened until I was afraid it would swallow me.

"Anger is ugly, Insoli," Asmodeus said. "It consumes."

"Stop calling me Insoli and Hex off!" I screamed at him. "Dmitri is dead and unless you're going to do something about that, get out!"

Asmodeus crouched and moved me aside. He had human hands with black nails, a touch warm and soft. "You released me," he said. "You have the right to compel a task in return, as payment."

"Leave," I whispered. "Just leave me alone."

Asmodeus picked up Dmitri's arm, touching Stephen's bite. I wanted to tear him limb from limb for touching Dmitri, but I was so weak it was a marathon effort to keep my eyes open.

"I believe I will interpret your request freely." He opened his own palm on one pointed nail and pressed it against Dmitri's wound. The blood sizzled, and the bite mark faded to a black crescent. The convulsions spread to Dmitri's whole body, the were half blending back to human.

Asmodeus stood. "And now I will honor your order, Insoli. Good parting." Golden smoke grew up around him, obscuring my view. Before he faded, I swear Asmodeus stretched out his hand to a second figure and that they shimmered away together in the smoke. I decided I was hallucinating, and finally slumped over next to Dmitri's body, too exhausted to keep awake any longer.

S omeone kicking me in the side woke me up. "Hex you!" I snarled before my eyes opened, batting at the foot.

Regan Lockhart glared down at me. I gasped and scrambled away from him. He smiled thinly. "Not the person you expected?"

"Lockhart, *person* doesn't apply to you even as a joke."

His hair was a brownish red now, the face more square and old Hollywood movie idol than his previous small frame, but the obsidian eyes and curled smirk were definitely Lockhart.

"You let Meggoth walk away. Under pack law, consorting with a daemon means death."

"His name is Asmodeus, and you try to kill me, you pull back a stump," I warned. I slid a glance to the spot where Dmitri had lain when I passed out. He was gone, a smear of blood the only remainder.

"Detective, your defensiveness is extremely unattractive," said Lockhart. "While I'd like nothing more than to rip your skin off and feed it to you for releasing Asmodeus, the higher-ups have determined you did us a *service* by removing Duncan." He rolled his eyes at the last part. I wondered if his higher-up was anything like Roenberg.

"So, what, are they going to pin a medal on me?" I asked wearily, tilting my too-heavy head back against the wall. Lockhart snorted.

"For dispatching a dangerous blood witch, they grant you life. As for the *favor* Asmodeus did you, that's yours to bear."

He looked down at his new palm and I saw a tattoo like the one Roenberg sported, only far more complex. Off to infiltrate another pack of blood witches. "You don't have to worry about *him* anymore," said Lockhart. "With Duncan dead, none of his apprentices will have enough energy to do much more than magick up a cup of black coffee."

"What are you, Regan, telepathic?" I asked churlishly, though I couldn't have cared less.

"Ask me again next time we meet," said Lockhart. "If you haven't figured it out." He nodded curtly at me once, and then blinked out of existence.

Come to think of it, I really didn't like the way he used the word *favor*.

I drifted in and out of a drugged kind of sleep until the real, human police found me. No one tried to arrest me for Thorpe's murder; they just wrapped me in a blanket and took me to the ambulance, where I passed out and woke up in a hospital bed two days later.

TWENTY-SEVEN

S unny jumped up so fast from her chair that she
knocked it over, tackling me in a hug that shook the
air from my sore chest.

"Ow," I said as she squeezed.

The small interrogation room at the Twenty-fourth
was as dingy as ever, but as Sunny pulled up a chair and
sat me in it, it was damn near beautiful.

"I thought you were dead!" were her first words.

"Why do you always, *always* assume the worst with
me?" I demanded. "I was unconscious in Sharpshin
Memorial, not shuffling off the mortal coil."

She grinned so wide I was afraid her face would
crack. "When Missing Persons called with your Jane
Doe report, Lieutenant McAllister was so excited he did
a little dance."

"I was a Jane Doe? Right, no ID. Wait. Mac danced?"

"Just a small jig," said Mac, sticking his head in.
"Very dignified." He grunted as I hugged him. "Damn it,
Wilder, is there anything else you can do to ruin me?"

"I'll get on that," I told him.

He had a file in his hand, with my name on the flap. "Why don't we sit down?"

The good mood that had sprung up when I saw Sunny wilted and died. Mac was here to tell me I was still fired.

"You stirred up the perfect shitstorm with Duncan, that's for sure," said Mac. "Roenberg is off the grid, as are most of the officers he took into Ghosttown with him. Internal Affairs is calling about that—and you— every five minutes." He tapped the file against his chin, deciding how to couch the next bit of news. "They've decided that pending an investigation, you're being placed on unpaid leave."

I let out a whoop. Sunny started and cocked her eyebrow at me. "But that's bad."

"Who cares?" I shouted. "I'm not fired!"

Mac smiled as much as Mac ever smiles and stood. "Let your cousin take you home," he said. "And stay out of trouble for a few weeks." He smiled as he ducked out of interrogation.

Sunny stood. "Let's go."

I bit my lip. "We can't."

"Why the Hex not?" Sunny demanded.

I stood, feeling my sore muscles complain eight different ways, and went to the door. "I told Rhoda that if she helped me I'd let you leave. As payment."

Sunny sat back down hard. "You did that? You actually agreed?"

"Don't jump for joy or anything," I told her. "But I thought you'd be a little more excited." Of course I knew Sunny would be happier with Rhoda, and my grandmother knew it, too. Didn't mean it didn't sting.

I jingled my car keys in my jacket pocket. "See you soon, Sunny. Don't be a stranger." I walked back to the parking lot.

"Good to see you alive and well, Detective!" Rick called as I passed his station.

"Likewise, Rick."

In the Fairlane, I leaned my head against the window frame, letting cool air from the bay wash the hospital smells off me. I started the engine and as I drove watched Nocturne flow by me in daytime, thinking how much paler everything looked in the sun.

I lay awake that night, staring straight up at the ceiling. I was never able to sleep in the first week of the waning moon, and now the cottage held Sunny's empty bedroom down the hall and a whole set of new memories. Lockhart appearing above me as I slept, the silver bullet hole in the kitchen wall, Dmitri waiting in the living room to make sure I was still alive.

Dmitri. I'd never had someone sacrifice himself for me, and I didn't like it. I didn't like him being dead. It wasn't right, or fair, or natural in any way.

Tears pricked and I rubbed my eyes fiercely with the corner of my pillow. Crap. I did not cry alone in the dark. Or any other time. But I hadn't even gotten to tell him good-bye, or thank you . . .

A low rumble from outside caught my attention, and I was out of bed, feet touching the floor silently, before I had time to think. Downstairs, slip the deadbolt, out the door.

I came around the corner of the house, where the beach access road ran past, and commanded, "Freeze!"

"Right back where we started, huh?" said Dmitri. He was astride his motorcycle, which grumbled under its breath.

My knees buckled. "Goddess . . ."

In a flash, he was propping me up. "Easy." He set me on my feet before backing away.

"You . . ." So many words fought to be first in line, but what came out was the oh-so-witty, "You're not dead."

Dmitri shrugged. "It's harder than it looks."

"Duncan killed you. I saw it."

He frowned. "Didn't feel great, but I lived through it."

"No, you didn't!" I exclaimed. This was my life—arguing with a man I might love about whether he was dead or not.

Dmitri sighed and pulled back the sleeve of his jacket: Stephen's bite. The scar was a glossy black crescent against his pale skin. "This thing is in me," he said. "It saved me. Don't suppose you'd happen to know how it got there, Luna."

I touched the scar with my fingertips and felt the distinctive *pop* of darkness. "Dmitri, I'm so sorry. There was nothing else to do."

"I saw the other side," he said softly. "It wasn't so bad. Olya . . . she was there. With him."

Guess I should start paying more attention to my hallucinations.

"It seemed peaceful," Dmitri said wistfully.

The tears came again, strong, and a twin pair made their way down my cheeks. "Dmitri . . ."

"Hey," he said quickly, rough thumb reaching out to wipe them away, "forget it. I just came to tell you I'm headed back to Ukraine."

My mouth worked in that attractive fish expression. "Why?"

"Pack elders are there," said Dmitri. "I've been changed into something that's not a were. It's magick, and magick from outside the pack is unnatural. The elders will judge me and do what pack law commands."

"Like what, take you out on the steppe and pull an Old Yeller?"

He walked back to his bike. "Good-bye, Luna."

"I didn't want you to die," I said. I wanted so badly to run to him and wrap him in a fierce kiss and beg him to never leave me, but I just stood there staring at my flip-flops while he got back on his motorcycle.

"I'm glad," he said. "And I don't blame you at all." He kicked the clutch and then released it again, shutting the bike off. "You know, Luna, you could come with me. I could give you the bite right now and you'd be a Red-back. Whatever happens, you could be there."

I didn't run, I just walked slowly across the crushed shells and took his face in my hands. "I am what I am, Dmitri. And we'll both do what we have to." I kissed him gently, barely a brush of lips. "You'd better come back to me."

He pulled my head down and returned my kiss for a long moment. "Promise."

With that, I stepped back and watched his taillights disappear down the beach road. When they finally winked out, I headed back to the cottage, but changed direction and went down on the beach instead, sitting on a driftwood log at the edge of the surf.

Dmitri alive. Asmodeus free. Alistair dead. Case closed.

I let myself enjoy the feeling of having done something right for a change and tried to ignore the pit of loss that was already growing where Dmitri had been. The waning moon gilded the surf, and cold sluiced around my feet.

"Thank you," I whispered upward. "For Lilia, Marina, Katya, and Olya. And for me, too."

I decided then I would no longer fear the phase. Tonight I would sleep without nightmares, under the light of the waning moon. I was Insoli. And that was fine.

Coming in September 2008

PURE BLOOD by Caitlin Kittredge

In the shadows of Nocturne City, witches lurk and werewolves prowl, and homicide detective Luna Wilder must keep the peace. Now bodies are turning up all over town, the murders linked by a cryptic message. . . . *We see with empty eyes.*

To make matters worse, Luna can't get Dmitri Sandovsky out of her mind. The last time he helped Luna with a case, he suffered a demon bite that infected him with a mysterious illness, and the pack elders have forbidden Dmitri from associating with Luna.

But Luna will need his help when high-level witches start turning up dead. Because a war is brewing between rival clans of blood witches and caster witches—a magical gang war with the power to burn Nocturne City to the ground . . .

Read on for a preview

ONE

I'm not a patient person under the best of circumstances. Standing next to a dead man on a cold city sidewalk is not one of them. Add in the fact that I was the only homicide detective on the scene, and had been standing around stamping my feet and rubbing my hands together for almost half an hour, and you could kiss any patience I started the night with good-bye.

I grabbed Officer Martinez by the elbow as he walked past, headed to his patrol car.

"Where in seven hells is CSU?"

He shrugged. "Sorry, Detective Wilder. There was a drive-by shooting on Archer Avenue. Could be another forty minutes. We're low priority tonight."

I looked back at the dead man. Under the flickering sodium light his cheeks were gray hollows and his eyes receded until there was only black. He was thin, with grayish skin that puddled around his neck and wrists. A tan uniform shirt did nothing to cover the track marks on his forearms, between his fingers, in the fold of his elbow . . . everywhere. If I took off his shoes, I'd find them in his ankles, his toes, and anywhere else a vein might be hiding.

A simple OD doesn't usually warrant a homicide detective, but I had been driving to work and picked up the call. It was a block away, so I swung by. By the way the dead guy smelled, I was wishing I hadn't. He was stale—stale skin, stale sweat, the tang of cooked heroin burning the back of my mouth as I inhaled.

"CSU is on the way, Detective!" Martinez called from his patrol car. I rolled my shoulders. Thank the gods. I was in a bad neighborhood with limited backup, and someone in the dark row houses that lined the street was probably itching to shoot me right this second.

"You want a cup of coffee, Detective? I got a thermos in the prowler."

I shook my head at Martinez, who looked sweetly disappointed. He was baby-faced, stocky and short, but had blazing black eyes and big hands that could probably snap a suspect in half.

"I don't drink the stuff."

"Something a little stronger?" He pulled his blue satin jacket aside to show me an engraved silver flask. My mouth quirked.

"Your captain know you have that?"

"Don't ask about the captain's late-night lady visitors, he won't ask about what you do on patrol." Martinez grinned back at me. "Hey, don't take this as a come-on or nothin', but you look familiar. You didn't just transfer in, did you?"

I sighed. It had to happen sooner or later. Savvy editors had slapped my headshot from the police academy on the front page of every major newspaper in Nocturne City. Above the fold. "I've been on medical leave for three months. Just got back today."

"Three months . . ." Martinez's gears ground for a second and then he blurted out, "Hex! You're that cop that killed the DA!"

"*Former* DA," I growled, "and it's not like he didn't try to kill me—*and* call a daemon—before I took action."

"Holy shit," said Martinez, slapping his leg. "We got all your clippings up in the locker room at the precinct house. There was a pool whether they'd let you back on the force or Section-8 you."

I had an unpleasant flash of Dr. Merriman, my department-appointed psychiatrist, and beat it back. "Can I assume you bet against me?"

"Hell no," said Martinez. "You're a tough bi—er, lady. I knew you'd be back."

"Your confidence is touching," I told him, and turned back to the body. Suddenly, the company of a dead junkie didn't seem so bad. At least he couldn't point and whisper.

I was going through the black messenger bag emblazoned with a fancy winged-foot logo and the legend MESSENGER OF THE GODS when the CSU van pulled up.

A black Lincoln with the seal of the city and medical examiner parked behind the van, and Bart Kronen exited after a fight with his seatbelt. He brought a canvas tote bag holding the tools of his trade and waved to me with his free hand.

"Good to have you back, Detective! What present have you got for me this evening?"

"Nothing exciting, I'm afraid," I said as a CSU camera clicked and lit the scene to blinding daylight with a flash. "Just your standard street OD." I gestured to the one lit row house a block away. "I figured he came out of that shooting gallery and dropped dead before he realized he'd gone past the point of no return."

Kronen checked the man's pulse perfunctorily and then wiggled the arm. It moved like a store mannequin, all stiff joints. "Rigor is fixed, skin is close to ambient temperature . . . dead less than six hours. Can't be more specific, I'm afraid."

I shrugged. "Makes no difference to me, unless someone jabbed him with that needle against his will."

Kronen flashed his light over the man's hands and fingernails. "No trace evidence that I can see." He lifted the lids of the staring eyes and examined them. The dead man had had green eyes, a bright grassy color that was already fading.

The pain caught my gut, a physical sensation to go with a memory of dark green eyes and shaggy auburn hair falling across them like autumn leaves on a deep pond. *Hex you, Dmitri. Hex you and the ground you walk on.*

"Now this is interesting, Detective. Detective?"

As quickly as he'd come, he was gone, fading into a cloud of clove smoke and gravelly laughter.

I crouched next to Kronen, trying not to wince when he poked the dead junkie's eyeball with a rubber-tipped finger.

"See this here?" He indicated spidery columns of red drifting across the white.

"Little late for drops," I said. Kronen's mouth curled in displeasure. I stopped smiling.

"This is petichial hemorrhaging," he said. "A bursting of miniature blood vessels on the surface of the eye."

"So?" I said. Kronen snapped off his light and stood, fixing his tie and expansive waistband.

"This is not consistent with a heroin overdose. Petichia usually occur when the brain is deprived of oxygen."

"He wasn't strangled," I said defensively. "He's just dead." I was competent, dammit. I didn't need to be walked through my own crime scene like a first-year patrol officer. I'd know if someone was strangled, thank you.

Kronen went about tucking all of his accoutrements back into their case, and he pulled out a clipboard, initialed a report of a white male, dead on the scene, and handed it to me to sign as the ranking responding officer.

"I have no idea what could have happened to him," he said. "But once I do the post, I'm sure all will be revealed. In the meantime, do you . . . detect . . . anything?"

My pen froze mid-signature. "Exactly what's that supposed to mean, Bart?"

He spread his hands. "Well, after the incident with Alistair Duncan certain . . . rumors have been flying heavily. If you can put your abilities to good use, it might speed a cause-of-death determination along."

I flung the pen down and shoved the clipboard back at him. "I don't know what you think you know, Bart, but you're barking up the wrong damn tree." He looked like a perturbed owl, eyes wide as I snarled, "I'm not a trick dog, so screw your assumptions," and stormed away up the street.

My hands were shaking, and I compensated by stomping my motorcycle boots on the pavement. I'm a werewolf, and thanks to the debacle with Alistair Duncan, anyone who read the *Nocturne Inquirer* knew it, which included most of the department.

Kronen probably had no idea he was being insensitive, and I was a bitch for snarling at him, but since the Hex Riots, weres and witches don't enjoy the best reputation. Or any kind, except as the thing under your bed that you pretend doesn't exist.

And Hex it, I *wasn't* a hound dog that could sniff

clues on cue. Being were didn't mean a shiny package of heightened senses that made my job easier. It was that, and uncontrollable rage and strength that could separate someone's head from their neck if I ever let myself off lockdown.

I'd only met one person who knew what that felt like, and he was somewhere on the other side of the world.

I breathed in, out, and willed myself to turn around and go back to the scene, knowing that everyone currently clustered around the body was talking about me.

Down the street, light spilled out of the condemned row house as a door opened and another scarecrow started up the walk toward me. He saw the patrol car, Martinez, and the CSU techs. He used what was left of his brain and ran.

"Better and better," I muttered, taking off after the live junkie. I figured if he was sprinting he probably knew something about the dead one. I caught up with him after a block and used my arm like a battering ram to drive him into the iron fences marching up the sidewalk.

"Get off!" he yelled, shoving back and making me stumble off the curb. I windmilled and caught myself on a rusted-out Ford, panting in surprise. Not many plain humans can stand up to were strength.